MW01195576

THE
RIVER
IS
WAITING

THE
RIVER
IS
WAITING

A Novel

WALLY LAMB

**MARYSUE
RUCCI
BOOKS**

New York   London   Toronto   Sydney   New Delhi

**MARYSUE
RUCCI
BOOKS**

An Imprint of Simon & Schuster, LLC
1230 Avenue of the Americas
New York, NY 10020

First Marysue Rucci Books hardcover edition June 2025

MARYSUE RUCCI BOOKS and colophon are trademarks of Simon & Schuster, LLC

Simon & Schuster strongly believes in freedom of expression and stands against censorship in all its forms. For more information, visit BooksBelong.com.

For information about special discounts for bulk purchases, please contact Simon & Schuster Special Sales at 1-866-506-1949 or business@simonandschuster.com.

The Simon & Schuster Speakers Bureau can bring authors to your live event. For more information or to book an event, contact the Simon & Schuster Speakers Bureau at 1-866-248-3049 or visit our website at www.simonspeakers.com.

Interior design by Hope Herr-Cardillo

Manufactured in the United States of America

1   3   5   7   9   10   8   6   4   2

Library of Congress Cataloging-in-Publication Data has been applied for.

ISBN 978-1-6680-0639-9
ISBN 978-1-6680-0641-2 (ebook)

For Christine, the love of my life

Suffering comes to us as an interrogator. It asks, "Who are you?"

—David A. Fiensy

PART ONE:

The Unimaginable

CHAPTER ONE

—

April 27, 2017

It's six a.m. and I'm the first one up. Spotify's playing that Chainsmokers song I like. *If we go down, then we go down together . . .* I take an Ativan and chase my morning coffee with a couple of splashes of hundred-proof Captain Morgan. I return the bottle to its hiding place inside the twenty-quart lobster pot we never use, put the lid on, and put it back in the cabinet above the fridge that Emily can't reach without the step stool. Then I fill the twins' sippy cups and start making French toast for breakfast. *If we go down, then we go down together.* I cut the music so I can listen for the kids, but that song's probably going to play in my head all morning.

Emily's up now and in the bathroom, getting ready for work. When the shower stops, I hear the twins babbling to each other in the nursery we converted from my studio almost two years ago. My easel, canvases, and paints had been exiled to the space behind the basement stairs. It wasn't much of a sacrifice. I made my living as a commercial artist and had been struggling after hours and on weekends to make "serious" art, but after the babies were born, the last thing I felt like doing was staring at a blank canvas and waiting for some abstraction to move from my brain down my arm to my brush to see what came out. Maisie was the alpha twin; Niko, who would learn to creep, walk, and say words after his sister did, was the beta. In the developmental race, Niko always came in second, but, as their personalities began to emerge, his sister became our more serious, more driven twin and he was our mischievous little laughing boy. I loved them more deeply every day for who each was becoming. How could some artistic indulgence of mine have competed with what our lovemaking had created? It wasn't even close.

"Yoo-hoo, peekaboo!" I call in to them, playing now-you-see-me-now-you-don't at the doorway into their room. "Daddy!" they say simultaneously. Their delight at seeing me fills me with momentary joy—my elation aided, I guess, by the benzo and booze. I lift them, one after the other, out of the crib they share. The twins often hold on to each other as they sleep and sometimes even suck each other's thumb. I lay them on their backs on the carpet and take off their diapers. Both are sodden and Maisie's has two pellet-sized poops. As I wet-wipe and rediaper them, I say, "Hey, Miss Maisie, where's your nose?" We were playing that game yesterday. "Very good! And how about you, Mr. Niko? Where's your ear?" He puts his finger to his nose. "Nooo!" I groan in mock horror. "You can't hear with your nose!" Both kids giggle. I start singing "Wheels on the Bus," that song Emily sometimes sings with them when they're in the tub. Maisie listens attentively and does a few of the gestures with me while her brother kicks his legs and blows spit bubbles. I lift them up, one in each arm, and walk them into the kitchen just as the smoke alarm starts screaming.

The room is hazy and smells of burnt French toast. Frightened by the blare of the alarm, both kids begin crying. From down the hall, Emily calls, "Corby?" and I call back, "Everything's good. I got it!" I slide the kids into their high chairs and snap their trays in place. Point up at the alarm and tell them Daddy's going to stop the noise. "Watch," I say. Climbing onto the step stool, I reach up and silence the damned thing. "Daddy to the rescue!" I announce. Jumping off the stool, I do a little dance that turns their fear into laughter. "Daddy funny!" Maisie says. In my best Elvis imitation, I slur, "Thank you. Thank you very much." Of the two of us, I'm the fun parent and these two are my best audience. When I give them their sippy cups, I blow raspberries against their necks. They lift their shoulders and squeal with delight.

By the time Emily comes into the kitchen, I've already put her coffee and a stack of French toast on the table, the older pieces on the bottom and the fresh slices I'd made to replace the burnt ones on top. "Mama!" Niko shouts. Emily kisses the top of his head. "How's my favorite boy today?" she asks. Then, turning to his sister, she kisses her head, too, and says, "And how's my favorite girl?" She loves both of our kids, of course, but she favors Niko, whose emerging personality is like mine. Maisie is clearly her mother's daughter. She's less silly, more self-sufficient. Niko and I are the needy ones.

As Emily sits down to eat, I feel a surge of guilt thinking back to a morning a few weeks earlier. Emily told me she and some of the other teachers were going to Fiesta's after school for drinks and an early dinner. "I'll be home by seven, seven thirty at the latest," she'd said. I reminded her that Friday is family night. "I'll have had them all day. Not to mention all week. Did it occur to you when you were making your plans that I might need a break?"

She gave my shoulder a sympathetic squeeze. "I know you do, Corby, but Amber's really struggling right now. People have already RSVP'd to the wedding. She's been fitted for her dress. Their honeymoon is booked." Amber's a fellow teacher who was going to get married next month until her fiancé told her he was gay. "He completely blindsided her. She just really needs our support right now."

"And I don't?"

She stared at me, shaking her head. "If you're going to make a big deal about a couple of hours, then fine," she said. "I'll tell the others I can't make it."

"No, you go ahead, babe. Fiesta's, that Mexican place, right? Enjoy yourself. Have a margarita on me. What the hell? Have three or four. Get hammered."

She was almost out the door when she pivoted, her eyes flashing. "That's your thing, not mine." Touché.

She said goodbye to the kids but not to me. At the front window, I watched her get into her car, slam the door, and drive off. My regret kicked in a few minutes later—probably before she'd even pulled into the school parking lot. I texted her: *Sorry I was being a jerk. Go out with the others and help your friend. No worries.*

Her terse return text—*K Thx*—let me know she was still pissed, which, in turn, pissed me off all over again and made me feel justified in taking another Ativan to calm down. That was what that doctor prescribed them for, wasn't it?

Emily didn't get home that evening until after nine. I heard her in the kitchen before I saw her. "Hi, Corby," she called. "I got you an order of chicken enchiladas if you haven't eaten yet." I hadn't eaten but told her I had. "Okay, I'll put them in the fridge and you can have them tomorrow." She entered the living room with that tipsy glow she gets on the rare occasion when she has a second glass of wine, but her face deflated when she saw Niko asleep on my lap instead of in the crib. "He's sick," I said. "Earache."

She sat down on the couch beside us, stroked his hair, and asked whether I'd taken his temperature. "A hundred and one," I told her. The thermometer actually read one-hundred-point-four but I'd added the extra sixth-tenths of a degree. Yeah, I can be that small.

"Did you give him any Tylenol?"

I nodded. "About an hour ago. So how did group-therapy-with-nachos go?"

Instead of answering, she stood and picked up empties from the coffee table. She'd mentioned before that she doesn't like me drinking beer at night if I'm watching the kids, but she didn't call me on it that night. Her guilt was at a satisfactory level.

I'm sure Emily is keeping track of my nighttime beer consumption, but I'm confident she's unaware that I've started drinking the hard stuff during the day. Tuesday is when the recycling truck comes down our street, so I've begun hiding the empty liquor bottles until then. I wait until she leaves for school, then take them out of hiding and bring the blue box out to the curb, feeling embarrassed by the evidence of my growing reliance on alcohol but proud of myself for pulling off my daytime drinking deception. She knows I'm taking that prescription for my nerves, of course. In fact, she was the one who urged me to see someone because I'd become so edgy and sleep-deprived. What she doesn't know is that I've begun taking more than "one before bedtime and/or as needed."

I tell myself that "and/or as needed" is the loophole I can use if that doctor questions my need for an early refill. I'm not too worried about my growing reliance on "better living through chemistry." It's just a stopgap thing until my situation turns around. It's not like I'm addicted to benzos *or* booze. There was that DUI, but there were extenuating circumstances: namely that I lost my job that day. Everything will right itself once I get back to work. And okay, maybe I'm not looking for another position as hard as I was at the start, but I'll get back on the hunt soon.

The morning after Niko's earache, he was back to his rambunctious self and Maisie wasn't sick yet. I let Emily know I wasn't over it yet, communicating in single syllables. Emily took the kids to lunch and then over to the playscape in the park while I watched basketball. March Madness. Gonzaga versus Xavier, Oregon versus Kansas—but I didn't have skin in either of those games. Back when I worked at Creative Strategies, Declan from Accounting was always in charge of the brackets pool and he or Charlie, one of the salesmen, would have the rest of us over to watch the games. I haven't been gone that long, but neither had bothered to see whether I still wanted in. Out of sight, out of mind, I guess.

I stretched out on the couch with my six-pack of Sam Adams on the floor for company. What was that TV show where you could "phone a friend" for help? Who would I have called? My friendships at Creative hadn't lasted past my being employed there. My high school and college buddies and I hadn't stayed in touch. I had never been that close with the guys on my softball team. Try maintaining your male friendships when you've got two-year-old twins and have lost your job. While every other dude is out in the world, working during the week and hanging

with his bros on the weekends, I'm Mr. Mom twenty-four seven for a
couple of toddlers.

By midafternoon, I was half in the bag. Emily and the twins were still
out—probably over at her mother's. When I got up to take a piss, I swayed
a little on my way to the bathroom. Mid-pee, I saw the envelope she'd left,
propped against that stupid doll with the crocheted skirt that covered the
toilet paper roll. We'd both laughed at it after Emily's great-aunt Charlotte
gave it to her one Christmas, but for some reason it's survived several purges
of domestic detritus.

Inside the envelope was a letter on lined paper. *Hey Babe. I'm sorry
about yesterday. You were right. I should have asked you if you minded my
going out after work instead of telling you I was going. I hope you realize
how much I appreciate your caring for the twins while you look for another
job. I know it's hard. And I know you're going to find another position soon,
Corby. I hope you realize what a talented artist you are and a great dad, too.
Let's do pizza tonight. Hope we can have some close time after the kids are
asleep. XOXO, me.*

I appreciated what she'd written, particularly her offer of "close time"—
code for makeup sex. And sure enough, we had it that night, but it was a
bust. As usual, we did her first, but she was taking so long that I gave up,
got on top, and plugged in. Went from zero to sixty and was pounding away
when she grabbed my wrist and whispered, "Hey, take it easy." I stopped
cold, began losing my hard-on, and pulled out. Threw on my robe and
headed out the door, thinking, shit, man, I can't do anything right. Can't
find work, can't get through the day without drinking and drugging, and
now I can't even satisfy my wife. "Where are you going?" she said. "Come
on. Let's wait a few minutes and try again."

I appreciated the offer. I still love her. Still want her. A dozen years and
two kids after that summer we met, I still can't believe she said yes when I
asked her out that first time. Or that she committed to me when I drove
cross-country to California and showed up out of the blue at her college

apartment. And that she's *stayed* committed. Of the two of us, I definitely got the better deal. And here she was in our bed, offering me kindness and understanding. So of course I sabotage myself. "Not feeling it," I told her. "I'll take a rain check."

I went downstairs. Walked around in the kitchen, opened the fridge. I microwaved those enchiladas she had gotten me but kept them in so long, they were dry and tough. After a few bites, I scraped the rest into the garbage. Reached up for the lobster pot and made myself a stiff drink instead. By the time I got back to bed, Emily was asleep. In all the years we'd been together, I don't think we'd ever been this much out of sync.

But the next day, things got better. We sat on the floor and played with the kids. Danced with them to that silly "Baby Shark" song. When they went down for their afternoon naps, we went back to bed and tried again—successfully, this time, for both of us. We cooked supper together, the twins watching us as they wandered around underfoot. Things have been better since then. The usual minor ups and downs but nothing more. Marriage is all about that seesaw ride, isn't it? We're okay.

———

Now Emily cuts two slices of French toast into bite-sized squares, dotting each piece with syrup. "Yum, yum, yum," she says, divvying up the finger food between the kids. I love watching her with them, more so when I'm feeling relaxed like this. Maisie resembles her mother: dark hair, dark eyes, Em's dad's Mediterranean complexion. At her twenty-four-month checkup, she was in the thirtieth percentile for both height and weight, so she's probably going to be petite like Emily. Niko's got my reddish hair and lighter skin tone; his height and weight are a little higher than average, the pediatrician said, but compared to his sister, he looks like a bruiser. Turning to me, Emily asks why the smoke alarm went off. I hold up the two burnt pieces I threw on the counter, dangling them like puppets. "Here you go," I say, sliding the new stuff from the pan onto a plate. "Be right back." I head to the bathroom and brush my teeth so she doesn't smell my breath. I wait half a minute or so, then flush and walk back into the kitchen. She asks me what I'm smiling about.

"What?"

"You're smiling. What are you thinking about?"

"What am I thinking about? I don't know. Nothing much." I'm smiling because, thanks to the rum and Ativan, I'm pleasantly buzzed.

Maisie, the more fastidious eater, finishes without making a mess, but her brother's bib is saturated with milk and he has somehow managed to get syrup in his left eyebrow. Half of his breakfast is on the floor. Emily looks at the clock, then starts cleaning up the mess. "You know something, kiddo?" she asks Niko. "I think Mommy and Daddy should get one of those Roomba things and program it to follow you around all day. Would you like that?" Without having any idea what she's talking about, he nods enthusiastically. I tell Emily to leave it, that I'll clean up. "That would be great," she says. "I'm running a little late." She heads back to the bathroom to brush her teeth and blow-dry her hair.

Just before she leaves for work, Emily addresses the twins. "Be good kiddos for Daddy and Grammy today. No naughty stuff, okay?" She models the correct response, a head nod, which they both mirror back to her.

"Too bad we can't get that in writing," I quip. The day before, Niko led his sister in a game of crayon-scribbling on the kitchen linoleum and it was a bitch to scour off those marks without scratching the surface, which I did anyway.

"Okay, I'm off," she says. "Wish I could stay home with you guys. Love you."

"Love you, too." I made sure to start the breakfast dishes when I saw she was about to leave. Better a sudsy-handed wave goodbye than a boozy kiss. "Have fun on your field trip." She's just finished a dinosaur unit with her third graders and is taking them to the Peabody Museum to see prehistoric bones and footprints.

"Good luck with those leads, babe," she says. "Maybe today's the day, huh?"

I shrug. "Maybe."

Theoretically, I'll be job hunting today, although, truth be told, I've pretty much surrendered to the status quo. When I hear Emily's car back down the driveway, then accelerate, I say, aloud to no one in particular, "There goes the family breadwinner." Then I reach up for the lobster pot, take it down, and refresh my coffee-and-Captain cocktail. Get the twins dressed and pack the diaper bag. "Guess what?" I tell them. "Today is a Grandma day." Maisie claps her hands, but Niko shakes his head and says, "No Gamma! No Gamma!"

"Dude, I feel your pain," I tell him, chuckling. Emily's father once referred to his ex-wife as "the iron butterfly."

I lied to Betsy, telling her I'd drop them off somewhere around eight thirty so I can chase down a couple of imaginary leads, one of them in Massachusetts, north of Boston. Traffic permitting, I said, I'll pick them up sometime between three and four. I added the "traffic permitting" caveat as a cushion in case I need an extra hour to sober up.

I've lied to Emily, too—told her that after I drop the kids off at her mom's, I'll send out another round of résumés, make some follow-up calls, and then drive over to Manchester because Hobby Lobby has advertised an opening in their framing department. In truth, having been defeated by several months' worth of humiliation in my search for employment, and now dreading the possibility of actually *getting* the Hobby Lobby job and having to mat and frame people's shitty, mass-produced poster art at a big-box store, I will *not* be driving to Manchester or doing anything else on my make-believe agenda.

When I was laid off from the two-person art department of the advertising firm where I'd worked for five years, Rhonda, my manager, delivered the news at lunchtime and told me to take the afternoon off. In fairness, she didn't realize she was shitcanning me on Maisie and Niko's first birthday, for which we'd planned a party with the two grandmas, plus a few of our neighbors, and some of Emily's work friends. (The year before, it was Rhonda who had arranged for the lunchtime celebration of the twins' birth: cake, gift cards, packs of Huggies, jokes about sleeplessness.) "I want you to know that it's not about the quality of your work, Corby," Rhonda assured me as she raised the ax and let it drop. "It's about the company's bottom line. It was a difficult decision, but I was told I couldn't keep you both." And, of course, she wasn't about to lay off Brianne, the golden child who'd been hired three years after me but had been getting assigned to the bigger accounts. Like me, Brianne had been a scholarship student at the Rhode Island School of Design, but unlike me, she had graduated with honors and won awards for her work, whereas I'd quit midway through my senior year and driven across the country to secure Emily's love.

For a while now, I've been nurturing this scenario whereby a bigger and more lucrative agency lures Brianne away from Creative and I get my old job back and excel, showing them what a foolish mistake they made when they let me go. What's that called? Magical thinking? Meanwhile, my unemployment benefit has run out, and we've refinanced our mortgage and done three sessions of marriage counseling. Last month, we acknowledged the twins' second birthday with presents, cake, and candles but skipped the expense of a party. Hey, it is what it is, as they say. With an assist from rum and Ativan, I've lately held panic at bay by embracing the Alfred E. Neuman philosophy: What? Me worry? So after I drop off the kids, I'll be heading to the liquor store for another fifth of the Captain, then back home to consume it while watching some daytime TV: CNN, *The People's Court*, *The Price Is Right*, and, if I can find it again, that station that carries reruns of *Saved by the Bell*. Once my rum-and-benzo minivacation *really* kicks in, I might watch some porn and jerk off, maybe grab a nap. I'll pick up Maisie and Niko at Betsy's sometime around four. Start cooking supper by the time Emily gets home or, more likely, pick up Chinese or Chipotle for dinner, plus McNuggets for the twins. There's starting to be an embarrassing number of Happy Meal toys gathering on the windowsill in the playroom. That's my plan. But none of this will happen.

I put the bag I packed for the twins' day at their grandmother's on the bottom porch step, then go back inside. Brush my teeth and gargle twice so that Betsy won't smell anything when I drop them off. It's a chilly morning, so I put the kids' hats and spring jackets on. Lock the front door and walk them out to the driveway. The usual order of buckling the twins into their car seats is Niko first because he's the more restless of the two. But the order gets turned around this morning when I see Niko on his belly, watching a swarm of ants in the driveway crawl over and around a piece of cookie that got dropped the day before. I buckle Maisie in. Then I remember the bag on the porch step and hustle back to get it. I place the bag on the passenger's seat up front. Wave to our across-the-street neighbors, Shawn and Linda McNally, as they pull into their driveway. Linda gets out of the car shaking a paper bag. "Mr. Big Spender just took me out for breakfast," she calls over to me. "Egg McMuffin to go. Woo-hoo!"

I laugh. Promise Shawn I'll return the maul I'd borrowed from him. The weekend before, I finally finished splitting and stacking that half cord of wood that had been delivered a few months ago. "Yeah, good," he says, instead of "no rush" or "not a problem." Some guys are so possessive of their tools. Linda's outgoing, but Shawn always seems standoffish. Suspicious, almost. Toward me, anyway. He's a recently retired state cop. That probably explains it. I have the feeling that "Make America Great Again" sign on their lawn last year was his idea, not hers.

"How are my two little sweetie pies?" Linda asks.

"You mean double trouble? They got ahold of some crayons yesterday and scrawled all over the kitchen floor. When I busted them and asked, 'Did you two do this?' Maisie looked at her brother and he shook his head, so she did, too. The little monsters were still holding on to their Crayolas."

"Gonna be artists like their daddy," she says, laughing.

"Or politicians," I say. "They've already got the fibbing thing down."

Linda concurs. "When he was three, our Russell took a Magic Marker to our brand-new duvet. Swore up and down that he didn't do it—that it must have been his sister, Jill, who hadn't even started to creep yet. He almost didn't live to see age four." I roll my eyes and laugh. Ask her how Russell likes living out in Colorado. "Fine," she says. "He's been taking classes and bartending part-time but he just got a 'real' job at a TV station in Fort Collins."

I tell her to say hi from Emily and me next time she speaks to him. "Well, I better get going," I say. "Have a good one."

I climb into our CRV, start it up, and put it in reverse. When I feel the slight resistance at the rear right wheel, I figure a piece of the wood I stacked must have fallen off the pile; that's what the obstruction must be. What are they yelling about over there? I pull ahead a few feet, then back up again, depressing the gas pedal just enough to make it over the obstacle. In the rearview mirror, I see them running toward us, arms waving. What the fuck, man? Why is she screaming?

And then I know.

CHAPTER TWO

—

Summer 2005

Emily and I met the year before my desperate cross-country drive to save our relationship. We'd both gotten summer jobs at Olde Mistick Village, a self-consciously quaint New England Colonial-era tourist trap with a town green, a duck pond, and small shops selling the kind of high-end stuff and souvenirs that nobody really needs. I was on the two-man landscaping crew and Emily was working the front counter at a bakery where they sold these oversized molasses cookies I liked, Joe Froggers, cellophane-wrapped in a basket on the counter. That was what I bought the first time I went in there: a coffee and a Joe Frogger. "Nope," she said, looking at the cookie I'd selected. She put it back in the basket and replaced it with another. "This one's bigger. Hey, do you think there's a Mrs. Coffee?"

"Uh . . . what?" She was wicked cute but a little weird.

She tapped her painted fingernail against the carafe she was holding, the place where it said Mr. Coffee. "I mean, you hear a lot about Mrs. Santa Claus and Mrs. Doubtfire but never anything about Mrs. Coffee. Do you think he has a wife?" I shrugged. Gave her a half-smile. "By the way, I'm Emily."

"Hey," I said, catching up. "I'm Corby. I think Mr. Coffee's a bachelor but he's got a thing for Mrs. Butterworth."

"That slut?" she said. "I hope he's using protection because she's also got something going on with Mr. Peanut. Three seventy-five." I handed her a five and told her to keep the change. "You know who you kind of look like? Except he's not a redhead? Heath Ledger."

"Wasn't he Billy Bob's son in that prison film? Shoots himself in the head after his father humiliates him? What was the name of that movie?"

She shrugs. Says she's thinking about *10 Things I Hate About You* Heath Ledger. "You're not as hot though, so don't get a swelled head about it."

"Okay," I promised. For the rest of my shift that day, I thought about her as I picked up litter with my trash stabber and hosed off the walkways around the duck pond. Stupid birds. Why couldn't they just shit in the water? I figured she probably had a boyfriend.

Every lunchtime after that, I bought another Joe Frogger, but mostly I went into the bakery to flirt with Emily. She had dark wavy hair, big brown eyes, olive complexion. She had a cute little heart-shaped butt below the bow tied at the back of her apron, too. And a low, sexy voice you wouldn't expect to come out of someone not much over five feet tall. If there was a line at the register, I'd look at her and calculate which pigments I'd use to capture her skin tone: bronze, beige, maybe some flecks of Mediterranean green and Tuscany yellow. Not that it was likely she'd ever pose for me. How could I ask her to do that without sounding pervy?

"You eat many more of those, you're going to turn amphibian," she warned me one time about my cookie consumption. "As a matter of fact, you're looking a little green around the gills." She had a great deadpan delivery.

"Actually, we only have gills when we're tadpoles," I said. "As adults, we breathe through our skin." It was some random fact I remembered my father telling me out by the stream across from our house after I'd just caught a frog.

Another time at the bakery, I was standing in line behind a woman and her little kid. "You see that guy in back of you?" Emily asked the kid. "He's part human and part frog." The kid swiveled around and faced me with a skeptical smile. When I nodded and gave him a couple of ribbit-ribbits, the smile dropped off his face.

I think that was the day I finally got the balls to ask her out. Half the summer was over by then and she hadn't once mentioned a boyfriend. "You get off work at six, right? I was wondering if you wanted to grab something to eat this Friday and maybe go down to the Andrea? There's an R.E.M. cover band playing there this weekend. I saw them in Providence last semester. They're pretty decent." I could feel my face getting hot while she kept me waiting.

"Sorry. I've got plans," she finally said.

"Oh, okay. No worries."

"Yeah, on Fridays my mother and I get into our pj's early and play Scrabble."

Scrabble with Mom? Seriously? If she wasn't interested, she could at least have left me with a little bit of dignity. "Sure. No problem," I said. "Well, back to work." I couldn't get out of there fast enough.

"Hey, Red?" she called. "You planning to pay for that cookie?"

I looked down and, sure enough, I was holding a Joe Frogger. "Oh. Sorry," I said. Flustered, I pulled a five out of my wallet and handed it to her.

"You know I'm kidding, right? I'd be eternally grateful if you rescued me from another Friday night of board games and jammies. And did you say food? Do you know what I've been dying for all summer?" I shrugged. "Fried clams."

"I was thinking pizza, but yeah, that's cool. Strips or whole bellies?"

"Whole bellies," she said. "Eating clam strips is like stopping at kissing."

Whoa, I was taken aback by her cheeky remark and she noticed. Laughed and told me I looked shocked. "Shocked?" I said. "Who's shocked?"

I spent that afternoon weeding and deadheading the flower beds, thinking about what kind of signal Emily might have been sending me with that crack about kissing. I was doing math in my head, too. A couple of whole-belly clam dinners were going to cost three times as much as a pizza, I figured. But whatever.

For a lot of guys my age, sex was all about hookups, the more the better. Not me. The summer I met Emily, I'd had sex with a grand total of three women.

On that first date, we ate in the car at the clam shack she suggested. I didn't dare tell her, but I preferred strips to whole bellies. "Are you done?" she asked. I told her yeah, I just wasn't that hungry for some reason. Those bellies in my mouth felt too squishy. She ate the rest of mine and all of hers. Dipped her fries in tartar sauce rather than ketchup and polished them off, too.

On our way to the dance club, we talked about school. I told her I'd just finished my junior year at RISD with so-so grades except for Advanced Studio and Topics in Architectural Drawing. She said she was going into her senior year at UCLA, majoring in Educational Studies, and that she'd wanted to be a teacher since she was a kid. "Except for a brief time when I was eight and thought I'd like to be a nun." She'd gone to grammar school in Connecticut and high school in Southern California, where her parents had relocated to save their marriage. When it failed nevertheless, her mother returned to her family in Stonington, Connecticut. Emily had stayed in Cali with her dad so she could access the free tuition offered to state residents. She missed her mother, though, and was glad she got to stay with her during the summer.

"You closer to her than to your father?"

"Now I am, I guess. When I was growing up, I was a daddy's girl. Mom is Type A all the way and my dad's more laid-back. I was living at his place and commuting. But now his girlfriend Ana and her daughter have moved in with us. Ana's nice enough—it's not like we don't get along. But she and my dad kind of assumed I was their live-in nanny, so when I get back I'm sharing an apartment with some other UCLA students. How about you? Which parent are you closer to?"

"No contest," I said. "My dad's a dick." I didn't want to go into the particulars with her, so I changed the subject. At the bakery the week before, she'd mentioned that she was taking a night course at the UConn extension campus, so I asked her about that. "World Religions, right?"

She nodded. "I signed up for that class just to get my last gen-ed requirement out of the way, but it's been really interesting. This past week, we've been looking at Hinduism: karma, dharma, reincarnation." As she talked about the theory that we've all been here before in other forms, I pretended to be interested, but what I was really focused on was how good she smelled and how much I wanted to kiss those plump talking lips of hers and what it would be like to fuck her. "Don't you think?" she asked.

Busted. I had no idea how to answer her. "Possibly," I said.

At the Andrea, we danced a couple of times (she danced cooler than I did) and drank a few Heinekens, but the band was too loud for conversation. When they let rip with an eardrum-shattering cover of "What's the Frequency, Kenneth?" I pointed to the beach out back and she nodded. The just-past-full moon illuminated the shore that night. We dropped our shoes and her purse in the sand, threw my hoodie over them so they'd be concealed, and started walking. "So," she said. "You're closer to your mother than your dad. What's she like?"

"My mom? Well . . . she's got red hair like me except hers is starting to go gray. Good sense of humor, likes to garden." I edited out the more exotic stuff: that Mom grew her own weed and was into Tarot; that the summer between my high school graduation and my first year of college, she'd gotten a tattoo, turned Wiccan, and told me she might be bisexual. "She's a bit of a free spirit," I added.

"Does she work?"

"Yeah. Waitresses at Newport Creamery. She's been there for years. Has a bunch of regulars she jokes with. What's your mom like?"

She said, "Well, she reads a lot and writes poetry that she never lets anyone see. Vacuums her apartment twice a week and hates that I'm such a slob. She belongs to this women's church group where they get together and sew patchwork quilts."

"Girls Gone Wild, huh? So if you wanted to be a nun, you guys must be Catholic. Right?"

"Nope. I'd been over at my friend Erin Houlihan's house when her aunt was visiting. Sister Julia: she was young and pretty and had just taken her final vows. When I got home, I told my mother that Erin and I had decided to enter the convent when we were old enough. She reminded me that we were Methodists, not Catholics, and did I know that nuns had to shave their heads and kneel on hard surfaces when they prayed, sometimes for hours at a time? I decided Erin would have to go it alone."

She laughed at the memory. "My grandfather was a brigadier general in the army, and both Mom's brothers were commissioned officers. My uncle Frank worked at the Pentagon until he retired. The whole family votes Republican, including Mom."

"Like mother, like daughter?" I asked.

"Politically? Oh God, no. I can't even go there with her about politics. What about you? Were you Bush or Gore?" When I said I hadn't bothered to vote because all politicians were the same, she punched my arm. Hard! "That attitude is part of the problem, you chooch. I can tell I have a lot of work to do if I'm going to straighten *you* out." As in, maybe you and I might have a future? That this night might go somewhere?

"Maybe you should have been a nun after all," I said. "You've already got the scolding thing down and you can land a pretty decent punch. Plus you're pretty enough to rock a shaved head."

She said she bet I used that line with all the girls. "All *what* girls," I said.

"Oh, come off it. Those broad shoulders and the lanky frame? Those long lashes that any girl would kill to have?"

Her compliments made me feel embarrassed but pleased. "Lanky?" I said. "Gawky, you mean."

She scoffed. "Cute butt, too. Not that I noticed." When she reached over and slipped her small hand in mine, I folded my fingers around it. Had it happened as early as that? Was that the moment—the gesture—that made me fall in love with her?

By the time we got back to the place where we'd left our stuff, the tide had crept further in and soaked everything. "No biggie," she said. "Most of my stuff's in my other purse and folding money dries."

Up at the Andrea, the band must have been taking a break. The jukebox was playing an old tune that I recognized. *You are here and warm / But I could look away and you'd be gone* . . . We decided not to go back inside. Holding our wet shoes, we walked barefoot to the parking lot. Made out in my car, touching each other until the windows fogged up and I was getting close to launching. She whispered that we'd better stop. "Is that what you want?" I whispered back.

"No," she said. "But yes."

When I dropped her back at her mom's, I asked her, on a scale of one to five, how good a time she'd had. "Five," she said. "You?" I told her ten.

The following morning, I was still asleep when my phone rang. I squinted at the time: seven fifteen. Who the fuck . . . ?

"Yeah?"

"Good morning," she said. "Thanks again for last night. Hey, would you like to go out for breakfast? I was thinking the Aero Diner on Route Two in half an hour?"

I said yes, swung my legs out of bed, and headed for the shower. After toweling off, I looked at my naked self in the mirror. Long eyelashes? Check. Broad shoulders? Nah. Average, maybe. Nothing special. But because the work I was doing that summer was physical, my stomach looked cut and my biceps were bigger. Still, I had a T-shirt tan—not cool. And an overbite, as the hygienist always reminded me when I got my teeth cleaned. And in my opinion, my frame was still on the scrawny side. It was a draw, I figured, and slipped on some clean boxers. What counted was that Emily liked what she saw. I glanced again at the clock. I had fifteen minutes to get to that diner on Route Two and there'd probably be beach traffic. There was no time to shave, so I hoped she liked the scruffy look.

Apparently, she did. We got together almost every night for the rest of that dwindling summer. Went to the beach half a dozen times. Made love whenever the opportunity let us, given that we were both staying with our moms.

Emily's mom was iffy about me from the beginning, and she wasn't exactly reassured when she found a couple of the nude sketches I'd done of Emily. "He could post these on the internet," she warned her daughter. "How many schools would hire you to teach if these went public?"

Emily's theory was that Betsy would come around once she got to know me better, so I went over there for dinner one rainy Sunday in the middle of August. Emily made a lasagna and Betsy contributed a green salad with nothing in it besides arugula, oil, and lemon juice. Hope she hasn't tired herself out making it, I thought. To impress her, I had splurged on a thirty-dollar bottle of red wine and purposely left the price tag on, but I could have saved my money. Betsy barely touched her lips to her glass. After I'd finished a second helping of lasagna, Emily said she'd made a blueberry pie for dessert. When she stood and started clearing the plates, I got up to help her. Betsy insisted I sit back down because I was their guest.

With Em in the kitchen, that left the two of us. After an awkward several seconds, I said, "So your daughter says you write poetry."

"Oh, here and there," she said. "I'm much more of a reader than a writer."

"Yeah? What's your favorite book?"

"Oh goodness, I have so many. I've been rereading *Jane Eyre*. That's one of my favorites. *Masterpiece Theatre* has been running a marvelous series based on the book. I don't suppose you've seen it."

"No, but my mother's been watching it," I told her. Which was a lie. For Mom, must-see TV on Sunday nights was *Desperate Housewives*.

"So tell me," she said. "Is art something you're hoping to make your living doing?"

"Maybe," I said. "I'm not really into planning my future at this point. I guess I'm more of a live-for-today kind of person."

"Aha. Then you're the grasshopper, not the ant." When I shrugged, she said, "Aesop's Fables. You're very young, aren't you?"

As in immature and stupid, I figured. I poured myself more wine. A thirty-buck bottle of cabernet? *Some*one had better drink it. I felt like letting her know that my high school girlfriend's parents had been *crazy* about me; her dad had even taken me fishing. Where the hell was Emily?

Reaching for my glass, I knocked it over, spilling wine on their white tablecloth. Ignoring my apology, Betsy jumped up, rushed to the kitchen, and came back armed with paper towels, a dishcloth, and a bottle of club soda. Blotting, pouring, and scrubbing, she let me know that the tablecloth, a gift from her favorite aunt, would be ruined if the stain was allowed to set. "Again, I'm very, very sorry," I said. Instead of acknowledging my apology, she continued to scrub aggressively.

When Emily returned with the pie, she apologized that it was so juicy. She'd forgotten the cornstarch. Aware that blueberries stained, I ate my piece super carefully. As soon as I had my last bite, I stood and said I had to go. "Already?" Emily said. I made up a bullshit excuse about having to feed a neighbor's dog.

At the front door, I whispered to Emily that I was pretty sure I'd flunked the audition. "Good thing you're not dating her then," she quipped. "And don't worry about the stupid tablecloth. Big deal." When I kissed her, she kissed me back.

It was pouring by then and the ground was saturated. Backing up, I accidentally veered off their driveway and onto the lawn. Made a little bit of a rut, which by morning might not even be noticeable. And if it was, Betsy would have to just fucking get over it. *You're very young, aren't you?* What a bitch.

At the end of August, Emily and I promised each other we'd call and write as often as our upcoming semesters allowed. I'd fly out there for the four-day Thanksgiving break and she'd spend the month between semesters back at her mother's. So at the end of our Mistick Village summer, we returned to our schools on opposite coasts.

CHAPTER THREE

2006–2013

We talked to each other four or five times a week, ending calls with "I love you" and "I love you more." Thanksgiving out in California went well; Emily's dad, Pat, and his girlfriend, Ana, were cool and a lot friendlier than her mom. Emily flew back to Connecticut for Christmas at the end of the fall semester and I picked her up at the airport. When she came around the corner and saw me in the crowd, she made a mad dash, leapt into my arms, and bracketed her legs around my hips. A few of the people around us hooted and applauded.

We spent most of our three-week break together. Took the train into New York for the day to see the tree at Rockefeller Center and the holiday windows. Home again, we went tobogganing over at the golf course. We met my mother for lunch at Village Pizza because she wanted to meet Emily. She had invited us over to her place, but Mom's trailer was as messy as Betsy's place was neat and it sometimes smelled of cat pee, so I lied. Told her Emily was allergic to cats and that Ajax and Trixie might give her a sneezing attack. When we went Christmas shopping at the mall, Emily and I were looking in one of the jewelry store windows when a saleswoman came out to the entrance and said she could show us a much bigger selection of engagement rings inside. Emily blushed and shook her head. "Not quite there yet? Well, we have some lovely preengagement pieces and friendship rings. Come in and have a look." I told her no thanks and we walked away hand in hand. The next day I went back there and bought Emily a bracelet, fourteen-karat gold with a diamond chip.

We exchanged our gifts out in my car on Christmas Eve. "You sure you don't want to come in?" Emily asked. I didn't. I was going over to her mom's for Christmas dinner the next day and there was only so much Betsy I could take. Emily said she loved her bracelet and put it right on. She didn't say anything about the diamond chip and neither did I, but I hoped she'd gotten my intended message: a preview of coming attractions. For my present, Emily had reserved us a room at the Three Rivers Inn for New Year's Eve.

I had never stayed in a hotel room that fancy before. We made love in the warm, bubbling water of the hot tub and, later, in the plush bed. Emily had gone on the pill by then, so there was no fumbling with condoms. When she came, she burst out crying. "What?" I asked. "What's the matter?"

"Nothing's the matter. It's just . . . I don't know. I've never felt like this before."

"What do you mean—like this?"

"Like . . . feeling a little drunk when I haven't had anything to drink. I'm just so happy, Corby. It's a little overwhelming, in a good way."

Cuddling, we watched a show about the major events of the year just ending—Katrina, Iraq, the death of Pope John Paul, the birth of YouTube. Then the ball dropped in Times Square, we kissed the New Year hello, and fell asleep in each other's arms. Two days later, we were back at the airport, and I watched her plane take off and rise, flying her back to California.

While I was packing to go back to school, Mom came in with a tin of brownies. She told me how much she liked Emily. "But long-distance relationships can be pretty hard to sustain," she said.

"Yeah? I thought absence was supposed to make the heart grow fonder." I was being a wise guy, which Mom sometimes liked and sometimes didn't. And sometimes ignored if she was trying to make a point.

"I'm not trying to be a wet blanket, Corby," she said. "I just don't want you to get ahead of yourself with this girl. You're both very young and—"

"You know something, Mom? You worry too much. Maybe long-distance relationships get tricky for some couples, but that won't happen with us."

"Okay then. I just don't want to see you get hurt. And don't forget to share those brownies with some of the boys in your dorm. There's a dozen and a half."

"Any wacky weed in there, Mrs. Feelgood?" She gave me a look. "Okay. Thanks, Mom. And stop worrying about Emily and me. We're fine."

And things *were* fine for the first several weeks of the semester. When Emily's letters and callbacks began to taper off, I chalked it up to her student teaching. She had a forty-minute commute to her school, taught all day, and then drove back, prepared lessons and graded papers into the night. She and I were rock solid; she was just super busy. But then came the night when, over the phone, she said basically what my mother had said: that maybe we needed to tap the brakes on our relationship.

"I don't get where this is coming from," I said. "I thought being with me made you feel . . . intoxicated. Was that because you'd just gotten laid and were feeling the afterglow?" Instead of taking the bait, she let her silence do the talking. But I couldn't stop. "You breaking up with me? Is that what this is?"

"*No.* I'm just wondering if maybe we should slow down a little, you know?"

"Jesus Christ! How much more 'slowed down' can we be with you out in California, me in Rhode Island, and three thousand miles between us?"

"Corby, why do you sound so angry? All I'm saying is that maybe we both should have the freedom to go out with other people from time to time."

If there had been Skype or FaceTime back then, she would have seen my despair. "I don't need that kind of freedom because I know for sure that I want to share the rest of my life with you."

"Okay, but Corby, I'm just not sure we're in the same place about that. I don't even know what the rules are for us as a couple. It's confusing."

"So who is he?"

"Okay, if you must know, it's Brad Pitt. I couldn't resist."

"No, seriously. Who is he? And have you slept with him yet?"

"There's nobody else, Corby. You're jumping to conclusions."

"Am I?"

There was a long pause on her end. "One of my housemates? Mason? He and I were eating breakfast yesterday and he said, out of the blue, that he has feelings for me. Which was awkward because the only thing I feel toward him is annoyance. I mean, he clips his toenails in the living room. And when he's studying? He clears his throat so many times that I find myself counting instead of concentrating on what *I'm* supposed to be studying."

"Okay, who else?"

"No one else. The guy who runs the coffee shop I go to asked me if I wanted to go to some art show opening with him and I told him no, that I was seeing someone. But it's gotten me thinking that if—"

"If someone better comes along? You want to keep your options open?"

"Okay, forget I even said anything. And stop being so fucking insecure. Because this is already a really stressful time for me with student teaching, okay? The kids in one of my classes keep testing me. And their regular teacher's this hard-nosed disciplinarian who won't even let the kids breathe. Yesterday she told me that if my classroom management doesn't improve, she can't see how she'll be able to give me a good grade. But the thing is, she never leaves the room. She just sits on the sidelines and scowls. Whenever that class is coming up, I turn into a nervous wreck."

I didn't want to talk about her student teaching; I wanted to keep talking about *us*. As if I were qualified to give her advice about her situation, I said, "Just tell her you've got your own style and that you need her to leave the room when you have that class because it makes you nervous."

"Oh yeah, that would go over big," she said. "The thing I said about not knowing what the rules were? For us as a couple? What if some guy I know, someone who's just a friend, wants to go for a walk or to a movie. Is that—"

I barged in before she could finish. "Let me ask you something. That bracelet I gave you? Do you wear it or is it shoved in a drawer someplace?"

"I have it on right now, Corby. I wear it every day. Look, I know I'm not doing a very good job of explaining what I'm trying to say. But I'm just under so much pressure right now about the teaching stuff and—"

I told her I had to go but that we could talk later.

Hung up on her.

Paced back and forth. Guy at a coffee shop? I thought about that barista at the Starbucks on Angell Street: guy was so good-looking and gym-fit, you noticed him even if you're a dude. Mr. Personality, too, with dollar bills and fives stuffed into his tip jar. Like I'd have any chance if I had to compete against *that* guy.

I went downstairs and stormed out of the dorm. Hoofed it from campus into downtown Providence and bought a pack of cigarettes. I only smoked when I felt anxious about something, a habit I'd picked up one exam week in high school. For a good hour or more, I kept walking, smoking, and thinking about what I could do so I wouldn't lose her. By the time I got back, my throat burned from tar and nicotine but I had figured it out.

I'd never loved RISD and this semester *really* sucked. I'd gotten a D and a C-minus for midterm grades, the first in Spatial Geometry (if I wanted this much math, I'd have majored in it), the other in Ambient Interfaces (too many missed classes, plus the prof had an annoying laugh and bad breath). Then things had gone sour the first week of the new semester when I was hauled before the disciplinary referral board for something ridiculous that had happened before Christmas break. Having volunteered with some other guys to decorate the common area for the holidays, I'd gotten shit-faced. We all had, but I was the one who had written, in spray snow on the picture window, "Fuck you and the sleigh you rode in on." Some dean had walked by, seen it, and made a complaint. The students on the discipline committee—a trio of dweebs—listened to my lame defense about having exercised my First Amendment rights. "I'd like to think this is a *college*, not a *prison*," I said in closing. I concluded that me and RISD were a bad fit.

I didn't bother to withdraw; I just drove away in my rusted-out Chevy Chevette and headed west. I was that sure that Emily was the one for me and the grand gesture I was making was going to convince her that *I* was the one for her. How many other dudes would ditch their college education for love?

Even gunning it, the trek from Providence to San Diego took me almost four days and earned me two speeding tickets (one in Pennsylvania, the other just outside of Little Rock, Arkansas), plus a loitering fine somewhere along Route 40 for napping on the shoulder of a highway. I played the radio all the way out there—listening a billion times to Rihanna, CeeLo, and that sappy James Blunt song "You're Beautiful" on the pop stations and, as I drove west, Kenny Chesney, Rascal Flatts, and a bunch of stations hawking Jesus. The news was redundant, too—the Patriot Act gets renewed, the polar ice caps are shrinking, the trouble at Abu Ghraib prison. And if you're planning to go quail hunting with Dick Cheney, better think again.

When I couldn't stand the radio anymore, I'd turn it off and enjoy the silence for a while until my father's voice would start playing in my head. "But deciding to leave isn't the same as flunking out, Dad," I'd insisted, interrupting his usual refrain about me being a disappointment to him. That earworm had begun in middle school when I'd gotten caught shoplifting Upper Deck basketball cards at the hobby store in the mall. The night my buddies and I had gotten pinched at Lantern Hill for underage drinking I'd been an embarrassment to him and myself, he'd said. (Of course, when he picked me up at state police barracks, he reeked of scotch.) I'd humiliated him the day he found out I'd gotten fired from my summer job at the A&P for helping myself to handfuls of cooked shrimp while, instead of herding empty carriages out in the parking lot, I was chatting with the hot blond behind the fish counter. He reminded me that he'd gone out on a limb and asked one of his golfing buddies, an A&P district manager, to see that I'd get hired. He might as well just face it, he'd said: his son was a nonstarter, a slacker, a dud. During my freshman year at RISD, I'd gone to a counselor for a while because of my anxiety and we'd talked about my relationship with my father. "I don't get it, you know?" I told her. "Supposedly, his students love him. And last year his university gave him some big award for this program he started down in Haiti. But at home, until he left my mother and me, he was always riding my ass about something. Hers, too. She got it worse than I did."

"A lot of people are like that, Corby," she'd said. "They have a public persona that's different from who they are at home. Have you ever considered that you might have been the victim of verbal abuse?"

I'd stuck up for Dad. "He just wants to wake me up when he says shit like that. Give me a reality check."

"So are you saying you *are* a loser? That that *is* your reality? Because you and I haven't known each other for long, but I'd have to disagree."

Why had that shrink's attempt to defend me against my father during that session pissed me off? Why had I stopped going to see her after that?

But anyway, that flamboyant gesture I made—shitcanning school and driving cross-country to rescue Emily's and my relationship? It worked. "Oh my God," she said when she answered the door. "Corby? What the . . . ? Why . . . ?"

"Because the only thing that matters to me is you. Will you marry me?" When I began to cry, she reached up, put her hands on my shoulders, and pulled me close. Rested her head against my chest and said she didn't care that my showing up made no sense—that the only thing she knew was that she fucking loved me. As for marriage, she didn't say yes or no.

Emily's housemates weren't happy about my arrival, even though I began kicking in toward the rent. The shy one, Becky, tended to freak out if I went into the kitchen shirtless or left the bathroom wearing just a towel. Mason, the dude who had "feelings" for Emily, kept making cryptic remarks in my presence that Em said were passive-aggressive. Odessa's beef was that I left dirty dishes in the sink, which I had done like maybe two times, tops. They had a meeting one afternoon when Emily and I weren't around and voted us out of the house. Emily was hurt and I felt bad for her, but another part of me was like, hallelujah! No more having to put up with the bullshit of community living with these prima donnas.

We moved into a two-room apartment over a garage near campus. I started to love living in SoCal. The easygoing vibe, the unbelievable weather. Emily's student teaching went so well during her last month that she got an A and the principal at her school offered her a job for the following year. I'd gotten a job, too, selling suits at a Men's Wearhouse in Redlands. Every other weekend when I was off, I tried selling my paintings at the street fairs around the Embarcadero Pier. Most of the Saturday and Sunday tourists were buying seascapes and no one was interested in the abstract expressionist stuff I was doing at the time. I wasn't about to lower my standards and start churning out that kind of cheesy shit just because it sold. Instead, I lowered my standards and started sketching rock icons in charcoal—the usual suspects: Hendrix, Janis, Prince, Cobain. I got fifty bucks a pop for them. Sold three or four a day on average and put most of that money toward buying Emily an engagement ring. Making it official.

Emily didn't go back east to her mom's that summer; she stayed in Cali with me. I think it was mid-July when she developed something called deep vein thrombosis. Fearing a blood clot down the road, her doctor took her off the pill and prescribed a diaphragm instead. It wasn't until she got pregnant that we read the fine print that said diaphragms had a 4 percent failure rate if you'd used them correctly every time and a 12 to 18 percent failure rate if you hadn't. A few times in the heat of the moment we might have gotten careless, I don't really remember. But whatever the reason, the home test kit said Emily was pregnant. When I took a knee and showed her the diamond, she cried. Said yes. But when Emily called to tell her mom we were engaged, Betsy had news of her own. She had breast cancer and needed a mastectomy.

Between wanting to be there for her mom during her recuperation and wanting her mom closer during her pregnancy, Emily lobbied for us to go back east.

"You can fly back when she has her surgery, help out for a couple of weeks while she recuperates if you want, but you and I have a life out here now, babe," I said. "Maybe after the baby's born, your mother can come out here and—"

She shook her head. Told me her mom needed her and she needed her mom.

"Yeah, but what about the teaching job you just got? What are you going to do—resign before you've even started?"

And that's just what she did. I gave in. We rented and packed up a U-Haul trailer, typed Betsy's address into MapQuest, and hit the road. There went our California life.

The trip back east was hell. I had bought the cheapest trailer hitch kit that U-Haul sold and hadn't installed it right. We were just over the state line into Arizona when the trailer broke free, just missed the car behind us, and then went flying off the side of the highway and into a gulley. That set us back a whole day, plus the cost of a better hitch and a nondescript motel room that had bedbugs.

Emily's nausea came and went as we traveled all those miles. We fought. She had a couple of crying jags. We were driving through Missouri when she began spotting. The doctor we saw at an emergency room in Oklahoma City examined Emily, ordered an ultrasound to be on the safe side, and assured us that a little bleeding during the first trimester was something a lot of women experienced. "Maybe twenty-five percent. And most go on to deliver healthy babies down the line. So there's no need to panic, Mom and Dad. I think everything's going to be fine." In the blurry picture he gave us, the fetus looked like a lima bean with an eye. It was about an inch long, he said. Emily miscarried the next morning about a hundred miles outside of Nashville. She alternated between crying and sleeping and I tried to comfort her as best I knew how, but it was guesswork; I was in over my head. She said she didn't want to see another doctor. She just knew. All she wanted was to see her mom. So I fought sleep, pounded Red Bulls, and drove almost nonstop the rest of the way.

Betsy had good news: the cancer had been contained to her breast without having metastasized. She was solicitous with Emily and, surprisingly, with me, too. "Do you need a hug?" she asked me when we were alone together in her kitchen. I hesitated—I *didn't* want one because I kept picturing her severed breast on a stainless steel tray. But I told her I did so I wouldn't hurt her feelings. "No bear hugs," she warned. "I'm still pretty tender there." When she put her arms around me, I found myself unable to reciprocate. Instead of hugging her back, I reached around and gave her some little one-handed pats on her back.

Emily and I were married at the Stonington Town Hall on August the first. Emily's dad couldn't get there on short notice, but he mailed us a check and asked us to send pictures. Emily wore her sleeveless yellow sundress and I wore my lucky plaid shirt, the vest from my one suit, and my least faded jeans. Our witnesses were Em's high school friend LeeAnne and her boyfriend. Both of our mothers were there, my mom still in her waitress uniform because she'd had to dash over from her shift at Newport Creamery. Betsy was decked out like it was the big church wedding she had wanted her daughter to have. After the marriage license was signed, she sprang for lunch at the Floodtide, one of those upscale places where they put guys in toques at the carving stations and you get your Caesar salad tossed table side. No honeymoon; we both had job interviews.

West Vine Street Elementary hired Emily to teach third grade. That same week, I got my job as a graphic artist at Creative Strategies, a startup agency that was happy to hire me based on my portfolio and the fact that they could lowball me, salary-wise, because I had no degree. My RISD buddy Matt, the only one I'd stayed in touch with, had graduated, landed a job at Cutwater, one of the big agencies in Manhattan, and sublet an apartment in Brooklyn, where all the cool kids lived. My job was in working-class Connecticut and I presumed he was making a lot more than me. But it was a trade-off. I had lucked out at love and Matt hadn't—not yet, anyway. Had I not abandoned school to save my relationship, I would probably *not* be married to Emily. But I was. I was more in love with her than ever, and if she wasn't quite as committed to me as I was to her—something I worried about from time to time—it didn't mean she *wasn't* committed. She was just a little reserved, that was all. Not aloof like her mother—not by a long shot. She just held a little something back for herself, that was all. Nothing wrong with that.

We postponed getting pregnant again, telling ourselves that we had plenty of time, and that we both wanted to establish ourselves in our careers first. We needed to be practical, not impetuous or haphazard like the first time, she said. But fear was involved, too, I think—more so for Emily than for me. Having had that miscarriage under such difficult circumstances made her gun-shy. I asked her maybe three or four times if she wanted to talk about it, but she always just shook her head and got quiet. She still kidded with me, showed me that wise-ass side of her that I'd enjoyed so much during our first summer, but it surfaced less often. We were fifty-fifty on the household chores and sometimes when I did the laundry and put stuff away, I'd look at that blurry ultrasound photo she kept in her underwear drawer: the tiny lima bean of our nonbaby. It wasn't like Emily was hiding it; she knew that I knew it was there. She just never wanted to discuss it: that traumatic cross-country trip back east.

During the summer of 2014, we rented a cottage up in Truro on the Cape. It was during that week when Emily told me she thought she was ready to try again. We stopped using birth control and Em was pregnant by the end of that month. "If I were you two, I'd start shopping around for one of those double strollers," Emily's gynecologist told us the day we went in for the ultrasound. "What? Are you kidding us?" I said. I started laughing. When I glanced over at Emily, she looked scared.

CHAPTER FOUR

April 27, 2017

And now I know.

I swivel around and look in the back seat to prove to myself that I'm wrong. But there's Maisie, strapped in, clutching her Mr. Zebra. Niko's car seat is empty. Too late: the image of him on his belly behind the car, studying those ants.

Opening the door, I stumble out of the car, lose my balance, and fall to the ground. On hands and knees, I force myself to look beneath the undercarriage. See him and have to look away. I beg a god I don't believe in to make this not be happening. To make these shouts of denial not be coming from me but from some other child's father. I hear Shawn McNally's agitated plea to 911. See Linda coming around from the back of the car, her hand over her mouth. I go to my son, drop to my knees beside him, averting my eyes but then forcing myself to look again. He's on his side, his head turned to the left, a puddle of red under his crushed body. I watch the rapid rising and falling of his little chest—his fight to stay alive—and have to look away. This isn't happening, is it? Don't leave us, Niko. You have to hold on.

When I move to pick him up, cradle him, Shawn stops me. Tells me to leave him where he is. He pulls me up onto my feet and bear-hugs me. Maisie! She's still in the car. But no, she isn't. Linda's gotten her out and is holding her, shielding her from the horror. Looking confused and frightened, Maisie reaches for me. Taking her in my arms, I try to hold it in but can't. When I start to wail, she does, too. "What do I do?" I ask Linda. "I don't know what to do!"

"You need to call Emily," she says.

I shake my head. "I can't. How can I tell her it happened because of— "

"You have to tell her, Corby. She needs to know."

I nod and rummage in my pockets for my cell phone. "Must have forgotten my phone in the house," I tell Linda. "Can you hold her for a few more minutes?" She nods. "Daddy has to call Mommy first," I tell Maisie. "Then I can hold you." Feeling a surge of nausea, I run toward the house, trying not to hear her screams for Daddy.

Where is it? Where's my fucking phone? In a frenzy, I run from the kitchen to the bathroom, from our bedroom to the kids' room. I'm stopped by the photo on the shelf by their dresser: the two of them standing up in their crib, wearing the sleepers we gave away after they outgrew them. Maisie's smiling sweetly; Niko, the comedian, is making a goofy face. Oh God, what if . . . ? How can what's happening be real when twenty minutes earlier I was wiping syrup off his face and lifting him out of his high chair? I don't want to go back out there. I want to stay in here, in the safety of before it happened. Before I put it in reverse and . . .

In my second sweep, I see my phone sitting in plain sight on the kitchen counter. I grab it and tell it to call Emily, but it rings unanswered until Em's voice kicks in and says to leave her a message. I text her: *Emergency! Come home now.* There's no immediate text back. Goddammit! She must have turned her phone off. I run back outside.

The ambulance is here. The EMTs are bent over Niko, blocking my view. "Daddy!" Maisie screams. I stand there, confused about which kid to go to until Linda walks toward me holding out my daughter. Arlene from down the street is with her. I take Maisie and begin walking toward Niko until Arlene grabs my arm. "Are you thinking clearly?" she asks. "You don't want her to have to see this, do you?" I shake my head. Walk

Maisie to the far end of our lawn to shelter her—both of us—from what's happening on the driveway.

"It's okay, it's okay," I keep telling Maisie to stop her crying. "Everything's okay." This may be the biggest lie I've ever told in my life.

No! I tell myself. His sister *needs* him. His mother and I wouldn't be able to cope if . . . and Niko's a tough little guy. He's still breathing, still fighting to live. Emergency responders are *trained* and these two look like they know what they're doing. Maybe he'll need surgery when he gets to the hospital, but doctors perform miracles. He's going to make it. He *is*.

I look past the ambulance's flashing lights at the end of the driveway to the neighbors huddled together on the McNallys' front lawn. Arlene and her husband, J.G.; Dylan and Rashon, the couple who bought the Olmsteads' place; Mary Louise and her daughter, Jodi, who sometimes babysits for us. The week before, Jodi walked her new puppy over to let the twins see her. Why are they still working on him *here*? Get him in the ambulance! Get him to the hospital!

Two cruisers pull up in front of the house, one after the other. Two pairs of cops. The first pair walks to where it happened. Squatting, examining the right rear tire. One of them begins taking measurements, the other takes cell phone photos. The second pair of officers approach the neighbors. Linda McNally's voice is the only one that carries over to me. "We screamed for him to stop, but he didn't hear us!"

The police must have asked where I was, because I see Shawn McNally pointing in my direction. As they cross the street toward Maisie and me, Linda calls to them. "It was an *accident*! A terrible *accident*! He's a wonderful father!"

Oh God, Emily still doesn't know. "Someone call my wife's school!" I shout over to the neighbors. "West Vine Elementary! She's got a field trip today, but maybe they haven't left yet!" Rashon waves his cell phone at me and says he's on it.

"Hello, sir," the stocky older cop says. "This is Officer Longo and I'm Sergeant Fazio. You're the boy's father?"

"Yes."

"And you were the operator of the vehicle?"

"Yes."

He waits for me to compose myself. "This one yours, too?" he asks. I nod. "Twins."

"She and the victim?"

The *victim*? Don't call him that! "His name is Niko," I say.

The younger cop focuses his attention on Maisie. "I have a little girl just about your age," he says. "What's your name, sweetheart?"

Maisie buries her face against my chest and mumbles, "Don't see me."

"Think you can have someone else take her while we talk to you?" the sergeant asks. I nod. Call Jodi and her mom over. When I ask whether they can take care of Maisie for me, Mary Louise says of course, whatever I need.

"No! I want Daddy!" Maisie shouts. But Jodi reminds her about the new puppy. Does she want to come over to their house and play with Cupcake? Maisie hesitates, but then she nods and detaches herself from me. When I put her down, Jodi and her mom each take her by the hand. "We can keep her for as long you need us to," Mary Louise calls back as they walk her away. "We'll pray for Niko."

The sergeant does the talking. "We need to ask you some questions, Mr. . . . ?"

"Ledbetter." I pull out my wallet and, with a shaking hand, offer my driver's license. The younger one takes it. "I'll get started on this," he says. Walks toward their cruiser, my information in hand. The sergeant gets close to my face and says I should tell him exactly what happened and everything leading up to it. "And I need you to be as specific as you can, all right? Don't leave anything out, even if you think it might not be important."

I back up a step or two. Begin with the French toast, the smoke alarm, Emily's field trip, the plan to take them to my mother-in-law's. I listen to myself retell the lie I had told my wife: that I was planning to spend the day job-hunting. I don't mention anything about the liquor-laced coffee or the extra Ativan. When I finally stop talking, I notice he's looking down at my trembling hands.

At the end of the driveway, the EMTs are on their feet. They've placed Niko in the middle of an adult-sized stretcher and are rolling him into the back of their ambulance. One of them climbs in back with him. The other heads to the front and gets in the driver's seat. "I need to go with him to the hospital," I tell the sergeant. As the ambulance pulls away, lights flashing, I shout, "Hey! Hold up!" The siren begins blaring; they pick up speed. Turning back to the sergeant, I plead, "He needs me! I'm his dad!"

"Why don't Officer Longo and I give you a ride over there?" he says. "That way, you can continue telling us what happened."

"Yeah, but . . . I'll have to sign things, give them information. He might need surgery. Who knows how long we're going to be there? I should take my own car."

"You mean the SUV?" He shakes his head. "That stays put. When they get here, the detectives are going to want to have a look at it. And anyway, you're probably not in good shape to drive right now." My stomach heaves. I wait. "Too shook up maybe, huh? We'll give you a lift."

"I don't understand why detectives have to—"

"Standard procedure, sir. Especially if your boy doesn't make it. I'm not saying that's gonna happen but—"

"It's *not* going to happen! But he needs his father. I should be with him in that ambulance!"

"Is he conscious, Mr. Ledbetter?"

His question stops me cold. "What?"

"Because if he was unconscious, or if they sedated him, he wouldn't know one way or the other if you were there."

I just stand there, silenced by his logic, his fucking cruelty.

"Come on, Mr. Ledbetter," he says. "You're right. He's going to need his dad. His mother, too. Has she been contacted?" I say I'm not sure—that her phone is turned off but I had someone call the school. He probably got the office secretary.

"Okay, good, so let's go. Cruiser's over here." What's his name again? I glance at the name tag pinned to his shirt pocket. Fazio. Sergeant Fazio.

As he walks me toward the car, I hear the other cop talking into the radio. "He may be EtOH, too. Not sure, but it's a possibility. . . . Copy that. I'll see if I can get someone at the hospital to draw it for us."

"Officer Longo," Fazio says. Longo turns around, surprised to see us right there. Fazio opens the back door of the cruiser and tells me to watch my head. Then he walks around to the other side and gets in the back seat next to me. As Longo pulls away from the curb, I watch three people, a woman and two men, jump out of a white van that has pulled up in front of the house. I recognize her: one of the reporters from the local TV news. Fazio watches them, too, shaking his head. He advises me not to talk to any reporters, something I'm not about to do anyway.

"So why don't you give me the particulars again on the way over in case you forgot something," Fazio says. "That way you'll have the sequence of events clear in your head when our detective interviews you."

"But *you're* interviewing me," I say.

"Yeah, well, the thing is, you'll probably have to go through everything two or three times. There has to be an investigation so they can rule things out."

"What things?"

"Well, negligence, intentionality."

"Intentionality? Like I might have injured him on *purpose*? What kind of sick person would—"

"It happens, Mr. Ledbetter. You'd be surprised. But we're not accusing you of anything. The opposite, actually. We just want to help you to get your story straight so that when our detective interviews you—"

Longo interrupts him. "They've assigned Sykes. She's meeting us at the hospital."

"Copy that," Fazio says, as if his partner's said it from a radio, not the front seat. "So like I was saying, Corbin. Can I call you Corbin?" I shrug. "You want to get your story straight so that when Detective Sykes talks to you, she can determine that the injury to your son happened accidentally. Especially if your boy doesn't—"

"Don't keep saying that! Because he *will* make it! He's like a little bulldozer, that kid. Last week? He banged his head on the coffee table but got right up and kept going as if nothing happened. His sister's a different story, but Niko—"

"How did he bump his head?" Fazio asks.

"What? He fell. Clunked his head on the way down."

"What made him fall?"

"I don't know. Kids that age fall all the time. Why am I getting the feeling that you're reading into whatever I say?"

"I don't know, Mr. Ledbetter. Why *are* you getting that feeling?"

"Look," I tell him. "I don't think you get what I'm going through right now. I can't focus on these things you want me to talk about when part of me is still trying to convince myself that any of this is really happening. And all the other part can think about is what's going on at the hospital and how I'm going to break all this to my wife. And I'm trying not to lose it in front of you two, but . . . but . . ." And then my anguish overtakes me and losing it in front of them is exactly what I do.

When I get ahold of my composure, Fazio says, "Okay, Corbin. We can talk more about this when we get to the hospital."

"And what do you mean when you say I should get my *story* straight? I don't need to practice anything because it's not a story. It's what happened."

No reaction from the sergeant. Not so much as a fucking nod.

I lean forward. Address the driver's right shoulder. "Officer? When you were talking on the radio before, what were those initials you said?"

He glances in the rearview mirror at me.

"ET something. You said you'd bet that he was an ET something."

He keeps me waiting, then finally answers. "EtOH."

"Yeah. What's that stand for? Were you talking about my son's condition?"

"No, I wasn't. Hey, speaking of initials, I have a question for you, too.

When I fed your information into the system, it said you got a DUI a while back. What was that about?"

Sergeant Fazio looks over at me, waiting for my response. I tell him it happened the day I lost my job. "Company downsized. I stopped off at that tavern on North Main Street to drown my sorrows."

"Bid's?" Fazio says. "Was that where you stopped?"

"Yeah. I ran into some guy I know and we took turns buying pitchers. I was feeling no pain when I left, but I was still able to drive. Thought I was anyway. Got about halfway home when they pulled me over." I leave out the part about it being the twins' first birthday party and forgetting to pick up their cake.

"Bid's has great sandwiches, don't they?" Fazio says. "The Astro, the Supreme. Good bread, too. I like a crusty grinder bread better than the soft kind. And how about Betty's pickled eggs? Try not to pucker up when you're eating one of those babies." Up front, his partner is nodding.

It's surreal. My kid is fighting for his life and he's talking about sandwiches? I still haven't gotten an answer about what EtOH is, but I shut up after that. Close my eyes and try to imagine I'm not riding in the back of this squad car. That I dropped the kids off at Emily's mother's like we planned because I buckled both of them in and nothing bad has happened to Niko.

When I open my eyes again, we're moving at a faster clip past the Wendy's on Perkins Avenue, then the Little League field, then that laundromat Emily and I used to use before we could afford to buy our washer and dryer. It dawns on me that this is the same route we took after I phoned Dr. Delgado to tell him her contractions were coming about five minutes apart and getting more intense. "Time to rock 'n' roll then," he said. "I'll meet you there." Emily worked so hard in that delivery room. . . . Have they gotten ahold of her or is she still in the dark? Still on that bus heading to New Haven? She must be, or else she would have called me. Oh God, this is going to wipe her out. If he ends up disabled, in a wheelchair or something, how is she ever going to forgive me? How will I ever forgive *myself*? I start shaking, just a little at first, then uncontrollably.

At the emergency room entrance, I get out of the cruiser and run on wobbly legs, passing through the sliding glass doors. Sergeant Fazio is a few steps behind me; Officer Longo has dropped us off and gone to park.

"Corby! Corby, *wait*!" Emily is running toward me. "What's going on? The vice principal flagged down the bus just as we were turning onto the highway, but all he'd say on the way here was that there's a 'family emergency.' Is it my mother?" When I shake my head, her eyes go wide with fear. With a trembling hand, she reaches out and grabs my arm. "Please tell me it's not one of the kids."

CHAPTER FIVE

In tears, I tell her it's Niko. "He's hurt, Em. It's my fault. I'm so sorry."

Fear flashes in her eyes. "Hurt how? Did he break something? Were you in a car accident?" I shake my head. "What about Maisie?"

I tell her Maisie's fine, that I left her with Jodi and Mary Louise so I could be with him here at the hospital.

"I don't understand," she says. "Aren't you just getting here? Where is he?"

"The ambulance took him. When the EMTs got to the house, they worked on him in the driveway. Then they—"

"EMTs? Why were they called? Is it that serious?" I tell her yes, that he lost a lot of blood. She shakes her head vehemently. When her eyes roll back and her knees buckle, I catch her before she falls. She's back a few seconds later, demanding to know what happened and why I said it was my fault.

We're both crying now. "He was . . . he was belly-down on the driveway. Looking at ants. I remembered the bag I'd packed for them was on the step and I went back to . . . and the McNallys had just come back from . . . and it slipped my mind that I hadn't buckled both of them in yet. I'd gotten her strapped in but . . ."

"Oh no!" she shouts. "Oh, God!"

"So I started the car and—"

She closes her eyes tight and shakes her head. "Stop it, Corby! I can't hear this. Stop talking!" Then she embraces me, holding on for dear life.

"Listen. I think he's going to come out of this okay," I tell her. "Sometimes it looks worse than—"

"Please, just *stop!*"

I coax her into one of the chairs and tell her to take some deep breaths.

"I don't need deep breaths!" she snaps. "I need to find out what's happening! I need to see my son!"

I see Sergeant Fazio at the receptionist's window. Then he approaches us. "Excuse me, folks. Sorry to interrupt, but they need you to check in, answer some questions, give them your insurance information." Message delivered, he joins Longo, who's standing halfway across the room. With a shaky hand, Emily takes the card out of her wallet and hands it to me. I approach the window, answer the receptionist's questions, and ask her some, too. Is our little boy in surgery? Who's the doctor? When can we see him? She says she's sorry but she doesn't have that information. She imagines the doctor who's seeing him will be out to talk to us soon.

When I sit back down again, Emily asks if I got any answers from the receptionist. I shake my head. "Why are *they* here?" she asks, nodding toward the two cops. I tell her they gave me a ride here after the ambulance left, but beyond that I'm not sure. "I guess there may be an investigation." Emily says she can't believe this is happening. "I'm so scared, Corby," she says. "What if he ends up crippled? Or brain damaged? You said there was blood. Where was he bleeding from?"

"Don't go there, Em." She rests her elbows on her knees, covers her face with her hands, and sobs softly. I knead her shoulder for a minute or so, then stop. She sits up and leans against me.

In the silence that follows, I take in the waiting room: an elderly couple, a high school kid on crutches at the soda machine, a middle-aged woman with knitting in her lap, a homeless-looking guy. Like Peeping Toms, they've been watching us, but when I look back at them, they avert their eyes. Fazio and Longo do *not* look away. Emily and I are being watched.

A young woman in scrubs and a lab coat calls my name from the doorway. "That's me," I say. She tells me to follow her. Emily asks her whether she should come, too, that she's the mother. Looking confused, the woman says that won't be necessary and this won't take long. Emily nods, a puzzled look on her face. When she asks where they're taking me, I tell her I don't know. I follow the woman in the lab coat. Longo, the younger cop, gets up and starts walking behind us. Fazio stays in the waiting room with Emily.

"Were you in the ER just now? Do you know anything about my boy's condition?" I ask. The woman shakes her head. Says she's a phlebotomist and has been told to draw a couple of vials of my blood. "My blood? Is he going to need a transfusion? I know we're both O positive. That's good, right?" She nods. I look over my shoulder at Officer Longo. His face is unreadable.

We go into a small, windowless room. The phlebotomist motions toward a chair. I sit. Longo positions himself against the door. "You've had blood drawn before?" the woman asks. I tell her I've been a donor since high school. Nodding, she grabs my wrists and pokes at my veins. Then she pulls on latex gloves, readies the needle and the attached vial. "Little pinch," she says. She repeats the procedure twice more. "Okay, you're done," she says.

When I get back to Emily, her mother is in my chair. Betsy looks pale, red-eyed, and ready for combat. "Just answer me one thing," she says. "Why didn't you check to see that they were both buckled in before you put that car in reverse?"

"What the fuck are you implying, Betsy?" Realizing that I've raised my voice, I glance over at Fazio and Longo.

"I'm not implying anything," she hisses. "I'm asking you a simple question."

I look at Emily, hoping she'll defend me or tell her mother to stop with the third degree. Instead, she says, "That's the thing though, Corby. You *always* double-check. First you look in the rearview mirror. Then you turn your head and look back. It's second nature to you. I've seen you do it a million times. I just don't get why this morning . . ."

I stare at her, saying nothing. There's nothing *to* say.

A doctor enters the room and walks toward us. He's young, NBA-tall, blond crew cut. "Mr. and Mrs. Ledbetter?" We nod. He gets down on his haunches in front of us, pity overtaking his face. "I'm Dr. Stefanski, one of the ER docs."

"How is he?" Emily asks.

"You know what? Let's go someplace where we can talk in private. There's a family room just down the hall where we can have some privacy, or if you prefer, we can use the chapel."

"The family room," I say. Betsy tells him she's the boy's grandmother and wants to come, too. The doctor looks from me to Emily, who nods. "Of course," he says. He glances back at me as if to assess the family dynamic. "Follow me," he says. Mercifully, the two cops stay put.

We sit around a table on cushioned chairs, the doctor on one side, the three of us across from him, Emily between her mother and me. "I'm so sorry to have to tell you this, but your little guy didn't make it. He died in the ambulance on the way here. By the time he got to the ER, there was nothing we could do for him."

He's still talking—his lips keep moving—but I can't take it all in. I hear "broken pelvis" and "pancreas" and "small intestine," but I'm still on he *died*? Niko is *dead*? I'm hit with a strange sensation that I'm falling from some great height. Grab the arms of my chair to steady myself. Emily gets up, arms straitjacketed around herself, and, shaking her head, walks to a corner of the room. Her back is to us. To me. Betsy stands and goes to her. She places her hands on her daughter's shoulders and murmurs something that I can't quite hear. *I* should be the one comforting her; he's *our* little boy. But what kind of comfort can I offer when I'm the one who caused his death?

I turn back to the doctor. "I got distracted," I explain. "I always double-check before I start the car, but the one time . . ."

He nods and says he's a dad, too. He mentions something about two grief counselors on staff, one spiritual, the other a psychologist. Do we have a preference? Before I can answer, Emily pivots and approaches the table. "Where is my son?" she asks the doctor. "I need to see him."

He says she might want to think about that because of the nature of his injuries. "Maybe it would be better for you to remember him the way he looked before the accident." Turning to me, he says, "Don't you think so, Dad?" As horrifying as my last look at Niko was, at least he was still drawing breath. Fighting to live. I nod.

Emily shakes her head. "No, I *have* to see him. I'm his mother. I need to comfort him no matter what he looks like. He must be so scared." What she's saying makes no sense.

"I'll go with her," Betsy says.

The doctor hesitates, then says, "Come with me then."

The three of them start toward the door. When I stand to follow them, Betsy swivels around and says, "No! Not you." Ignoring her, I turn to Emily. She shakes her head. That falling sensation hits me again. After it passes, I go to the doorway and watch them head down the corridor. The doctor, walking between them, towers over both women. He says something to Emily and places his hand on her back—a gesture of comfort for the poor young mother whose husband has caused the death of their child. As they turn a corner and disappear from sight, it's all I can do not to shout out in agony.

The corridor is busy, hospital workers in scrubs, lab coats, carrying cups of coffee, food on foam trays. Two guys in scrubs chatter on either end of a gurney as they wheel a patient into an elevator. What time is it? Afternoon already? Morning still? I have no idea, but what would be the use of checking my phone to find out? Niko has died, no matter what time it is.

I go back into the meeting room, close the door to the corridor, and sit. Rub my burning eyes. . . . *I need to comfort him. He must be so scared.* Is she in denial? In shock?

I caused his death, but I lost him, too, Emily. Can we still hold each other, cry together? Grieve together? I let myself imagine that I *did* look back, saw his empty car seat, and got out of the car. Picked him up off the driveway and buckled him in. I see him over at Betsy's, playing with blocks, eating the Cheez-Its I packed and drinking from his juice box. See him over at the neighbors' house, laughing with Maisie at the antics of Jodi's new puppy.

Oh God, poor Maisie! They've hardly ever been apart. How can we ever explain Niko's abrupt disappearance? Will she remember him by the time she's four or five? Consciously? Subconsciously? And if she does remember him, what then? And what about later when she *can* understand? . . .

I'll go with her, Betsy said. *No! Not you.* What right did she have to put herself in charge? There's never been much love lost between Betsy and me; she disapproved of my having left college just shy of my degree, my claim on her daughter. I'm someone she tolerated for Emily's sake, although she warmed up a little after her grandkids were born. At least I was good for something. But ever since that day I got laid off and came home drunk to the kids' birthday party . . .

"I want you to know that it's not about the quality of your work, Corby. The layoff will begin in two weeks, but why don't you take the rest of the afternoon off?" Not wanting to give Emily the news that in another two weeks I'd be unemployed, I stopped off at Bid's for a few, then a few more. Then a guy from our summer softball team strolled in. "How are things going, Ledbetter?"

"No complaints. How about you?"

He bought the first pitcher, I got the second. "Yeah, I guess I'd better take off, too. Keep in touch, bro. Good seeing you, too."

I ended up getting that DUI and a ride home in a taxi. "Right here is good," I told the driver. Handed him a ten and got out six or seven houses down from our blue raised ranch. When I walked into the house, still three-quarters in the bag, I was momentarily confused. Had Rhonda called my wife with the news that she was shitcanning me? Why in the world did Emily think balloons were appropriate? "Where have you been?" she asked. "Everyone's going to be here in another twenty minutes. Don't tell me you forgot to pick up the kids' cake. Where's your car? Jesus Christ, Corby!"

Behind me, I heard a car door slam and when I looked around, there was Betsy, struggling a wooden rocking horse out of her back seat. "Need a hand?" I called, more to dodge the third degree from Emily than from any burning desire to come to the aid of my mother-in-law. When she handed over the rocking horse, she told me I smelled like a brewery. "You're soused, aren't you? At your children's birthday party? Honestly!" My father chimed in from somewhere. "Nonstarter. You're pathetic."

———

"Mr. Ledbetter?"

"Hmm?" I open my eyes to a blur of Black skin, close-cropped hair, huge hoop earrings. As she comes into focus, I take in the business suit, an ID hanging from the lanyard around her neck.

"Are you the grief counselor?" I ask.

"No, sir. I'm Detective Tunisia Sparks, Three Rivers PD." She flashes a badge. That's when I notice Sergeant Fazio and Officer Longo standing behind her, their hands behind their backs.

CHAPTER SIX

——

"I understand your little one didn't make it," Detective Sparks says. "I'm very sorry for your loss, sir." It sounds rote, but I manage a thank-you. "My officers tell me your wife wasn't at home when the accident occurred, but she's here in the hospital now. Is that correct?"

I nod. Tell her the doctor we talked to has taken Emily and her mother to see our son. "I think she's having trouble accepting that he's . . ." I squint hard but the tears come anyway. She waits, watching me. When I regain my composure, I apologize.

She shakes her head. "I can appreciate what a difficult time this must be for you, Mr. Ledbetter, but we need to go over some details about what happened. Okay?" I can't respond. "Your first name is Corbin, right? Can I call you Corbin?" I don't give a shit what she calls me.

"That's fine. But look, I've already told these officers everything."

She pulls up a chair and sits, facing me, close enough that our knees almost touch. "And I'll go through their report, of course. But I always like to hear things firsthand from the people who were involved. For their own protection. So why don't you tell me in your own words how it happened? Okay?"

"Yeah. Okay."

She slides a small notepad from her large black bag. Pulls out the pen stuck in the metal spiral. Says, "Go ahead. Whatever you can remember."

"Well, like I told these guys, I got the kids ready because they were going to my mother-in-law's. She was going to babysit them for the day. And I . . . buckled his sister, Maisie, into her car seat. See, I usually buckle him in first, *then* her, but he was looking at this swarm of ants in the driveway and . . . so I buckled her in first."

"They're twins. Right?"

"Yes."

"Any other children?" I shake my head.

"And these are your biological children, right? Yours and your wife's? Not stepchildren or children you adopted."

Why did that matter? "No, they're ours."

"How old?"

"Twenty-five months. Close to twenty-six."

"Okay, go on."

"So our neighbors from across the street drove into their driveway and when they got out of their car, they said something to me and—"

"Said what? Do you remember?"

"Nothing significant. Just chitchat."

"Can you be a little more specific?"

I nod. "Linda—the wife—called over and said they'd just picked up some breakfast at McDonald's. . . . And I remembered I had borrowed a splitting maul from Shawn, the husband, and I told him I'd bring it back to him."

Sergeant Fazio breaks in to tell her these were the two eyewitnesses and he has their names and contact info. Sparks nods and tells me to go on.

"Linda, the wife, asked how the twins were doing and I told her how they'd scribbled on the floor with crayons the day before. It was just friendly neighbor talk, know what I mean? But I guess our conversation distracted me. I got in the car and I must have just assumed . . . I must have thought . . ."

I close my eyes tight to squelch the tears I feel coming. Do the deep breathing thing. "This is just so fucking painful," I say. "He was still alive when they put him in the ambulance and I thought . . . And then I find out he died before he even got here. And now I'm here, answering your questions while my wife is . . . That doctor tried to talk her out of it, but she said she needed to see him. And what is it? Maybe an hour since we found out he didn't make it. You say you can appreciate how hard this must be, but then you pull out your notebook and make me relive . . ."

"Just doing my job, sir," she says.

"Yeah well, don't say you can appreciate how hard this is when you have no idea what it's like to know that your little boy has just died and it's your fault because you got distracted. Made a simple mistake."

We stare at each other, at a standstill until I ask her whether she has kids.

"I do, yes. Two daughters."

"What are their ages?"

"Twelve and fifteen. But let's stay focused, okay? The more we get sidetracked, the longer this interview's going to take."

I nod. All I want is for her to leave me alone. Leave *us* alone. Emily is bound to be a mess when she comes back from seeing him and I need to protect her from this third-degree bullshit.

Sparks flips to a new page in her notebook. "Okay, so let's back up a little. I'd like you to take me through your morning *before* the accident? You wake up, get out of bed, and . . ."

"I went out to the kitchen. Started making breakfast while my wife was getting ready for work. She's a teacher."

"And what about you, Corbin? What do you do for work?"

"I'm a commercial artist, but I was let go a while back. Laid off, not fired. I was planning to spend the day looking for another position, which is what I do on the days when my wife's mother can take the kids." It's a lie, yes, but in fairness, it's what I *had* been doing in good faith in the beginning. In all those weeks of trying, I'd only gotten as far as showing my portfolio twice. And neither of those times led to anything. "By the way," I tell her. "Corbin's my official name, but most people call me Corby."

"Okay," she says. "So on the days when your mother-in-law babysits, you do what? Send out résumés? Do internet searches? Make follow-up calls?"

"Yeah, all of that."

"And otherwise, you're the stay-at-home parent?"

"Yes. For now."

"Do you enjoy that role, Corby, or has it been difficult?"

"Not one or the other," I say. "Both."

She jots something down. "Okay, so you were making breakfast and your wife was getting ready for work. Then what?"

"I heard the twins babbling to each other. Amusing each other, you know? They almost always wake up in a good mood." She smiles. "So I went in to change them and pack the bag for their day with their grandmother. But I'd forgotten to turn off the burner and the friggin' smoke alarm started wailing, so—"

"Why do you think you forgot to do that, Corby? I would have thought, if you were going to leave the room, turning off the stove would be something you'd do automatically."

I shrug. "Don't know. I guess I was just spacing out a little."

"Huh," she says. "Were you drinking this morning, Corby?"

Curveball! Don't panic. "Was I drinking? Yeah. I was drinking coffee."

"But not alcohol?"

"At six thirty in the morning? No. Why would you—"

"Because Sergeant Fazio said he thought he smelled liquor on your breath when he and Officer Longo got to your house this morning."

I can feel the thumping of my heart. "I mean, it's probably . . . I had insomnia in the middle of last night. Woke up a little after two and couldn't get back to sleep for, I don't know, an hour and a half maybe? So I got up, had a stiff drink—well, one and a half—so that I could knock off again. Which I did." I look over at Fazio. "Maybe that's what you were smelling? Now that I think of it, I may have forgotten to brush my teeth when I got up." He stands there, poker-faced. Says nothing.

"What were you drinking to put yourself back to sleep, Corby?" Sparks wants to know. "Whiskey? Vodka?"

My palms feel clammy. I grab on to the arms of my chair so they won't see my hands shaking. "Rum."

"Okay. What proof?"

"I'm not sure." Another lie. I graduated from seventy to a hundred proof two or three bottles ago.

"And you said these were stiff drinks, so maybe the equivalent of four regular-sized pours?"

I shrug. "Probably more like three."

"Okay." She's writing all this down. "Any explanation for why your pupils would have been so dilated this morning?"

"Were they?" I shrug again. "I took an Ativan when I got up. I have a prescription."

"You took just one?"

"Uh, two maybe. Yeah, two, now that I think of it. I take them for anxiety."

"You were feeling anxious this morning?"

I nod. "I am a lot of mornings. Since I got laid off. I get nervous about our finances. That's why I have trouble sleeping some nights, too."

"So you're saying that when you can't sleep at night, you use alcohol. And when you feel anxious during the daytime, you take your medication?"

"Yeah. Although some nights when I have insomnia, I just take some over-the-counter thing like Tylenol PM. Which I don't like doing too much because when I wake up, I feel groggy."

"Do you ever take a drink *with* your anxiety medication?"

"Together? No. It says on the prescription bottle not to mix them like that." It does say that, although I've never paid that warning much attention. Lately, when one or the other hasn't been doing the trick, I combine them. I can still function fine. Coast through whatever I have to do. Whatever I have to deal with.

"And you're telling the truth about the alcohol. Right, Corby? Because those blood samples are going to tell the truth whether or not you're lying."

"Except I'm *not* lying! Jesus Christ, lady, I'm cooperating as much as I can under some fucking brutal circumstances."

"Hey," Fazio says. "Lower your voice. And watch your language."

Ignoring him, I get up and go to the door, then turn back to her. "What are you trying to get me to say? That my son is dead because I was drunk? Strung out on benzos? Because that's bullshit." And I mean it, too. I was fully functional, despite whatever those blood tests are going to say. It was an *accident*. And if they're getting ready to accuse me of something that isn't true, I'll get myself a lawyer before I say anything else.

I open the door and look down the corridor to see whether Emily and Betsy are coming back. Don't see them but, mercifully, there's a commotion coming from the other direction. That homeless guy from the waiting room is heading toward where we are, batting away the two guys in scrubs who are trying to subdue him. "Yeah, and you can go to hell if you think I'm gonna put up with *your* shit! You think I'm not onto you two? I know who you are."

"Excuse us," Fazio tells Detective Sparks. "We better see if we can give them an assist with this individual." And with that, he and Longo leave the room.

"All right, Corby," Sparks says. "I guess that's enough for now, provided you're willing to come down to the station for some follow-up questions. How about tomorrow afternoon at three? Do you think you'll be able to do that?"

"Yeah," I tell her. "If I have to."

"Oh, and your vehicle's been impounded so that the forensics team can examine it. Like I said, dot the i's and cross the t's. They'll probably have it for a couple of days. Would you like me to arrange for a cruiser to pick you up?"

I say no, that I can take my wife's car. "What are they looking for in my van? Empty booze bottles? Heroin in the glove compartment? Hey, maybe they can lift some DNA off the steering wheel so you can solve two or three outstanding crimes while you're at it."

She doesn't react, other than to say, "Okay then. Tomorrow at three."

She closes her notebook and drops it back in her bag. Stands. Thanks me for talking with her and asks me to extend her sympathy to my wife. Then, in the doorway, she turns back and says, "You know what I think, Corby? I think you were most likely drinking and maybe drugging, too, this morning. I hope those blood test results will prove me wrong, but if I'm not and your impairment is a contributing factor to—"

She stops when she realizes Emily and her mother have come up behind her. Steps aside and lets them come in. My head is spinning. Em has just come back from seeing our son's mangled, lifeless body. Did she just hear Sparks's accusation? Is the blood they drew going to prove what she suspects?

I'm nauseous, lightheaded. My heart is pounding. I order myself to refocus—to forget about Sparks and take care of my wife.

"How you doing?" I ask her.

"How do you *think* I'm doing, Corby?" She rushes me and begins shoving me, cursing me, punching me. When Betsy tries to pull her away from me, she resists, then collapses against me, taking short, ragged breaths between her sobs. I put my arms around her. "How can he be dead?" she cries out. "How could you have . . ."

When I look over Emily's shoulder, Detective Sparks is standing in the corridor, watching me.

CHAPTER SEVEN

—

We're at the hospital until midafternoon, signing paperwork, listening to both grief counselors' spiels, making decisions about what we will or won't let the hospital do with Niko's body. Some social worker whose office we've been sent to asks which funeral home should be notified once the body is ready for release. We have no idea. Niko isn't Niko anymore; he's just Niko's body.

Along with having to put up with all the hospital's procedures and permissions, there's a lot of sitting and waiting in uncomfortable silence, just Emily and me. We make Betsy a list of tasks neither Em nor I feel strong enough to handle: finding a funeral home, calling my mom to let her know what happened, picking up Maisie from Mary Louise's. "She's going to wonder where her brother is. What should I tell her?" Betsy wants to know. Emily and I look blankly at each other. One of the grief counselors addressed this but neither of us could focus on what she said. "Well, I read Dr. Rosemond's column in the paper faithfully," Betsy says. "He always has commonsense advice. I'll Google him and send you a link if I find something." Emily reads that column, too, usually taking exception to the doctor's advice about spanking and toilet training. Now she just nods and says, "Thanks, Mom."

In the midst of all the waiting, Emily and I don't say much to each other. We're both too numb, I guess, or maybe too bewildered and afraid of what's in store. I turn to her at one point and say I can't wrap my head around his not being here anymore. She looks at me without speaking, her expression unreadable. We've been brought to two or three offices by then and it hasn't escaped me that in each, she's put an empty chair between us.

All of this silence and separation frees my mind to wander. It's going to be on the news and in the papers. On social media, too—everyone giving their anonymous bullshit opinions. The circumstances around Niko's death are going to define who we are now. We'll be *that* family. I imagine wheeling my cart past shoppers in the grocery store. *That's the guy. Did you hear how it happened?*

Maybe we should move someplace where people wouldn't know us—where we wouldn't represent every parent's worst fear. Where Maisie won't have to be the *other* twin, the one who *didn't* die. . . . That detective is clearly out to get me. They can make those blood test results say whatever they want them to. I should probably get a lawyer—one that specializes in DUI arrests. What's the name of the attorney on that billboard I used to pass on my way to work? The one who boasts she can help clients BEAT DUI! But how many thousands will that cost? And I *wasn't* impaired, no matter what conclusion Sparks wants to jump to. I had a little bit of a buzz going on when I was making breakfast, but I'd come down from that by the time it happened.

When Betsy called my mother to give her the grim news, the two grandmothers coordinated their efforts, something that rarely happens. Mom watched Maisie while Betsy called around to a few funeral homes and got an appointment for the next morning. Now she's driven back to the hospital to pick us up and bring us home. Emily sits in the front seat, me in the back. Mid-ride, Betsy asks how she's feeling. "I have no idea," Emily says. "I'm just . . . blank."

"Well, I can't imagine a worse shock to the system, sweetheart," her mother notes. "At least it will be a relief to get home after that long ordeal at the hospital."

Emily shakes her head. "Home is the *last* place I want to be right now.

Whatever room I go into, he's going to be there. Whenever I see Maisie, I'll look around to see where he is."

"We'll figure it out," I promise. Neither woman responds. I'm the back-seat pariah—the guy who caused all this pain and loss.

When Betsy takes the left onto our street, I dread what I imagine we're about to see: yellow crime scene tape, reporters and cameramen waiting to ambush us. I dread the possibility that Niko's blood might still be there, something I'll need to shield Emily from having to see. But I'm relieved that our driveway has gone back to just being our driveway. Who scrubbed it clean of Niko's blood? The police? A neighbor—maybe Shawn McNally? I'm grateful to whoever it was.

My mom meets us at the door. She holds out her arms and wraps Emily in a long, silent embrace. Does the same with Betsy. Then she turns to me. Takes my hands in hers and squeezes. "Hey," she says, pulling me in closer. I fall against her, releasing the sobs I've been trying to hold in all afternoon. Trying to be the strong one for Emily. When I can finally speak, what comes out is, "Mom, how am I supposed to live with myself?"

"I know this is overwhelming right now, but once the initial shock—"

Emily cuts her off. "Where's Maisie? Is she asleep?"

"The poor kid was exhausted," Mom says. "She kept trying to fight it, but she couldn't keep her eyes open."

"The sitter said she wouldn't go down for a nap," Betsy says. "I wasn't sure if you wanted me to pay the girl or her mother and I had no idea what the going rate is these days. I tried to give them a twenty-dollar bill, but the mother kept saying no."

"You didn't put her in their crib, did you?" Emily asks Mom. The question sounds like an accusation.

Looking confused, my mother apologizes. "I just assumed that—"

"It's okay, Mom," I tell her. "Emily's probably thinking that, when she wakes up and her brother's not there—"

Emily cuts me off. "For Christ's sake, Corby. I'm standing right here. I can speak for myself." Addressing her own mother, she says, "I'm not going into that room right now. I *can't*. From now on, Maisie can sleep with me." Turning back to me, she says, "You'll need to sleep somewhere else. I don't want you rolling on top of her in your sleep, Corby. You're always so goddamned restless."

"Yeah, all right. I'll set up the sleeper sofa."

The kids curling up in our bed with us has never been an issue. But the message comes through loud and clear: she's going to keep Maisie safe from me.

Betsy says, "I'll get Maisie and put her on your bed."

Mom must sense the tension, because she changes the subject to the food neighbors have dropped off: a green salad, a fruit salad, a roast chicken, meatballs, brownies. "I took down all the names," she says. "Someone brought a lasagna and I've got that warming in the oven. Is anyone hungry?"

Emily shakes her head. "I just want to go lie down. I need to be there with Maisie when she wakes up." Betsy thinks she'll just go home. That leaves Mom and me. She suggests I pull out the sofa and grab some sheets so she can make up my bed for me; I tell her I'll get it later. "Okay," she says. "Come on then. You need to eat."

I tell her what I need is a drink. "How about you? You want a beer?"

"No thanks," she says. I can feel her watching me as I go over to the fridge. But instead of opening it and grabbing a beer, I take the soup pot out of the cabinet above, pull out the bottle, grab my mug, and pour myself a couple of inches. Drink half in one gulp and sit down to eat. Mom says nothing.

I eat a few bites of the lasagna and move the salad around on my plate. Then I ask her the question I'm not sure I want her to answer. "Did you call Dad?"

She shakes her head. Says she meant to, but the day got away from her. "I'll let him know tonight, unless you'd rather it came from you."

"So he can congratulate himself about having called it a long time ago: that his son's a loser? No thanks. I don't think I'm up for that right now."

"Oh, honey," she says. "I can't defend the way he treated you back then, but—"

"Why *should* you defend him? It's not like he treated you any better."

"I let all that go a long time ago, Corby. I just wish you could, too."

"You know how many times he's seen the twins? A grand total of once. He showed up unannounced with some presents that Natalie, Wife Number Three, had bought—newborn outfits that the kids had already outgrown. And he didn't drive here just to see them. He hadn't switched dentists when he moved to Rhode Island and was in town to get his teeth cleaned."

Mom purses her lips. "Eat before it gets cold," she says.

She doesn't seem to have an appetite either. At one point, she puts her fork down and asks if she can say something. I nod. "Niko's death is going to hurt like hell for a long while. There's no way around that. But you and Emily are going to have to weather this tragedy, keeping Niko in your hearts without letting his death paralyze you. Eventually, I mean. You'll have to move on for Maisie's sake."

"Yeah, you know what, Mom? I know you mean well, but the last thing I need right now is a pep talk." I grab my mug and take another good-sized gulp. Swish it around in my mouth, then swallow, letting the burn in my throat comfort me.

"Well, I'm sorry if that's what it sounded like, Corby, but I'm worried you won't be able to move forward if you allow yourself to be consumed with guilt."

"Except I *am* guilty, Mom. I'm the one who put the car in reverse."

"Okay. I'm sorry. I'm trying to say the right thing but instead I'm—"

"At the hospital today? This detective showed up to interview me and it looks like they're going to arrest me."

She shakes her head but I see the fear in her eyes. "For what? Being human enough to let your guard down for a couple of seconds? Anyone who knows you can vouch for the fact that you're a loving and capable father. Their primary caretaker."

"Mom, he *died* under my care."

She steeples her hands and places them against her mouth. I count the number of times I inhale and exhale as I wait for her response. "Do you think you need a lawyer?" she finally says.

"I don't know. Maybe. I have to go down to the police station tomorrow afternoon. They want to ask me more questions."

She goes over to the counter. Her back is to me, but I can tell from the way her shoulders are shaking that she's crying. After she's composed herself, she comes back and sits. "Do you remember thar horrible story in the news a few summers ago? About the mother who forgot her baby in the back seat of her hot car for hours because she'd gotten mixed up about what day it was? They didn't charge her with anything because they said she was only guilty of human error and that the death of her child was punishment enough."

"Yeah, I remember that," I say. "And I also remember everyone's outrage because they thought she'd gotten away with murder. Emily had her suspicions, too, I remember. And Jesus, they *crucified* that woman on social media."

"You know what?" she says. "I think I'd better just keep my mouth shut."

"I'm glad you're here, Mom. It's helpful to have you to talk to."

She smiles sadly, then gets up and starts clearing the table. I grab our plates and go to scrape the uneaten food into the garbage. Sitting at the top is the French toast I burned that morning. Without warning, that sensation I experienced earlier comes back. I'm falling in space, hurtling toward an inevitable crash. As I grab on to the counter to steady myself, the plates slip out of my hands and smash against the tile floor. "I'll get it," Mom says.

She grabs some paper towels, gets down on her knees, and starts scooping lasagna off the floor and stacking broken pieces of pottery. I crouch down beside her to help with the mess, but instead, a choking sob rises up from my throat and I burst into tears again.

She grasps my hands. "I know you're in unbearable pain, Corby. Time will help it become less intense, I promise, but for now all you can do is be there for your wife and daughter and keep putting one foot in front of the other."

"I love him so much, Mom. How can we not have him anymore?" She strokes my head and quiets my sobs. "And how is Emily ever going to forgive me?"

"She'll find a way because you need each other, Corby, and Maisie needs you both. You're a family."

Once the kitchen is cleaned up and the sofa bed is made, Mom says she's going to go home. At the door, she hands me a baggie with two pieces of candy inside. I look at her, puzzled. "Pot gummies," she says. She's always relied on weed, but years of waitressing have given her the back spasms that made her eligible for a medical marijuana card. "I'd rather you used these instead of drinking yourself to sleep," she says. "Don't forget, alcohol is a depressant and that's the last thing you need right now. I'll check with you tomorrow after the breakfast shift to see what you guys need. Just remember: you're going to get through this and you don't have to do it alone. Good night. Get some sleep. I'll call your father when I get home. He may already have heard, but if not, I'll let him know."

Standing at the front door, I watch her drive away. Across the street, there's an upstairs light on. Their downstairs is dark, except for a flickering light from a TV. I close my eyes and see a soundless movie of that morning: Shawn and Linda in my rearview mirror, running toward me, waving frantically. Why did I keep backing up? Why didn't I stop?

I close the door and lock it. Go into the bathroom and flush my mother's gummies down the toilet. What if Maisie somehow got ahold of one and put it in her mouth? Or what if I took one and they did another tox screen at the police station tomorrow? They probably already have me pegged as some kind of substance abuser. Having THC in my bloodstream won't do me any favors. If I have trouble getting back to sleep, I'll take a couple of my Ativan. How could they fault me for that when I have a fucking prescription?

As quietly as I can, I walk down the hall to our bedroom and stare at the light beneath the closed door. I hear Emily murmuring. Has Maisie woken up? Is Emily trying to soothe her? Emily's voice is just barely audible, but it suddenly dawns on me that she's singing. "*The wheels on the bus go round and round . . .*"

I knock softly. The singing stops. I hold my breath, waiting. I guess she's waiting, too—for me to go away. Then the song resumes. "*The wipers on the bus go swish, swish, swish all through the town.*"

Back in the living room, I flop down on the sofa bed, thinking I'll just rest my eyes before I get up and . . .

——

What the . . . ? What time is it? Why is my cell phone still ringing after I answered it? Oh, the landline. Someone's calling on the landline.

"Hullo?"

"Terrible. Just terrible, Corby. Natalie and I can't even imagine."

It's Dad, offering his version of condolences. He sounds drunk or on his way. "Your mother says the police questioned you and they want to talk to you some more. I hope you didn't say too much, but *do not* agree to any more questioning without your lawyer being present." When I tell him I don't have a lawyer, he says yes, I do. "You got a pencil? Take this name and number down. Rachel Dixon, eight-six-o-seven-seven-nine-four-six-eight-nine." He repeats the number, spells the name. "Her father, Bob, runs a charity golf tournament at our club and we write him a pretty nice check every year. Natalie knows him better than I do from Rotary, so she called him and he called her right back. Got you an appointment for eight a.m. tomorrow morning before she goes to court. Her dad says she's such a ballbuster in court that the prosecutors are practically in tears by the time she's through with them. Course, that's her father talking, so he's going to crow about his own kid."

Some do and some don't, I think. And some sons don't give their fathers anything to crow about. "Yeah, but hold on, Dad. How much is this going to cost?"

"Don't worry about that. We'll figure it out. First things first. Her office is downtown, across from the post office. Upstairs from some bakery," he says. "You got all this? Eight o'clock tomorrow morning. And don't be late. She's doing us a favor by squeezing you in. She told her father she's got a heavy docket tomorrow."

I know we have that appointment at the funeral home but can't remember what time of day, so I don't mention it. Plus, I'm supposed to go to the police station at three o'clock. I feel ambivalent about accepting his help but thank him anyway. "Least I could do. Hang in there, Corbin. Get some sleep."

He hangs up.

Now that I'm awake again, I'm *good* and awake. I look out the front window. No lights on across the street now. I go down the hall to our bedroom. I can still see the light beneath the door, but it's quiet in there. I go to knock but change my mind. If she's gotten to sleep, I don't want to wake her. Or Maisie. Niko sleeps—*slept*—through thunderstorms, but his sister will sometimes wake up scared, needing reassurance that we'll keep her safe. Needing to have us put on the light to show her that her brother is safe, too—asleep in their crib. How the hell will either of us be able to reassure her now?

I walk back down the hall and pace, from the kitchen to the living room, back and forth, back and forth until I stop to look at that framed photo of the twins in the bookcase—one of the gifts I'd given Emily for her thirty-fifth birthday. JC Penney was running a special at their portrait studio. I dressed the kids in their matching Carter's overalls that Betsy had bought them and bundled them up against the cold. We were early for our appointment, so I wheeled them to the food court to kill some time. Got myself a coffee and opened the bag of Pirate's Booty I'd brought along. A woman saw the double stroller and came over to have a look. "Twins?" she asked. I nodded, smiling. This happened a lot when we were out in public; strangers who otherwise would have walked right past would stop because they were twins.

"Boys or girls?" she asked.

"One of each. Girl on the left, boy on the right."

"Well, they certainly aren't identical." She leaned in and spoke directly to the kids, addressing Maisie first. "Sweetie, you must take after your mommy with that dark hair and those big brown eyes." Maisie watched her warily as she continued eating her Pirate's Booty. Turning to Niko, the woman said, "And you, young man, look just like your daddy. And I bet when you grow up, you're going to be just as handsome." I scoffed and said I wouldn't wish that on the poor kid. "Aha, handsome and modest," she said. "You tell your wife she's a lucky gal." Silvery gray hair, midfifties maybe. Compliments always fluster me so I was grateful when Niko started shouting "Bah! Bah! Bah!" and grabbed the Pirate's Booty bag, upending it. As I squatted down to scoop the mess off the floor, the woman said, "Daddy's got a nice behind, too." I didn't look up until I could feel my blush subsiding. By then, she'd walked two or three stores down and was looking in the window of Godiva Chocolates.

Holding the photo that was taken that day, I study Maisie's expression first. The photographer and I got a half-smile out of her, but I'm struck by the sadness in those big brown eyes. It's almost as if, at that instant, she foresaw her future as the surviving sibling, the solitary twin.

It takes me another couple of seconds before I can look directly at Niko. Other than our chestnut-colored hair, I've never been able to see that my son looks much like me, but now the resemblance is obvious. Despite the fact that I have no belief in an afterlife, I indulge myself with a little magical thinking. Imagine that when he died, his spirit rose from his broken body and escaped into the ether. "Hey, buddy," I whisper to his image. Choking back sobs, I tell him it's Daddy. "Where are you, silly head? Where did you go?"

Holding on to that framed photograph, I pace some more. Later, face down on the sofa bed, I twist, turn, and try to fall back to sleep. It's no use. As exhausted as my body feels, my mind is still wide-awake, replaying the events of the day just past and imagining all the shit that will be happening in the days to come: the appointment with that "ballbuster" lawyer, the continuing investigation, the dreaded decision about whether to bury or cremate his body, and how much everything is going to cost. I meant to avoid taking something to get to sleep, but I have to get free of the spinning hamster wheel in my head. A couple of those Ativan will knock me out for several hours. I can set the alarm on my phone so that I wake up in time to get to that lawyer's office. The SUV isn't here, so I'll have to take Emily's car. She's left her purse on the kitchen counter, so I get up, grab it, and fish around until I feel her keys. The problem is that my prescription bottle is in the nightstand on my side of the bed. When I go back down the hall, there's no light seeping out from under the door. Good. I'll tiptoe in, grab my prescription, and tiptoe out again. But the knob won't turn. She's locked me out.

I go back to the kitchen. I hadn't put the rum back yet. I fill my mug half-full. Take a couple of long gulps. Pour some more and drink that. I pull out my phone and set the alarm for quarter to seven. That will give me enough time to get cleaned up and dressed and drive to the lawyer's office. I'm already beginning to feel the booze's soothing embrace—the opening of the escape hatch that sleep will give me. As I begin to doze, I wonder what Mom thought when she saw that I'm hiding my liquor. She's in on my secret now, I figure, but I'm glad she didn't say anything.

CHAPTER EIGHT

—

April 28, 2017

I don't remember going into the twins' room, but that's where I wake up—a failed sentry face down on the carpet alongside the empty crib. That picture of the twins is on the floor beside my head and my cell phone is next to it. I grab the phone, squint at it, then realize the alarm hasn't gone off because I set it for six forty-five *p.m. Goddammit*, I heard my father say. *She's going out of her way to help you and you stand her up? You know something, Corbin? You could fuck up a wet dream.*

I stagger onto my feet, grab the crib rail to regain my balance. Hurry into the bathroom, splash cold water on my face, and take a big swig of Listerine. Tasting the burn of the alcohol, I swish and spit. Our bedroom door is still closed, but I don't have time to change anyway. No time to make myself a cup of badly needed coffee either. Out in the kitchen, the first thing I see is the empty rum bottle and the mug beside it. I retrieve Emily's car keys, scrawl her a note that I've got an early appointment with a lawyer. I rinse the mug and grab the bottle. Take it with me.

I know I'll be late, but she's allotted me fifteen minutes, so I might make it for the last six or seven. My hands on the steering wheel won't stop shaking and my headache is banging away like a jackhammer. When I'm about halfway there, the houses and stores give way to a wooded area. There's no one in back of me and no cars coming the opposite way. I pull over, grab the bottle, and fling it as far as I can into the woods. Hear the smash, then get back in the car. I've lost maybe a minute but figure it's time well spent.

I find her building, park down the street, and take the stairs two at a time. When I get to her office, I barge right in on her. Overweight, oversized glasses, fortyish. Her spiky hair is pink on top, shaved close on the sides. "Mr. Ledbetter," she says. She looks down at her watch. "You're late."

In the middle of my rambling apology, I become aware that she's checking out what a mess I am: slept-in clothes, crazy hair, shaky hands. "And then when I finally *did* get to sleep, it was like I fell into a coma or something." I don't mention that I got plastered and woke up on the floor in the twins' room.

"I'm so sorry for your loss, Mr. Ledbetter, especially under such tough circumstances. You must be going through hell right now." She's slipping manila folders into her attaché case as she speaks. "Unfortunately, I can't talk with you now. If you want me to represent you, we'll have to carve out a good hour, minimum, for an initial consultation. But did I hear that the police are questioning you about the circumstances of your son's death?"

I nod. Tell her I spoke with them yesterday and agreed to meet with them at their headquarters later today. Tell her, too, about how they had my blood drawn while I was at the hospital.

"Oh, shit," she says. She glances again at her oversized watch. Is that Wonder Woman on the dial? "So what are those test results going to show, Mr. Ledbetter?"

"Not that much. I had poured a couple of shots of rum into my morning coffee—just to take the edge off, you know? And I'd taken an Ativan. Which I have a prescription for. For anxiety." I'd taken two, actually, and just lied automatically.

"Why is it that you had to take the edge off first thing in the morning?"

"Why? Well, I've been out of work for about a year now so we've been getting by on one salary. And I—"

"Any DUIs in your history?"

"One. On the day I found out I was getting laid off, I stopped on the way home to—"

"Was your drinking why you lost your job?"

"No, not at all. The company was downsizing."

"And that's what your former employer would tell the police if they inquired?"

"Absolutely. I never had any drinking issues at work."

"Okay. Good. But just between you and me, would you say you have a drinking and drugging problem now? Maybe because of your unemployment?"

I shake my head. "Not really. No. What happened yesterday happened because I was distracted by my neighbors across the street. Like I told Detective Sparks—"

"Tunisia Sparks was who you talked to?"

"Yes. Why?"

She checks her watch again. "I don't have time to go into it now. I've got clients waiting over at the courthouse and I need to talk with them before they appear in front of the judge today. I'll be tied up for the rest of the day, but I should be able to make time for you tomorrow. Just call my receptionist, Virginia, and make an appointment." She hands me her card. "But in the meantime, here's what you need to do. Get ahold of Sparks and tell her you have to postpone your interview because you want your lawyer to be there and I'm not available today. That's all I want you to say. All right? Don't volunteer anything else. But make sure you mention me by name, okay? I've gone head-to-head with Sparks a number of times and my win-lose record against her is better than fifty percent. It won't hurt to put her on the defensive."

"So you're going to take my case then?"

"Unless you tell me otherwise. Come on. I'll walk you out."

I wait while she locks her outer office door, then follow her down the stairs. Out on the street, she stops at the front window of the cupcake bakery and says, "Their Death by Chocolate with ganache icing probably *will* kill me someday, but at least I'll die happy. Don't forget to call Ginny and make that appointment. Tell her I said it has to be tomorrow." I promise I will and thank her for her help.

We start off in opposite directions when she calls my name. I stop, walk back to her. "How many vials of blood did they draw from you at the hospital yesterday?" she asks. I hold up three fingers. "Okay, so they wanted you tested for both alcohol and chemical substances. Oh, and one more thing. After the accident happened, did you go back inside your house for any reason?"

I shrug. "Not that I can remember. Why?"

"Because, let's say—theoretically—that you were so shook up by what had just happened that you went inside and took a drink or another benzo to steady yourself. Or maybe you took one of each because you were so distraught."

"I *was* distraught," I tell her. "*I am.*"

"Yeah, but think again. Did you go back in the house after you realized what had happened?"

"Wait. Come to think of it, yeah, I did. To get my cell phone so that I could get ahold of my wife."

She nods approvingly. "Anyone see you do that?"

"Yeah. Some of the neighbors had come out when they heard the ambulance, saw the police cars. I was holding my little girl and had a woman from the neighborhood take her so that I could get my cell and call my wife."

"Did you reach her?"

I shake my head. "She had turned off her phone."

"Well, that must have made you crazy, huh? Your little boy is lying there, fighting for his life at that point. Right?" I nod. "You need to let his mother know, but you can't reach her. It's understandable that, at that point, your anxiety is so acute—so off the charts—that you might need to pop a pill or take a drink to try to hold yourself together."

I shake my head. "I might have, but I—"

She puts her hand up to stop me. "Like I said, I'm just talking theoretically. Because if that's what happened, it would be helpful—something we could use."

"What are you getting at?" I ask.

"Well, you told me you'd done a little drinking and drugging before your son got hurt. But if you did a little more *after* he was injured, then whatever those blood test results are going to say, a judge might rule that they're inadmissible. You know, theoretically speaking." I'm confused about what she's saying; her expression is unreadable. "Okay, gotta go. Talk to you tomorrow."

As I watch her hurry off, I figure it out. If I lie about what happened when I went back in the house—tell Sparks I couldn't face the fact that I'd just critically injured my son without "fortifying" myself—then there's a decent chance they'd have to invalidate the blood tests. Whatever they're planning to charge me with would be that much harder to prove. They might even decide it wouldn't be worth it to charge me at all. And with no arrest hanging over my head, I'll be motivated to drink less, cool it on the Ativan, get serious again about the job hunt. None of that will bring Niko back, but it would be a way forward for Emily, Maisie, and me.

Tempted by Attorney Dixon's "theoreticals" and still feeling the effects of my two a.m. alcohol binge, I walk the street for several minutes looking for my car before it hits me that I've taken Emily's. I didn't notice before that I parked across from a diner. I need coffee badly and I ate almost nothing the day before. "Large coffee, cream no sugar, and a corn muffin to go," I tell the woman at the register. Back in the car, I stuff half of the muffin in my mouth and wash it down with a big gulp of coffee. Take a second swig, a third. Ah, caffeine. . . . Glancing at the dashboard clock, I realize that at this time yesterday, Niko was still fighting for his life. What right do I have to be sitting here, enjoying the taste of coffee?

I start the car. The mirrors are still positioned for Emily, so as I pull out into traffic, I get a blast from someone's horn. Look again to make sure it's clear, then hit the gas and drive off in the opposite direction from home. If

I don't turn around, I might miss the meeting at the funeral home. It isn't right; I'm his father. But Emily will probably prefer to go with her mother. I'm not sure I could handle it anyway: bringing them his clothes, choosing a casket, deciding about calling hours, a service, cremation or burial.

I drive south without any destination in mind. . . .

Maisie will be up by now, missing her brother. She'll be confused, in need of reassurance, and where am I? Her daddy is missing, too—driving away from her because I'm a coward. They'll probably be better off without me. Maybe I should put the pedal to the metal and aim for some tree. But I'm too weak to do that, too.

I'm eight or nine miles past Three Rivers when the traffic begins to slow down near the exit for the Wequonnoc Moon Casino. Spur of the moment, I put on my blinker and follow the line of cars to the entrance, then to the massive parking lot. I have no idea why I'm doing this.

But the answer comes to me once I'm inside and have joined the stream of morning gamblers. As I walk past the craps tables, the clamoring slot machine halls and off-track betting parlors, I'm not the father who backed over his kid; I'm just some anonymous guy hoping, like everyone else, to score with Lady Luck. The problem is: even if nobody else knows who I am, *I* know. That calls for a drink. I go into one of the bars and sit down at a table for two. The cocktail waitress who comes toward me is wearing a fringed buckskin top and matching short shorts. "What can I get you?" she asks. I order a Jack and Coke.

Waiting for my drink, I look around. Two old duffers at the end of the bar are talking Red Sox—their hopes that Rajai Davis's base-stealing will do for Boston what he did for Cleveland last year. A trio of older ladies are sharing laughs and cocktails at a table halfway across the floor from me. Two of them are silver-haired, the third is wearing one of those cancer-victim headscarves. A couple closer to my age sits on the other side of the bar. They're drinking Bloody Marys and his hands are all over her. Honeymooners, I figure, or cheating on their spouses. Everyone in here is clueless. What does baseball matter? Or fucking someone else's wife? Do those other two women think their friend is the only one whose days are numbered? Why should we all still be alive when my little boy is dead?

I look up at the four soundless TVs above the bar, each tuned to something different: Fox News, CNN, a rerun of a Sox game on NESN, and one of the local stations—the morning news. I watch the anchor's lips move. Read the crawl at the bottom of the screen: "Tragedy in Three Rivers." The picture changes to a reporter holding a microphone—the one who arrived as I was leaving for the hospital in the back of that cruiser yesterday. She's standing across the road from our house. Over her shoulder, I see my SUV, a perimeter of yellow crime tape, a huddle of neighbors.

"Run a tab, sir?" the waitress asks. She's already placed my drink on the table. Looking at it, not at her, I say, "Sure. Why not?" Taking a sip, I glance back at the TV screen. There's Emily's Facebook profile picture of the four of us. When the camera zooms in on me, I'm confronted with the smiling face of the son of a bitch who killed his son. I look away, gulp down my drink, slap a twenty on the table, and get the fuck out of there. Out in the parking lot, I break into a run.

Back in Emily's car, I check my phone. She's texted: *You still at the lawyer's? Sorry I shut you out last nite. Couldn't deal. Funeral home appt is @ 1:00. Plz be back in time. I can't do this by myself.*

I shake my head no. Pull out of the lot and turn right, heading farther south. It's like that thing they say before the plane takes off? Put on your own mask before you help anyone else. She'll have to call her mother, have Betsy take her to the funeral parlor. Ignoring the highway entrance toward New London, I take the back road that runs parallel with the Wequonnoc river. I think again about what that lawyer—*my* lawyer—implied: if I lie about why I went back in the house, those test results might get tossed. Can I out-and-out lie like that? Why the hell not? Everyone lies to cover their asses. The cops who claimed self-defense when they shot that black guy in the back. The politicians: "We have credible intelligence that Saddam has stockpiled weapons of mass destruction." "I did not have sex with that woman, Miss Lewinsky." Trump lies every time he opens his mouth and we all just shake our heads and let him get away with it.

But can I pull it off? Lie to Detective Sparks or some prosecutor, some judge? Maybe. Since my drinking has ticked up, I've become a pretty good sneak. Hiding my bottles until recycling day, lying about how I'm still looking for work. Keeping my Ativan prescription at the back of my nightstand drawer so she won't question why my supply is nearly gone. Even throwing that rum bottle into the woods on my way to Dixon's office. Disposing of the proof that I had a few yesterday morning so that Emily won't assume I was impaired when I started the car. I mean yeah, I *have* been overdoing the booze and the benzos a little, and sure, I need to cut back. But I was in control when I put the car in reverse. It happened because the McNallys distracted me. How could I live with myself otherwise?

It's after ten now. The river is playing peekaboo, sparkling in the sun one minute, hiding behind thickets of trees and brambles the next. I roll down the window so I can hear it move. I let that sound steer me to the river's edge. Why have I come here? What am I looking for?

CHAPTER NINE

——

At the river's edge I watch and listen to the moving water for a while. Am I absolutely sure I wasn't under the influence when it happened? Would it dishonor Niko if I lied to Sparks? I close my eyes and take myself back to that afternoon when I got my first glimpse of him, on a screen in Dr. Delgado's office. We knew by then that we were having twins, each of them in their own amniotic sac. During a previous visit, I'd asked the doctor if he thought they had any awareness of each other. He turned the question over to Emily. "What do you think, Mama? You're the expert on these two." She smiled at me and said she was sure they did.

As we watched the blurry ultrasound movie, I was moved by the miracle of a rapidly beating heart. "Is that the boy or the girl in front?" I asked Delgado's nurse. "The boy," she said, pointing at something. "There's his little penis."

The night Emily's water broke, I drove her to the hospital. Held her hand as they wheeled her to the delivery room, then suited up in the paper gown they handed me. Stretched the gloves over my hands. She worked so hard, so bravely, all night long to push our two children into the world. She'd read all the baby books and was determined that both would have vaginal births. She didn't want to take an anesthetic because she wanted to be alert and ready to see them and hold them as soon as they appeared.

At last, in the first light of morning, I saw between Emily's legs the crowning of a small head with its dark matted hair. The firstborn twin: who would it be? "Breathe, Emily. Now push. Deep breath. Smaller push." Out came more of the head, then the neck, the top of a shoulder. It amazed me that some version of what I was witnessing was how everyone, past and present, entered the world. It was profound.

"One last push now, Emily!" and the rest of our daughter slid out in a whoosh of blood and fluid. Her body was bluish and I was afraid something was wrong. Then she squawked and, as her lungs took in air, she turned pink, her head first, then little by little the rest of her, down to her toes. The baby nurse—her name was Maureen—placed her on Emily's chest and, turning to me, asked whether Maisie was a keeper. "Hell, yes," I told her, laughing as my tears fell. Emily was laughing and crying, too.

I open my eyes now and start hiking along the riverbank, following the direction of the rushing water. . . .

As Maisie was carried to the other side of the room to be cleaned up and bundled in a warm blanket, Dr. Delgado turned his attention to delivering Niko. But there was a problem: he'd shifted and was positioned now to come out bottom first, knees bent. Emily's exhaustion was a concern at this point, plus there was the complication of what would be a breech delivery unless he could be turned. Doctor Delgado made two unsuccessful attempts to shift him when Maureen said the heartbeat was weakening and dropping quickly. Dr. Delgado decided an emergency C-section was necessary; Emily sobbed and protested but I managed to talk down her opposition. It all happened so fast! Emily was rushed to an operating room and I followed. Another nurse put up a screen to block my view when I saw the doctor grab a scalpel. As his hand disappeared behind the screen, I got weak-kneed. "You all right, Dad?" the nurse asked. I nodded, embarrassed to have any attention on me. Seconds later, Niko was wailing away, pink and perfect. My son! I had a son! . . .

The riverbank turns sandy for a while, then gives way to a stretch that bulges with wild vegetation: arborvitae, hemlock, skunk cabbage, forsythia. Somewhere nearby a woodpecker is tap-tapping away, hunting for insects, eggs, and larvae. *They also peck to declare their territory or drum for a mate,*

I hear my father say—a remnant of some long-ago walk in the woods when I was seven or eight. Those nature walks were one of the few aspects of my dad's parenting that I'd been looking forward to replicating with my daughter and son once they were old enough.

A day or so after we brought the babies home from the hospital, Niko gave us another scare, and as first-time parents, Emily and I were worst-case-scenario worriers. Maisie took to breastfeeding right away, but Niko was cranky and jittery and didn't seem to get the hang of sucking. His skin and the whites of his eyes were turning yellowish and we grew scared. We drove to Dr. Delgado's office without an appointment. The nurse practitioner said words like "bilirubin" and "jaundice," and the next thing we knew, Niko was demoted back to the hospital for treatment under a phototherapy lamp. His yellowish cast faded away soon after and, home again, he suddenly mastered his mother's nipple and established himself as the chowhound twin. He began to thrive.

Emily and I were fascinated with every stage of the kids' development during that first year. Their growing awareness of each other. Their smiles in recognition of our faces, our voices. Their ability to turn over and then creep. The days when Maisie, and then her brother, let go of the furniture and took their first wobbly steps before falling into my open arms. In all these achievements, Maisie led and Niko followed. But there was one exception. Niko was the twinkly-eyed scamp who taught his more serious sister the pleasure of laughter. Maisie thought he was hilarious and we did, too. I took a cell phone video of him swaying and dancing to some song on the radio, another of him deliberately teasing us. The twins were exhausting but fascinating, too; each day brought new discoveries, new mastery of skills, as they learned how to negotiate their world. One night, I heard Emily call me from the twins' room. "I want you to see something," she said. She was standing at the crib. "Look at them, Corby." They were sleeping side by side, sucking each other's thumb. I put my arm around her and pulled her closer. "We made these two," she said. . . .

Now I wipe my eyes on my shirtsleeve. Tell myself to turn around and drive back home. Instead, I keep walking. Is what I did going to destroy our marriage? Mom said I need to figure out how to forgive myself if I'm going to move forward. But what if I can't? What if Emily decides she wants to move forward without me? I pick up a flat stone at my feet and pitch it into the water. Watch it jump along the surface once, twice, three times before it sinks. Skipping stones was one of the boyhood skills my father taught me, a pleasure Niko will never know—one of the thousands of things I've deprived him of. I see him lying in the driveway, breathing bravely, just minutes away from dying in the back of that ambulance. How can I not blame myself? How can I have failed my son far more disastrously than my father failed me?

I've been hiking for about a mile when I come upon a boulder lodged in the middle of the river, the water churning and rushing around it. A large, long-beaked, spindly-legged bird—an egret?—stands atop the rock, still as a statue as it watches the water. I stop. Stare at it as I speak to my dead son.

"Hey, little man, can you hear me? Where did you go?" I drop to my knees at the water's edge and begin to cry. "You had so much of your life left to live, Niko, so much waiting for you. How can I still be in the world when you're not? I don't deserve your forgiveness, but if I could know that . . . somehow . . ."

I plunge my hands into the cold water and claw the bottom. Scoop up handfuls of gravel and fling them at my face. Make a fist and punch myself in the chest. Do it again, harder. The hurt of it feels right.

"Niko, what's going to happen if I tell the truth? Will your mother leave me? Will I go to prison?" I deliver another punch, harder still. "But how can I live inside my skin if I keep lying about why you died? If I devalue your life like that?" I slam my knuckles against my forehead once, twice, three times. "I don't want to lie anymore, Niko, but I'm scared of losing them both. What should I do?"

I don't realize I'm shouting the last, pleading with my dead son, until I see that bird on the rock turn its head and look across the rushing water at me. Then with slow, deep wingbeats, it takes flight, its neck tucked into its body, its legs trailing behind it. It's not an egret. It's a majestic great blue heron. I watch it soar, flying farther and farther away from me until all I can see are the indifferent clouds and the hard blue sky.

I hike back to where I parked Emily's car. Get in, grab my phone, and text her: *Coming home now. Should be back in time.*

———

At the funeral home, we're met by solicitous husband-and-wife morticians who make no references to the circumstances of our son's death but mostly address Emily. I just sit there, one hand cupped around my wife's shoulder, the other fisting the tissue they've offered me. I nod in agreement with whatever Emily decides: a private, secular service; no calling hours; no to embalming; no to cremation. He is to be buried in the forty-two-inch "Precious Moments" casket—twenty-inch gauge steel construction, blue crepe interior, embroidery on the inner lid. Ours for $1,999.

On the way back to the house, I ask how Maisie's been that morning. "She kept saying his name," Emily says. "Looking for him. It's been brutal." She drops open the glove compartment and grabs some napkins. Wipes her tears, blows her nose.

"Did she ask where I was?"

"Once," she says. "It was mostly about him."

"Who's with her?" I ask.

"My mother."

I pull in behind Betsy's car and keep the motor running. Emily gets out and comes around to the driver's side. "You coming in?" she asks. I tell her I have to do something first. She nods and starts toward the house.

I roll down the window and call her name. When she comes back, I say there's something I need to tell her. She waits. I take a deep breath and say, "I started drinking during the day a while back. Liquor, not just beer. In the afternoon and the morning both, hiding the bottles from you. And I've been lying about looking for a job. I kind of gave up on that a while ago. Surrendered, I guess you'd say. And that prescription I got for my anxiety? I've been overdoing that, too. I think I may be addicted. I'm sorry."

She just stands there, wide-eyed, trying to take it in.

"Yesterday? When it happened? I was already kind of wasted. I was . . . I started drinking when I was making breakfast. My lawyer has an idea about how I might beat getting charged, but I can't lie anymore. Not to you, not to the police."

She doesn't cry or yell or call me a son of a bitch. Her face betrays no emotion whatsoever when she says, "I can't have you living here anymore."

"You mean temporarily, right? Can we discuss it?"

"No. I'll pack some of your things and you can pick them up." She turns away and walks toward the house. After the front door closes, I back up, put the car in drive, and head to the police station.

In the parking lot, I pull into one of the visitor spaces and head toward the building. Halfway there that falling sensation comes over me again and I have to stop and put my hand on someone's truck fender to steady myself. It passes quickly and I keep going. I see Detective Sparks walking in ahead of me. She's holding a coffee in one hand, her cell phone in the other. "No means no, Chanel," I hear her say. "I don't care what your boyfriend wants."

I follow her into the lobby. Call her name. When she turns around, she says, "Oh, hi. You're early. We agreed that you'd come in later this afternoon. We're still waiting for those results to come back from the lab."

I tell her there's no need. "You were right. I'd been drinking and drugging yesterday morning when I got in the car. That was why I didn't check the back seat before I started backing up. Why he died. I guess you better arrest me."

CHAPTER TEN

—

May 5, 2017

Eight days after Niko's death, I'm brought before the court on the charge of second-degree involuntary manslaughter due to operating a motor vehicle while under the influence of alcohol and a controlled substance. Because I plead guilty, there will be no trial. A probation officer will be assigned to research and write a presentence investigation report, partly based on his or her assessment of my degree of remorse and the sincerity of my resolve to rehabilitate myself. I will be sentenced at a future date. "Could be several weeks from now," Attorney Dixon explains. Where I will spend those weeks—in or out of jail—is the judge's decision, to be made on the day I'm arraigned.

Rachel Dixon makes the case before Superior Court Judge Vincent Pelto that, prior to sentencing, I should remain out of jail on a bond-free Promise to Appear. "He's a low flight risk, Your Honor, and has no long list of priors. He attended his first Alcoholics Anonymous meeting yesterday and plans to continue going daily. He and the boy's mother have an appointment with a bereavement counselor in hopes that they can work on things together. For the time being, Mr. Ledbetter is living at his mother's residence, but he sees his daughter every day and his stabilizing presence is helping the child cope with the loss of her twin brother. In addition, Mr. Ledbetter has filled out applications for stopgap employment and is hoping to find work soon. The efforts my client already has made to rehabilitate himself are impressive and we are confident that, during the next weeks, these efforts can continue if he is not detained in a presentence lockup facility."

All of what my lawyer is saying is true, but the judge's face is unreadable. Not so the prosecutor's. Bettina Reitland is smirking. Dixon and Reitland are probably both in their midforties but, physically, they're a study in opposites. Attorney Dixon is short, squat, and pink-haired. Attorney Reitland is tall and fit. Her sleek black hair falls to her shoulders and her sleeveless black dress shows off some powerful-looking biceps and calves. As she stands to counter Dixon's argument, her smirk falls away, replaced by a look of earnest intent.

"That's an impressive number of mitigating factors, Your Honor," she begins. "But as you know, it's *highly* unusual for someone who's been charged with a violent crime to be granted a no-cost bail and released on his own recognizance. And although the defendant has no long *list* of priors, there is a previous DUI on his record. Despite the suspension of his license, who's to say he won't drink and drive again and harm or kill someone else?"

I cringe at the gut shot she's just landed, but she isn't done yet.

"Attorney Dixon makes the point that, if prior to his sentencing, he has daily contact with the Ledbetters' surviving child, this will help her cope with the sudden absence of her twin brother. That may or may not be so; neither Attorney Dixon nor I have expertise in child psychology. But let's keep in mind that little Niko Ledbetter's 'absence' is the result of his father's negligence while he was drugged and intoxicated."

I look over at Emily. Her face is turned away from me, but Betsy is nodding in agreement with Reitland.

"I would also remind the court that *applying* for jobs is not the same as being hired and working responsibly at them over time. And I can't help but wonder why, if Mr. Ledbetter is so motivated to find stopgap employment now, he didn't look for temporary work in the nine months between the time he was laid off and the day he committed the crime for which he's been charged."

Turning to me, Judge Pelto asks whether I want to respond. Dixon attempts to intervene on my behalf, but I say I'd like to answer him. "I *was* looking for work," I tell the judge. "But there was nothing in my field."

"What field is that?" he asks.

"Commercial art. I sent out résumés and went to interviews pretty steadily, but I couldn't find anything. Plus, I was the stay-at-home parent for our kids. When my wife and I were both working, we had daycare for the twins. Once we were down to one income, we couldn't afford it anymore, so I took care of the kids. And when I was out looking for work, my mother-in-law babysat for us."

The judge asks what kinds of jobs I've filled out applications for since my arrest. "You name it, Your Honor. Third-shift convenience store clerk; warehouse worker at Lowe's, Home Depot, and Target; packer at the Amazon warehouse; nighttime group home supervisor. I've gotten a couple of callbacks, but I've been waiting to follow up because I didn't know what was going to happen here today. In terms of, you know, my availability."

Judge Pelto looks back and forth between me and Reitland. "So let's say you *do* get hired for one of these jobs, Mr. Ledbetter," he says. "With your driver's license revoked, have you thought about how you'll get back and forth to work? And for that matter, what about transportation to and from your AA and NA meetings?"

"Well, if I get a second- or third-shift job, my mother says she can drive me. She works the morning shift at Newport Creamery and gets home by one thirty or two. I can also check out the bus route. Ride a bike if I have to. And in a pinch, there's Lyft or Uber. And the AA meeting I went to yesterday is at a church a couple of miles away from where I'm staying. I can walk there if I can't get a ride."

I wipe the sweat off my top lip and wait. The judge shuffles the papers on his desk. He seems satisfied with what I just said; I'm optimistic. So I'm surprised when he renders his decision that I can be released on a Promise to Appear, but only after I've posted a $25,000 bond. He flips through a calendar and schedules my sentencing hearing for July twentieth—eleven weeks from today. "That's almost twice the number of weeks we usually set for sentencing, but I want to see how successful you are at keeping up with these efforts you're beginning to make." Turning to the attorneys, he asks, "Does that work for you two?" Dixon checks her calendar and nods. Reitland says that's during her vacation. "Okay, let's see what else we've got," the judge says. The date is switched to August first.

Later that day, while I wait in a holding cell with a guy muttering to himself, my mother drives to the courthouse and cosigns my bail agreement, surrendering the deed to her trailer as collateral. "Okay, Ledbetter, you're free to go," some anonymous sheriff announces.

Driving me back to her place, Mom says, "Emily packed up some of your things and dropped them off. I put them in the spare room. There's a futon in there so that can be your bedroom for now. You'll have to ignore all the dream-catcher materials. I have a bunch more to do for the crafts show that's coming up."

"How does she seem?" I ask.

"Emily? Pretty brave, I'd say. And sad."

"Angry?"

She shakes her head. "More like determined she's going to get through this one way or another. Stoic, I guess you'd say. She told me some of the other teachers have donated their sick days so she's taking some time off from work to figure things out. Which I think will be good for her and Maisie, too."

"So what do you think the odds are that she's going to divorce me?" Mom declines to speculate or give an opinion. "I wish Betsy thought like you," I tell her. "I'm sure she's not holding back *her* opinion."

"Well, honey, Emily's going to decide for herself what she needs to do, and whatever that is, I think we're just going to have to respect that decision."

"Yeah, well . . ."

"Oh, and she said to tell you your appointment with that grief counselor is at four o'clock Wednesday, so she can swing by and pick you up at a quarter of."

"Okay. Maybe that's a good sign. Plus, she's letting me see Maisie at the house every afternoon. She says she'll stick around while I'm there but not, like, *supervise* the visit. Which would be kind of weird, you know? For Maisie?"

Mom says she thinks *that's* a hopeful sign.

"Yeah, maybe. Hey, by the way, thanks."

She looks over at me. "It's fine, Corby. I just hope you're not going to feel too claustrophobic. It's a small room, and with all those hoops and feathers and beads and skeins of colored thread in there—"

I tell her I mean because she posted my bail and got me out of there.

"Oh, that. It's no big deal as long as you're not planning to skip out of the country on us. I'd hate to end up sleeping on a park bench."

"It *is* a big deal. Putting up your home like that? It's a *huge* deal and I appreciate it. I love you, Mom."

"I love you, too." Her eyes brim with tears. "I just wish it didn't have to be so goddamned hard for you. Indicting you for a crime when it was an *accident*?"

"Yeah, but Mom—"

"I'm not saying you were faultless, but what good would it do to send you to prison? I'd like to know how many other people in that courtroom today have driven drunk or stoned and gotten away with it, including that holier-than-thou prosecutor. The way she was scoffing at the efforts you've made was infuriating."

"That's her job, Mom. Like it or not."

"Okay, fine, do your job then," she huffs. "But lose the attitude, lady."

I can't help but smile. "Yeah, Reitland. You better watch out now that you've pissed off Mama Bear."

"Damn right," she says. "She better not come in for breakfast some morning and get one of my tables. She might end up with eggs in her lap."

We pass the next mile or so in silence until Mom asks me what I'm thinking about. "I'm having trouble reading Emily," I tell her. "I can't tell if she thinks I should get a prison sentence."

Mom says she doesn't believe Emily would want that. "It's understandable that she's angry, but she's not vindictive. And you've lost your son, too. I'm sure she feels that's punishment enough."

"And you've lost your grandson," I say. "How are *you* doing?"

She smiles sadly. "Sometimes in the middle of the day, even in the middle of a busy shift, it'll hit me that he's really gone and I have to go in back and take a couple of minutes no matter who's waiting for me to bring their food to the table or refill their coffee cup. It's the same kind of grief I felt after my brother Warren got killed in Vietnam. I'll be okay for a while. Then it clobbers you like a wave you didn't see coming. Crashes into you and pulls you under so that, for a few seconds, you can't breathe."

I nod. Say nothing.

"Oh, Corby, I just loved that little guy. Maisie's just as precious, but Niko reminded me so much of you."

May 8, 2017

"I used to use alcohol to drown out my problems," the woman says. "Then it finally dawned on me that my problems were better swimmers than I was." A few people chuckle. Others nod. She tells us it had happened little by little. First, she lost the cosmetics company she and her husband had started. Then she lost the husband, followed by her friends, her dignity, her freedom. "I got a six-month sentence for writing bad checks and three 'failures to appear' because I couldn't manage to sober up when it was time to go before the judge. I was a hot mess, believe me."

Her hard-luck story and her appearance don't match up. She's stylish, professionally dressed, midforties, maybe. Those look like expensive shoes she's wearing. I noticed a Benz convertible in the parking lot on the way in and figure it might be hers. I'd never have pegged her for being a lush with a prison record.

"I had tried AA before and was convinced it just didn't work for me.

But the only reason it didn't was because I wanted to keep drinking. It's amazing how we lie to everyone including ourselves. Right? But I hadn't hit bottom yet. That happened while I was in prison when I got this letter notifying me that my parental rights were being revoked."

I lean forward, jolted by what she's just said. Can they do that? And who is "they"? Her ex? The court? DCF?

"But after I lost my girls, I got serious about my sobriety. I was *motivated*, okay? It took me five years, but I got them back. One's a high school sophomore now and the other's in her first year of college. I've got a good job in real estate, own my own condo, and lease a car that's fun to drive. I had lost all these things because of my obsession with booze. It's like they say. When you're an active alcoholic, you give up everything for one thing. But when you commit to sobriety, you give up one thing for everything. Okay, thanks for listening. I'll share the time."

Nice story, but her kids didn't die because of her. Niko will never get to kindergarten, let alone high school or college. I look at the door, wondering whether I can get up and leave without much notice.

"Thanks, Priscilla," the stocky guy at the front table says. "Who else?" Three or four hands go up, but he looks past them and seems to be eyeballing me. "What about you?" he says.

"Me?" I can feel my face flush. My arrest was front-page news the week before and I don't want anyone connecting the dots. "No thanks. I'll just listen."

"All right. Want to tell us your name at least?" I shake my head. "Fair enough. Troy, you had your hand up. Why don't you go?"

Troy tells a grim story about witnessing a lot of "grisly shit" while fighting in the war in Afghanistan. "I started shooting heroin while I was there," he says. "And I was addicted to alcohol, too, by the time I came home. I didn't think this back then, but now I realize I was drinking and doing smack to treat my PTSD."

What he's saying makes me think of Luke Lebeau, this kid in high school who sat in front of me in homeroom. He joined the army right after graduation, fought in Iraq, and lost his shit. Walked around town all day talking to himself.

"Me and a buddy bought a bar together, but we were both using and ignoring the bills that kept piling up. It failed after about a year. Then my girlfriend kicked me to the curb. My grandmother paid for my ninety-day rehab in New Mexico and let me live with her after I got discharged. The deal was, I'd be a caregiver for her husband, my stepgrandpa, who had this disease called Lewy body dementia. I liked the guy and took pretty good care of him, but Gram fired my ass when she realized I was stealing her jewelry and pawning it to pay for my bad habits. She didn't press charges like my dad wanted her to, but my whole family cut me off.

"I went down fast after that. Slept in a tent by the river when the weather was decent, sometimes by myself and sometimes with women I'd pick up in dive bars or at the soup kitchen. When it rained, I'd find an unlocked car and sleep in that. In winter, I'd make the rounds at the shelters. The best ones would let you take a shower, give you breakfast in the morning. But those places fill up fast, so I'd usually end up at the ones where all you got was heat and a mat on the floor.

"Anyway, one day while I was waiting in line for the soup kitchen to open, I started puking up blood. Collapsed and woke up in the ER. When they found out I'd been in the army, they shipped me downstate to the VA hospital. One of the docs there gave it to me straight. Said if I didn't stop pouring poison down my throat and sticking it in my arm, I was going to die from an OD or cirrhosis or maybe a gastric hemorrhage. Or maybe I'd end up with a wet brain, drooling and babbling in some locked ward somewhere. So what do I do as soon as I get out of there? Hitchhiked back home and panhandled until I had scrounged enough money to buy myself a speedball and a quart of bottom-shelf bourbon. The next day, sick as a dog, I wandered into a meeting in some church basement—not to get saved but because I knew they'd have coffee and cookies, maybe even doughnuts. Anyways, that was the day, six years ago now, when the miracle happened. I haven't had a drink since. I'm not patting myself on the back, though. It wasn't me who got me sober. It was my higher power coming to me through all of you."

Well, good for him that he's stayed sober, and if he wants to believe in miracles, why not? But if I keep coming to these meetings, which I've promised Emily, my mom, and my attorney I'll do, they better not try to shove religion down my throat. I want to get sober, not "saved" by some imaginary god that's supposedly pulling the puppet strings. He sure as hell hasn't handed *me* any miracles.

This is my second meeting and, just like the first, when time is up, everyone stands, gets in a circle, and takes hold of one another's hands. Someone says, "Who keeps us sober?" and everyone starts reciting the Lord's Prayer. I do the hand-holding thing but, for the second day in a row, I keep my mouth shut. I can't pray to something I don't believe in.

Outside again, while I wait for my mother to pick me up, I watch a bunch of the others, laughing and lighting up like it's a cocktail party without the cocktails. I'm right about who's driving the Mercedes. She taps the brake as she sidles up beside me. "Keep coming," she says. "It gets easier." I smile at that small, simple act of kindness.

A guy from the meeting walks toward me. Scraggly beard and bushy eyebrows, early sixties maybe. Plaid flannel shirt, Mets ball cap. "I recognize who you are from the TV," he says.

I tense up, thinking I'm about to be called a baby killer or something.

"Here," he says. "In case you want to talk." He hands me a Taco Bell napkin with his name, Dale Tebbins, and his number written diagonally across it. I say thanks, fold it, and shove it into a back pocket of my jeans. He starts to walk away, then turns around and comes back. "Something similar happened to me, more or less, so I might get the hell you're probably going through more than most," he says. "I was driving drunk with my niece in the back seat. Ran a red light and got T-boned by a Hummer. I walked away without a scratch, but the accident brain-damaged Kayla. She was eight then. Died five years later."

I stand there, unable to think of anything to say.

"Day at a time, my friend. You can always drink tomorrow if you need to. Just don't drink today. Well, I better get going. Give me a call if you need to." I watch him walk down a row of cars and climb into a blue pickup truck. He waves as he drives out of the parking lot. I wave back.

———

During my scheduled visit with Maisie, Emily is true to her word. She doesn't leave the house, but she doesn't hover over us either. Maisie is subdued but seems okay. I make her half of a grilled cheese for lunch, her favorite, and cut up some carrot sticks. Get her to grin a little when I balance one of the sticks above my top lip and say it's my orange mustache. After lunch, we cuddle up on the sofa and watch TV: *Peppa Pig, Daniel Tiger's Neighborhood*. When it's nap time, I tell her to pick out a story. She chooses not one but two: her own favorite, *The Very Hungry Caterpillar*, and her brother's, *Where's Spot?* The door to the twins' room is still closed, so at nap time I figure the crib is still off-limits. I put Maisie in the middle of Emily's and my bed, kiss her, and tell her I love her.

As I'm leaving the room, she says, "Niko?" I turn back and face her, at a loss for words. There's no way to explain death to a little girl who's two. Instead, I hurry into the living room, grab that framed picture of the two of them, then go back and show her. "Niko," she says. She touches his face behind the glass and smiles. That's when I lose it.

That thing my mother said about grief? How it's like a wave that clobbers you so that you go under and can't catch your breath? That's how it felt when Maisie touched her brother's photograph. Emily and I had agreed that my daily visits would end when Maisie went down for her afternoon nap. I need to compose myself before Emily sees me crying. That woman at the AA meeting had had her parental rights taken away. If I want to stay in my daughter's life, I need these visits to go smoothly. I grab my jacket, go outside, and sit on the porch step to wait for Mom to pick me up.

Emily opens the door. "It's raining," she says. "Why don't you wait inside?"

"No, I'm okay," I tell her. "Thanks, though." It's weird how polite and careful we're being with each other. I'm relieved when she goes back inside.

When I see the McNallys' garage door open and Shawn's car backing out, I brace myself. What am I supposed to say to him now that my confession and arrest have been in the paper and on TV? What's *he* going to say to *me*? What happens, though, is that neither of us speaks. He backs into the street, shifts, and drives off, pretending he didn't see me. Part of me feels shame, another part feels relief.

For the rest of that afternoon and into the evening, I keep hearing Maisie's question. "Niko?" Where is Niko? Where did Niko go? My mother showed me where she kept her weed if I want any, but I don't need to get mellow. I need to get hammered. But Mom's gotten rid of her alcohol; I've already checked. By eight o'clock, I'm craving a drink so bad that I start getting the sweats. And not just *a* drink. A number of them, one after another, enough to make me too drunk to feel the pain that my life has become and the pain I've caused everyone else.

Mom went to bed early—to read, she said, but her workday starts at four in the morning so she's probably asleep already. I crack open her door and sure enough, her breathing is rhythmic and she doesn't stir. I fight the urge for another half hour or so, then give up, pull on my jacket, and grab my wallet and phone. There's a liquor store in that strip mall on Sachem Turnpike. If I hustle, I can make it there before closing time. Outside, I break into a jog, each step bringing me closer to relief.

I walked away without a scratch, but the accident brain-damaged Kayla. . . . Anyways, that was the day when the miracle happened. . . . You can always drink tomorrow if you need to. Just don't drink today.

I stop. Stand there shaking and baking until I reach into my back pocket and feel that napkin he gave me. With a shaky finger, I punch in the digits. Listen to it ring once, twice, three times, four. I'm about to hang up when there's a click.

"Hello?"

"Dale? It's Corby . . . guy from the meeting today? You said I could call?"

Ten minutes later, his truck pulls up in front of the Cumberland Farms where I told him I'd be waiting. When he asks me whether I've been drinking, I'm able to say no. He asks whether I'm telling him the truth and I say yes. I don't take offense; drunks know what good liars other drunks can be. But I'm not bullshitting him.

Over coffee and pie at the Pilot truck stop off Exit 93, he fills me in on his story. "My sister Gina was in the middle of a divorce and she and Kayla had moved in with me. Gina worked long hours, so I was pitching in—helping Kayla with her homework, giving her rides, stuff like that. My sister knew I wasn't the best babysitter—no secret I was a boozer—but at that point, her options were limited. I was on disability from work, so I was around and I had promised her I wouldn't let Kayla get in the car if I'd been drinking.

"Gina was supposed to get back in time to take her to gymnastics that day, but something came up at work. Attendance at practice was mandatory for some show. At first, I thought I'd call the kid a cab, but then I decided I was feeling no pain but not really drunk. I could get her there and maybe get one of the mothers to drop her off when practice was over. That was fourteen years ago, but to this day, I remember starting the car and watching her run across the lawn toward me in the polka-dot leotard I bought her for her birthday. She had a pretty limited life, thanks to me. In and out of hospitals and Easter Seals. Her walking and talking were compromised and she had all kinds of learning problems. Died from an aneurysm when she was thirteen. She'd be twenty-two now if she had lived.

"The thing is, you never get over it—that hard a loss and the fact that you caused it. There's always going to be sadness and shame around it. You just have to figure out how to live with yourself without drinking over it. At least that was what *I* had to do." When I ask him about his sister, he says she moved out to Colorado. Got married again, didn't have any more kids. "She still won't have anything to do with me. When I got to my ninth step, Gina was the first person on my list that I had to make amends to, but she told me she wasn't having it. Said I could take my amends and shove it. I was pretty bummed out about that, but my sponsor said her not accepting it didn't matter. I couldn't control what her reaction was going to be. What mattered was that I had *offered* her my amends."

Dale and I talk for about an hour. Then he drives me back to my mother's. As he pulls into the trailer park, he says, "Oh, one more thing. Today, at the end of the meeting, I noticed you weren't saying the Lord's Prayer."

"Yeah, I'm not really big on the higher-power thing," I say.

"I hear you. I love AA, but I tune out a lot of the God stuff. The closest I get to believing in a higher power is when I look out at the ocean while I'm surf casting. See something that's much bigger than I am. Something that's been here a lot longer than me and is going to be here long after I'm gone. What I'm saying is, you don't need to turn into a Holy Roller in order to get saved. Just keep coming to meetings and don't drink. My first sponsor was a religious man—a deacon in his church. He used to say to me, 'Dale, you don't have to believe as long as you believe that *I* believe.' "
He stops talking and lets that sink in. Finally, he says, "So. You all right?"

"Yeah. Thanks."

He nods. "And you're not going to drink tonight. Right? We got a deal?"

I take a deep breath. "Deal," I say.

CHAPTER ELEVEN

—

May 9, 2017

Rachel Dixon's wife, Sandy, a psychiatric social worker, was the one who recommended Emily and I see Dr. Beena Patel, a licensed clinical psychologist who'd done extensive work counseling grieving couples. Emily was skeptical but compliant; I was desperate to try anything that might help us ease the pain.

When we step into Dr. Patel's office, she holds out her hand to welcome us. Her sari, honeydew green, is draped over a white short-sleeved T-shirt, her hair is salt-and-pepper. "Please sit down," she says, indicating the gray-and-white-striped love seat opposite her matching armchair. Once we're seated, I reach over and take Emily's hand, a gesture she tolerates for about five seconds before she withdraws it. This does not escape our grief counselor's watchful eye.

"May I first of all offer you both my deepest condolences," she says. Emily and I nod, mumbling our thanks. "How long ago did the accident happen?"

"Twelve days ago," Emily says.

From the other side of the room, I hear what sounds like a train whistle. "I put some water to boil just before you came in," she says. "Tea? I have chamomile and jasmine." Emily declines. I say either one. "Let's have jasmine then." She takes two small cups from a shelf, lifts the kettle off a glowing hot plate, and pours the steaming water into a colorful teapot.

"Ah, the aroma of jasmine always carries me back to my childhood in India."

"India?" I say. "Really? I would have guessed Scandinavia." Emily looks over at me, disgusted. I apologize, explaining that I make stupid jokes when I'm nervous.

"No apology necessary," Dr. Patel says. "I like jokes, especially silly ones." She cocks her head and gives me a benign smile. "And there's no need to be nervous, Corbin. This is a safe place for you both."

I nod. Ask whether she could call me Corby.

"Of course. Now, I understand you'll be appearing before a judge for sentencing in several weeks. Correct?"

"Yeah, although I've already been drawn and quartered on Facebook and Twitter, as my mother-in-law has dutifully reported to Emily."

Dr. Patel looks at Emily, who looks away from her. "Well, that is not the case here, Corby. My job is to help, not judge." Emily rolls her eyes.

Trying to break through my wife's resistance, I say, "I mean, don't get me wrong. I *deserve* to be judged. I put *both* our kids at risk when I started drinking while I was taking care of them."

"And drugging yourself, too," Emily mumbles. "Don't forget *that* little detail."

Dr. Patel looks back and forth between us.

"Right," I say. "And Niko died because of it. Emily, the shame and guilt I feel—the pain this is putting you through—is going to be a life sentence for me. And it should." I turn from my wife to Dr. Patel. "But there's a bigger picture."

"Meaning?" Dr. Patel asks.

"That I've been a loving father, too. A pretty *good* father up until—"

"Until you weren't!" Emily snaps. "Don't make yourself sound like Father of the Year. Or like you're a victim because of what people are saying on Facebook. Because you're *not* the victim, Corby. Niko was."

Close to tears, I snap back at her. "You think I don't know that? You think that's slipped my mind?"

Dr. Patel waits for one of us to speak, but when we don't, she says, "Let's take a breath. I think our tea must be finished steeping. I'll be right back."

While we wait, Emily checks her phone and I scan the degrees on Dr. Patel's wall. Oxford University, the University of Chicago. There's a plaque from the National Alliance on Mental Illness, a teaching award from Yale.

When she's back, I nod toward the wall. "That's a pretty impressive collection you've got up there," I say.

"Well, I'm afraid my accomplishments in the kitchen are much less so," she says, placing a plate of cookies on the table in front of us. "These are *nankhatai*—Indian butter cookies."

I take one; Emily doesn't. Dr. Patel says she'd like to turn to Emily now. "Corby has told us that his feelings of shame and guilt will be 'a life sentence,' but—"

"That's typical. Our son is dead, but he's focused on himself."

I flinch but don't respond. "Tell us what *you're* feeling, Emily," Dr. Patel says.

"What *I'm* feeling? I'm feeling so overwhelmed with grief that I have to remind myself to breathe. That I have to force myself to get out of bed in the morning."

"That's understandable, and good for you that you're making that effort," Patel says. "What other feelings are you experiencing?"

"Anger. Confusion. Guilt. And that's just for starters."

"It's understandable that, this close to so profound a tragedy, your emotions would be all over the place," Patel says.

"Please don't call him 'a tragedy.' He has a name: Niko." She looks over at me. "*Had* a name," she says.

"So noted," Patel says. "Now I'd like us to examine your anger a little more closely. Would that be all right?"

Emily sighs impatiently but finally nods.

"Good. Thank you, Emily. Let me first tell you that I have done grief work with other mothers who have lost a child. If the death was unexpected, rather than anticipated because of the child's terminal illness, these mothers, understandably, feel angry about a situation that has been thrust upon them out of the blue. Some of these grieving mothers direct their outrage at fate or, if they are women of faith, at God because they feel He has betrayed their devotion to Him. Depending on the circumstances surrounding the death, others feel angry with themselves or with their child's father. Can you tell us what or whom—"

"Corby!"

"Because?"

"Isn't it obvious?"

Dr. Patel suggests it might be useful if Emily says what she needs to say directly to me. When she turns to me, I brace myself, determined to face her.

She keeps me waiting, but I can tell from her rapid breathing that her anger is rising. "You betrayed my trust," she finally says. "I assumed our kids would be safe in their father's care, but Niko's not here anymore because of your stupid self-pity. 'Oh, poor me. I lost my job and can't find another one. And now I have to take care of our kids because we can't afford daycare. Boo-hoo. I might as well just get wasted.'"

My hands clench up and my stomach tightens, but I'll be damned if I'm going to lose it. When I ask Patel whether I can respond, she nods. "I started drinking because I was depressed, Emily, not because I resented taking care of the kids. Was it easy being the stay-at-home parent? Not always. But there were parts about it that I really loved. It was amazing to watch their development from day to day. I bonded with Niko and Maisie in a way I never would have otherwise."

"Too bad they weren't your priority then."

"Emily, they *were*."

"No, your priority was numbing your self-pity with alcohol and drugs, or as you like to put it, 'checking out,' which sounds a lot nicer than getting behind the wheel while you were incapacitated and backing over our son." She begins to sob. "And because of that, I'm never going to see him again, cuddle with him, tickle his tummy when I'm changing his diaper and hear his giggle. I won't be able to go to his swimming lessons, his T-ball games. Send him off to high school, then college. Watch him become whoever he was going to be. You took all of that away from me, Corby. You put the car in reverse and stole him from me."

I can't do it. Can't keep facing her, watching the grim truth come out of her angry mouth, but she doesn't stop. I look at Patel, my eyes begging her to intervene, but she lets it go on. Lets Emily lash out, then wail from the pain. When Em stands up and walks toward the door, I assume she's storming out of the session. But then she pivots, comes back, and sits down again. Having unleashed some of her pain seems to have calmed her down.

"And the thing that's so confusing is that I love you and feel sorry for you because of the shame you must have to carry, which I can't even begin to imagine. But I hate you, too, Corby, for breaking that trust I thought I could rely on."

"You don't think I hate *myself*, Emily?" Calm down. Lower your voice. "Babe, you and I have a history," I remind her. "And sure, we've had our ups and downs, but until recently—"

"That's a pretty big 'until recently,' don't you think?"

"All I'm saying is—"

"Don't you *dare* dismiss my son's death like that! Don't you fucking *dare*!"

"*Your* son? He was *our* son, Emily!" Inhale, exhale. Once, twice, three times.

She sits there, fuming. Glances over at Patel, then turns back to me. "I get that you were depressed about your career. And that me bringing home a paycheck while you took care of the kids all day wasn't a great fit for you. Bruised your fragile male ego or whatever. But do you think it was easy for me to drive away from them every morning? Or when I got home, having to give up bath time on school nights because I had hours of work to get to? Because one of us had to be the grown-up? And then having to get into bed and listen to you complain about how exhausted *you* were?"

"Babe, the arrangement was situational. Temporary until I could—"

"You know what's *not* temporary, Corby? One of my babies is dead!" Her face is flushed, contorted with anger. "That's permanent. Do you remember how that doctor advised me not to go to him in that hospital morgue? But I wouldn't listen. I needed to see him, be with him. And now all I can see is his damaged body, my little live wire lying there ashen and still."

When Dr. Patel asks me whether I want to respond to what she's just said, I shake my head. What words are there to soothe the pain I've inflicted on her? Turning to Emily, Patel asks whether there's anything else she wants to say to me. She nods, turns, and looks me in the eye. Her words are more measured now, more sad than angry. "People lose jobs all the time without falling apart and causing everything else to fall apart around them," she says. "Without causing the death of one of their children. I just can't imagine how I'm ever going to be able to forgive you so that we can salvage what's left. And I'll be honest with you, Corby. I'm not sure I *want* to."

We're both crying now, and when I look over at Patel, I see that her eyes are wet, too. This comforts me somehow. For a minute or more, the three of us sit in silence with what's just been said. Dr. Patel is the first to speak.

"When a child dies, no matter the circumstances, it puts a terrible strain on the parents' relationship. How could it not? But the fact that you are here together is, in my opinion, a hopeful sign. Let's visualize that hope as a flickering candle flame. It may stabilize and keep burning or be snuffed out. It depends on your willingness to do the hard work of sustaining your relationship under extremely difficult circumstances, or your decision to end it and move on.

"I also would like to point out that, although you have lost the *same* child, your relationship with him will have been different. Corby, perhaps you can keep in mind that Niko's and his sister's bodies grew inside of, and emerged from, Emily's body. Before you had your first glimpse of them in the delivery room, your son and daughter had an intimate nine-month bond with their mother."

When I reach over and cup Emily's shoulder, she shifts her body away from me. Dr. Patel observes this without dropping a beat.

"And Emily, fathers and sons bond as well, but differently. More often than not, as the male child grows, he observes and begins to emulate his father's way of being in the world. So I would encourage you both to keep in mind that female grief and male grief in response to the death of a child manifest differently. Because men are conditioned to be strong and stoic, their bereavement tends to be internalized and private. Conversely, women are allowed and encouraged to express their feelings more openly. The danger for you as a couple is that you might not understand that there are these differences. A mother might incorrectly conclude that her child's father cares less deeply about his death or rebounds more quickly and she resents him for it, whereas the father might wish that the child's mother would rein in her emotions. These are general patterns that don't apply to all couples, of course. The important thing is to keep talking to each other—to not get so mired in your own pain that you fail to understand the pain your partner is feeling."

"I know Corby's in pain," Emily tells her. "But Niko is dead because he chose to impair his judgment that morning." She looks from Patel to me. "And it was a *choice*, Corby, so I'm sorry, but empathizing with your grief right now isn't something I can do because my anger is in the way."

I nod. Mumble that I understand. But do I? Would I be able to empathize with her if she had been the driver?

"And I want to apologize to you, Emily," Dr. Patel says, "if I've seemed not to acknowledge that your anger is as legitimate as your grief. I assure you that I *do* acknowledge this, and if we continue working together, that is something we would surely wish to address." Emily nods, but just barely.

Dr. Patel says our time for today is just about up. "Should you both wish to continue with the work we began today, I would request that next time I see each of you separately. After that, we can reconvene for another joint session. But whether it's with me or another therapist, I strongly recommend that you continue to undergo counseling.

"You should probably avoid sexual intimacy," she says, "until you're *both* ready. Holding each other and crying together might be a far more useful form of intimacy for now."

If we could ever manage to do that, I think; we're nowhere near being able to do that now.

"And you should consider joining a grief group with other parents who have lost a child. Perhaps most importantly, you should take comfort in knowing that suffering as acute as yours is today will lessen over time.

"And Emily, I encourage you to do what you can to replace the image of your son as he looked in death with memories of him during happy times. Look at photographs, footprints. Watch videos, share stories about him. This may make others feel uncomfortable. They might become tongue-tied trying to think of what to say. But their discomfort is not your problem. Your challenge is to survive this early stage of grief while your pain is so raw and intense. And by all means, talk about Niko with your daughter if you can."

Emily nods compliantly.

Dr. Patel flips through her notes. "Ah, I knew I wanted to return to something before you go. Emily, when you were speaking before about the many emotions you've been feeling, you identified one of them as guilt. Can you say what it is that's making you feel guilty?"

Emily looks over at me and seems to be deliberating about whether or not to say it. She opens her mouth, closes it again, and then speaks. "I wondered if Corby might have been drinking during the day. It was only a hunch, but maybe I should have asked him about it. Confronted him about it. Maybe if I had . . ."

I'm too stunned to say anything. Too confused to react. Patel says, "Well, you and I will want to explore that during our one-to-one session if you choose to continue the work we began today. I do have one last question I'd like each of you to answer. If we move forward with this process, what would you hope to gain from it?"

I go first. "I want to save our marriage."

"And you, Emily?"

"I'm looking for clarity." When Patel asks her whether she can be more specific, she says she doesn't know whether she can stay married to me. Turning to me, she says, "I guess it depends on whether or not I can ever forgive you."

At her office door, Dr. Patel takes each of us by the hand. "You both did some important work today and I would very much like to keep working with you. If that is to be, I suggest we focus first on Niko's death as a *traumatic* experience. Trauma is different than grief. So perhaps the grieving process can be put on hold while we look at ways to deal with the trauma. Then we can explore grieving in a constructive way that will give clarity to you, Emily, and make it more likely, Corby, that your relationship can be saved and maybe even strengthened. Talk it over and give me a call if you think that would be worthwhile. Then we can set up some appointments."

I ask her whether, in the meantime, there are any websites she'd recommend we look at. Dr. Patel advises that we should not put too much stock in information on the internet. Not everything on there is reliable. "But off the top of my head, there's the Butterfly Project, which might be helpful. It's a British website for health givers on how to help the parents of twins or multiples cope when one has died—how to cherish and meet the needs of the living child or children while grieving, in their terminology, the 'butterfly baby.' You might find something useful on that website. Or not. The most valuable work, in my opinion, can be done right here."

In the car on the way back to my mother's place, neither of us speaks for the first couple of miles. "Well, what did you think?" I finally ask.

"I think you were trying hard to win the popularity contest."

"What the hell does that mean?"

"It means you were trying to come off as the reasonable husband who has a difficult wife. I bet she saw right through that."

"I was just trying to take in what she was saying, Em. Stay open-minded."

"The 'butterfly baby'?" she says, shaking her head. "Are we supposed to pretend he didn't die? That he just hatched and migrated to Mexico? That's ridiculous."

"Yeah, but how do you feel about the session other than that?"

"I thought the tea party at the beginning was a little weird."

"I guess she was just trying to put us at ease," I say. "How do you feel about continuing with her?"

She shrugs. Says she has to think about it. "But not if you're going to keep sucking up to her." I manage to hold my tongue. "And what about how much this is going to cost? I assume her services come with a price tag."

"Yeah, but if it helps . . ." I reach out to touch her, then stop. Decide not to risk it. "You want to go get coffee or something and talk?"

She shakes her head. Says she needs to get back for Maisie. Glancing out the driver's-side window, she says, "They're really developing this area out here. Price Chopper, Lowe's, Starbucks. When did all this happen?"

In other words, let's change the subject. But aren't we *supposed* to talk about it? Acknowledge each other's feelings? "I think it was good that you vented back there, Em. The more you deal with your anger—"

She looks over at me, frowning. "Don't fucking patronize me."

"What do you mean? How am I patronizing you?"

"By sounding like *you're* the therapist. 'It's good you vented, Emily. You need to deal with your anger.' You're not the shrink, Corby. You're the *problem*."

"I know I am. Believe me. If I could exchange my life for his, I'd do it in a second." She offers no reaction other than hitting the gas a little harder.

Another couple of miles and two red-light stops pass by in silence before I say that I'd like to continue with Dr. Patel. "At least for the time before my sentencing hearing. And if I get lucky and don't have to go to prison, maybe after that, too. She seems to know what she's doing. And those one-to-one sessions are a good idea. Can't hurt, right?"

Her only response is an impatient sigh.

"I was surprised, though, when you said you suspected I might be day-drinking. I thought I'd been so good at keeping it from you."

"Shut up, Corby. That hour was hard enough without having to listen to your fucking analysis of it." She was driving about ten miles over the speed limit, but now it's more like fifteen or sixteen.

"Yeah, okay. But you don't need to feel guilty about not saying anything. If you had, I would have just denied it."

"Please just *stop!*" she says. She's white-knuckling the steering wheel.

"You might want to slow down a little," I tell her. "I've seen cops in unmarked cars along this stretch."

"Shut up! Shut up! Shut up!" Her hand flies at me, bats me on the side of my head. With her hand off the wheel, her car veers into the lane of oncoming traffic.

"Jesus! Watch where you're going!" I shout. She corrects her course and drives on for a couple of minutes. Then she pulls onto the shoulder, stops the car, puts her head against the steering wheel, and sobs. Again, I resist the impulse to touch her.

"It's okay," I say. "Nothing happened. It's okay."

She mumbles an apology and drives back onto the road.

"We're going to get through this, Emily. I love you."

She just keeps driving.

CHAPTER TWELVE

—

July 26, 2017

At Attorney Dixon's suggestion, I arrive at her office building to read and discuss the report that Probation Officer Jonathan Gonzalez filed after having completed my presentence investigation. Before climbing the stairs, I stop first at that bakery on the ground floor and buy her one of those Death by Chocolate cupcakes I remember she loves. "I'm touched but goddamn you, Ledbetter," she says when I hand her the treat. "I just started doing keto. Oh well, my wife will enjoy it. She eats like a lumberjack without gaining an ounce." She hands me the PSI report. "Tell me what you think," she says. My sentencing hearing is in a week.

Officer Gonzalez has done a thorough job. He's included the police reports filed by Sergeant Fazio and Officer Longo, Detective Sparks, and the officer who arrested me for my earlier DUI. The toxicology reports based on the blood draw they'd taken from me at the hospital are in there, too. Gonzalez notes that I had not sought treatment for my substance abuse before the "event" for which I have been charged, but he's attached photocopies of the scrawled signatures of chairs from the various AA and NA meetings I've been attending since then. Gonzalez has also accessed and included my lackluster school records, not only from RISD but also from Three Rivers High School, which includes the information that I was suspended during my sophomore year for streaking during an outdoor assembly. There's no mention that I did this on a dare from Ethan Martineau, the police chief's grandson.

Also attached are letters of support from Rhonda Tolliver, my former boss at Creative Strategies, Michael McGee, the shift supervisor at the Amazon warehouse where I work now, my AA sponsor, Dale Tebbins, and Dr. Patel, who has written that my participation in our grief counseling sessions has led to genuine progress and that "a prison sentence will serve only to impede or perhaps even arrest the positive changes he has begun to make."

In addition to all that, Officer Gonzalez interviewed me twice to evaluate the degree to which he feels I exhibit remorse and the will to rehabilitate myself. Both of the times I sat in his office, I was confronted by the framed picture of him, his wife, and their three kids and worried that he might not be able to empathize with a failed father like me. But in his conclusion, Gonzalez wrote this: "I am convinced that Mr. Ledbetter is genuinely contrite and that his efforts to address his addictions have been serious and sincere."

When I look up from the report, Dixon is shaking her head and smirking. "Streaking, Ledbetter? Seriously?"

"Youthful idiocy," I say, shrugging. "Plus I got a hundred bucks from the kid who dared me."

"Oh, well then," Dixon says. "Other than the tox report and public nudity, I'd say this is pretty positive." She tells me it is fairly unusual for the person writing the PSI to avoid making a sentencing recommendation. "Which could work in your favor. Judges are free to ignore the probation officer's recommendations, but mostly they tend to follow those guidelines. If Gonzalez had suggested you serve time, that would have upped your chance of going to prison. That's the good news."

"You saying there's bad news?"

"Maybe, maybe not. I think you had a shot at avoiding time in with Judge Pelto, but his mother's gone into hospice down in Florida. He's on temporary leave so he can be with her. Judge Palazzolo is subbing in for him.

She's not a hanging judge by any means, but she's no softie either. She could go either way. Guess we'll have to argue like hell on your behalf, then wait and see. Of course, Reitland's going to argue just as hard that you should do time; that's what prosecutors do and she's not above getting nasty sometimes. I tell you what, though, Ledbetter. However this plays out, you've made some legit efforts during these twelve weeks. You were one hell of a hot mess when you walked into my office that first time, but I've noticed some real changes. It's not easy for a cynic like me to admit this, but I'm impressed."

The unexpected compliment flusters me. Mumbling a thank-you, I look down at her desk to avoid looking at her. That's when I noticed that, while I was reading the PSI report, she's scarfed down half of her chocolate cupcake.

July 27, 2017

Dr. Patel asks me how many of these episodes I've had.

"Two. Both of them at night."

"Can you say what precipitated them?"

"Insomnia, I guess. The first time, I couldn't *get* to sleep and the other time I woke up and couldn't get *back* to sleep. The longer I stayed awake, the more anxious I got about what's going to happen. It got so bad, I started getting the shakes and panting like I couldn't catch my breath."

"You were hyperventilating," she says.

"Yeah, and my heart was pounding so fast, it felt like it might explode. I didn't know what the hell was going on."

"Well, as frightening as they feel while you're experiencing them, panic attacks aren't fatal *and* they can be managed."

Her calming voice, the aroma of the tea she's poured, the colorful sari—peacock blues and greens: being in her presence is soothing. She's what—in her sixties maybe? Wedding ring, so there's a husband. Kids? Grandkids? There's a bit of mystery to her.

"You mention your anxiety about the future is a trigger for these attacks. Can you be more specific?"

I look over her shoulder at the thing mounted on the wall behind her, the source of the sound of trickling water. I ask her whether it's new. She says no, I just must not have noticed it during my earlier appointments. "Now, again, tell me more about why the future is making you so anxious."

"If I get sentenced to prison, I've got fear of the unknown about that. And fear of what I *do* know from watching shows like *Oz* and *The Wire*."

"Television programs might not be your best source of information," she says.

"No, but I look at a lot of stuff on the internet, too. Things ex-cons write about after they're released. It's pretty bleak."

"Perhaps you should look less at these things. Wait until you're in a position to judge the experience for yourself, if indeed you end up having that experience."

"Yeah, makes sense. But that's not the only thing I get scared about."

"No? What else?"

"Let's say I go to prison for however long they're going to give me. But eventually I get out and then what? I couldn't find another job as a commercial artist *before* all the bad stuff happened. What are my chances going to be when I have a prison record? I'm probably going to end up making minimum wage. Wearing a paper hat and asking people if they want chips and a soda with their sub."

"That's your biggest worry, Corby? That you'll end up working in the fast-food industry?"

I shake my head.

"Then what *is* troubling you the most?"

"You know."

Patel says she needs to hear it from me.

"I'm afraid she's never going to be able to forgive me and let me come home. That she's going to want to cut her losses and divorce me. Maybe keep me from our daughter because she doesn't think she'd be safe with me back in the picture? And in the middle of freaking out about everything that *could* happen, I start going back to what *did* happen."

"The accident?"

"You can say it. The day I backed up my car and killed my own son."

She cocks her head. Frowns a little. "That seems harsh, don't you think? Putting it that way?"

I shrug. "It's the truth, isn't it? What difference does it make how you put it?"

"Well, legally, it could mean the difference between involuntary manslaughter and homicide. The former indicates it was accidental, the latter implies intent."

"Involuntary manslaughter *while under the influence*. Don't forget that little detail."

She stares at me; I stare back. If she's trying to make me feel uncomfortable, it's working. To break the impasse, I get up and go over to that thing on her wall. Up close, I see it's a kind of fountain. Water comes out of a spout at the top, spilling down the ribs of a slate slab. A metal base at the bottom catches the water. It's got smooth white stones in it and the water splashing down on them is what makes the sound. "This is cool," I tell her.

"Glad you like it," she says. "But since our time together is limited, might we return to the business at hand?"

I go back to my chair and sit down. Wait.

"Corby, I'm wondering why you requested this appointment. Is it because you wanted to talk about your panic attacks or because you want me to participate in cudgeling you? Because it seems to me that you're doing a fine job of that all by yourself." She suggests that I try to be kinder to myself—put some work into self-forgiveness.

"Tall order," I tell her. "Before? When you said these panic attacks can be managed? How would that work?"

Instead, she asks me to describe what happens when I go back to the day of the tragedy. Is it a memory or does it feel like I'm experiencing it again?

"It's like . . . I relive it. I hear the neighbors across the street screaming for me to stop. . . . See him lying there beneath the car, his little chest heaving as he tries to . . . I hear the sirens, the cops asking me if I'm 'the operator of the vehicle.'"

"You're having flashbacks then. Yes?"

I nod. I'm close to tears. "Yes."

"Are these flashbacks part of what's been triggering your panic episodes?"

"Yeah. . . . Yes."

"Well then, let's figure out how these might be short-circuited before they get to the point of debilitating you. Wouldn't it be lovely if you could exert some control over these traumatic memories and your fears about what's to come?"

I nod. When my tears start falling in earnest, she apologizes for having run out of tissues during her previous appointment. I tell her no problem and wipe away the wetness with my sleeve.

"Okay then. Medication is one way to quiet these demons." She scans her notes. "Now, you have had a problem with benzodiazepines, so we would want to steer clear of those. But there are SSRIs that I could ask one of the psychiatrists I consult with to prescribe for you. Maybe Paxil or Zoloft. They're antidepressants as opposed to the kind of antianxiety medication you ran afoul of."

I shake my head. Tell her I don't want to mess with drugs of any kind.

"Very well then. Good. There are deep breathing exercises you can do when you feel the onset of an attack. And grounding techniques. I have instructions for both if you'll give me a minute." She pulls a tattered, overstuffed manila folder from her desk drawer and riffles through it, loose pages spilling to the floor. "If I am reincarnated as another human in my next life, instead of a baboon or a garden slug, I should like to be an *organized* homo sapien, ha ha. Ah, here we go."

She hands me what she was looking for. I glance at the sheet about breathing exercises. Tell her we learned a version of these when we were taking Lamaze classes. And that they had helped Emily when she went into labor.

She nods. "As one concentrates on the air passing in and out of the body, you are simultaneously distracted from the pain and your body relaxes. And in your case, if you can put yourself into a state of relaxation, you may then be able to get to sleep.

"Now as for the other paper you have there—the one about grounding techniques—these will also refocus you away from the disorientation of a panic attack. Instead of flashing back to the tragedy or losing yourself in fears about the unknowable future, you bring yourself back to the here and now. For example, you might hold an object that's within your reach. Look at it, feel its texture, perhaps even touch your tongue to it and taste it." I shoot her a skeptical look. "As it says on the sheet, there's a formula you can follow."

"A formula?"

"Based on the five senses. You concentrate on five things you can see. A calendar, for example. A photograph. Then four things you can touch or feel: your shoe, a book, anything within reach. Then three things you hear, two things you can smell, and one thing you can taste. What you are doing is giving your mind something to do other than surrender to the terror."

I ask her whether I can keep the printouts. "Oh yes, they're yours," she says. Stoops to pick up the papers that have fallen to the floor. Smiles at one of them. "Aha, here's a lovely bit of synchronicity," she says. "Read this quote for me, please." She hands it to me—it's from some woman I've never heard of. I'm reading it silently when she says, "No, no. Aloud, please."

" 'Worrying is carrying tomorrow's load with today's strength—carrying two days at once. It is moving into tomorrow ahead of time. Worry does not empty tomorrow of its sorrow; it empties today of its strength.'—Corrie ten Boom."

"Well?"

"Well what?"

"Do you see the wisdom in what she is saying?"

"I guess. But . . ."

"Yes?"

"No disrespect, but I assume this is the 'wisdom' of someone who's never had to be facing the probability of being warehoused in prison, then coming out to find that he's lost—"

"Warehoused?" she says, frowning. "Corby, you are not an inanimate object. You're a living, evolving person, and if prison is to be in your future, one way to face it is to embrace the possibility that you can learn from the experience."

"Right. Okay. Good point." Better to agree with her than to argue against the educational value of life in the slammer. "I just wish we could go back to the way it used to be so that . . ."

"So that what?"

I shake my head and shrug. What's the point of even saying it?

She reaches across the table. Takes my hands in hers and gives them a gentle squeeze. "Well, nothing *can* go back to the way it once was, if by that you mean before the accident. The death of your son is a terrible reality that cannot be denied. But you can certainly have a life worth living, whether or not your marriage survives. For your daughter's sake as well as your own. Do you see Emily as a vindictive person?"

I shake my head. "She's kind, good-hearted. She's a wonderful teacher. A great mom, too, although she'd probably give me an argument about that. She always used to say that I was the better parent. But I dealt her such a terrible blow, you know? And it's changed her. Made her bitter, which I understand. But I still love her so much. Having her and Maisie back is all I want."

"Well, I have no crystal ball, so I cannot promise you your marriage will remain intact. And to be blunt, in situations like yours and Emily's, the odds may be against it. The death of a child often results in a couple divorcing, especially—"

"If one of them backed over him. Crushed the life out of him."

She shakes her head and smiles sadly. "I was going to say, especially since mourning a lost child is such a complicated and personal thing. As I've mentioned before, two parents will often grieve quite differently from one another and grow apart. But you just told me that Emily is not a vengeful person, which is good news, I think. I doubt she would want to mount some custody battle to deprive you of your daughter because it would also deprive your daughter of her father."

She glances at her watch. "I'm afraid it's time for us to end our session, Corby, but I hope we can speak again before your sentencing hearing. I used to be one of the psychologists in rotation at Yates. If you do have to go to prison, I know you'll be in good hands with Dr. Clegg or Dr. Kandrow. And whoever the new hire is, I'm sure that person will be able to help you, too. And in the meantime, I wish you the best of luck in ridding yourself of your panic episodes." She smiles and crosses her fingers.

I get up. Thank her and start to leave. Then I stop and turn back.

"You know the woman who wrote that quote you gave me?" I ask.

"Corrie ten Boom. Yes?"

"What kind of a name is that? Native American?"

She shakes her head. "She was from the Netherlands. She and her family were part of the Dutch resistance and hid many Jews from the Gestapo during Hitler's reign. When they were caught, she, her sister, and their father were arrested and sent to a concentration camp. Of the three, Corrie was the only one who survived. So you see, she did know a thing or two about life in captivity after all."

"No shit?" I say, forgetting my promise to myself not to swear in front of her.

"No shit," she says.

I wave the folded handouts at her and thank her again.

That same night, during another battle against sleeplessness, I feel an attack coming on. I do the breathing exercises. Grab the Big Book off my nightstand and do the five-senses thing. Then I turn on the light, grab that quote Dr. Patel gave me, and read it over and over like a mantra: "Worrying does not empty tomorrow of its sorrow; it empties today of its strength." After a while, I start to feel calmer. . . .

In the morning, I wake up to the sun winking through the slats of the venetian blinds and realize it worked. It fucking worked!

CHAPTER THIRTEEN

———

August 1, 2017

"All rise!" the bailiff commands. "This court is now in session, Judge Rose-marie Palazzolo presiding." She's tiny and very tan. Big black-rimmed glasses. She looks back at me and scowls.

Bettina Reitland goes first. "There's a name for it," she says. "Backover. It happens more than you'd think: on average, about fifty children a week, according to the statistics. Forty-eight of them survive; two don't. The age of the victim is most often between one year and two and the person most often responsible is the victim's mother or father. Usually, the grief that comes from losing a child, coupled with the horror of being the parent who caused the death, is punishment enough. The police will often conclude that it was accidental and decline to press charges."

Get ready, I tell myself. Here it comes.

"But in this case, that didn't happen. Why, Your Honor? Because Mr. Ledbetter, having consumed excesses of alcohol and an antianxiety medication *before nine o'clock in the morning*, got into his vehicle, started the engine, put the car in reverse, and backed over his twenty-six-month-old son, Niko, who was playing in the driveway. The defendant has stated that he misremembered having buckled both Niko and his twin sister in their car seats before operating his vehicle. 'Misremembered.' Well, that happens to all of us. But the guilty plea Mr. Ledbetter has entered is

tantamount to his admission that the tragedy was the result of his prior-
itizing his intoxication over the safety of his children."

This is all true, but it's too painful to hear, so I try as best I can to tune
her out. Say the serenity prayer. Look past Attorney Dixon, who's sitting
to my right, and scan the gallery for Emily. She's seated with her mother,
across the aisle and one row back. It breaks my heart to see how pale and
drawn she looks. During my last visit, when I'd asked her how much weight
she'd lost, she'd shrugged and said she had no appetite—that she mainly
just ate Kind bars and a few bites of whatever she'd fixed for Maisie. I keep
hoping she'll glance over at me, but she just keeps looking straight ahead.
Is she listening to Reitland's case against me? Letting her mind wander?
I can't tell. Betsy is looking over at me, though, as cold and stone-faced
as ever. It's even money on whether or not she hopes I go to prison, but I
doubt she'd shed many tears if that's the outcome today.

I look over my shoulder at the other side of the gallery and there's
Mom. And to my surprise, Dad is sitting next to her. I'm grateful to him
for having covered my lawyer's fees, but I expected nothing more than
checkbook support. His presence here must be costing him pain as well as
money. As a kid, I sometimes would fantasize that Dad came back home
to us and, in his absence, had turned nice. Now here he is, reunited with
Mom at last, because of their loser son's colossal failure.

I look around for Dr. Patel but don't see her. She told me she'd come
today if she could. But hey, she's a busy lady; I understand. Still, it would
have been a comfort to have her here. In our one-to-one sessions after
Emily bowed out of couples work, Dr. Patel helped me cope with the
difficult waiting time between the day I was arrested and today. And now
the wait is almost over. I'll probably know in under an hour whether or
not I'm going to prison.

My sponsor, Dale, has come as promised. He's sitting by himself in
the back row. In the weeks we've been working together on my sobriety,
I had one slip—took a few swigs from the pint bottle of bourbon one of
my coworkers at the Amazon warehouse held out to me on the sneak.

When I called Dale to confess, he said, "Progress not perfection, Corby, but you need to share this at the meeting tomorrow. Remember what the Big Book says about rigorous honesty." It was hard to do, but I did it and was moved by the number of people who surrounded me after the meeting was over to offer me encouragement and volunteer their own stories about going out and coming back. I'd been counting sober days and had gotten to thirty-seven when I slipped and demoted myself back to zero. There have been no slips since, thanks in large part to Dale's support, so sitting in the courtroom now, I'm at day number fifty-five.

Reluctantly, I tune back in to Reitland's reasons why I should be incarcerated.

"Within an hour of Sergeant Fazio's and Officer Longo's observations at the scene, Mr. Ledbetter's blood was drawn and later analyzed. The results show that he had operated his vehicle while under the influence of an excess of the benzodiazepine he had been prescribed and a blood-alcohol level of point-zero-nine."

Turning from the judge, Reitland takes a few steps toward Dixon and me. "I suspect Mr. Ledbetter's attorney will attempt to establish that her client was a good and loving father, and that may have been true until the day when, suddenly and irrevocably, *he was not.*"

It hits me that her phrasing is the same as Emily's that day in Dr. Patel's office. Is that a coincidence or has Reitland conferred with my wife? I've assumed that Emily doesn't want me to have to go to prison. Have I been wrong?

"Your Honor, a little boy with his whole life ahead of him would be alive today had his father not started his car that morning while his judgment was impaired by alcohol *and* an addictive prescription drug that, while not classified as a narcotic, may produce narcotic effects on the central nervous system. Corbin Ledbetter must be held accountable for that fatal decision. Keep in mind that this is his *second* DUI, so I think it's fair to assume his first had no preventive effect.

"Let's also keep in mind that the tragedy for which Mr. Ledbetter is responsible has created a ripple effect of profound grief not only for himself but also for his son's mother, the boy's grandparents, and the Ledbetters' extended family, their friends, and their neighbors. Two of those neighbors, Shawn and Linda McNally, who witnessed and tried to stop the tragedy from happening, have put their house on the market. I spoke recently with Mrs. McNally, who says their decision to move out of what had always been a peaceful and safe neighborhood has been motivated by the depression she has struggled with since she could not prevent little Niko's death in the seconds before his fatal injury. As I said, a ripple effect."

When Reitland says she wishes to read a letter from Niko's maternal grandmother, I see Emily turn toward her mother with wide-eyed surprise. It's obvious she didn't see this coming. Ignoring her daughter's reaction, Betsy looks straight ahead, a study in stern self-righteousness.

In her letter, Betsy asks the court to keep in mind the depth of her daughter's suffering and the physical and emotional toll Niko's death has taken, the result of the reckless and irresponsible choice I made on the morning in question—a choice that robbed her grandson of his life. Her letter ends with a question: If the law doesn't hold me accountable by sentencing me to prison, doesn't that then devalue the precious life I took?

Emily's audible sob draws my attention and everyone else's. Really, Betsy? She wasn't in enough pain already?

"And Niko's grandmother is right," Reitland says. "The average life expectancy of an American male in two thousand seventeen is seventy-eight-point-eighty-seven. Actuarially speaking, Mr. Ledbetter's action that morning deprived his son of seventy-six years and two months of his allotted life. And that's merely by today's life expectancy calculation. Who knows what future medical advances might have extended the victim's life well beyond seventy-eight years?"

When I look at my attorney, she rolls her eyes. "Bullshit," she whispers. "I'm not letting her get away with that."

"And let's not forget the individual who may end up paying the highest price of all as a result of Corbin Ledbetter's negligence: his two-year-old daughter, Niko's twin sister, Maisie."

Leave my daughter the fuck out of this!

Dixon must sense how much this has triggered me, because she reaches over and covers my fist with her hand. "Calm down," she whispers. "Leave it to me when it's my turn." So instead of shouting out in protest, I take a few deep breaths and focus instead on Dixon's pen, the veins in my hand, the wedding ring on my finger.

"Her twin brother's death has no doubt left little Maisie with a profound sense of loss that she can neither understand nor articulate. And what about her future when she can better understand who her father took away from her? Niko was her soulmate and companion from their time together in utero until April the twenty-seventh of this year when he abruptly went missing from her life."

Here, she pivots away from the judge and faces me. I look away from her. Shift in my seat. She takes several steps toward me until she's standing just a few feet away. My heart is thumping. I sense she's about to go in for the kill.

"At the defendant's arraignment several weeks ago, I admitted I have no expertise in child psychology. Since then, however, I have familiarized myself with several studies about how the death of a co-twin puts the surviving twin at greater risk for future psychiatric problems. The damage is particularly acute if the loss occurs during the child's preverbal stage. The trauma Maisie no doubt has been suffering since the abrupt disappearance of her soulmate is likely to have serious repercussions into her adolescence and adulthood. As one article stated, 'The mind will likely forget the traumatic event, but the body will remember.' The bottom line, Your Honor," she says, "is that we must not deny the defendant's victim, little Niko Ledbetter, or his sister, the justice they deserve."

Dixon stands and objects. "Your Honor, may I remind you that Attorney Reitland has no credentials as a child psychiatrist or a PhD in behavioral science. Nor has she solicited any such expert to affirm her suppositions. This is pure speculation, based on articles I suspect she's read in mainstream periodicals like *Psychology Today* or articles on the internet. And even if these were valid sources, which I suspect they're not, the points being made are not germane to the specifics of this case."

Judge Palazzolo sustains the objection.

I lose it then. Cover my face with my hands and sob. Because I've been scared about the impact of Niko's death on Maisie. I, too, have searched the internet and found some of the same studies she's talking about now. Other than confiding to Dr. Patel about my fears concerning Maisie's future, I've kept what I found to myself, so I'm unprepared when Reitland so publicly exposes those bleak findings about surviving twins. I keep struggling to compose myself, but the shame of having probably doomed *both* of my kids in different ways keeps me in its grip. I think I have a handle on it, then start up again. This lasts for a couple of minutes.

"Miss Dixon, does your client need a fifteen-minute recess?" the judge asks. Before Rachel can answer, I shake my head vehemently. Say I'm all right, that I want to keep going if I can just have another minute. One of the sheriffs places a box of tissues in front of me. I wipe my eyes, blow my nose, and get control of myself again.

"Ready to resume, Mr. Ledbetter?" the judge asks.

"Yes, Your Honor. Thank you. Sorry for the interruption."

"Not at all," she says. "Attorney Dixon?"

Rachel has washed the pink out of her hair and dressed professionally in a gray pantsuit. There's not a whole lot she can do for me, given my admission to Detective Sparks and my decision to plead guilty, forgoing the lie that could have rendered those tox-screen results inadmissible. Addressing the judge, she paints a sympathetic picture of the extenuating circumstances and mitigating factors that argue for leniency. She portrays me as a talented commercial artist who was an asset to the company that employed me, as was expressed in the letter of support from my former manager, Rhonda Tolliver. She also references letters of support from my supervisor at the warehouse where I've been working, my AA sponsor, Dale, and Dr. Patel.

"I trust you have read these letters, Your Honor, but if I may, I would like to read aloud a few lines from Dr. Patel's letter," Dixon says. Judge Palazzolo nods.

"Initially, the patient came to me with his spouse for bereavement counseling. Mrs. Ledbetter elected not to continue counseling, but Mr. Ledbetter has attended eight more sessions. In that time, I have found him to be remorseful about the cause of his son's death and serious about rehabilitating himself. In the time I have been treating him, Mr. Ledbetter has made very good progress. If he is sentenced to prison, I am concerned that his progress may be arrested or, worse, that he may regress."

Whatever the judge's reaction is, I see her grab a pen and make a note.

Dixon then emphasizes my virtues as a stay-at-home dad and the twins' primary caretaker: our visits to the park, story hour at the library, our participation in the YMCA's toddlers' swimming class, my disinclination to use the TV as a babysitter. She says my "brutal honesty" in having confessed to Detective Sparks about my impairment on the morning in question is evidence of my underlying good character and asks that the judge take this into consideration before she renders her decision. She also points out that, for the past twelve weeks, I have been attending AA and NA meetings faithfully, as indicated by the signatures of the various chairpersons of those meetings, and that I trained and have been working successfully as a "picker-packer" at the Amazon warehouse in Waterford for the past nine weeks. I have no doubt that Dixon is the crackerjack defense attorney her father described to my father, but she's pretty much been hamstrung by the confession of the guy she was hired to defend.

Attorney Dixon asks Judge Palazzolo to disregard Reitland's predictions about Niko's lifespan and Maisie's future emotional state, as these are purely speculative and should have no bearing on the judge's decision "unless Attorney Reitland has access to a crystal ball and can *know* the future rather than merely making predictions.

"Finally," Attorney Dixon says, "there can be no greater punishment for Corbin Ledbetter to endure than getting out of bed each and every day for the rest of his life having to face the fact that he is responsible for his son's death and the heartbreaking loss he has inflicted on his loved ones. I think it's impossible for us to imagine the degree of guilt, shame, and remorse that is, and will be, this man's daily burden. Your Honor, don't you think that's prison enough?"

Dixon instructed me to look at Judge Palazzolo when she said that and, if I had any tears left, to shed them then. Unable to do either, I bow my head and stare at the floor.

Reitland could have asked for the maximum of ten years in prison; instead, she has asked for six. Attorney Dixon has requested a suspension of my entire sentence, three years of probation, and community service. Judge Palazzolo says she needs a few minutes of silent deliberation before rendering her decision. "All rise!" the bailiff calls as she stands and heads, slump-shouldered, back to her chambers.

While we wait, Dixon speaks some hollow words of encouragement. I thank her, try to smile, and ask her what happened to her pink hair. "Gone with the wind," she says. "My wife hated it." After that, we two wait in silence.

"All rise!"

Judge Palazzolo speaks more to the gallery than to me. "In some cases, sentencing someone for a crime that's been committed is not a difficult decision to make. Cut-and-dried, you might say; just follow the guide-lines. But cases like this one are more complex, more difficult. They're the ones that can keep you up at night, before and after you've rendered your decision."

She turns then to me. "Mr. Ledbetter, I sympathize with you and your family; you have all had to endure an unfathomable loss. Nevertheless, I cannot unhear Attorney Reitland's argument that, in order for your little boy to have the justice to which he is entitled, the state must hold you accountable for the tragedy that resulted from your having broken the law. That said, I am *not* granting the prosecutor her request that you serve six years in prison. My decision is that you are to be incarcerated for a period of five years, suspended after three, and another three years. I will not mandate your attendance at twelve-step meetings during your incarceration because I believe recovery from addiction must be self-motivated, not ordered by the state. That said, I sincerely hope that this is something you will want to continue to work on for yourself and your family. Good luck, Mr. Ledbetter. I wish you well."

And with that, she gavels my case to a close and exits the courtroom.

Two court sheriffs approach with cuffs and shackles. I look over my shoulder at Emily, hoping to make eye contact, but she is already heading for the exit with her mother. From there I look over at my parents, still seated. Mom is glum but stoic. Dad's in tears. Who would have thought?

And there behind them is Dr. Patel, who has come after all. Her hands are clasped in front of her, and when she sees that I've spotted her, she offers me the gift of a compassionate smile.

Outside, I squint in the bright summer sunshine. I'm boosted up and into the back of a transport van. A few minutes later, I'm on my way to Yates Correctional Institution, where I will spend the next thirty-six months of my life.

PART TWO:

Day by Day by Day by Day by Day

CHAPTER FOURTEEN

August 1, 2017
Day 1 of 1,095

Inside the transport van, I'm chained to two other prisoners. The guy next to me is snoring and the guy next to him has puke all over his shirtfront. It's sweltering in here and the stench is so bad, I hope I don't start vomiting, too. "Good to go," someone calls. Car doors slam, the engine starts, and the van lurches forward, rolling out of the courthouse parking lot and onto a downtown street. From behind a caged window, I watch a blur of trees and cars, storefronts and pedestrians—glimpses of the freedom I've just lost.

Two or three miles into the trip, the snoring guy startles himself awake, yanking the chain and me with it. Turning to his left, he gives me a bleary-eyed once-over. "Where'd you come from?" he wants to know. When I tell him, he says he got picked up in Bridgeport and the guy to his right was in Hartford lockup. "Can you believe my shit luck?" he says. "This is my second bid and both times I get stuck next to some dope-sick junkie. At least this one didn't get any on me." The other guy groans. "Not yet anyway. This your first joyride in the ice cream truck?"

"What?"

"Never mind. You just answered me."

The "joyride" lasts somewhere between thirty and forty minutes and I'm nauseous for most of them. The van slows, takes a left, and enters the compound. When it stops at Admittance and Discharge, I'm unchained from the other two, helped down from the back door, and unshackled by a new guard. First stop: getting fingerprinted and having my ID picture taken. After that, there's the humiliation of a strip search and a supervised shower. The guard who's watching me tells me to hold out my hand. When I do, he squirts delousing shampoo into it and tells me to wash my hair, pits, and pubes thoroughly; the assumption, I guess, is that if you're a prisoner, you probably have lice. I scrub myself and rinse, but the chemical stink of that shampoo stays with me. Watching the CO bag up the clothes and shoes I wore to court and being handed recycled prison underwear, tan hospital scrubs, and used, laceless sneakers is a painful reality check about my new existence.

Next, I'm led to a small room where two other admits are seated before a TV. One of them is the guy I'd been chained to on the trip from the courthouse, the other looks like he should be in high school. One of the two COs guarding us, the white one, shoves a cassette into the VCR below it and a Connecticut Department of Correction orientation video begins. It covers DOC's rules and regulations, how the commissary system works, how to make collect calls and arrange for visitors, what happens when you get a disciplinary ticket. Cell phones are strictly forbidden and there is no access to the internet. I miss a lot of information because the audio has a low buzz and the officers keep chatting with each other without bothering to lower their voices. Staticky lines keep running through the picture. When the video is over, the Black officer asks us whether there are any questions, but neither he nor his buddy bother to look up to see that I've raised my hand. Although I'm still pretty much in the dark regarding prison policies, I've already learned two things: officers are indifferent to the questions of the guys in their custody and, technologically speaking, DOC is still in the Dark Ages.

The guards who ran the video hand us off to three other COs. One gives each of us a "survival kit"—a brown paper bag holding bedding and hygiene stuff that's supposed to hold us over until someone on the outside funds our commissary account. Another distributes our newly laminated

IDs and tells us to clip them to our shirts and make sure we're wearing them whenever we leave our cells. "Ledbetter?" the third guard, an older guy, says as he approaches me. "They got you in B Block. I'm Lieutenant Cavagnero." When I hold out my hand, he shakes his head. "No physical contact between offenders and staff unless it's a restraint situation," he says. "Come on. Follow me."

As we cross the yard, I notice that most of the inmates along the walkway are Black or Brown. Cavagnero asks me how much time they've given me. When I tell him, I brace for the question I assume is coming next: What was I convicted of? Instead, he gives me some practical advice. "You'll do okay as long as you cooperate with staff and keep a low profile. Nobody likes a showboat. And be careful who you trust. Not too many choirboys doing time at this place." He says I'm lucky they've assigned me to B Block. "It's one of the older buildings, so the roof is slate, sturdier than shingles, and the plumbing's got copper pipe rather than PVC. With plastic, the cement that bonds the joints together breaks down so you get leaks. Lots of headaches in the newer blocks because they were built on the cheap." Jesus, I'm just trying to hold it together and he's giving me a plumbing lesson.

"Oh, and as far as the racial stuff that goes on in your block, my advice is to stay out of it," he says. "Some of the white guys will probably try and recruit you because in B, they're a minority. But don't pick a side. Stay neutral." Which is exactly what I plan to do.

"Any questions?" he asks me.

"Yeah, I was wondering. Do they have AA meetings here?"

He nods but says he doesn't know where or when they meet. I should check with my counselor.

Inside the building, Cavagnero points out the first-floor facilities as we pass by them: a GED classroom, a rec room with TV and foosball, a fitness room with a stationary bike and weights. When I glance in at the brawny white guys lifting and spotting each other, I get the side-eye from a couple of them. After we've moved past, I hear one of them out me as the guy who killed his kid. "Flat as a pancake," someone else says. "Whoops. Sorry, Junior."

Lieutenant Cavagnero looks over and sees me swiping at the tears in my eyes. "I been working this job for seventeen years, so nothing much fazes me by now," he says. "But I can still get surprised by how mean some of these guys can get after they've been in here awhile, especially where kids are involved. See, most of them have kids themselves, so they tend to target someone who they think has harmed a kid. Makes them feel superior. I know what you're here for, so you're probably going to get a lot of that kind of hazing at first, but don't let them see that they can get to you. Just try and shake it off."

Shake it off that they're joking about my little boy's death? How do I do that?

We climb the stairs to the third tier. Cavagnero calls to the CO behind the control desk to open 3-E. I hear an electric pop and follow Lieutenant Cavagnero into the living space I'll be sharing with the burly, grandfatherly looking guy who's seated on the toilet. Turning to me, he says, "You're the baby killer, right?"

I take a breath.

"Be nice, Pug," Cavagnero says. "See you guys tomorrow." The cell door bangs shut.

"Here's how it's gonna go," Pug says. "Bottom bunk is mine. Don't let me catch you sitting on it. Don't speak to me in the morning before chow time. Don't ask to borrow any of my shit and don't play my radio or my TV when I'm at work. And when I'm watching TV, keep your mouth shut. My last cellie didn't think I meant it until I got sick of his yapping and dislocated his fucking shoulder. You got all that?"

"Yeah," I say. "No problem."

I glance over at what he's stuck to the cinder-block wall: an American flag poster with Trump's face in the middle of it, a centerfold picture of two tattooed, nearly naked biker chicks kissing each other, some family photos of what I guess are his wife and kids. Beneath this display is a TV hookup:

a coaxial cable poking out of the cinder-block wall connected to a set that's got a small screen and a clear plastic outer shell that exposes the insides.

"On the chow, ladies!" someone outside the cell bellows.

Pug walks over to the door and stands. "Supper's four o'clock here. You gonna eat?" I go over and stand behind him, waiting, too. "Don't do that," he says.

Have I just broken one of his rules? "Don't do what?"

"Get behind me where I can't see you. Someone's standing close to me, I need to see them. I don't know you from Adam."

I nod in agreement, wondering whether paranoia comes with the territory around here. To change the subject, I ask him whether the dining hall is in this building or somewhere else.

He laughs at the question. "The dining hall? You expecting silverware and fancy dishes? Someone asking you what kind of cocktail you want?"

"No, I just—"

"In here, it's usually two slices of white bread and some kind of slop ladled onto a Styrofoam tray. You shovel it in with a plastic spork. And you better eat fast. They're supposed to give us twenty minutes, but we're lucky if it's twelve or thirteen. They like to rush us out of there and get us locked back in our cells so they can sit around on their asses until their shift's over. Play Candy Crush or watch porn on the phones they're not supposed to bring in here. And don't let them catch you trying to walk out of the chow hall with food you didn't finish. They'll give you a ticket if they catch you with 'takeout.' Doesn't mean you can't do it. Just don't get caught."

I hear that electronic pop again. Pug pushes the door open and holds it for me. "You know what?" I say. "On second thought, I'm not that hungry."

"Whatever," he says, and joins the others tramping through the corridor.

While he's gone, I try to settle in a little. My craving for a chemical escape hatch had been subsiding since I got clean and sober, but being in prison for a couple of hours has made my urges come roaring back. I begin to shake from needing a stiff drink or a couple of Ativan right about now. Start wondering whether there's a black market here so that I might be able to score some benzos. If I could get ahold of something, I'd take it no matter what I promised Emily. No matter what Dale advised me to do to quiet the urge.

I dump the stuff from my survival kit onto my mattress: a worn pair of shower flip-flops, a rolled-up set of paper-thin sheets, a shabby-looking towel. There's some travel-sized hygiene stuff—soap, shampoo, toothpaste and a two-inch toothbrush, plus three commissary-order sheets and one of those little pencils like they give out at minigolf. I scoop up that stuff and drop it into the empty storage box that must be mine. Make up my bed. Check out the view of the outside from the skinny slit of a back window: a parking lot, a dying spruce tree, a couple of dumpsters, a scurrying rat. When I turn around again, I take in the size of the cell; it's about the same dimensions as our bathroom on Butternut Avenue. *Her* bathroom for the next three years. Is Maisie okay? Poor kid. She must really miss her brother. Does she miss me?

By the time Pug gets back, I'm curled up on my upper bunk, facing the wall so he won't see that I've been crying. "Here," he says. Whatever he's just thrown at me hits me on the hip. I reach back and grab it—a granola bar. I tell him thanks. Peel off the wrapper and stuff half of it in my mouth. Have I eaten anything since before Mom and I left for the courthouse this morning? I can't remember. God, it's still the same day? Hard to believe.

I hear the TV go on—the nightly news: Trump's bromance with Kim Jong Un, how "zero tolerance" is separating kids and their parents at the border. After the commercials, there's a story about a white guy who's gunned down Black seniors at a supermarket in Kentucky. Pug starts singing that old Queen song, "*And another one's gone, and another one's gone. Another one bites the dust.*"

"Jesus Christ," I mutter under my breath—or thought I did until I realize that Pug is standing next to my bed.

"Something the matter?" he asks.

I don't answer him at first, but when I can sense that he's still standing there waiting, I raise my head, turn around, and face him. Tell him I don't think people getting shot and killed is something to sing about.

"No?" he says. "That's interesting coming from a guy who killed his own kid."

My instinct is to jump off the bunk and get into it with this scumbag. But I hear Lieutenant Cavagnero's advice to shake it off. Don't give them the satisfaction of seeing that they're getting to you. I turn my back to him and mumble, "Yeah, okay, Pug. Whatever."

But he's not letting it go. "Let me explain something to you, buddy boy," he says. "Educate you a little. The spooks and their amigos sneaking in here from Mexico both breed like flies. They think that as soon as they outnumber us, they'll be in charge. Except they're sadly mistaken. This is our country, not theirs. We're the ones who made America what it is, and if we have to get into a race war against them and their pansy-ass sympathizers to remind them of that reality, then that's what we're gonna do. And if you know what's good for you, you better fucking decide which side you're on because race traitors get dealt with in here and it ain't pretty."

I deserve to be punished for the death of my son; I know that. I just don't know how I'm going to survive in this place for the next three years.

CHAPTER FIFTEEN

—

August 2017
Days 2–22 of 1,095

It doesn't take me long to observe that Yates prison assigns white guys to cells with other white guys, that Blacks are paired with Blacks, and that Latinos become the bunkies of other Latinos—doesn't matter whether one is a Spanish-speaking Mexican, the other a Brazilian whose language is Portuguese, or a Haitian who speaks French. Here at Yates, cell assignments are all about the melanin.

It doesn't matter to me what race my fellow inmates are or where they came from; I'm intimidated by almost everyone walking the grounds here. Most of them scowl as they walk past me and half of them don't so much walk as strut, their bodies chiseled and bulging with muscles. I'm no featherweight, but I could get squashed like a bug in here.

Pug does his best to fuel my fear. He tells me about how one white inmate's face was bludgeoned beyond recognition by a Black guy who got slashed in return. "And some guys with a score to settle? They'll whittle a toothbrush into a shiv and somebody ends up getting stabbed in the eye or the neck. One guy over in D Block got stuck in the heart by one of the spooks on his tier and he bled out on the spot. And when it gets around here what you're in here for, you better hope no one hears 'dead kid' and mistakes you for an Uncle Chester."

"What's that?" I ask.

"Someone who gets his rocks off by diddling little kids. They get the worst of it. A lot of the guys here were the victims of those pervs when they were kids. The COs hate 'em, too, so they look the other way when something's going down out in the yard or someplace where there's no cameras. I'm not saying someone's *gonna* mistake you for a Chester the Molester. I'm just saying you better watch your back. They hear you killed a kid, they might jump to conclusions, you know? And watch out for the spooks. Where they come from, everyone's shootin' and killin' each other, OD'ing on smack and dying, so they don't value life like we do. It's the law of the jungle with the jungle bunnies."

I coexist uneasily and warily with my fellow Caucasian bunkie by saying very little, obeying his rules, and acknowledging that he is the alpha dog of Cell 3-E. The one time I accidentally break one of Pug's edicts, we're headed for the shower room. It slips my mind that I'm not supposed to walk behind him where he can't see me. Reeling around, he shoves me against the wall, his fist cocked until he pulls his punch at the last second, possibly sparing me a broken jaw.

There's no such thing as relaxing in Pug's presence, so the only relief I get is when he goes off the compound for his job. He's part of a work crew that picks up litter on the sides of the highway. This keeps him out of our cell for six or seven hours at a time most weekdays. Rainy days and weekends are a different story; he watches TV, naps, plays solitaire, and masturbates to the skin magazines he keeps hidden in his lockbox. Privacy isn't one of his priorities when he's having sex with himself. I guess it would be futile anyway, given the dimensions of our cell and the fact that he talks dirty to get himself there and shouts when he arrives.

Another of Pug's weekend activities is rolling makeshift cigarettes. On his trash-collecting detail during the week, he pockets the discarded butts he finds. Then on Saturday, he removes whatever unburned tobacco is still in them, separates the pile into smaller piles, and rolls each of them in two layers of toilet paper. After that, he'll light up on the sneak whenever an opportunity presents itself.

I learn from the tier's gossip, Manny something, that Pug's real name is Albert Liggett. A mechanic on the outside, he caught six years in here for operating a "chop shop" for car thieves out of New York City. I begin to notice that Pug lets his racist comments rip when it's just the two of us, but he watches his mouth outside our cell. He's particularly cautious around Black inmates, and one morning, when I'm sitting across from Manny at morning chow, I find out why. During Pug's first year here, he was out in the yard talking with one of his cronies when he referred to Blacks on welfare as "lazy porch monkeys." The next day, he was on the walkway when someone jumped him from behind, choked him until he passed out, and left him in a heap. According to Manny, Pug spent some time in the medical unit because of a cartilage fracture in his larynx. His paranoia about someone creeping up behind him is no doubt triggered by the fact that his assailant was never identified. "How do you know all this stuff?" I'd asked Manny. He said he's naturally curious and his radar is always up.

Almost two weeks in, I'm just barely holding on in here. Stifled crying jags, insomnia. Except for chow time, I stay in our cell and pretty much detach from the day-to-day. I make a visitors' list like they told me to do—put down Emily's and Maisie's names, plus my mom, and my AA sponsor, Dale. I hesitate before adding my father to the list, but at the last minute, I write down his name, too. When I give the list to one of the counselors, she says it will take about four or five weeks before I can expect visitors.

"Why so long?" I ask.

That makes her smile. "Because everyone whose name's on here has to be checked out and approved. Or denied if there's a felony conviction on their record. Nothing in here moves fast. It helps if you realize that and develop some patience."

"Hey, I was told to ask you about AA and NA meetings in here. Is there a list?"

"Good question," she says. "I'll have to get back to you."

Walking out of her office, I remember that Dale did prison time for the drunk driving that led to his niece's injuries and her eventual death. I figure I won't be seeing my sponsor for another three years or talking to him either. I forgot to write down his number and I don't have an address where I can write to him.

No visitors for five more weeks and no phone calls either until someone sets up and funds an account with that rip-off prison telephone service company out of Texas that everyone gripes about. Once that's done, I can make collect calls, but until then it's snail mail. I bum paper, envelopes, and a couple of stamps from Manny and write to my mom, asking her to fund my account so I can talk with her and Emily and Maisie—at least let my daughter hear my voice. I worry that Emily might not even take my call.

I write to my father, too—reluctantly.

Dear Dad,

I hope you're doing well, getting out to the golf course and the hiking trails during this nice weather. Prison takes some getting used to, but I'm okay—settling in here, more or less.

I'm writing to thank you for a couple of things. First, I appreciate that you and Natalie arranged for Attorney Dixon to represent me. And thank you for paying for her services. I'm grateful to you for taking care of that. I also appreciate that you came to court to support me the day they sentenced me. I'm sorry you had to see me getting carted off in chains. No father should have to witness that, but I appreciate that you were there.

If you want to write to me while I'm here, the return address and my prison # are on the envelope. I also put you on my visitors' list. It will take about a month to get you approved to come here, but no sweat if you'd rather not. I'll understand.

Yours truly,
Corby

My loneliness and my fear of the system and the people in it are making me crazy. I spend the long daytime hours pacing the confines of our cell or tucked in on myself on the top bunk. I've become hypersensitive to noise, so I skip a lot of meals to avoid the din in the chow hall. When hunger forces me to go, I usually end up sitting with Manny, whose cell is three down from Pug's and mine.

Manny seems decent enough, harmless, but he never shuts up. I sit there, shoveling in whatever looks edible and not saying anything to anyone. Meanwhile, Manny spends most of his eating time yapping away, so that when the guards shout for us to clear out, he watches where they're looking as he hides bread or cake up his sweatshirt sleeve, drops a chicken leg or half of a meat pie down his pants.

Throughout the day, after every meal and until lights-out at night, the guards count us to make sure no one has gone missing. *Mis*count us half the time, and when the numbers don't come out right, everything stops until they do. Once the count clears, we get on-the-hour "common time." The CO at the control desk pops all the cell doors simultaneously, allowing us five minutes out in the corridor—just enough time to make a quick collect call on the phone, or fill a Styrofoam cup with lukewarm water from the communal hot pot so you can make tea, instant coffee, or ramen, or just shoot the shit with someone other than your bunkie. None of this applies to me. My phone account hasn't been funded yet, I have no packets of instant coffee or noodles, and I don't want to talk to any of these guys anyway. I stay in my cell.

On odd-numbered days, our tier gets thirty minutes out in the yard for fresh air, exercise, and sunshine. I try it once, but I basically just stand there by myself, watching some Black guys playing a roughneck game of basketball with a netless hoop. A couple of the older inmates are playing checkers, and a bunch of the weight room bros are gathered around a picnic table, cheering on an arm-wrestling match between two of their own. It feels like I'm back in middle school, watching all the cliques I don't belong to. Three poker-faced COs—one Black, two white—oversee us all like playground supervisors.

Having become more aware of the racial divide at this place, I notice that Manny is hanging with six or seven guys who are Black, white, and Brown—the queer clique from the looks of it. For once, he isn't monopolizing the conversation. The person holding court is a tall, skinny, light-skinned Black dude with loud, affected speech and what sounds like a Jamaican accent. He's wearing red lipstick, blue eye makeup, uniform pants rolled up to midcalf. There's a purple feather boa around his neck that, apparently, the COs aren't interested in confiscating. "So I said gurl, if I went down on that monster, I'd get lockjaw!" Having seen the attitude toward gays around here, I kind of admire his "fuck you" declaration of queerness in the midst of all this prison yard machismo.

I look away when he catches me staring at him. Too late. "Hey there, handsome! I'm Jheri Curl. Like what you see?" I try for an expression of bored indifference but can feel myself blushing. "I got some junk in the trunk for you, baby. Can you go deep the way I like it? Never can tell what you white boys got until showtime." Hoots and laughter from the others except for Manny. He says something I can't hear. Whatever it is, the drag queen says, "I was just jokin' with Uptight Whitey was all. Can't a gurl have a little fun out here?"

I look over at the COs to see whether they've picked up on any of this, but they're occupied with their own conversation. When the hell are they going to let us go back to our cells? Thirty minutes? It feels like we've been out here for an hour.

Halfway across the yard, a skirmish breaks out and I follow some of the others who are gearing up to watch the show. Two guys are yelling at each other in Spanish. When it escalates into a shoving match, the three guards move in, separating them and threatening each with pepper spray if they don't knock it off. One guy is compliant. The other one launches a hawker that lands on the shoe of his opponent. The CO who cuffs him escorts him out of the yard.

"Hey, Ledbetter!" someone calls. Who knows my name?

"Yeah?"

My eyes find two white guys walking toward me. The older one has a shaved head and a bushy salt-and-pepper beard. I've seen the younger one talking with Pug in the shower room a couple of times. Naked, this guy is covered front and back with tattoos: the Confederate flag on his left pec, on his right one a circle and cross. An angry-looking American eagle takes flight on the entirety of his broad back, along with the words "White Pride Worldwide."

The older guy does the talking. "I'm Wes and this is Gunnar. We want to discuss something with you. Let's get out of earshot."

"Nah. I'm good," I say. "How do you know my name?"

"Made it our business to find out," he says. He lowers his voice. "Look, you're new here, but you must have figured out by now that the spics, the spades, and the half-breeds outnumber us. Now that presents a clear and present danger to us three and every other white guy doing time here. Know what I'm saying?"

Play dumb, I tell myself. Shake my head.

"Then let me spell it out for you. You can already hear the beat of the jungle drum at this place and we've got reliable intel that the 'libtard' governor of this fucking state is pushing the commissioner to appoint a nigger as the next warden here. The nigs are already coddled at this institution and it'll get a whole lot worse if *that* happens. Sooner or later there's gonna be a war breaking out at a lot of prisons around the country, including this one."

I look over and see the Black CO, McGreavy, eagle-eyeing us. I've got to walk away from these crackpots or I'll be lumped with them.

"You better decide where your loyalty's at," the tattooed one says. "Wes and me just want to advise you not to betray your race."

Is this a threat or a recruitment spiel? Whatever it is, before I can respond, I'm saved by McGreavy's whistle. "Rec time's over!" he shouts. His wingman—I think his name is Yarnall—claps his hands and shouts, "Let's go! Back inside!" I'm relieved that "outdoor recess" is finally over. This is what I get for venturing outside my cell, but I don't plan on making *that* mistake again.

Manny comes up from behind me as I enter the building. "Don't let Jheri get to you," he says. "She's got a big mouth, but she's harmless."

I shrug. "Where did 'she' get that drag queen makeup from? Is that stuff listed on the commissary order sheet?"

Manny shakes his head and laughs. "After you've been here awhile, you get pretty good at improvising. You'd be surprised how much dye you can suck out of Starburst gummies, Jolly Ranchers, and strawberry Twizzlers. By the way, I don't know if you noticed, but I was the one who got Jheri to stop teasing you."

"Yeah, thanks," I say. But if Manny thinks this is going to make us buddies, he's mistaken. By now I've seen some of the shitty treatment gay guys get at this place, from COs as well as other inmates. I don't want to be associated with them any more than I want to hang out with the racist frat boys I just met. I haven't met anyone at Yates who *isn't* a liability. I have nothing in common with any of these guys, and yet I'm one of them. I have to admit that I sometimes catch myself thinking I'm better than them—that *they* deserve to be here but I don't. But who am I kidding? The opposite is true. How many of them caused the death of their own child?

When I get back to our cell, Pug's there. Back early from work, he's using a magazine to fan away the smoke from his roadkill cigarette. "What are you going to do if someday a CO walks in here and sees this haze? Smells it?" It's the first time I've challenged him.

"I'll probably throw *you* under the bus," he says. "Claim that you were the one who was lighting up." He says it like it's a joke, but I know he'd do just that.

That night, when I climb up to my bunk, I smell something. Shit. My sheet is smeared with feces and there's a turd sitting on my pillow.

———

By my third week, I've picked up on some of the slang you hear at this place. A private note wrapped up tight and thrown from one prisoner to another is a "kite" that arrives "airmail." If you die in prison before your sentence is up, you've gotten a "back-door parole." You'll catch "dinner and a show" when a fight breaks out in the chow hall and you watch the guards pepper-spray the brawlers. Crapping into your cell's toilet is "feeding the warden." It's part gallows humor and part survival mechanism. It also serves as a kind of antidote to the bullshit euphemisms the institution loves to hide behind. Take the name of this place for instance: the Yates Correctional Institution. The only thing most of the staff is interested in "correcting" is a new inmate's assumption that he might be something more than a worthless piece of shit with a felony conviction and an inmate number. I know I deserve to be here. But if you want to fix yourself while you're doing time at Yates, I think you're pretty much on your own.

The days here are bad enough, but the nights are worse. Pug snores and sometimes shouts out in his sleep and his restlessness shakes my bunk as well as his. Some nights I can't get to sleep and other nights I can't stay asleep because of it. Either way, I'm awake for hours, silently asking my baby boy and baby girl for forgiveness or pleading with Emily not to give up on me. As the hours crawl by, my desperation reawakens my craving for the benzos and booze that used to allow me to drift into merciful unconsciousness. Now, instead of sleep, I experience night sweats, tightness in my chest, palpitations, shallow breathing.

When I finally doze off for an hour or two, I sometimes wake up startled by disturbing dreams: my father screaming at my mother and me as we cower together on the kitchen floor; Michael Jackson laughing as I beg him to stop dangling Niko upside down over a balcony railing. One night I'm awakened by the smell of burnt toast that isn't really there. Next thing I know, I'm lying there reliving in painful detail what happened that morning: the smoke alarm, Niko's fascination with the ants in the driveway, Linda McNally waving her McDonald's bag from across the street, me putting the CRV in reverse without checking the back seat. I begin to dread the sun going down. Nighttime is when the fire burns most fiercely inside my head and I'm at a loss to know how to put it out.

Toward the end of my third week here, I hear a commotion downstairs on tier two—shouting and yelling, some guard on the intercom squawking, "Code Purple! Building B, first floor! Code Purple!" The emergency turns out to be an inmate's suicide. He's torn his sheets into strips and braided them into a makeshift rope. Then, during one of the breaks outside his cell, he tied one end of his rope to a stair railing and, at the other end, slipped the noose he'd fashioned over his head, tightened it, and jumped into the stairwell.

Returning from a commissary pickup, Manny witnesses the jump and the guy's dying struggle. At chow that night he's bug-eyed as he provides all the gruesome details. "This wasn't any half-assed cry for help. He wanted out of here. He was swinging back and forth between the first and second tier, his body twitching and jerking all over the place. They called maintenance to get a ladder over here, but by the time it arrived, he'd stopped moving. I tell you, I seen a lot of dead people at wakes and shit, but not anyone *dying* in front of me. By the time they cut him down, his whole head was purple like an eggplant."

Someone at the table says the guy's last name was Hogan and that he was doing time here for Assault One. "Found out his half brother was boning his wife and went after the mofo with a pipe wrench."

Another guy says he can't picture Hogan.

"Skinny white dude, thirties, horn-rimmed glasses."

"Oh, him? He didn't seem like the type."

"There's a type? Don't think so, bro. I heard he just found out the wifey was divorcing him and suing for sole custody of their kids."

"That's cold, man. She must feel like shit now."

"Probably why he did it. Give her a big fuck-you on his way out."

Nods all around. I look down at my half-eaten meal and say nothing.

That night I wrestle again with insomnia. Emily might divorce me, and if that happens, I'll just have to accept it. But she'd never withhold Maisie from me. That wouldn't happen. Would it?

At chow the next night, the conversation's about Hogan again—specifically, the removal of his corpse. Pug says, "You ever notice how they always do the 'back-door paroles' during third shift? Probably because in the daytime some reporter or politician might see another one going out in a body bag. Next thing you know, there'd be a front-page story about why these hang-ups keep happening. Nothing DOC hates more than bad publicity. Somebody ought to write a book about all the shit that goes on around here that nobody knows about."

After that, the conversation shifts to other matters: Yankees versus Red Sox, predictions about when the next lockdown is going to be, whether or not some female CO has gotten breast implants. My mind is still on Hogan.

Maybe he was smarter than the rest of us, I think. At least he found a way out of this hellhole. The table goes silent and everyone's looking at me, some of them with sporkfuls of food on the way to their mouths. That's when I realize I didn't just think it. I said it out loud.

A guy at the other end asks Manny what my name is. When he tells him, the guy says, "Well, son of a bitch, Ledbetter. I guess you ain't a deaf-mute after all." They all snicker and go back to eating. Everyone, that is, except Manny. He isn't shoveling in the slop on his tray or running his mouth for once. He's just staring at me.

A couple of minutes later, one of the guards shouts, "That's it, gentlemen! Head 'em up and move 'em out!" And like a herd of obedient cattle, we all stand and walk our trays over to the garbage cans.

Manny catches up to me on the walkway heading back to B Block. I've been doing the math in my head: a three-year sentence minus the three weeks I've done leaves a hundred and fifty-three more weeks. I can't do it. "You all right, Corby?" Manny asks. It's the first time since I got here that someone's called me by my first name. Without looking at him, I tell him I'm fine.

Dying would free me from my unbearable guilt. And sometimes I indulge myself by imagining that Niko is alive again in some other place unknowable to the still-living. Reunited by death, he and I will laugh and play together, run after each other. But allowing myself this fantasy is inevitably followed by intense feelings of heartache and loss. . . .

How will Emily react to my death? She'll grieve, sure, but will she also feel relieved to be done with me? Free to move on? And what about Maisie? Emily's promised that my daughter and I will stay connected through photos and drawings, but she's said she will *not* bring her here for in-person visits. If I last three years at this place, by the time I get out, she'll be five and I'll be a stranger. I might as well admit it: they'll both be better off without me complicating their lives. . . .

Mom will take it hard, but she's strong and has a lot of friends who'll support her. And if my father feels any regrets, well, that will be on him to deal with. Or not. Dad's pretty good about intellectualizing his way around difficult truths.

Over the next couple of days and nights, my flirtation with suicide becomes an obsession. Thinking about it energizes me, but then the adrenaline subsides and I crash, the prospect of my death triggering sobs I have to stifle with my pillow pressed against my face.

How should I do it? *Purple like an eggplant.* Not by hanging myself in the stairwell, I know that. There's no way I'd make it a public spectacle. Sleeping pills would be an easy way out, but how would I get ahold of enough? . . . Maybe I can find something in our cell that has a sharp edge, hack away at a vein, and bleed out during the hours when Pug is at work. But no. Some CO might see the blood during count and intervene. He'd be a hero and I'd be a failure at one more thing. . . .

What about death by suffocation? Plastic trash bags used for something other than trash are contraband, which makes them a hot commodity here at Yates. The workout guys fill them with water and lift them during lockdowns when the weight room's off-limits; the alkies use them as toilet tank liners for the jailhouse hooch they ferment from a mixture of bread, sugar, water, and fruit rinds. "Tastes like shit," Pug has said. "But if someone's desperate to get cocked, 'pruno' will do the trick." I'm repulsed by the thought of drinking homemade booze distilled in a toilet tank but wonder whether I'd be able to resist it if it was put in front of me. Pathetic but probably not. Before I got here, I read the Big Book promise that the obsession to drink gets lifted for those who follow the program, but I haven't been to a meeting since my sentencing. Lieutenant Cavagnero said they have AA here, but that counselor never got back to me before she transferred out of here and I haven't followed through with anyone else. It won't really matter, I figure, if I kill myself. My addictions will die along with me.

I know Pug has access to those clear plastic bags at work because I've watched him bring a couple back to our cell, fold them, and stash them in his lockbox. The problem is, he never forgets to lock the fucking thing. But DeShaun, an inmate who works janitorial on our tier, has a small side business going, swapping trash bags for commissary: candy bars, soup packets, styling gel. I won't have anything to barter with until my commissary account gets set up, but maybe then I can make a trade. If I do, then work up enough courage, I can pull it tight around my head and suffocate myself in minutes. I've heard both arguments about suicide: that it's the coward's way out and that it takes amazing courage. I go with the second theory, but once I commit to it, I better have the balls to follow through.

My crying jags continue on and off that night and into the next day, but I'm dry-eyed and quiet, lying face-down on my top bunk, when the door pops and Lieutenant Cavagnero enters the cell. I sit up, swing my legs over the side, and watch him walk to the window, his back to me.

In my limited interactions with the guards at Yates, there seem to be two types. The gung-ho cowboys just arrived from their academy training are eager to demonstrate what hard-asses they can be if their authority gets challenged. The older guards are easier to deal with because they have nothing to prove; they're just focused on getting through their shift without any hassles or complications. Cavagnero is one of the second type, but why is he here? I don't think officers make house calls.

When he turns and faces me, he says, "So how's it going, Ledbetter?"

I shrug. Say, "It's going." Pug has advised me that the less said to the guards, the better—that none of them can be trusted, especially the friendly ones.

"You been here, what? A couple of weeks now?"

"Three and change," I say.

He sits down on my lockbox like a chummy uncle or something. "Big adjustment for you, I bet. How are you and Liggett getting along?"

"All right, I guess." After all the kowtowing I've done, has Pug complained about me anyway? Is that what this is about?

Cavagnero nods. "That's good. He can get a little prickly sometimes. He and his last roommate had some dust-ups, one of them a humdinger. They both went to seg for that one and when they got out, we moved Cappy to D Block."

"Yeah, well, Pug expects to be the boss. He made that clear from day one."

"You have a problem with that?"

I shake my head.

"So listen, some of us have noticed you don't circulate much. Skip a lot of meals. Stay put in here during common time. Someone said the only time they saw you out on the yard, you just stood there and didn't talk to anyone."

Not true. I had a conversation with a couple of racist assholes and got hit on by a drag queen. And who's this "someone"? One of the guards? Has Manny opened his big mouth about me? I tell Cavagnero I'm more of a loner than a socializer.

"Uh-huh. So we were just wondering. You depressed?"

"Sometimes. This place is pretty depressing. Why?"

Instead of answering my question, he asks me another one. "What about your people on the outside? Friends? Family? Much contact there? You getting some support?" I tell him I'm still waiting to get my phone account funded and the people on my visitors' list approved. "No contact yet then, huh? Well, that stuff takes a little time, but like you said, it's only been three weeks. Right?"

"Right."

"But you wouldn't say you're overly depressed, would you?"

"*Overly* depressed? What do you mean?"

"Well, like if, for example, you were thinking about hurting yourself."

"Oh. No, then," I say. "Not overly." Now I get it. He's trying to find out whether I'm going to become another Hogan.

He smiles, stands up, and walks toward the door. Then he turns back. "Because if you were, you could talk to someone—a counselor or one of the visiting psychologists. There's usually a waiting list to get an appointment, but I could probably help you jump the line if you're struggling. Or you could talk to me."

I nod. Thank him.

"And look, it gets easier to be here once you've gotten your bearings, made a couple of friends you can trust. These first weeks are the hardest for guys like you: first-time offenders who never imagined they'd end up here. For a lot of the guys doing time, it's just part of the life. They start in juvie, then graduate to big-boy jail. Do some time and cycle out, commit another crime and cycle back in. Some of them get so they *prefer* being on the inside. But for guys like you, it's a whole new experience. Takes getting used to, but then it's okay. Right?"

"Right," I say. "I'll keep that in mind."

"Good. Okay, nice talking to you, Ledbetter. Have a good evening."

"Yup. You too."

A few seconds after he's gone, I hear his voice again, coming through the tray trap in our steel cell door. "Hey, Ledbetter?"

"Yeah?"

"Keep the faith."

"Uh-huh. Thanks."

Lying there, I start wondering about Cavagnero's motivation for visiting me. Have I just been offered some genuine compassion? It's in short supply around here, so it's nice to think so. Keep the faith: Was he pushing religion? Or has he been sent here to try to prevent any future bad publicity Yates might get if there's a second suicide within a week? Don't trust any of them, Pug said.

Later that afternoon, during one of our tier's five-minute breaks for common time, I go out on the corridor to show them I'm not isolating. That's what they want to see, right? There are just a few others out here, talking and laughing together halfway down the corridor. One of them is DeShaun. And there, maybe ten steps away from me, is his cleaning cart, parked by itself with a box of garbage bags on the top. Opportunity seems to be whispering, *Do it. This is a sign. Don't be a wuss.* I look around to see whether the coast is clear, then yank out two of the bags, fist them, and walk back in my cell.

That night, after lights-out, I make my plan. I'll do it in the morning. Once Pug leaves for work, I'll grab that stubby little pencil in my survival kit and use the backs of those commissary order sheets to write notes to Emily and my mother, explaining why this is the best thing for all of us. . . . I'll double up the bags in case I accidentally poke a hole in one or try to claw my way out before I lose consciousness. If everything goes the way it should, I'll be dead before the midmorning count. That's probably when they'll discover me. By chow time, I'll most likely be the topic of conversation. *I can't place him. Kept to himself. Killed his own kid.* A week later, I'll just be another "back-door parolee" whose name nobody will remember. With my decision made and my plan in place, I feel relief. I pull one of the plastic bags from beneath my pillow, unfold it, and place it loosely against my face. It rises and falls with each breath I take, almost as if I've given it life. In the morning, it will return the favor and give me death. My way out of here is just hours away.

CHAPTER SIXTEEN

August 2017
Days 23–28 of 1,095

I'm poked awake. Someone's shining a light in my face. As my eyes adjust, I realize there are two of them, but I can only see them in silhouette. Who are they? Is this a home invasion? Then it hits me like a brick to the head. I'm not at home, I'm in prison; these must be guards. But bed checks are done by one officer, not two. From his bottom bunk, Pug asks what the fuck is going on. "Doesn't concern you, Liggett. Go back to sleep," one of them says. I don't know what's going on either, but if it's not about him, then it's about me. I'm poked again, blinded by the flashlight's beam. "Let's go. You going to cooperate or do we need to pull you down off there?"

Disoriented, I slip off my bunk and onto the floor. A wave of nausea hits me as I'm led out of our cell. By the lights in the corridor, I can see the guards now, but neither is familiar. One of them cuffs me; the other holds a fistful of plastic in my face. "What were you planning to do with these, Ledbetter? Huh? Check out early?" I'm too scared to answer. Flanked by the two of them, I'm walked down the two flights of stairs and out of B Block.

Outside it's foggy and cold; crickets are chirping like crazy and there's an opaque half-moon. Barefoot and shivering in only my underpants, I ask where they're taking me. Neither one answers. Their flashlights lead us along the walkway until I see the medical building rising out of the fog.

Inside, we stop at the front desk. "Ledbetter," one of the guards says. The receiving officer puts down his Game Boy and stands. He's short, slight, bearded. His name tag says O'Brien. "Is he belligerent?" he asks. The other two shake their heads. He grabs a ring of keys from a plywood board and comes out from behind his desk. Says, "Okay, follow me."

The four of us head down a hallway, then take a right, passing a sign that says Psychiatric Unit. I've heard that having to go to seg is bad, but being locked up in the "ding wing" is worse. What fresh hell is this going to be?

"Take him to number two," O'Brien says. "I'll be right there." The other officers walk me to a cell that says Observation #Two. I watch O'Brien unlock a cabinet and take out some bulky blue thing. When he rejoins us, he unlocks the observation cell and motions me in. He and the escorts follow.

"Drop your underwear and put this on," O'Brien says. He and one of the escorts hold out the blue thing—a sleeveless wraparound garment. O'Brien tells me to put my arms through the holes. I ask him what it's for. "Safety smock," he says. "So you can't hurt yourself." When one of the escorts quips that it's "noose-proof," O'Brien frowns. I slip my arms through the holes and feel the weight and bulk of the thing—four or five pounds of some sturdy, nylon-like material. O'Brien pulls the front straps and Velcros the garment around me. "Too tight," I tell him. "Can you loosen it a little?" He shakes his head and says it's supposed to be tight. I lock eyes with him. "Why am I here?" I ask. It's more of a plea than a question. Because he doesn't look away, he suddenly seems more human than robotic.

"An emergency order's come down to put you in administrative seg-regation."

"Why? What did I do?"

"It's not what you did," he says. "It's what they think you might do.

You're on a seventy-two-hour suicide watch." I deny that I'm suicidal—so emphatically that I half believe myself. "Someone's made a mistake."

"That's for a clinician to decide," he says. "I'm just following orders."

"We done here?" one of the escorts asks. O'Brien nods. They leave the cell. O'Brien starts to leave, too, but he stops at the door. "Maybe it *is* a mistake. But if I were you, I'd just go with it and cooperate. You cause a stink and those seventy-two hours might be just the beginning. You see that up there?" My eyes follow his pointing finger to a surveillance camera mounted to the ceiling. "You're being observed and evaluated by staff. Behave yourself, okay? Get some sleep." Having offered that little bit of kindness, he closes the door and locks me in.

I look around, but there isn't much to see. Bare concrete walls, a thin plastic mattress on the cement floor. No sheet. I stare up at the bright-as-hell halogen lights overhead and the surveillance camera. Two cameras, actually. They're watching me from more than one angle. I feel something move across my bare foot. It's an ant. I would bend down and flick it off if this fucking safety suit wasn't so bulky. It crawls down my ankle and across the cell. Disappears into a crack where the wall meets the floor.

How did they figure out what I was planning? Had I flunked my interview with Cavagnero? Did it get back to them that I said Hogan was better off than the rest of us? Maybe a camera in the corridor caught my spontaneous grab of those plastic bags from the janitor's cart and someone put two and two together?

———

I open my eyes; somehow I've slept. There's no way of knowing how many hours I can subtract from the seventy-two I have to stay in this goddamn cell under the glare of those fucking lights. They never go off and those surveillance cameras never stop watching me. With no way to escape the reason I'm in prison, Niko's death hits me full force. I drank and drugged that morning and robbed him of his life. Stole him away from his mother and sister. I deserve this shame I'm feeling. Deserve to have had my suicide attempt thwarted. Big Brother's up there, watching my every move to make sure I don't cheat them of the thirty-six months of suffering I owe them.

———

At some point I start pacing, counting the number of times I've gone around the cell. One thousand, seven hundred and twelve. When I stop, I lean against one of the walls and begin to doze on and off. I'm awakened by the sound of the door being unlocked. Are they letting me out? Have seventy-two hours slipped by? I gaze up at the cameras, then at the unfamiliar CO who has entered the cell. He's carrying a Styrofoam tray of food: powdered scrambled egg, oatmeal, two slices of bread, and a foil-covered plastic container of apple juice. Breakfast food. So it's morning? Is the sun up? When I ask what day it is, the CO doesn't answer. He puts the tray on the floor, comes over to me, and removes the safety smock. "Eat up," he says.

Naked, I sit cross-legged on the mattress, look up at the cameras again, and try as best I can to cover my privates with the tray. When I tell the guard the kitchen forgot to give me a utensil to eat with, he says, "You're on suicide watch; you eat with your fingers." Seriously? How the hell would I be able to harm myself using a plastic spork? I put handfuls of the eggs and the oatmeal on the two slices of bread. Fold them together and eat them like they're tacos. Take small sips of apple juice to help swallow it down.

After I'm finished eating, I tell the CO that I need to go. Instead of leading me to a bathroom outside the cell, he points to a drain in the corner. When I say I need to take a crap, too, he points again to the drain. After I've pissed then squatted to relieve myself, I'm given nothing to wipe my butt with before he puts the safety suit back on. How is making someone who's suicidal live under these conditions supposed to make him *not* want to kill himself? True, the observation cell is a place where it's just about impossible to harm my body. But it's likely to accelerate my *wanting* to do myself in. When I start to whimper involuntarily, I turn over, facing the floor to keep the watchers from seeing my face.

———

The ants come and go. I don't mind the black ones so much, but the smaller red ones bite. To fend them off, I start pacing the perimeter of the cell again. This time, instead of counting, I think about all the other suicidal inmates who have had to wear this smock before me. How many of them, I wonder, are still alive? How many killed themselves after they got out of here? I can't predict what I'm going to do. . . .

———

In an attempt to elude my watchers, I get down on the floor and pull that dirty mattress on top of me. Bang my head against the floor once, twice, three times. Within a few minutes, a female guard comes in and screams that if I don't stop what I'm doing, I will have to be therapeutically restrained. "You think you'll enjoy lying spread-eagle on your back and having cuffs around your wrists and ankles? Having a helmet strapped onto your head so that you don't bash your brains in?" I begin to cry, begging her not to do this, promising her I'll be good, the way I used to beg and promise my father when he screamed at me for whatever offense I'd committed. "I'm sorry," I keep saying. "Please. I won't do it again. I promise."

———

I have no idea how many of those seventy-two hours of observation have passed when a clinician arrives to interview me. Accompanied by the same CO who threatened me with five-point restraint, he is carrying a stool in one hand, a clipboard in the other. She's carrying a stool, too. "You want this off him, right?" the CO asks the shrink. When he nods, she approaches, frees me from the safety smock, and hands me a small towel so I can cover my genitals. "I'll be right outside the door if there's a problem," she promises the doctor. Before she exits, she turns and smiles at me as if she *isn't* the enemy.

He's an older man, balding, fat. "Good morning, Mr. Ledbetter. I'm Dr. Blankenship. I'm here to ask you some questions and evaluate your need for further psychiatric treatment or your readiness to return to general population." The combination of his high-pitched voice and his body like the fat one in Laurel and Hardy, I worry I might break into nervous laughter.

He sits down on his stool and invites me to sit on the other one. After small-talking to me for a moment or two, he gets down to business, reading questions from his clipboard and nodding when I respond. I do my best to offer him whatever lies, truths, and half-truths will get me the hell out of here.

"Are you hearing voices, Mr. Ledbetter?"

"Voices? No."

"Do you feel like you want to die?"

"No."

"Have you been contemplating suicide recently?"

"No. I think that was someone's mistaken assumption."

"Have you ever contemplated suicide in the past?"

"Never seriously."

"Seriously or not, have you ever thought about how you might do it?"

"No."

"Are you aware of the recent inmate suicide in this building?"

"Yes."

"Has it troubled you?"

"Well, I felt sorry for the guy if he was that desperate."

"Would you say you became preoccupied with thinking about what he did?"

"Preoccupied? No."

"On a scale of one to five, how fearful do you feel about your future?"

"I don't know. Maybe a three?"

"Do you frequently have feelings of despair?"

"Frequently? No. Occasionally maybe. Everyone has bad days, right?"

"And when you do feel despair, one to five, how intense is that emotion?"

"Out of five? I don't know. Two? Three?"

"Do you miss your family, Mr. Ledbetter?"

"Yes."

"One to five, what would you say your anxiety level has been here at Yates?"

"I don't know. Three, I guess. Sometimes four. I have trouble sleeping here and while I'm awake, I start worrying about everything. But that's normal, right?"

Again, he nods. "Have you formed any friendships since you've been here?"

"Friendships? Not really. Well, one or two, I guess."

He asks me several more questions. Then he stands up, says he has what he needs and that he's enjoyed our conversation.

Our conversation? It's felt more like an inquisition. I decide to go for broke. "So what's the verdict?"

He says he's going to put me down as a short-term EDP. When I ask him what that means, he says it's an acronym for "emotionally disturbed person." The good news, he says, is that he considers my agitated emotional state to have been short-term and that I don't present any signs of being an imminent danger to myself.

"Okay. So what happens next?"

"Well, I'm ordering your release from observation. And I'm going to put you on some medication that should help you with your anxiety."

I wince a little, undetectably, I hope. "What kind?"

"One of the benzodiazepines. There are several: Xanax, Librium, Ativan. Do you have a history of taking any of those?"

I tell him no. An addict's first instinct is to lie and his second instinct is to justify the deceit. If all you get in prison is this hit-and-run psychiatric care by a shrink who takes your word for it rather than checking your record, then you're being handed a gift—an opportunity.

"Okay, I'll write you a script for Xanax." He picks up his stool. "Good luck, Mr. Ledbetter." He knocks on the door and waits for the CO to unlock it.

I want so badly for him to leave that I start to shake. But his *not* leaving yet is an opportunity, too. The Big Book says we can only be saved if we practice "rigorous honesty." I made a promise to Emily that I'd stay clean. How will I be able to sit across from her in the visiting room and *not* confess that I'm back on benzos? If I have any hope of fighting against what my addiction has cost us, I need to keep that promise because getting hooked again would dishonor our marriage and our dead son.

I hear the key in the lock. The door opens. "No, wait," I say. "Don't write that prescription."

Blankenship raises his eyebrows. "Why not? I think it can help you."

"No. No thanks. I don't want to take it. I'm good."

"You sure? All right then. Your call."

When they let me out of the observation cell an hour later, I'm given a pair of scrubs to wear on my way back to B Block. That CO, O'Brien, is back behind the desk where patients check in and out. "Do I have to wait for an escort?" I ask.

He smiles and shakes his head. "Go on, get out of here. B Block, right? I'll radio them to expect you. Take care of yourself."

"Yeah, thanks. Hey, can you tell me what time it is?" He says it's two thirty-five. "And what day is it?" It's Monday, he says. I thank him again.

Walking out of the building into a bright late-summer day, I feel a lightness in my step the likes of which I've not experienced here at Yates. Maybe it's relief that I've been released from that medieval dungeon or maybe it's because I've mustered the strength to resist getting back on that hamster wheel of dependence on benzos. My sobriety has held.

When I enter Block B, I pass the weight room, where the same guys are lifting, spotting, and doing crunches to take control of *some*thing. I take the stairs a couple at a time. Walking into Cell 3-E, I wonder for a few seconds whether I'm in the wrong place. Pug's TV is gone and so are his posters, replaced by ones of Donna Summer, Lady Gaga, and Kermit the Frog waving a rainbow flag.

I look from the posters to the familiar face that appears in the top bunk. Apparently, it's no longer mine. "Hey there, roomie," Manny says. "Welcome back to the living." When I ask him what's going on, he fills me in on what I've missed.

Pug is gone, transferred out of here, he says. Opening and examining inmates' mail was part of CO McGreavy's job. He discovered that Pug was on the receiving end of unmarked bulletins from Vanguard America and the East Coast Knights of the True Invisible Empire. In addition to confiscating these materials, McGreavy let it be known to a couple of Black inmates he's friendly with that Pug was getting this White Power crap. Two days ago, while Pug was walking back to the block after work, someone shoved him to the ground and whacked him in the face so hard that it broke some of his teeth and deadened an eye. McGreavy is heading up the investigation, but so far the assailant hasn't been identified. According to the rumors that have been circulating, the weapon used against Pug was a sock with three tins of mackerel inside it. Pug was moved to protective custody, then transferred yesterday to Northwest CI.

———

My sheets, pillow, and blanket have been moved to the bottom bunk. The bed is made. Two pieces of mail have been placed on my pillow. I open the one from my mother first. It contains the welcome news that my phone and commissary accounts have been set up and that she has deposited one hundred dollars in each. She also has contacted my father and gotten a promise from him that he will match these amounts. "Can't wait to talk with you and find out how things are going," Mom has written.

The other letter takes me by surprise. It's from Dr. Patel. She writes that, because she was a visiting psychologist at Yates, "I know from my former patients how challenging prison life can be, especially in the early weeks." She is writing, she says, to offer me a few simple suggestions that she hopes will help me as I transition to institutional life.

First, Corby, try as best you can to live in the present, not the past or the future. Don't allow yourself to become too preoccupied with the tragic circumstances that have led to your imprisonment. What's done is done and cannot be changed. Likewise, you should not allow yourself to become too focused on what might happen after you're released. Doing so will rob you of the energy you need to get through each day in real time.

Secondly, you will have a more positive experience in prison if you respect the mind/body connection. Avoid the processed foods available from the commissary; sugar, saturated fats, and carbohydrates may provide short-term satisfaction, but they can affect your moods in negative ways. Exercise as often as you can and reap the benefits of fresh air and sunshine whenever they are available. Keep your mind engaged and active through reading. It can guard against lapses of negative thinking and offer you a temporary escape from your restrictive environment.

Finally, my friend, do keep busy. There are many jobs available to inmates at Yates. Look around and find work that you might enjoy. Toward that end, I have an idea. One of my friends when I worked there was the prison librarian, Fagie Millman. She is a positive person and would be a wonderful work supervisor if she has positions available. I will email her and ask her to be on the lookout for you should you have any interest in working a library job, but you should feel no pressure if my idea doesn't suit you.

In closing, I ask you to think about this: every person who enters prison must make the choice of moving toward the dark or the light. Many people who are serving time further imprison themselves with dark thoughts and dark deeds, but both paths are available to you. Seek the light, dear Corby. Move toward the light.

CHAPTER SEVENTEEN

September 2017
Days 47–48 of 1,095

What's weird about Yates Correctional is that it's seven buildings plopped down between a busy four-lane road and twenty-five acres of woods and wetlands—what could be described as a nature preserve if it wasn't part of a prison. Deer graze out back; coyotes and weasels prowl; wild turkeys mill for seeds and roost in the trees to elude nighttime predators. The name of the game out there is survival of the fittest, the fastest, the cleverest, the most alert. By my seventh week at Yates, I've figured out that this is more or less the name of the game inside this place as well.

I promised Emily that prison wasn't going to get in the way of my recovery, but I haven't yet gotten to a meeting here or even figured out how to make that happen. My visitors' list has finally been approved, and if Emily comes to see me soon, I don't want to have to sit across from her and lie or admit that I haven't yet made good on my pledge. I had a close call when I almost let that shrink put me on Xanax, but my determination to stay clean overruled my desire to use. One of the AA Promises says, "We are going to know a new freedom and a new happiness." Well, happiness is a tall order when you're in prison, but I'm less preoccupied about drinking or drugging now, so I guess that's a kind of freedom. And the longer I can stay clean and sober, the more fortified I'll be against surrender.

But I'm put to the test the following Saturday morning. "Not many of us know about this," Manny whispers. "And you said you were in AA before you got here, so this probably doesn't interest you, but I figured I'd let you know about it. There's real booze at the rec station, not toilet tank hooch."

The week before, he says, a guard smuggled in a handle of 86-proof tequila for Butler, but he got paroled unexpectedly the next morning before he had the chance to even crack open the bottle. There was no way he'd be able to sneak it out during his discharge, but he didn't want to just pour it down the sink. Instead, he poured it into the broken twelve-cup hot pot in the rec area. The plan, Manny says, is that, starting with the nine a.m. five-on-the-hour break outside of our cells, us guys who know about it will line up to pour some "hot water" into our disposable cups, supposedly for our instant coffee or noodles.

I tell myself I have no intention of screwing with my sobriety, but when Manny returns from his first visit to the hot pot, his breath permeates the air in our confined space, and the smell of alcohol begins flirting with me, coaxing me to ignore my resolve and indulge. In a way, it would be stupid to pass up a rare opportunity like this or hesitate until it's all gone. "We are not saints," the Big Book says. "Progress, not perfection." Approaching the eleven a.m. break, our end of the tier has come alive with the sound of loud talk, laughter, and the inebriated pleasure of "sticking it to the man." I used to love that about getting drunk back in high school: the way when, two or three drinks in, your buzz would free you from your worries and inhibitions and let you just float above your sucky reality for a while. My craving for some of that tequila intensifies until I end up waiting by our cell door, Styrofoam cup in hand.

When the door pops, I hustle to the rec area and am fourth in line from the spigot that's going to allow me an 86-proof minivacation. While I stand here waiting, my effort is to block out the three reasons why I *shouldn't* drink—Emily, Maisie, and, most of all, Niko—and I start getting the shakes. I don't just *want* some of that tequila; I *need* to have it. But then, with only Pacheco between me and my alcoholic deliverance, I watch my thumb punch through the bottom of my cup. Feeling conflicting emotions of despair and relief, I leave the line.

Back in our cell, I flop face-first onto my bunk, rattled by how close I came, thanks to the "stinkin' thinkin'" we addicts are warned about.

"Hey," Manny says. "You okay?"

I murmur that I'm fine.

"Should I not have told you the secret?" he asks.

Again, I say I'm fine.

Several seconds go by before I raise my head and look over at him. He's staring back at me. "You sure?"

"Jesus Christ, Manny, I don't need a shrink and I already have a mother!"

"Okay, okay. Just asking. I'm not that crazy about alcohol either, to tell you the truth. Give me a dance club and some party drugs, and booze can go fuck itself."

I don't sleep for shit that night. The next day, Sunday, Captain Graham is working the control desk. A woman of imposing height and weight, Delia Graham is legendary around here for having single-handedly broken up a fight between two gangbangers, fracturing the arm of one and putting the other in a collar for a sprained neck. The word on Graham is that she'll treat you decently as long as you don't piss her off.

On the way back from chow, I stop and, on impulse, ask her whether she knows what I need to do to get to an AA meeting.

"Friend of Bill's?" she asks, which might mean she's in the program, too. I nod. "Okay, let's see now. There's something about that somewhere in this mess. Whenever I work this desk, I gotta put everything back in order. Next time I'm here, same thing. All the men working this desk expect Mama to get things neat again. Probably treated like princes when they were kids. Not my sons. By the time they left home, they knew how to cook, clean, do laundry, wash and wax the kitchen floor. My daughters-in-law are always thanking me for the way their men got brought up." She seems to be talking to herself, not me, so I say nothing as I watch her shuffle through a handful of notices. "Okay, here we go," she says, holding up a sheet of salmon-colored paper. "Says there's a meeting in D Block, second floor, immediately following seven a.m. Sunday Mass." She glances at her wristwatch. "Which is just about now." When I ask her whether I can go, she says, "You spoze to put in a request at least twenty-four hours before. But since you didn't know that, I'll write you a pass and radio them that you're not on the list but you're coming. Make sure you check in with the officer when you get there."

"Thanks very much," I tell her.

She shrugs. "When you need a meeting, you need a meeting."

I walk to the end of the corridor and wait for her to buzz me through the exit door. When she does, I turn back to wave, but she's busy sorting and straightening up the mess the others have left her. I start down the stairs.

Outside, walking toward D Block, I imagine a chapel of some sort, but when I reach the building's second floor, I see that "church" is a setup in the corridor. The "pews" are rows of beat-up plastic chairs and the altar's a sheet of plywood resting on two sawhorses. There are at least twenty guys in attendance—more than I would have guessed. The guard at the desk behind the altar is thumbing through a car magazine, drinking from a bottle of Gatorade, and paying no attention to the service. I hand him my pass and hold up my ID. Without looking at me or lowering his voice, he says, "Better late than never, huh? You staying for the meeting?" I nod. "Take a seat then."

There's an empty chair at the end of the third row. I sit and watch, feeling a small measure of gratitude for the priest's emerald-green robe—a dash of color amidst the gray cinder-block walls and our drab tan uniforms. I can see from the whispered conversations and muffled laughter that some of "the faithful" have come here not to pray but to socialize. I watch a grizzled-looking muscleman up at the altar fill a tray of those little paper ketchup cups from a bottle of what I'm guessing is grape juice. Dude has long, bleached-blond hair and, from the looks of it, is going for that Dog the Bounty Hunter look. Out of nowhere, I recall how, when I'd fill their sippy cups with grape juice, the twins would pucker up and giggle, showing each other their purple tongues. I catch myself smiling a little until my guilt delivers a roundhouse punch so unexpected that it takes my breath away. If I had any right to happy memories about my kids, I wouldn't be here.

The priest raises what I recognize as one of the chow hall trays. It's piled with broken pieces of white bread. "This is my body, which is given for you. Do this in remembrance of me," he calls, his voice traveling down the long corridor. Next, he raises a Styrofoam cup, a few sizes larger than the one I came close to filling with tequila the day before. "This is the cup of my blood, the blood of the new and everlasting covenant." I hear my father say, *Pure fantasy. How can people be so gullible?*

Someone rings a bell and eleven or twelve believers get up and form an orderly line to the front. Dog the Bounty Hunter stands next to the priest, holding his tray of juice shots. "The body of Christ," the priest says as he places bread onto the cupped hands of the first guy in line. "Amen," the guy answers. Puts it in his mouth, slugs down the grape juice, crumples the paper cup, and tosses it in the wastebasket below.

"The body of Christ."

"Amen."

"The body of Christ."

"Amen."

There are some tough-looking dudes in this Communion line, but they seem as pious as monks. Thinking again about the line I stood in the day before, I shift uncomfortably. Do these guys crave some kind of absolution the way I craved that tequila? I hope the AA meeting after this isn't going to push the God stuff too hard. I don't feel contemptuous of religion like my father does, but I'm skeptical that some savior "if He were sought" is anything more than wishful thinking. I remember what my sponsor's sponsor said to him: "Dale, you don't have to believe as long as you believe that *I* believe." Or what Dale told me about his own belief: that the closest he comes to feeling the presence of a higher power is when he looks out at the vastness of the ocean when he's surf casting.

My attention shifts to the three-man choir up front, one of them strumming a guitar. The song is familiar, but I can't remember where I know it from. The middle singer looks familiar, too, and when he steps forward and begins his solo, I do a double take. It's that Jamaican guy, Jheri Curl, who tried to embarrass me the first day I went out in the yard. *To see Thee more clearly, love Thee more dearly, follow Thee more nearly, day by day.* He's toned down his look for church—no eye makeup, no lipstick courtesy of strawberry Twizzlers. And he has a damn good singing voice. The other two join in as the song wraps up. *Day by day by day by day by day.*

After the ones in line have been served, Dog and the three choir members receive their communion, then take their seats. Jheri Curl's is directly in front of mine. I'm looking at the long vertical scar running down the back of his shaved head when I feel something hit my sneaker. Glancing down, I see the kite. At the far end of my row, a bearish-looking bald guy is pointing at . . . Jheri?

"Him?" I mouth, and his head bobs up and down. I tap Jheri on the shoulder and slip him the kite. He unfolds and reads it, then places two fingers to his lips and sends off a kiss to the sender. A hookup, I figure. *Spirituality now and sinning later on*, my father's voice says. *What hypocritical bullshit.*

When church is over, about half the guys stay behind, stacking some of the chairs against the wall and arranging others in a circle. I'm surprised to see that when the priest takes off his robe, he's dressed like the rest of us: tan scrubs, state-issued sneakers, prison ID pinned to his shirt.

A younger guy named Javier calls the meeting to order. He leads the eleven of us in the serenity prayer and reads a couple of announcements. When he asks whether anyone is new, I raise my hand, volunteer my first name, and tell the others I'm cross-addicted. "Welcome," some of them say. "Glad you're here."

Javier passes me a Big Book and asks me to read "How It Works." "Chapter five, pages fifty-eight through sixty," he says. I read the description of the twelve steps and end with that part about how, although no human power can save us from our addiction, "God can and will if He is sought." Everyone else chimes in on that last part. They sound more convinced than I am.

Javier says his topic for today's meeting is how we can resist temptation. Most of the guys who share say a lot of the same stuff I heard at the meetings I attended before my sentencing: talk to your sponsor; pray for strength from your higher power; "move a muscle, change a thought." One guy says he wants to remind us that while we're sitting in here, our addiction is doing push-ups out in the yard, getting ready for the day when we're discharged. The priest, whom everyone calls Father Andy, shares that he got his fourth DUI on his drive back from a ninety-day rehab. I half-want to tell them about my close call the day before, but I don't know whether I can trust these guys and I don't want anyone on my tier to get in trouble if someone ignores the "what's said in here stays in here" rule. Besides, I can't quite say how or why I was able to resist at the last minute. When my thumb poked through the bottom of that cup, had it been a voluntary act or an involuntary one?

I'm the only one who doesn't share. Still, walking back to B Block, I feel pretty good about having gone to that meeting. Calmer than I've felt in a long time. Maybe I'll put in a request to go back next Sunday. It would beat sitting in our cell, worrying about how Emily and Maisie are doing or trying not to listen to Manny's music or one of his monologues. Last week I added earplugs to my commissary order.

"Where you been?" he asks when I get back from the meeting. What business is it of his? I tell him, straight-faced, that the warden invited me over to her place for tea and cookies. He looks so hurt by my sarcasm that

I fess up. He says he's proud of me for going, which creeps me out a little. I sure as hell don't need *his* approval.

Before lights-out, I read Dr. Patel's letter for the umpteenth time. Reading can be *a temporary escape from your restrictive environment. . . . There are many jobs available to inmates at Yates. . . . the prison librarian, Fagie Millman . . .*

CHAPTER EIGHTEEN

—

September 2017
Day 53 of 1,095

I let a week go by before I get a pass from my counselor and find my way to the library on the top floor of the main building. Coincidentally, that guy Javier who chaired last Sunday's meeting is working the circulation desk.

"Hey, there," he says. "Corby, right?" I nod, pleased that he remembers my name. I ask whether he knows of any job openings. "Here, you mean? You'd have to check with the boss about that," he says. He points to the small office behind him. "Door's open, so you can knock and go right in."

Fagie Millman has no eyebrows; that and the headscarf that's riding back from her forehead reveal her baldness that says cancer treatments. She's warm and welcoming and remembers my name from Dr. Patel's email, but says she doesn't have any open slots. "I'm happy to add your name to my waiting list," she says. "There are three ahead of you, but one of my current workers has applied for a job in food prep and is waiting to hear back. And there's always a chance that someone will become eligible for early parole." In the meantime, she says, I should feel free to browse. "And here, have one," she says, holding out a plate of chocolate chip cookies. "After he retired, my husband, Howie, was bored out of his mind until he discovered he likes to bake. I'd weigh a thousand pounds if I ate everything that comes out of our oven. Warden Rickerby frowns on my bringing in goodies for you fellas, but nuts to her. What's she going to do? Fire me after twenty-eight years?"

I thank her, take a cookie, and tell her I have a two-hour pass. Does she mind if I hang around and do some reading? She says she'd be delighted. Handing me a pencil and a slip of paper, she has me write down my name and inmate number. When I hand it back to her, she compliments me on my legible handwriting. Makes me smile when she says that. At Yates, you take whatever praise you can get.

The collection's pretty thin. I browse through sci-fi, biography, nature. When I read the titles on the shelf labeled "Local Interest," I pull out something called *Connecticut's Carceral History 1773–2012*. On the cover are two photos: one of New-Gate, the state's first prison, the other of this place. I'm curious about New-Gate. When the state turned it into a museum, Emily took her sixth-grade class on a field trip there and came home with a brochure. From what I remember, the prison had been a copper mine before it housed crooks, killers, and British prisoners of war. Yates is bleak enough, but from the pictures in the book I'm holding, the conditions at New-Gate were practically inhuman.

I sit down at a table on the opposite end of an older Black inmate seated in a wheelchair. Short gray dreads, horn-rimmed glasses drooping halfway down his nose, faded US Navy tattoo. He's mouthing the words as he reads, tracing each line with his finger. When he looks up at me, I nod a hello. He nods back, not smiling, and holds up the paperback he's reading, *Charcoal Joe*. He asks whether I've ever read any Easy Rawlins books. "Can't say that I have," I tell him. "I've heard of that author, though."

I can tell from his "pfft" that I haven't won any points with that answer. "The author's Walter Mosley. Easy Rawlins is the *character*. Who you think writes all them *Tarzan* books? Tarzan?"

Yeah, whatever, Gramps. I give him a half-smile and crack open *Connecticut's Carceral History*. The introduction describes how the public's attitudes about prison is a pendulum that swings back and forth between punishment and rehabilitation, depending on which way the political winds are blowing. The book was published in 2012, when Obama was president. I remember reading about him visiting some prison and telling the inmates that some of them were there because they'd made the same kind of mistakes that he made when he was young. His message was all about hope and change and getting past those mistakes. Now that Trump's in the White House, the political winds have shifted so abruptly, you could get whiplash.

I flip to the back of the book. Turns out the author, Nathan Kipp, was a prisoner at Yates who came here at nineteen for a gang-related assault. Started taking correspondence courses while he was here and ended up as a college professor. It says *Connecticut's Carceral History* was his doctoral thesis. In his author photo, he looks early forties maybe. Bald-headed, full beard, arms folded across his chest. Despite his achievements, there's a sadness in his eyes. Did he always have that look or did he earn it in here?

I open the front and read the dedication: "To those who live in prisons of their own or others' making." He's inscribed this copy to Fagie Millman, thanking her for believing in him before he believed in himself. Nice.

I skip the rest of the introduction and dip into the history. The first chapter says that in the 1600s, the Puritans believed crime and sinning were the same thing, and that punishment was more about public humiliation than keeping people locked up. Thieves, blasphemers, drunks, liars, adulterers, idolaters, practitioners of witchcraft or Quakerism could be lashed, put in stocks, branded on the forehead with a red-hot iron, or banished to the wilderness. The most egregious transgressors could have an ear severed or be escorted to the gallows, where they would meet the noose.

Kipp writes that New-Gate was the first of its kind in Colonial America: a state prison. At New-Gate, the book says, incarcerated men were forced to live seventy-five feet underground in the caves and shafts of the converted mine, and that the facility was later replaced by Westfield Penitentiary, a four-story brick fortress built by New-Gate prisoners who were then locked up there.

In a way, it's not that different from what happens at this place. A lot of the guys here work for Prison Industries, making office furniture and body armor, assembling electronics, doing DMV data entry—all for a whopping fifty cents an hour. I overheard some guy in the shower room griping to his buddy that from the twentysomething dollars a month he earns "working for the man," they take out for taxes, victim restitution, and program costs.

The book says that by 1850, the prison population had far outgrown the Westfield facility, leading to overcrowding, escapes, brawls, and the stabbing death of a controversial warden. Deemed ineffective with the now more violent population, the penitentiary system was abandoned and the pendulum swung back to a more punitive—

"If I was you, I'd begin at the beginning."

I jump a little; I forgot about the old guy on the other side of the table. I look over at him, confused. "*Devil in a Blue Dress.* Start there."

"Oh," I said. "Mosley. Right."

"There's over a dozen Easy Rawlins stories. And he's got other series, too."

I'm more interested in what this guy looks like than what he's saying. His dreads are more salt than pepper. Smooth caramel-colored skin, hands as big as catcher's mitts. He's big and broad-shouldered with a body gone to fat on prison food, but he must have had a fullback's body when he was younger. I feel my right hand moving under the table as if I'm sketching him. When he stops talking and wheels himself over to the back window, I look at the other books on his side of the table: James Baldwin's *The Fire Next Time*, a biography of Satchel Paige, *The New Jim Crow: Mass Incarceration in the Age of Colorblindness*. Dude's reading a lot more than detective fiction. When he wheels back to the table, I ask him whether he's planning to read all of those. "Gonna *re*read Baldwin," he says. "For the others, I got a system. Give everything the fifty-pages test. If I like what I'm reading, I keep going. If I don't, I stop. What are you—in your thirties?" Thirty-five, I tell him. "Well, I ain't got as much time left as you, so I'm choosy. What's that you're reading?"

When I hold up the book, he says *he* could've written that one—that he's a walking history of this place. "Been here since nineteen hundred and eighty-two. Much better back then. They used to let us go fishing in the river, swim when the weather was hot, play softball. They supervised us, sure, and you had to *earn* them privileges. They didn't just hand 'em to you. But back then, we was treated like more than just our crime. The warden? Warden Hayden Barnes? He used to put on a hot dog roast for us on the Fourth of July and him and his deputy would do the cooking.

"And get this. If you didn't have no tickets for a year, you could enter a drawing to win an overnight in the trailer with your missus so that you and her could have some private time. Enjoy some marital relations, know what I'm saying? The time I won, January of '84, my wife, Mary, brought in some home cooking in a picnic basket. We have four kids and the youngest one got made in the trailer that night after my belly was full up with baked Virginia ham, sweet potato pie, and peach cobbler."

"Nineteen eighty-four? That's the year I was two."

"That right?" As in, so what? "You got kids?" he asks.

"Two," I say, then catch myself. "Well, one, actually. A daughter." I feel my face flush as he stares at me, puzzled. Luckily, Mrs. Millman comes toward us, rescuing me with her plate of cookies.

"Corby, I see you've met one of our favorite patrons," she says. "Lester, how about a cookie or two?" I note that in her domain, we're patrons, not offenders.

"How 'bout a half dozen?" Lester says, laughing at his own joke.

"Well, three, maybe. You don't want to ruin your boyish figure." They both chuckle. "How about you, Corby? Another cookie?" I thank her but say no. "Well, come up to the desk if you change your mind."

After she walks away, Lester keeps looking at me as he eats his cookie. "First you said you had two kids and then you said one. The other one die?"

I take a deep breath and say, "Yes, our little boy. He and his sister were twins."

"That right? Terrible thing for a parent, huh? What'd he die from?"

I wish Lester hadn't just asked me, but something about him makes me feel I can risk being vulnerable. "DUI accident," I said. "It's why I'm in here." Not wanting to watch his reaction as he takes in what I just said, I look away, groping for a change of subject. "So when you first got here, Yates had softball games and conjugal visits? Why is it so different now? What happened?"

I watch as his face shifts gears from sadness to anger. "Crack happened," he says. "Crack and the politics that went with it. Instead of the War on Drugs, they might as well have called it what it was: a war on the 'hood. Population at this place almost doubled, and a lot of the new arrivals was young Black boys eighteen, nineteen who were going to have to do the rest of their growing up in here."

He shakes his head. "It got so overcrowded that they turned the gym in A Block into a dormitory with them plastic sleigh beds all over the floor. One toilet and one shower for fifty young men? Pfft. After DOC started getting complaints about the conditions, they'd stack them sleigh beds and roll 'em out of sight when the inspectors were coming. Load the dormitory guys onto buses and drive 'em around the compound until after the inspection was over. Went from bad to worse after Johnston got elected governor. That was when the hammer really came down. They started training the new COs like they was military—and like we was the enemy. The officers carried sticks before, but you almost never saw them use 'em until Johnston's goons showed up. They gave 'em pepper spray, too. Brought in the dogs for riot training."

"Was that when they built the newer cell blocks?" I ask. "After the place got so overcrowded?"

"Uh-huh. Those things got slapped together on the cheap by Fusaro Construction. And it was no coincidence that they got the contract because Johnston and Nick Fusaro were brothers-in-law and sailing buddies. Fusaro cashed in big-time for those concrete-and-cinder-block pieces of shit, and now everyone who lives there has to put up with leaky roofs, shitty plumbing, and black mold. You know why people driving by out front don't see them newer buildings? Because the state don't *want* the public to see 'em, know what I'm saying?"

I nod. "Out of sight, out of mind."

Before I lost my job at Creative Strategies, Yates was just a place I'd drive past on my way to work. Morning traffic along the four-lane Woodruff Parkway usually moved along slowly, so I'd get more than just a passing glimpse of the fifteen-foot-high chain-link fence wrapped around the massive Greek Revival fortress and the two four-story cell blocks on either side. It seemed as imposing a structure as you'd *hope* dangerous criminals would be locked away in. The manicured lawn and landscaping on the law abiders' side of the fence implied that the facility was orderly and well managed. Unless you were paying close attention—and I wasn't—you wouldn't even know those other, newer blocks existed. Or that they'd been a legacy of the crack epidemic and the Johnston administration, and that they were falling apart.

"Mind if I ask you something?" Lester says. "How much time they give you for doing what you did?" When I say three years, a shadow creeps across his face. He goes back to reading his book. Not wanting our conversation to end, I nod toward his copy of *Maybe I'll Pitch Forever* and tell him I read someplace that DiMaggio said Satchel Paige was the best pitcher he ever went up against.

No response. Okay, I get the message. He's done chatting; he wants to read.

When it's almost time to head back to our block, I go up to the desk to check out *Connecticut's Carceral History* and *Devil in a Blue Dress*. Javier's reading something, too. Shaking his head, he slaps his book down and says, "It pisses me off, you know? What those fuckers did when they came over here and took charge?" I pick up the book and read the title: *Native American Genocide: The U.S. Government's Systematic Efforts to Eradicate Indigenous Populations.*

Javier tells me he's half Nipmuc on his mother's side and a quarter Wequonnoc on his father's. "You Indian?" he asks me.

"Just a fraction, I guess. My mom had her DNA analyzed a while back and it said her people mostly came from the British Isles but that she was six percent Native on her father's side."

"Yeah? Which tribe?"

"I don't think it was that specific. Northeastern Indigenous, I think it said."

"Probably Algonquin or Mohawk then. Maybe even Wequonnoc. Book says that back in the sixteen hundreds, the Colonists tried to wipe out the Wequonnoc in a land grab."

"Really? I grew up around here, but we never learned *that* in school."

"Yeah, 'the man' likes to rewrite history because the truth makes him look so bad. You should read this book if you got Indian blood."

"Just a couple of drops, though. But yeah, I'll check it out after you're done with it." He says I can take it now—that it makes him so mad, he needs to stop. "Okay, thanks," I tell him.

He checks out the three books and stamps my pass. "Okay, later, brah," he says. "You coming to the meeting next Sunday?"

I tell him I hope to.

CHAPTER NINETEEN

October 2017
Days 66–87 of 1,095

Emanuel "Manny" DellaVecchia is Russian-Jewish on his mother's side and Sicilian on his father's. Some relative of his mother's used to be a big-deal Vegas comedian in the late fifties and early sixties, Manny says, but these days he's parked in a nursing home and pretty much out of it. Manny and his sister, Gloria, have been told they're in his will and are going to inherit some motel in Jersey that the uncle owns. That's where Manny's planning to live when he gets out.

Manny's Nonna DellaVecchia was a hustler, he tells me. She sold sheet pizzas from her kitchen window in East Harlem every Friday and made extra money running numbers and undoing _il mal occhio_ for unlucky _paesani_ who'd been cursed with the evil eye. "I watched her do the ritual once," Manny says. "This sad sack comes to the door and tells her he got fired from the shoe factory, walked home early, and found his wife in bed with a traveling scissors grinder. Nonna sits him down at her kitchen table and puts a bowl of water in front of him. Dribbles a few drops of olive oil into the water, and 'reads' the results. 'Yeah, you got it bad,' she tells the poor slob. She ties a string to the stem of a red pepper, dangles it in front of him, and starts saying this singsong prayer in Italian. The longer it goes on, the louder her voice gets and her eyes start rolling in her head like pictures in a slot machine. Finally, she stops praying and bangs her fist three times on the tabletop. Tells the guy he's cured."

"Spooky," I say. "Did it work?"

"Don't know if it worked for him, but it worked for her. She charged him three bucks and told him to pay her 'cashier,' which was me. He hands me a two-dollar bill and four quarters. Nonna let me keep two of the quarters, so I walked down to the store and bought myself a can of Hawaiian Punch and ten pieces of Dubble Bubble."

"There were two-dollar bills?" I ask.

"Yeah. Thomas Jefferson on the front, I think. They must have stopped making them. You never see them anymore."

I tell him I've been reading this book that says Jefferson owned slaves and fathered children by one of them. "And he owned them, too!"

Manny shrugs and turns on the TV. "*Dancing with the Stars* is coming on and it's Disney night. I love it when they do that theme."

"I mean, 'All men are created equal' but if the kids you father are half Black, then they're your property? And Jefferson's a hero? Gets his face on US currency? How fucked-up is that?"

But as usual, Manny and I are on different wavelengths. "If that show had started ten years earlier, I could have *totally* been on it. As a professional dancer, I mean, not a celebrity. When I danced for Carnival Cruises, I did a little choreography, too, but my contract wasn't renewed because I was better than the head choreographer and he was jealous."

Well, Manny might be unplugged from social justice issues, but as far as cellmates go, I could do worse. In fact, I *have* done worse when I lived with Pug. *Much* worse. In comparison, a cellie who talks too much, acts like my parent sometimes, and "borrows" from me occasionally isn't so bad. He owns who he is; I respect that. And he's pretty well-liked around here; he doesn't get targeted the way some gay inmates do. He hooks up from time to time, but I don't know the details and don't want to. Shortly after we became cellmates, he offered to "service" me, but I told him no thanks, I was a do-it-yourselfer. He laughed and backed right off. It's been a nonissue ever since.

Manny can be funny as hell—especially when he's telling stories about his checkered job history. In addition to his gig as a cruise ship dancer, he's been a tuxedoed partner to rich old lady ballroom dancers and a deejay at gay clubs in New York and Connecticut. "The pay was only so-so, but I could make as much as a grand a week dealing coke and molly," he told me.

When I asked him what molly was, he looked at me in disbelief. "Ecstasy. X. Disco biscuits. For fuck's sake, Corby, where were you in the eighties?"

"Elementary school," I said. "I don't think they covered disco biscuits in the kindergarten curriculum."

That shut him up. Manny's touchy about his age, which I know for a fact is fifty-three, not "midforties" like he claims.

This is his second prison bid here at Yates. The first happened as a result of a sting at some rave he was working. "One minute I'm selling blow to these two gorgeous cubs, shirtless and sweaty from dancing. Next thing I know, they're pulling on their DEA T-shirts and shoving me into the back of an unmarked cruiser." He got five years because his lawyer was an idiot, he says. "Before I went in, I'd have everyone in the house up and dancing their asses off to Madonna and Whitney and Wham! By the time I made parole, it was all flannel shirts and fucking Nirvana. Fucking Beck. Fucking Radiohead. 'I'm a creep, I'm a weirdo.' 'I'm a loser, baby, so why don't you kill me?' How's anyone supposed to dance to *that* shit?"

Luckily, he says, he got his certified nursing assistant license while he was on the inside and, after his release, landed a job at a nursing home, taking temps and BPs and schlepping food trays "until word got out about how fabulous I was. When the recreation director went out on maternity leave, I saw my opportunity and went for it. I organized wheelchair conga and Thursday afternoon karaoke. They made me interim director. And I want to tell you, Corby, those old broads loved me and one of the men, too—Leon. He wanted to 'adopt' me, which would have put me on easy street, but his family got wind of it and had me fired." That was when Manny went back to working the clubs and dealing, he says. Got arrested for the same shit as before. "Second offense, ten years this time, suspended after seven."

Even before we became cellmates, Manny had appointed himself my Yates CI mentor. It's not like I didn't need some guidance back then; I was a stranger in a strange land, and my instinct was to stay curled up in a ball on my bunk, not speaking to anybody. Manny saw that I was isolating so he reached out. And I appreciated it, but he was such a fucking know-it-all about everything that it got annoying, especially after we became cellies.

Case in point: after my account finally got funded, I filled out my first commissary request sheet but forgot to order a lock for my storage box. "Never, *ever* leave your stuff unlocked around here," he lectured me. "I mean, come on, man. Use your head. People in here are crooks. Get yourself a lock ASAP, and until it comes in, put your initials on *everything*." Standing there, getting chewed out like that, I was my nine- or ten-year-old self again, having to listen to my father make me feel stupid for not knowing something. *Did I tell you to bring me a* Phillips *screwdriver, Corby? No, I just said "screwdriver," which means a flathead screwdriver. If I wanted a Phillips screwdriver, I would have said so. You're probably the only boy your age who doesn't know the difference between the two.*

The day after Manny gives me shit about the lockbox, I come back from my shower and catch him with his hand inside my open bag of M&M's. "Isn't that a C.L. on the bag?" I asked him. "It stands for Corby Ledbetter, doesn't it?"

Without dropping a beat, he said, "Oh, I thought it stood for cock lover, so I assumed it was mine. You can't get Grindr in here and you have to get the word out *some*how. Did you order M&M's, too?" He flashes me a guilty smile and gives me back my candy. "I was only eating the green ones," he says. "I figured you wouldn't notice." As restitution, he gives me six postage stamps and two foil packets of mayonnaise. When I tell him I don't like mayo, he says he doesn't either.

After a while, I begin to distance myself from Manny. The problem is that he's started to act like he owns me. It's not enough that we share a six-by-nine-foot cell. He also makes sure we sit together in the chow hall and stay in close range out in the yard. I don't want to hurt the guy's feelings, but I need to get out from under his wing. I start talking with some of the guys on our tier that he's warned me against. I pretty much know by now who I should avoid and these guys are fine. Gets me a little breathing space. And maybe it's homophobic for me to think this, but I don't want guys making assumptions about the two of us either.

———

Manny tells me he's starting to come down with one of his migraines—that he's getting an aura or something. He climbs up onto his bunk, lies on his back, and closes his eyes. It's our tier's day to have time out on the yard. I feel bad about his suffering but grateful for the opportunity to go out there without him for once.

Outside, I walk over to the picnic table where my new buddies are starting a poker game. "Deal you in?" Boudreaux asks. I tell him sure and grab a seat.

"We were just talking about Angel's girlfriend," Pacheco says. "You ever see her, Ledbetter?" I shake my head. "You one lucky mofo, Angel," he tells him. "That chick's a Jamaican Stormy Daniels."

"'Cept my boo's titties ain't fake," Angel assures him. "Only thing gets implanted in her is me, know what I'm sayin'?"

Lobo flashes his missing-teeth grin. "Yeah, man. Bury the meatstick. Right?"

Boudreaux rolls his eyes. "Lobo, you cray-cray. After all that meth you done, your brain cells probably ain't even in double digits anymore." He may have a point. Lobo's pretty slow on the draw. His nickname is short for lobotomy.

He counters with, "Whadda *you* know, Boudreaux? You're so dumb, you probably don't even know 'Meatstick' is a Phish song."

"Thass right, Einstein. I don't know it 'cause I don't listen to no lame-ass white-boy music."

"Your loss, motherfucker," Lobo says. "I been to nine Phish shows and every one of them was fuckin' *epic*. Hey, Ledbetter. I bet *you're* into Phish. Right?" He and I are the only two white guys in the game.

I shrug. "Never paid them much attention." I turn to Angel. "What's the story, bro? We got thirty minutes out here. You going to deal or what?"

Angel deals the flop. I have a decent hand and I'm a pretty good bluffer, so I bet. Boudreaux and Angel both call. Lobo and Pacheco fold.

"Who *you* like then?" Lobo asks me.

"Me? Musically? . . . The Killers, Drive-By Truckers, Jason Isbell, Amy Winehouse."

Boudreaux's eyes bug out. "Amy Winehouse? She dead, man. Thass messin' with some bad juju." Andre Boudreaux, a New Orleans Cajun, is superstitious as hell. Angel's his cellie and he told me the last time the COs did room searches, they confiscated Boudreaux's hoodoo shit and he was afraid to leave their cell because bad luck might chase him down.

Angel says, "Hey, Ledbetter, how come we don't hear no bruthas on that list of music you like?" In my defense, I tell him I like a lot of old-school R & B.

"Then what about Wu-Tang or NWA? They old-school."

"Older than that," I tell him. "Smokey Robinson, the Temptations, Aretha. Some rap's okay, though."

"Yeah? Like who?"

"Kendrick Lamar, Common. I used to like OutKast. Are they still around?"

Angel ignores the question. "Tupac versus Biggie? Where you at on that?"

I tell him I'm neutral. "And anyway, I'm a convicted felon, so I'm not allowed to vote. Are we going to finish this hand before break's over or what?"

Angel deals the turn. My luck's still running. Boudreaux folds and it's down to just Angel and me. When he deals the river, it gives me a full house without even having to bluff. I show my hand, then reach across the table and scoop up my winnings: commissary shit everyone's thrown into the pot. I'm now the proud owner of three teriyaki beef sticks, five instant coffee packets, two envelopes of spicy vegetable ramen, and a minitube of athlete's foot cream.

When I get back to our cell, Manny's curled up in the fetal position on his bunk with a towel over his head. "Bad?" I ask him.

He whispers that it feels like there's a jackhammer pounding inside his head, and when he opens his eyes, the lights make him nauseous. I ask whether there's anything I can do, anything I can get him. "The wastebasket," he says. "I keep thinking I might puke. I just wish everyone would turn their music down. The noise is killing me."

"Here you go," I tell him, propping the empty wastebasket against his hip. I feel for the guy but you can't miss the irony of it. When it comes to playing the music he likes, no one jacks up the volume more than Manny.

———

I squint over at the digital clock. It's 3:03 a.m. Sure, I'd rather be asleep than awake, but sometimes I don't mind these middle-of-the-night bouts of sleeplessness. During the daytime, the cell block can get so noisy you can't hear yourself think. Gets even louder in the evening from all the bickering, card game chatter, hip-hop, and shouting TVs. But at three in the morning, I can hear it: the Wequonnoc river at the rear of the prison property, flowing past this place.

AA says we need to have faith in "a god of our understanding," so let's say for example's sake that some undefinable spirit *does* exist—that it's not all just random. Maybe that spirit is speaking to me through the sound of moving water. And maybe that sound is telling me to trust that not everything is stuck and stagnant—that forward movement is possible. That by the time I've done my three years here, the sun will come up and light the path that leads me back to my wife and daughter.

I don't know. Sometimes I think we're all wandering in the dark and that it's random and pointless. But I'm trying to open my mind to the possibility of some deeper truths. Trying to see the light and move in that direction. At lights-out earlier tonight, the skies opened up and it began pouring like crazy. I don't hear the rain now, but the river is roaring back there. Clamoring to be heard.

———

I can't get out of second gear today because I was up half the night, so pretty much all I've been doing today is watching TV in our cell. Manny's rallied after his migraine yesterday and he's full of pep. When I start dozing off midafternoon, he taps me on the shoulder and asks whether I want him to wake me up when it's time to go eat. I shake my head, then fall into a deeper sleep. I don't wake up until a couple of hours later when I hear him come back from chow.

"Well, Corbs, you missed all the action," he says. "Dinner and a show. You know that tall skinhead with all the White Power tats?"

"Gunnar," I say. "He was one of the ones who tried to recruit me for the big race war."

"Yeah, him. So McGreavy was on supper patrol and there's no love lost between those two. McGreavy tells Gunnar which table to sit at and the dude ignores him and parks himself at the table where his neo-Nazi pals are at. But McGreavy's not going to let it go, okay? Not when the guy's just openly defied him in front of everyone. He goes over there and gets in his face. Gives him a direct order to move to the other table, but Gunnar just keeps eating and ignoring him. The showdown starts getting everyone's attention. Then the other guard working chow goes over there to give McGreavy an assist. He's one of those gung-ho newer hires. Blond crew cut, ripped, cocky attitude."

"Piccardy?"

"Yeah, him. He goes over there and says, 'Offender, you've just been given a direct order, so you'd better comply unless you want to—'

"Doesn't even finish what he's saying when Gunnar stands up, grabs his tray, and says, 'I have no problem complying when a white officer gives me a command, but I'm not taking orders from some spook wearing a sewn-on badge.'

"McGreavy goes up to Gunnar and pulls out his stick, probably just to scare him. Only Gunnar isn't acting scared. Everyone's standing up now because it looks like something's about to go down. Then Gunnar drops his tray on the floor, grabs McGreavy by his shoulders, and fuckin' headbutts him! McGreavy loses his balance and starts falling backward, but what's-his-name, Piccardy, catches him before he hits the floor in front of everyone. Except now it's on! Everyone starts egging them on, cheering, 'Fight! Fight! Fight!' A few of Gunnar's buddies stand up, ready to rumble, but so do three of McGreavy's homies—those Black cons he's chummy with. Then before any punches get thrown, Piccardy gets fuckin' trigger-happy and pepper-sprays Gunnar and his boys!

"He must have radioed for help, too, because pretty soon here come the storm troopers, wearing their helmets, face shields, and riot shit. You can tell they're just itching to use some of their riot training, but the big showdown has already fizzled because of the pepper spray. The White Power assholes get shackled, belly-chained, and dragged out of there, but the whole room stays, like, *energized*. Right?

"McGreavy must have felt he had to save face and remind everyone who's still in charge, so he announces that chow time's over and orders us back to our units. We all started bitchin' because we've only been there for like ten minutes and some guys haven't even gotten through the line yet. But Piccardy backs him up so that's that. They're the bosses and we aren't, so we all got up and headed for the door. And it was Jamaican meat pie night, too, those cocksuckers. I was stuffing mine down so fast, I started choking."

I shake my head. Tell him I'm glad I missed the show but sorry I missed the meat pies, which is one of the best meals they serve over in chow.

"I got you, dawg," Manny says. "A lot of guys left them on their trays, so I grabbed a few on my way out." I watch as he pulls a meat pie out of his sweatshirt like a fucking magician. I put my hand out and he tosses it to me. I take a bite and watch him pull another one out of his pants.

"Hey, thanks," I tell him.

He gives me a garbled "no problem," his mouth full of meat, gravy, and crust.

So yeah, Manny's helicopter-parenting me can be annoying sometimes, but at other times it feels kind of good to be taken care of. Other than my poker buddies, he's the closest thing I've got to a friend in here. And like I said, he's a whole hell of a lot better than Pug.

CHAPTER TWENTY

November 2017
Days 94–95 of 1,095

I'm surprised when I glance at the wall clock behind the circulation desk and see that my two-hour library furlough is almost up. I've only got twenty more pages of *Devil in a Blue Dress* left to read, but I better get back to our block. Standing and looking around, I realize that most everyone who was here when I checked in has left. Now it's just me and Lester. Should I go over and say hi or leave him alone? When he looks up at me, I walk toward him, smiling.

"Hey there. Nice to see you again."

"Uh-huh." No smile back.

I hold up the Walter Mosley book he recommended. "Hey, look what I'm reading. It's a real page-turner. Thanks for the tip."

"Yup." He returns to his book.

Instead of taking the hint, I just stand there. "Well, I've got to get going. But hey, next time we're both here, I'd love to pick your brain a little."

"Oh yeah? You a cannibal or something?"

"Ha ha. No, but the last time we talked, you said you were a walking history of this place. I'd like to hear more about that."

He says nothing.

"And uh, I'm an artist, okay? That was how I used to make my living. So I was wondering if, when you tell me more about the way things used to be, I could sketch you while I'm listening." Frowning, he asks why I'd want to do that. "Well, because you've got an interesting face."

"Do I? What's interesting about it?"

"Well, it's the face of someone who's learned a thing or two about life. A face of wisdom, I guess you could say. So while you're telling me about some of your experiences, I'd like to try and capture that quality. Do a couple of quick sketches if you wouldn't mind."

"Yeah, I *would* mind," he says. "A kindly old black man with a face of wisdom? You want me to sing 'Zip-a-Dee-Doo-Dah' while you're making your pictures?"

"Uh . . . what do you mean?"

"I mean you ain't turning me into your Uncle Remus or your magical Negro 'cause I ain't neither one of them. So, no. You can't 'pick my brain' and you can't 'capture' me either."

I stand there, dissed and dumbfounded. Why's he being so hostile? What did I do? What did I say?

I go up to the desk to return the book about Connecticut prisons, renew the Easy Rawlins one, get my pass stamped, and get the hell out of there. "Hey, what's the deal with Lester?" I ask Javier.

"What are you talking about?"

"Last time I was here, he was friendly, talkative. But just now, I thought he was going to bite my head off."

Javier says he gets moody sometimes. Suffers from depression. "Why wouldn't he get depressed with the kind of sentence they gave him? Fifty years? That's a lifetime. Mrs. M says he's gone to the parole board maybe fifteen, sixteen times to try and get his sentence reduced but it's always no." He reaches for my book. Renews it and stamps my pass. "Hey, did you ever read that other book I checked out for you?"

"*American Genocide*? No, I haven't gotten to it yet. You need it back?"

"No, you can keep it for a while. Let me know when you're done with it. I'd be curious about what you think." I tell him okay and I'm out of there.

Walking back, I keep thinking about Lester—how he's been stuck in here for decades. Is he in touch with his kids? Is his wife still alive? If he's practically a lifer, what did he do? And why'd he get so ornery? *You ain't turning me into your Uncle Remus or your magical Negro.* What the fuck, man? Just because I asked whether I could sketch him? It's not like *I* told him he couldn't get his sentence reduced. And if he thought I was being racist, he was mistaken. Someone says you have a face of wisdom, that's a *compliment*, Lester.

That night, maybe five minutes after lights-out, I ask Manny whether he's still awake. When he says yes, I ask him whether he knows an older inmate named Lester. "Big Black guy, uses a wheelchair?"

"Lester Wiggins? Sure. Everyone knows Lester. He's like a legend in here."

"I saw him in the library today. He says he's been at Yates since 1982."

"Yeah, with a fifty-year sentence. I suck at math. What's 1982 plus fifty?"

"Uh . . . twenty thirty-two. So he's got about fourteen more years to go?"

"If he lasts that long. I heard Lester's got a lot of health problems."

"What the fuck did he do to get a fifty-year sentence?"

Manny says he heard he was active in some Black liberation group back in the seventies. "A couple of their members held up an armored car and shot one of the guards. The guy died the next day. The way I heard it, they wanted to try Lester for murder along with the other two, but they couldn't pin it on him. So they got him on something else."

"What?"

"He was married, but he had a girlfriend on the side—a white woman who was a hanger-on with that Black Power group. Some judge's daughter. Owned a sports car, and one night, when Lester was driving it, they crashed into a bridge abutment."

"Did she die?"

"No, but one of her arms got so mangled, they had to amputate."

"Was the accident what put Lester in a wheelchair?"

"Nah, he's only been using that for the past few years. I don't think he got hurt much in the accident, but she got a prosthetic arm so they trumped up the charges and put him in here for the long haul."

That's when I begin to understand Lester's about-face from my first library visit to this one. For the death of my son, they gave me three years. Lester got fifty years because a judge's daughter lost an arm and, I'm guessing, because she was white. Three years as opposed to fifty. No wonder he's bitter. No wonder he went off on the stupid white guy who asked whether he could "capture" him.

———

This call originates from a Connecticut Correctional facility. Press 1 now if you wish to accept this call from . . . Corby Ledbetter. *If you wish to decline—*

"Corby? Hi."

"Hey. Thanks for picking up. Pleasant surprise."

"Surprise?"

"Yeah. I haven't talked to you in over a month. I was starting to think maybe you didn't want to talk to me anymore."

"Why would you say that?"

"Well, you know. I *am* a jailbird."

"If that's supposed to be funny, it's not. Actually, I'm relieved to hear your voice. How's it going?"

"Oh, you know. Fun times down here. You been getting my letters?"

"I've gotten two. God, that first one was . . . when you wrote that you weren't sure you wanted to live anymore because you didn't think you could survive for three years in there. And that same day, the TV news said the police were investigating another suicide at Yates. I lost it, Corby. I was so scared it was you that I went out in the backyard, wailing and walking around in circles."

"Oh, jeez. I'm sorry, Em. That suicide was a guy from our block, but on another tier. I'll spare you the details. But listen, things are a little better now. I guess I'm getting used to the place."

"Your second letter said you got a new cellmate. I was relieved to read that. Your first one sounded horrible."

"And I held back some stuff. But this new bunkie's all right. Kind of annoying but harmless enough. Actually, I sent you *four* letters—so you should be getting the others pretty soon. Oh, and I've been going to meetings. That's been helpful. There's this one I like that meets on Sunday after church and—"

"You're going to church?"

"No. Only the first time because I got there early. It's interesting, though, the way they improvise around here. The service is set up in a corridor. The altar's a sheet of plywood on top of two sawhorses. Kind of surprising who gets into the Communion line. I'm no expert on Catholic Masses, but I'm guessing this is a pretty unconventional one. The priest is doing time like the rest of us. But enough of that. How's Maisie?"

"Good, overall, I think. I upped her daycare to four days a week and she still goes to my mom's on Friday."

"How's she adjusting?"

"Well, some days she's fine when I drop her off and some days she resists. Which is typical, I think. She balks at going to my mother's sometimes, too."

"The girl's got good instincts, huh?"

"Don't start, Corby. I know she's not your favorite person, but Mom's been super helpful these three months."

"And super happy that I'm out of the picture, I bet. Okay. Sorry. Is Maisie still asking about Niko?"

"Not as much as before. Hard to tell, but I wonder if her memory of him is fading. I'm not sure if I should let it happen or try to keep those memories alive."

"I guess you just have to play it by ear. Take your cues from her."

"And I can run it by Dr. Patel. I'm seeing her this coming Tuesday."

"Really? Wow. What for?"

"Just some things I want to work on."

Like what, I wonder, but I know not to ask.

"By the way, Maisie's been talking about you a lot lately. Daddy this, Daddy that. We look at photos, watch videos on my phone. Niko's in some of them, too, but her focus is on you. It's all about her daddy."

With my free hand, I swipe away the tears in my eyes. One of my nagging fears is that my daughter's memory of me will fade away over time. "God, I miss her so much, Em. Miss both of you. I know how busy you are, how much you're balancing, but I haven't seen you since I came here. Maybe some weekend soon—"

"I want to see you, Corby, but to tell you the truth, I dread having to see you at *that* place. But I *am* going to visit. I promise."

"That would mean a lot. And maybe Maisie could—"

"Please don't start that again, Corby. I've made myself very clear on this subject. I'm *not* bringing my daughter inside a men's prison."

Our daughter, I want to say, but I drop it. Ask her whether she's talked to my mother recently. When she says she hasn't, I remind her that Mom has said she'd be happy to babysit Maisie. Neither of us says anything for several seconds. Then the canned voice breaks the silence.

You have one minute remaining.

"I still can't believe they cut your calls off at ten minutes," she says.

"Well, lots of times there's a line of guys waiting to use the phone, so I can understand that. What I *don't* appreciate is that Big Brother can listen in on our conversations in the interest of 'safety and security.' That's their excuse for everything they say no to. 'Sorry, it's a matter of safety and security.' Man, they love that phrase."

"But that's an invasion of privacy."

"No such thing as privacy at this place. I learned that the first day I got here when they strip-searched me. Oh, hey, before I forget, in one of the letters you haven't gotten yet, I ask you for a favor. Could you go on Amazon and order me a sketchbook and some charcoal drawing sticks— the skinny ones? I was thinking about drawing some cartoons for Maisie, maybe making them into a story for her."

"That's a great idea," she says.

"And when you order them, have them shipped right to the prison. They won't let you carry in something when you visit or send a package from a home address. It has to be sent directly from the retailer. And don't send me a sketchbook with one of those spiral binders. They'll deny it because of the metal. You'd be surprised how creative some of the guys in here can get if—"

And that's it. Cut off without any goodbyes or I-love-yous. When your ten minutes are up, they're up.

So why is she seeing Dr. Patel? That time we went for grief counseling, she was negative about her. I wanted to keep going—I *did* keep going—but Emily opted out. I remember at the end of that first session when Dr. Patel asked her what she hoped to get out of therapy if we continued. Em said she wanted to get clear about whether or not she could find a way to forgive me—and that if she couldn't, she didn't think our marriage could survive. Is that what this appointment is about? Is that why she doesn't pick up half the times I call? Is she leaning toward divorcing me? I have a sinking feeling that's what it is. And if I'm right, how's that going to affect my relationship with Maisie? Emily won't let me see her while I'm here. What happens if, when I finally get out of here, I'm a virtual stranger to my daughter? Whether she divorces me or not, I'm still Maisie's father. Emily can't deny that.

PART THREE:

A Simple Stone

CHAPTER TWENTY-ONE

—

August 2018
Day 367 of 1,095

I flip the calendar page and do the math in my head: 1,095 minus 367 equals 728 more days to go before I can reclaim my life—some version of it anyway.

I think back to how scared and confused I was a year ago. Those first weeks were brutal: the taunts, the isolation, my fear and distrust of everyone, including my cellmate, Pug. I knew I deserved to be here, but I didn't think I could survive in this place for three years. Suicide seemed like the only other option. A few months ago, I found out how they knew my plan: Manny had predicted it and gone to Lieutenant Cavagnero. Had I known this at the time, I would have been furious about his butting in. Now I'm grateful.

As I acclimated to my strange new surroundings, things got easier. I kept my head down, learned the system and the culture, got out of my own head so much. There's plenty of cruelty going on inside this place, but no one's targeted me in any significant way and Manny, as irritating as he can be sometimes, is a friend.

In the past twelve months, I've weathered the soul-crushing boredom of institutional lockdowns, a bedbug infestation on our tier, witnessing the stabbing of one inmate by another on the walkway, and, worst of all, the inability to see Maisie. My two most difficult days in here were April 27, the first anniversary of Niko's death, and March 30, the twins' birthday. Maisie turned three that day and Niko remained the age he'd been the day he died: twenty-five months. I called Emily both days to commiserate, but she didn't pick up.

I've tried as much as possible in the past year to heed the advice Dr. Patel gave me in that letter she sent: exercise the body and the mind. I've been faithful to my workout routine and kept a list of the books I've read—twenty-three of them. I've "moved toward the light" by attending thirty-seven AA or NA meetings, plus ninety-minute classes on meditation and yoga. No luck getting a job yet, but I keep checking at the library. There's still one guy ahead of me on the waiting list. I've been less successful in following Dr. Patel's advice to live in the present. I can't always stop my memory from replaying that morning: Niko watching the ants, my innocuous chat with the McNallys, my hand shifting the car into reverse. Nor can I always stop from imagining best- and worst-case scenarios about what happens when I finally walk out of here in another 728 days.

But one year's been served. I can't lose sight of that.

CHAPTER TWENTY-TWO

—

September 2018
Day 409 of 1,095

The intercom clicks on. What now?

"Ledbetter?"

"Yeah?"

"You've got a visit. I'll buzz you out."

Is it Emily? If so, it will only be the fourth time she's come to see me. But it's Thursday. The other times have all been on the weekend. I doubt she'd drive here on a school night. Plus, she would have been away from Maisie all day. It's probably my mom again; she tries to get here every few weeks. God, I hope it's not my father. He cried that day in court when they handcuffed me and took me away, but he hasn't visited or written to me once since I've been here. Okay, so much the better. The last thing I need to see is his look of disdain as he surveys the room, taking in where all my failures have landed me.

Walking along the connecting bridge from our block to the visiting room in the main building, I see Angel ahead of me. He must have a visitor, too. Maybe it's that hot girlfriend of his that everyone's always talking about. . . . I've been careful not to pressure Emily about visiting more often. It's hard to tell from a monitored ten-minute phone conversation how she's feeling about me. About us. We mostly talk about safe stuff and there are a lot of awkward pauses. If I could see her face-to-face more often, I might be able to read her better. I know she's stretched to the max—single-parenting, teaching, taking care of the house, going to therapy. But three visits in over a year? Some of the women who come here visit their men twice a week. Should I be reading the tea leaves?

When Mom came to see me last Sunday, the visiting room was humming, but tonight there's only five of us lining up at the entrance, waiting to be let in: that Sikh dude, Angel, Praise, that skinny mixed-race kid who looks like he belongs in juvie jail, and me. The Sikh's wearing his turban; I heard he sued the state and won the right to wear it based on religious grounds. Looks like he's got a shiner, probably courtesy of one of the "patriotic" idiots around here who think he deserves a beatdown because they mistake him for a Muslim. This kid in front of me is fidgety, nerdy-looking, braces. Reminds me of that character Urkel on whatever that show was. He's going to be low-hanging fruit for one of the con men around here who'll become his buddy so he can shake him down for whatever he's looking for. How the fuck old is he, anyway? He looks about fourteen or fifteen, but he's got to be at least eighteen if he's here.

"Hey, Praise," Angel says. "How's your pops doing? I ain't seen him around lately." Praise's real first name is Cornell. He's on the janitorial crew and his nickname's short for "Praise Jesus!" which he'll shout in the middle of mopping the corridor or cleaning the shower room. Doesn't hurt anyone, but that booming voice can make you jump if you're not expecting it.

"Ornery as ever," he says. "Wheels himself to the library every day, checks out a bunch of books, reads half the night, wheels himself over to the med line in the morning, and goes back to the library. That's about it."

"You talking about Lester Wiggins?" I ask him. "Lester's your father? I met him a while back." He gives me the once-over before he nods. Wow, father and son doing time in the same prison. Must be weird for both of them.

I shuffle my feet a little, wondering what the holdup is. If our visitors have already checked in, why are we just standing here? I look out at the empty sally port, then back at the guys I'm playing hurry-up-and-wait with. That's when I notice that Juvie's got a long scabby cut on the inside of his left arm. It looks infected. Forget prison; if that cut is self-inflicted, he probably needs to be in an adolescent psych unit someplace. I know I shouldn't say anything, but my parenting instinct kicks in. "How did that happen?" I ask him.

He swivels around with that deer-in-the-headlights look and sees that I'm staring at his cut. He looks away and says nothing.

"This place gets easier after you've been here awhile. That's been my experience anyway. You sentenced yet?" He shakes his head, still not looking at me. "Well, you might want to get over to the med unit. Have one of the nurses put some antibacterial ointment on that." If he's cutting himself, maybe they can connect him to one of the visiting shrinks.

"You a doctor?" he asks, turning and facing me.

I smile. "Far from it," I tell him.

"Then why don't you mind your own motherfucking business?"

Angel lets out a laugh. "Dang! Little fuckboy just bitch-slapped *you*, Ledbetter." So much for my fatherly instincts. Now I feel like jacking up the little shit for embarrassing me. Guess I'm getting institutionalized.

Praise leans in. Warns the kid that things will go easier for him if he loses the attitude. "I had to learn that lesson the hard way. Came in here when I was eighteen and had to get the badass attitude beaten out of me three or four times before it sunk in. How old are you, anyway?"

Instead of answering him, the kid crosses his arms and rolls his eyes. Up at the front of the line, the Sikh just shakes his head. But Praise—Cornell—hasn't given up yet. "You got a name?" he asks.

"Yeah."

"So what is it then? Rumpelstiltskin?"

A half-grin betrays the kid's sullen act. "It's Solomon," he says.

"Well, get wise, Solomon. It's hard enough in here. Don't make things harder for yourself."

The door buzzes. We enter the visiting room and take seats at the long, wide tables. That's the rule: inmates seated before they let the visitors in. Once they enter, we can stand for a quick embrace, but then everyone sits, with our company on one side, us on the other, everyone's hands on the table where the guards can see them. I don't recognize either of these two. The Black CO's probably a newbie. Young, butch-looking, her pant legs tucked into her boots. She's wearing that fresh-out-of-the-academy scowl to let us know she's not taking any shit from us. They must teach them that face before they let them graduate. . . . The white guard's older, probably a transfer from another facility. He's got the Gen X essentials: goatee, gut slackening into middle age. Looks like the type who was more into Nine Inch Nails than Nirvana back in the day. Probably did a couple of semesters of college before he packed it in. Decided to become a state cop instead but bombed out at the police academy and ended up here. Hates his job, cheats on his wife, smokes a little weed after work. . . . No. Stop it, Ledbetter. Don't be such a smart-ass. What's he done to you?

Okay, here come the visitors into the sally port. The steel door they've just passed through closes behind them and they stand there, waving and waiting to be buzzed in to where we are. I don't see who my visitor is, but not everyone is visible in that window. The Indian-looking woman has to be Mrs. Sikh. Someone's brought an antsy little kid with them; I see his head bobbing up and down. Little dude looks like he's about four, maybe a year and a half older than Niko. . . . I can't believe I still do that sometimes. Forget he's gone. Must be denial still. Last time we talked, Emily said when she goes into CVS to get diapers, she sometimes has to remind herself that a box of thirty-eight is going to last twice as long as before. I told her I was surprised Maisie's still wearing diapers, since she'd started to master toilet training a year ago.

"Well, she's regressed, okay?" Emily snapped. "Her pediatrician said it's probably because of the big changes that have been foisted on her, and that I shouldn't make an issue of it. And frankly, I'd rather change a diaper than have to wash and dry the wet sheets and make the bed with clean ones. If that's cheating, then too bad."

"Babe, I wasn't criticizing you. I'm sorry if it sounded like that. I know you're stretched to the max. I'm in awe of everything you're handling by yourself while I'm in here. Jesus, Em. It must be exhausting. I don't know how you do it all."

"Everything except toilet training," she said.

"No, Dr. Ritchie's right. She'll use the toilet when she's good and ready."

"Oh, shut up, Corby." It was pretty much monosyllables after that until our ten-minute phone call was up. . . .

Goatee Guard signals to some invisible CO who's working the door. Our visitors are buzzed in. As they enter, Butch calls out the rules like she's issuing threats. I still don't see anyone I know.

The gray-haired woman walking toward Cornell is the one who's brought the little guy. Must be his grandma. She's wearing a work smock; probably drove here from her job at a nursing home or whatever. The little dude breaks free and runs toward Cornell. "Slow down, Ezekiel! They don't want nobody runnin' in here!"

Mr. and Mrs. Sikh share a polite embrace. She touches the bruise under his eye with her fingertips. I swallow hard; tenderness isn't something you see much of around here.

Angel's sitting a couple of chairs down from me and here comes the hot girlfriend, tossing back her long, multicolored braids. She's wearing skintight jeans and a blouse that stops just north of her belly button. From the way her boobs are wobbling around under there, I'm guessing no bra. The room is hers and she knows it; even the two COs on the platform are watching the show. As she passes by me, I get a whiff of her perfume and a head toss that makes those braids go flying. Nice ass, too. Shit, man, I'm getting as bad as all the other horndogs around here.

What I don't get is why they called me down here if I don't have a visitor. Juvie's got the same situation. Well, I'm in no hurry to go back. Manny's been gassy all afternoon and there's no avoiding the sound or the stink of it, so I'll just sit here until it dawns on someone that I'm chilling in the visiting room without a visitor. I wonder who stood up Juvie. His mother? Father? That kid's messed up.

At the next table over, Cornell and his wife are holding hands and praying. His back is to me, but I can see she's got her eyes closed. The little guy grabs his opportunity. Scoots off his chair and goes running between the tables toward the place where they keep the kids' toys. Cornell's wife's eyes pop open. She gives the guards a quick look, then shouts "Ezekiel! Get back here or those *po*lice up there gonna arrest you!" Then it's Cornell to the rescue. "Hey, Zeke. You wanna see a magic trick?"

It's fun watching this kid, but it's painful, too. Emily said she wouldn't consider bringing Maisie here to visit. That's another thing I've tried not to pressure her about. In the pictures Emily sends me, her face is getting more angular and her hair looks thicker. Mom's taken care of her a few times—not as often as she'd like to, she says. Betsy's the alpha babysitter. Mom said Maisie's talking a blue streak now. "And singing, too. 'Row Row Row Your Boat,' 'The Eensy Weensy Spider,' the ABC song."

"Do you think she misses me?"

"I'm sure she does, but she's doing fine, sweetheart. Don't worry."

I *want* her to be doing fine. I just don't want her to forget me.

When Emily finally visits me again, she'll be surprised that I've grown a beard. It's come in pretty good—darker than the hair on my head, more brown than auburn with a little bit of gray in it. Not much, just a patch. I like the not-shaving part, but it gets itchy. You can't have scissors here, and I've given up trying to trim it with those stupid little nail clippers, so I'm just letting it grow. The Mountain Man look is in around here anyway. The only other time I grew a beard was when we were living out in California. Emily liked it—said it made me look sexy. Sometimes I think if we had just stayed out there instead of moving back east when Betsy got sick, then all the bad shit never would have happened. . . .

It's all women visiting tonight. Wives, girlfriends, moms. I think women are just braver than men. They'll put up with the pain of seeing one of their own stuck inside this place out of *love*. Most men won't. Or can't. Instead, they make excuses. My dad was a world-class excuse maker long before I landed here. That day he moved out on Mom and me, he sat down next to me on my bed, all buddy-buddy, and tried to convince me that his leaving was Mom's fault, not his, because she was a pothead and because our house was always messy and he just couldn't take it anymore. What was I? Thirteen? Even then I knew he was full of it. What I *couldn't* decide was whether he believed his own bs or whether it was just something he was trying to make me believe. Either way, I got it. Accepted that some kids got a soccer-coach-and-take-you-fishing kind of dad and some of us got the short straw. The indifferent dad and, in my case, the tenured professor who had gone off to play house with his pregnant grad assistant who lost the baby anyway. I mean, Jesus Christ, he had to leave because the house was messy? Hire a fucking cleaning lady! A professor screws his student and knocks her up? Use a condom, you fucking cliché! . . . Okay, stop! That stuff's ancient history. And anyway, what good does it do to keep prosecuting *him* when *I'm* here because of my own way-more-colossal failure as a father? I mean, fuck, Corby, when it comes to fathers who failed their kids, look who's talking. . . .

The steel door into this room starts its noisy opening. Whoever's about to come in is either my visitor or Junior's.

Nope. Don't know her. She looks around, then starts walking toward the kid.

But a few minutes later, the door grinds open again and there's Emily! I wave. She looks around the room, sees me, and waves back. Walking toward me now, she's smiling but I can tell from her eyes that she's upset.

"Wow. I can't believe you're here on a Thursday. I've missed you, Em. Can I get a hug?" She nods and we reach for each other, arms extended across the table. It's awkward embracing like that, plus her body feels rigid. And bony. Jesus, how much weight has she lost? When I rub the back of her neck, her body unclenches and she tears up. "Hey," I whisper.

She lets go before I do. Wipes at her eyes, composes herself. "Have a seat, Em. When they called me down here, I thought it would probably be my mom. And then, when nobody showed up, I thought, well, whoever it was must have changed their mind. But here you are. God, I can't believe it."

"I *said* I'd visit you when I could, Corby. I couldn't get here any sooner."

She sounds defensive. "No, no. I know how busy you are. I just meant I didn't expect you'd be able to come on a weeknight. Hey, remember, we have to keep our hands on the table where the goons can see them."

She glances over at the two COs up there on their platform, talking to each other. "I can't believe they have women guards here," she says. "Why would a woman want to work at a place like this?"

I shrug. "How's Maisie?"

"She's okay."

"Still have her ear infection?"

"No. She finished her amoxicillin a few days ago so I'm sure it's cleared up. She's been more needy, though. She really enjoyed those two days when I stayed home with her, but now every day on the way to daycare she starts whimpering. And she keeps claiming that another kid is pinching her. Mrs. Matteson says it's not really happening."

"That's weird. Why would she make up something like that?"

"Who knows? Anxiety, maybe. Either that or she might be trying to guilt-trip me. When I picked her up this afternoon and told her Amelia was going to take care of her tonight, she started claiming that her ear hurts again. I'm sure she's faking it, but I still felt like Bad Mother of the Year when I drove off. I mean, what if her ear *does* hurt? What if some bratty kid *is* pinching her?"

"Wouldn't it be easier if you visited on the weekend? It's busier then but—"

"I'm here tonight because I can't visit this coming Saturday. I'm at that all-day curriculum conference in Sturbridge I told you about. I'm more or less expected to go because I'm the math coordinator. The district's going all in on this Eureka program next year, so they want a couple of us to try it out and report back about how it went. And Sunday's the day I catch up with all the things I have to let go during the week."

I nod, commiserating. "Marcia going with you to the conference?"

"No. She's on child-rearing leave. I told you that, Corby."

"Yeah, I guess you did. So you're flying solo then?"

"No. The new teacher and I are riding up together."

"New as in first-year teacher? How's she doing?"

"*He's* doing great. The kids love Evan. He's a natural. He goes out and plays with them at recess. All my third-grade girls have crushes on him because he's young and cute. I had to intercept love notes from two of them this week."

It's the first time she's fully smiled since she got here. Maybe someone else is crushing on this Evan, too. "So is this guy right out of college?"

She shakes her head. "He taught at another school for three years, but he was low man on the totem pole, so when their enrollment went down, he got RIF'd."

"Laid off, right? You teachers and your acronyms. How old is he?"

"Twenty-four, I think. Maybe twenty-five."

"Married?"

"Single. Well, divorced. Why?"

"No reason. Just wondering. Hey?"

"What?"

"I love you so much, Emily."

"Love you, too," she says, but she looks uncomfortable saying it.

A disturbance at the far end of the next table distracts us. "But *listen* to me, Mom! Just *listen* to me!" It's Juvie, shouting at his mother. She says something to him that you can't hear. "Yeah, but you're not even listening to me!" He's got everyone's attention, including the COs.

"They had no business putting that kid in this place," I tell Em. "He's hostile and I think he may be cutting himself. He gave me some shit when we were waiting to come in here. He doesn't even look old enough to be in prison."

"They arrested him on his eighteenth birthday," Emily says. "I was talking to his stepmother when we were waiting to be let in here. Do you know what he did?" I shake my head. Not sure I want to know. "He took his father's gun, walked to the dog pound near where they live, and shot six dogs who were out in their pens."

"Jesus Christ, what was *that* about?"

She shrugs. When I look over there, Juvie's got his face against the table. He starts choking back these strange, hiccupy sobs. The stepmother reaches out to comfort him, then must remember the rule: no touching except for the beginning and ending hugs. Her hand freezes in the space between them. You'd think one of the COs would go over there, try to calm things down, but they stay put and stare. From her perch, Butch calls, "Quiet over there. Being able to have visitors is a privilege!"

Shaking her head, Emily says, "I hate this place. How can you stand it?"

"I didn't think I could at first." Jolted back to that suicide-watch cell, I flinch. "But you figure it out, you know? Learn the ropes, keep yourself busy. Calculate who to trust and who not to. I've been going to the library, doing a lot of reading. I applied for a job there, but I'm still on a waiting list. Hey, can I ask you something?" She nods. "I notice you're not wearing your rings. Is that—"

"I left them in the car because I knew I was going to have to go through that metal detector. I forgot they have lockers where you can put all your stuff."

"But what about when you're not here? Do you wear them at school? Or when you go to the grocery store?"

"I don't have time to go to the grocery store anymore, Corby. I order online and have our groceries delivered."

"Yeah, but—"

"The answer is yes. I still wear them because we're still married."

She seems annoyed that I asked, but I'm in it now so I might as well go for broke. "Do you think we're going to be able to weather this? *Stay* married?"

She stares down at her hands on the table and keeps me waiting so long that I withdraw the question. "Moving on, do you notice anything different about me?"

"Your beard," she says.

"And? When I grew one before out in California, you liked it. Thought it looked sexy, remember?"

"Well, you kept it trimmed back then. Your hair's longer now and it doesn't look like you comb it much. You kind of look like the Unabomber."

Ouch. But I cover my feelings with a laugh. "Not exactly the look I was going for, but hey."

"I honestly don't know if we can weather this," she says.

"Is that why you're seeing Dr. Patel? Trying to figure it out?"

"Be fair, Corby. When you were seeing her those times, I didn't ask you what you two were talking about. What I discuss with her is private."

"No, you're right. But just tell me. Are you leaning one way or another? Because I know your mother's probably weighing in on—"

She looks up at me. "Stop it. My mother doesn't get a vote and—"

"How about me? Do I get one?"

She gets hives when she's stressed and there's a splotch blossoming on her neck now. "Stop pressuring me, Corby. I haven't decided anything, all right? I'm just living day by day, doing what I have to do. I don't have the luxury of focusing on the future, so I need you to stop this right now."

"Got it. Sorry. So tell me—"

She interrupts me to ask whether I know why she was the last one to enter the visiting room. I shake my head. "Because I kept triggering the stupid metal detector." Her voice is shaky and the splotch on her neck has spread. "He kept making me go through it again and again, and I kept telling him it was the machine, not me. But it *was* me. There was a Hershey's Kiss in my pants pocket and the foil kept triggering it. So I felt like an idiot."

"Oh, jeez. I'm so sorry, babe."

"But that stupid guard didn't have to treat me like I was trying to sneak something in to you. Plus, he was getting way too personal. 'Don't get your panties in a twist, Emily.' 'If your bra is underwired, maybe you should take it off and try again.' Ugh."

"He was saying shit like that? And calling you by your first name?

That's *way* out of line." Now *I'm* shaky. My hands are fists. "Did you get his name? Check out his name tag?"

"No, but another guard said his name. Perkins, maybe? It began with a *P*."

"Piccardy? Young guy in good shape? Blond, military-looking haircut?"

"That sounds like him."

"He's one of the newer ones, but he's already proven that he's a total dick. Struts around here letting everyone know he lifts competitively. I hear the muscleheads who hang out in the weight room can't stand him. Maybe I should write up a complaint. Let staff know the kind of stuff he was saying to you."

She shakes her head. "No, don't. It's not worth it."

"Let him get away with disrespecting my wife? No way."

"But it could come back at you. What if he retaliates?"

"So what? There's a procedure for stuff like this. And if he tries to give me shit, I'll have *two* things to grieve him about. I'm not powerless, Emily."

"I'm not saying you are, but please just let it go."

I answer her with a slight nod, which isn't the same as promising her. Maybe instead of writing him up, I'll confront him directly. I look around the room, fuming but trying not to let that jerk ruin our visit. That's when I notice what's going on with Angel and his girlfriend over there. With her back to the guards, she's managed to undo the top buttons of her blouse. She's got one hand still on the table and with the other, she's fondling her breast, fingering her nipple. Angel's got one hand on the table, too, and one hand under it. Well, hey bro, if you want to risk it, then go for it. I just hope Emily doesn't notice.

I look back at Em and take a chance on another touchy subject. "Oh, hey, before I forget, two Saturdays from now, they're having Family Picture Day again? They bring in a photographer and I thought maybe you and—"

She shakes her head. "She's not coming here, Corby. End of subject."

"Yeah, I figured you'd say no. Just thought I'd ask because I want to see her so badly. The separation's one of the roughest things about being here."

"You know what? Instead of thinking about what *you* want, why don't you think about how scary and confusing it would be for *her*." She's gritting her teeth. "She's three years old. She doesn't need to see the inside of a men's prison. And do you really want to memorialize your time in here with a father-daughter photograph—the two of you posed against these cheerful gray cinder-block walls, you wearing your prison scrubs? Not to mention that if I brought her here, she'd be exposed to hepatitis and MRSA and whatever else is in the air at this germ factory?"

"Emily, kids visit here all the time and I haven't heard of any of them getting sick or traumatized. Look at that little dude over there. He's not focused on this being prison. He's just happy to see his gramps and play with the toys over there in the kids' corner."

"I wouldn't want her touching *anything* in here, especially toys and books that every other kid's been handling. Let's change the subject."

"Babe, can I just tell you what I keep worrying about? That if she doesn't get to see me while I'm here, when I get out, she might not even remember me. That I'll say something to her and she'll hide behind your leg like I'm some stranger she needs to be afraid of."

"Oh, for Christ's sake, Corby. Give me a *little* credit, will you? We look at pictures of you on my iPad and my phone, mention you in her bedtime prayers. And those drawings you've been sending her? We put them in her 'Daddy folder.' Take them out and look at them sometimes. And her favorite—the ones of her and her dolls having their tea party? That one's Scotch-taped to her bedroom wall. She insisted."

"Well, lucky you, Emily. You can use Scotch tape. It's contraband here. I had to swipe a couple of globs of Manny's Fixodent so that I could stick my pictures of you and her to my wall. I don't think you understand how much it hurts not to see her."

She straps her arms around herself, tight as a straitjacket. "Oh, I think I can. I haven't seen my little boy since a year ago last April."

Her remark lands so hard that I jump up from my chair. It falls back
on the floor, making a racket. "Hey, table four!" Goatee calls from up on
his platform. "Pick it up and sit back down!"

"Yeah, no problem. Sorry."

Then Juvie—Solomon—starts up again. "Shut up! Just leave and don't
come back! *He* wanted me, but you never did! I wish *you* were the one who
died." His screams are bouncing off the cinder-block walls.

The guards rush over there and post themselves on either side of him.
"Visit's over, Clapp," Goatee Guy shouts. "Get up. You're going back to
your cell." When the kid refuses, they start pulling him off his chair. He
resists. Grabs hold of the table with one hand and tries taking a swipe at
Butch with the other. Then Piccardy appears out of nowhere, grabs him
from behind, and squeezes him so hard that the kid cries out in pain.
As he's dragged toward the door kicking and screaming, he yells, "I hate
everyone at this place and when I get out of here, I'm going to get a gun
and kill all of you *and* your dogs!"

The kid's mother is crying. Emily looks so stricken, she may never
come back here. Butch reenters the room and announces that visiting
time is over. "Door!"

Everyone's company stands up: Mrs. Sikh, Angel's girlfriend, Praise's
wife and the little guy, Juvie's stepmom, Emily. When she gives me a quick
hug, I pull her closer, reluctant to let go of her. When I do, she joins the
others, walking like sheep toward the opening door. Emily's arm is around
the stepmom. "See you next time, Grampy!" Cornell's grandson calls to
him. He's the only one who doesn't seem upset.

After the room's been cleared of visitors, Butch says, "All right, offenders. Back to your units!"

"But we had ten more minutes," the Sikh says.

"You heard me," she says. "Back to your units."

But she forgot a step: the required post-visit strip search before we
go back.

Solomon's already left the building, but the rest of us wait our turn to participate in the DOC humiliation ritual. At least this CO is one of the older ones who's probably counting down the days to retirement. They don't hassle you the way some of the younger ones do. They keep it perfunctory. You just do what you need to do and try to go someplace else until they're done.

He points to the Sikh first. Tells him to take off his turban, too. After he searches him and sends him on his way, he examines Cornell, then Angel. I'm last. "You guys left early," he says. "Trouble in there?" As if he hasn't most likely watched what went down on that closed-circuit TV mounted to the wall or seen them haul Solomon out of there.

Without answering him, I take off my shoes and socks. Flare out my toes. Open my mouth wide to let him look down my throat. Touch my tongue to the roof of my mouth so he can see under it. Pull off my shirt. Drop trou. Cup my balls and lift them. Turn around, spread my ass cheeks, cough when he tells me to. "Okay," he says. I put my clothes back on and he sends me on my way.

Back in our cell, I flop down face-first on my mattress. "Who'd you have visiting you?" Manny asks. I tell him my wife.

"Yeah? I know you've been wanting to see her again. Good visit?"

I don't answer.

CHAPTER TWENTY-THREE

October 2018
Day 429 of 1,095

Officer Kyle Piccardy arrived at Yates after his uncle, Deputy Warden Geoffrey Zabrowski, got him transferred here from the women's prison, the better to keep an eye on him. According to the jailhouse scuttlebutt—which is often more reliable than not—Officer Piccardy, a newlywed not long out of the training academy, had been indulging in a little third-shift sex with one of the women in his custody. She was a pedigreed grifter who was open to a deal. Some strings got pulled somewhere and an agreement was brokered. In exchange for staying silent about the fact that Piccardy had knocked her up, she received a sentence reduction. I guess you'd call it a win-win-win situation. She waltzed out of prison and supposedly got the abortion, Piccardy got to save his job and his marriage, and Corrections dodged a front-page sex scandal. The only losers are the men of Yates CI who now have to put up with Piccardy.

Piccardy and his best buddy, Anselmo, are on shift tonight. Each is a dick, but when they're working a shift together, it's worse. Cavagnero's at the control desk, and when he pops open our doors, Piccardy shouts, "On the chow, girls! Chop chop!" Some of the other COs resort to name-calling, too—address us as vermin, losers, garbage—but Anselmo and Piccardy's ridicule is usually gender-based; to them we're ladies, bitches, pussies, cunts. One time, something set Anselmo off and he yelled down the tier that we should all tell our mothers we should have been abortions. Makes you wonder what kind of relationships these two have with the women in their lives.

Manny pushes our door open and asks whether I'm coming. I've got to take a leak, so I tell him to go ahead, I'll catch up. Toss him a shoe to keep the door propped open so I don't get locked in.

I pee, flush, remove the shoe. Leaving the cell, I run smack into Piccardy. I haven't seen him since the night Emily visited and the sight of him triggers my resentment about the way he treated her. "Propping open a cell door, Ledbetter? You looking for a ticket?" I bow my head and walk toward the others. "Hey! I just asked you a question. You think you can ignore an officer?"

I stop. He catches up and puts his face a few inches from mine—classic CO intimidation. "Sorry, Officer. I thought your question was rhetorical. But no, I'm not looking for a ticket."

"You thought my question was *what*?"

"Rhetorical. It just means—"

"I don't give a flying fuck what it means. You think your college-boy vocabulary makes you superior around here?"

Oh boy, here we go. "No, sir."

"Hey, by the way, how's your wife doing, Ledbetter? How's Emily?" My brain tells me to keep my mouth shut, but his saying her first name has just made it personal. "Tell her for me that the next time she comes here, she should remember to take the candy out of her pockets first."

I feel my heart pound and my adrenaline spike from an impulse to wipe that smirk off his fucking face. I'm not sure what's going to happen, but I know my body's in danger of overruling my brain.

"Yeah, she mentioned that you were hassling her," I tell him. "Making her go through the metal detector over and over and suggesting it might not go off if she removed her bra. I guess you'd call that sexual harassment. Right?"

He snickers, but at the same time wraps his hand around his stick in case he needs to start swinging it. I guess I'd be paranoid, too, if I knew a bunch of convicted felons would love to take a pop at me. "Let me assure you, Inmate Ledbetter, that when your wife kept triggering the detector, my actions were one hundred percent professional. If she told you otherwise, all I can say is I'm not responsible for whatever she was imagining. But I do feel sorry for the women whose men are here. They have needs, too, so if Emily enjoyed her little fantasy, then no harm, no foul."

I'm out on a limb, but I'm in it now, so I might as well finish. "I'm warning you, Piccardy. If you ever—"

He grabs me by my shoulders and backs me against the wall. "Better stop right there, Ledbetter." His face comes so close to mine, I can see his stubble and a small scar on his chin. "Because if what's about to come out of your mouth is a threat, me and some of my fellow officers can make your life here a whole lot harder than it is now." He lets me go and backs up a couple of steps.

It's all I can do to hold back from going at him, but I saw what happened to that con who threw his urine at a guard. They clubbed him so bad, his face was unrecognizable. "All I'm saying is—and this is a statement of fact, not a threat—all I'm saying is, if you hassle her again, I'll write you up." It sounds pathetic, even to me. Bother my wife and I'll squeal on you.

"Okay, you do that, big man. Make sure you spell my name right. There's two *c*'s in Piccardy. And my badge number is 1537. Think you can remember that or should I write it down for you?"

Up ahead, Anselmo's walking backward and watching us. "Everything okay back there, Officer?" he calls.

"Yeah, there's an annoying little gnat flying around me, but it's nothing I can't handle." Turning back to me, he says, "Now if I were you, Ledbetter, I'd catch up to your girlfriends before I send you back to your cell with one of those leftover court lunches that have been hanging around the office for a few days."

I catch up with Manny just before we reach the chow hall. "What was that about?" he asks. I tell him I'm not in the mood to play Twenty Questions so he can blab it all over the place. He puts on his hurt face. "Did it occur to you that I might have asked because I was worried about you?" he says. I don't answer him. I'm not pissed at Manny. I'm pissed at myself for not just letting it go. In trying to defend Emily, I handed Piccardy an opportunity to mock her *and* me. By challenging that idiot's authority, I might have just stepped in it.

Inside the chow hall, I go through the line. Get a sad little chicken leg that's more bone than meat, plus rice, canned peas, white bread, and cake. I sit between Angel and Lobo. Slouch over the table and shovel it in without really tasting it.

"What did Piccardy want back there?" Angel asks.

"He wanted to suck your dick."

"No, seriously, brah. Him and his sidekick keep talking to each other over there and looking at you."

"Not your problem," I tell him.

"Hope it's not yours either, but if I was you, I'd stay out of their way."

"Hey, Ledbetter?" Lobo says. "You gonna eat your cake?"

———

Back in B Block, I'm walking past the control desk when Lieutenant Cavagnero calls my name. "I want to talk to you about something, but I've got to finish this paperwork first. I'll call you up in a few."

"Got it," I tell him. Is this going to be about my exchange with Piccardy?

The squawk box clicks on maybe fifteen minutes later. "Come on up, Ledbetter," Cavagnero says. He pops the door and I walk up the corridor. Oh shit. Piccardy's standing at the desk, too. What is this about to be? A trial? A slap on the wrist? But I'm wrong; it's just Piccardy showing Cavagnero what an asshole he is.

"Average body fat for a guy my age is fourteen to sixteen percent, okay? And you know what mine is? *Six* percent. That's elite-athlete range. The calipers don't lie. You don't get a number like that from eating pizza."

"Well, good for you, Piccardy," the lieutenant says, like he doesn't care one way or the other. He takes another bite of the pepperoni slice he's been working on and nods to me. "Okay, Piccardy, I've got to talk to Ledbetter here. Why don't you take your dinner break?"

Realizing that I've been standing behind him, Piccardy sneers and tells Cavagnero that he's had to put me on notice. "The trouble with Ledbetter here is that he thinks it's an equal playing field between custody officers and convicted felons." And with that, he walks away.

"What's that about?" Cavagnero asks me. "No, on second thought, don't tell me. I'm off shift in another twenty minutes and I want to coast out of here without any complications, so change of subject. You know I supervise the grounds crew, right?" I nod. "Haven't you been looking for a job?" I tell him I'm on the waiting list for a library job but there haven't been any openings. "Well, with Boudreaux leaving, I'll have an open slot. We've got the big fall cleanup coming up and I don't want to be short-staffed. The others on the crew are good guys. I can see you fitting in. You interested?"

I think of Dr. Patel's advice: move your body. "Yeah, definitely. Thanks."

"You bet. We'll start you on Monday then. After breakfast, meet us at the barn behind the medical unit. I'll get you put on the list so they don't give you a hard time at the walk gate."

"Cool. I'll be there. Thanks again."

"Oh, and one more thing. Have you run into that young kid who's here? Solomon Clapp?" I roll my eyes and tell him I have. "He's been taking a lot of bullying down on tier two, so they're moving him."

"To this tier?"

"Yeah. Boudreaux's getting released tomorrow, so I thought maybe we could give Clapp his bed."

"Bunk in with Daugherty then?"

"Uh-huh. Do you think that would work?"

"I don't know Daugherty that well. He's a little shifty, but I don't think he's the bullying type. So yeah, that would probably be okay." Better the kid becomes Daugherty's headache than mine, which is where I thought Cavagnero might be heading.

"Okay, we'll give it a try then. Oh, and one more thing."

Uh-oh, another one more thing. Brace yourself, Corby.

"The kid's really struggling. Probably never should have been placed here."

"That's a 'definite,' not a 'probably,'" I say. "If you ask me."

"So what I thought was, I'd put him on the grounds crew, too. Keep him busy, get him outside, have him use up some of that negative energy he's got. And I figured you could keep an eye on him for me when, you know, I'm not always in the immediate vicinity. Not counting you and him, I got six other guys I've gotta keep an eye on, and when they're spread out over a ten-acre property, I can't be everywhere at once. So I'm going to pair you and the kid up."

I tell him no disrespect but I think that's a bad idea. Explain that the only contact I had with Juvie was when we were waiting to go into the visiting room. "He looked like he might have been cutting himself and when I asked him about it, he told me to mind my fucking business. Then, during his visit with his mom, he went off on her something fierce. Got so out of control that they had to drag him out of there kicking and screaming."

"Yeah, everyone says the kid's a loose cannon."

"You know who might have more luck dealing with him? Praise."

"Praise? Who's that?"

"Cornell Wiggins. Lester's son. Janitorial."

The lieutenant looks away, rubs his chin, then looks back. "Yeah, I'm not *asking* you to do this, Corby. If you want the crew job, you partner up with the kid."

"Guess I misunderstood then. I thought you were asking me my opinion."

He shakes his head. "I'm an officer and you're an offender, not my consultant."

What the fuck? First he consults with me about whether he should put the kid in with Daugherty. Then I'm *not* his consultant?

"I don't expect you to be his shrink or anything. I just need someone I can trust who'll supervise his work and watch out for him. Make sure he doesn't get bullied. So what do you say? You taking the crew job?"

Cavagnero and I have had a good relationship up to now. He's just called me by my first name, something no other CO has done. He said I was someone who could be trusted. And despite the strings he's attached, he's offering me a job.

"All right, I'll do it. But he's not going to like it."

"No? It might surprise you that, when I told him I was putting him on the crew, and that I might match you two up as work buddies, he asked me if you were the one who looked like Jase Robertson. And I said, 'Son of a gun. You're right. He does.' So he said, yeah, all right, if he *had* to be on the crew, which he didn't *want* to be, then okay, you could be his buddy."

"Come on, Lieutenant," I said. "I'm sure he doesn't know who I am."

"Yes, he does. Says he read it on your ID one night when you guys were waiting at the visiting room door."

I shrug. "So who's Jase Robertson?"

"Guess you're not a *Duck Dynasty* fan, huh? He's one of the commander's sons. Reddish-brown hair, bushy beard, needs a haircut. He's a good-looking cuss under all that brush."

"Well, I guess that's better than looking like the Unabomber," I said.

"What?"

"Nothing. Just thinking out loud. Anything else?"

"Yeah. Piccardy's pulled a double shift tonight. Whatever his beef is, just stay out of his way. I don't know him that well, but he doesn't strike me as the forgive-and-forget type. Someone you do not want to cross."

That evening, about an hour before lights-out, I hear a key in the lock. Manny and I are both stretched out on our bunks, reading. The cell door opens and, fuck, it's Piccardy and Anselmo. "Room inspection," Anselmo announces.

"During third shift on a Monday? That never happens," Manny says.

"Does now," Anselmo tells him.

After Piccardy orders me to unlock my storage box, he and his wingman start rummaging through my property, supposedly hunting for contraband. Piccardy grabs one of my grape Gatorades, twists the cap off, and helps himself to a couple of swigs. They toss everything onto the floor, but there's nothing they can nail me on. So far, they're leaving Manny's stuff alone, which is good for him. He's got lots of shit they could write him up for, but I'm pretty sure this performance is for my benefit.

Anselmo grabs my books, fans the pages, and tosses them onto the pile on the floor. Piccardy starts leafing through the drawings in my sketchbook, including the ones I've been working on for Maisie. He watches for my reaction as he rips them out, throws them on the floor, and "accidentally" spills Gatorade on them. But I hold it in, keep my face expressionless. I'll be goddamned if I'll give him what he wants.

"Hey, those are for his kid," Manny protests.

"Yeah? Which one? The dead one or the one he *didn't* kill?" Piccardy says.

The remark makes me jump off my bunk, ready to fight. From the bunk above, Manny says, "Let it go, Corby."

"Stay the fuck out of it, Twinkle Toes," Anselmo warns him. "Unless you want us to rip into *your* shit."

Piccardy crouches and looks under my bunk. "Well, looky looky what we've got here, Officer Anselmo," he says. He pulls out the two thirteen-gallon garbage bags I've been using as part of my workout when we're in lockdown. As barbell replacements, they're kind of wobbly and take getting used to, but they do the trick as far as giving you a decent pump. Half the guys on the tier use water bags for exercise. Technically, they're contraband, but most of the COs let it go as long as they're kept out of sight. "Pick up that one," Piccardy orders me, nudging the bag on the left with the toe of his boot. When I do, he unfastens the set of keys from his belt and slashes the bag. Water gushes out onto my feet and spreads across the floor. "Now pick up the other one," he says. I don't.

"Something wrong with your hearing, Ledbetter?" Anselmo says. "Officer Piccardy just gave you a direct order."

When I pick up the second bag, Piccardy rips a gash in that one, too. As soon as the bag is empty, he nods at Anselmo and the two of them slosh to the door. "Have a nice evening, ladies," Piccardy says. "And Ledbetter, tell Emily I said hi."

There's over an inch of water covering our cell floor now and half the property they've pulled out of my box will probably have to be tossed. It's going to be a bitch to mop everything up. My laundry just came back today, so it kills me to have to throw my two clean towels and my government-issued sweatshirt onto the mess to sop it up. I don't know whether this is the end of it or whether he's going to write me up for having the contraband bags. "You just witnessed that whole thing. If I file a complaint about them, will you back me up?" I ask Manny.

He shakes his head. "It's two officers against two offenders. Even if their superiors believe us, they won't admit it. It'll just get dismissed and those idiots will ratchet up the retaliation. You can't win against them, Corbs. That's how it works in here. Let it go."

When I look down at the mess Piccardy made of Maisie's drawings, a cartoon heron looks back up at me. *Tell Emily I said hi. . . . Which one? The dead one or the one he* didn't *kill?* . . . I have half of a pad left and three or four pencil stubs. After the ruined drawings dry off, I'll copy them. Improve on them, too. I'm not going to let Piccardy defeat me.

Tossing and turning in my bunk after lights-out, I think about how much I'd like a benzo and a chaser right about now. I recall that thing Cavagnero said about Solomon: the kid almost goes out of his way to get bullied. . . . This grudge Piccardy has against me started when I defended Emily's honor after she told me not to, so maybe I went out of my way to ask for trouble, too. Why? Isn't having to be stuck in here for three years punishment enough without kicking the hornet's nest? . . . But can I *ever* be punished enough for having killed our little boy? Lieutenant Cavagnero is right. If it's not too late, my best bet would be to steer clear of them both. And Manny's probably right, too. The way the system works in here, I couldn't win against Piccardy, even if he wasn't the deputy warden's nephew.

In my dream that night, I'm not in prison. Piccardy is walking ahead of me on an unfamiliar street. I tap him on the shoulder, and when he turns around, I cold-cock him. He staggers, then falls flat on his back. His arms and legs flail as if he's an overturned beetle. I wake up smiling.

CHAPTER TWENTY-FOUR

October–November 2018
Day 443 of 1,095

My new job on the grounds crew means six hours of freedom from the confines of our cell, fresh air to cleanse my lungs of the stagnant junk everyone breathes inside the block, October sunshine, and the reassuring sound of the river passing by at the back of the property. And since the work is physical—mowing and raking, picking up litter, sweeping and hosing down the walkways—I start sleeping better. Occasionally I'll make it all the way through the night now, a minor miracle.

At noon, when Lieutenant Cavagnero blows his whistle, we walk back to the barn and he passes out our bag lunches. They're way better than the stale court lunches we probably would get otherwise. Cavagnero is friends with the culinary arts teacher who has his students make them for us. The day before, we got Italian hoagies and the day before that, it was BLTs. Bacon at this place? I thought I was dreaming. Today it's chicken salad on a roll, chips, and an oversized oatmeal cookie.

I like the other guys I'm working with—Israel, Tito, Ratchford, Harjeet, Pacheco, and Spence. They're a good-natured bunch, easy to get along with. And of course, Manny's got the scoop on all of them. Israel's a former drug trafficker—a federal prisoner being housed here while he waits for his trial to start. Harjeet, who's Indian, is in for credit card fraud. He's the grandson of an old movie star, Sabu the Elephant Boy. There's a John Prine song about Sabu, but Harjeet says he's never heard it. Ratchford's doing time for bigamy. Two wives, eight kids. Manny says that back in the eighties, Spence was promised he'd be the next big thing in professional wrestling. After his career tanked, he started doing heroin and drifted into porn. The sex-crime cops nailed him after he performed in a film about a threesome with two sisters who turned out to be sixteen and seventeen. Statutory rape times two.

Angel says Tito's a former gang member who turned Pentecostal. Angel was working the parking lot at some tent revival thing, he says, jacking shit from unlocked cars when he poked his head in the tent to see what the commotion was. "And I seen the spirit coming over Tito. I'm telling you, that was some spooky shit. First, he stands there shakin' and bakin'. Then he drops to his knees and howls like a motherfucking coyote. And when the preacher put his hand on his shoulder, Tito starts babbling in some crazy language I never heard before. And I grew up in the Bronx. I didn't know there was a language I *hadn't* heard."

When I suggested that Tito must have gotten paid for that performance, Angel said, "Hey, I seen what happened and you didn't, Ledbetter. What makes you the expert?" I feel appropriately chastised for sounding like my cynical father.

"Yeah, well, if the spirit entered him, it must have left later on, because he's in here for aggravated assault," Pacheco says. "Found out his girlfriend was cheating on him, tracked down the guy, and slammed his head against a wall a couple of times. They had to put the dude in a coma until the swelling in his brain went down." Someone at the table asks Pacheco how he knew all that. "Because the family offered to pay me if I fucked up Tito while he's in here. I wouldn't do it, though. I don't need commissary money that bad."

So work-wise, things are good. Of course, I might be singing a different tune when Solomon joins us.

Day 456 of 1,095

Dear Emily,

Thanks for sending me those pictures of Maisie. I loved that one of her in her bunny costume. Damn, that daughter of ours is a cutie!

Hey, good news. I finally got the sketch pads and charcoal sticks you ordered from Amazon a while ago. When an inmate gets a package, it has to be opened and examined first, so whatever comes in can sit in the mail room for days or even weeks before you get it. The Pony Express probably delivered things faster back in the day. But anyway, now that I have the drawing stuff, I'm thinking about doing a bunch of sketches that I can make into a kids' book for Maisie. Does she still love giraffes? Maybe I'll draw her a story about a giraffe family and put her in it. She can be their next-door neighbor or something—maybe best friends with one of the giraffe kids. I was thinking about putting Niko in the story, too, but decided not to. I drew one quick sketch of him and had to stop. It was too hard.

I started my new job a couple of weeks ago and I like it a lot. Next week this kid Solomon joins us. Remember him? The one who flipped out in the visiting room that time. Being his "work buddy" was a condition of my getting on the crew. The lieutenant who supervises us is a nice guy—not your typical CO. He actually treats us like we're humans. He says he thinks I'd be a good influence on the kid. I don't know about that, but I'm pretty sure Solomon's going to be a high-maintenance headache for me, especially if the other guys start busting his chops. He gets a lot of that in here because of what he did and because he's such a fish out of water. To be continued.

Speaking of headaches, that dumbass CO who gave you a hard time at the metal detector has been riding my ass. I know you said *to drop it, but I couldn't let him get away with disrespecting you like that so I called him out. A couple of nights ago, he and his shift partner treated me to a surprise shakedown (an unannounced cell inspection). They didn't touch Manny's stuff, but they dumped all my property out of my box, threw it on the floor, and ruined some of it, including a couple of the drawings I'd started doing for Maisie. Nice guys, huh? I know it's useless to get into a pissing contest with the guards at this place because the deck is stacked in their favor. Still, if those two keep it up, I'm not just going to sit back and take it. Don't worry, though. Nothing I can't handle.*

How are your sessions with Dr. Patel going? I was thinking about that one time we saw her together. I remember when she asked you what you wanted to work on, you said you needed to figure out if you could ever forgive me. And if you couldn't, you didn't think we could stay married. I'll be honest, Em. It scares me to think you might be coming to that conclusion. Just remember, we have a history and we've shared a lot of love through good times and bad before we lost Niko. I've always needed you more than you needed me—I admit that—but I hope it doesn't mean you don't need me at all. I'm getting ahead of myself, but let's say we stay together while I'm in here. Maybe when I get out, we could sell the house, pull up stakes, and move back to SoCal. Just a thought. I liked hanging out with your dad and his girlfriend (forget her name) when we lived out there. Do you guys still talk on Sunday nights? If you think of it, ask your father about the job market out there. Maybe if it's better than the East Coast, I can get something in my field that offers a decent salary and health insurance. I know you won't have a problem getting work. Schools always need good teachers and you're one of the best.

Halloween's this coming Wednesday, right? Next thing you know it will be Thanksgiving and then Christmas. No inmate visits on either of those days, same as last year, so that a lot of the staff can be home with their families. Nothing special about the holidays for us—they're just regular days. I wish to hell I could be with you and Maisie for Christmas, trim the tree and all that stuff, but after my three years are up, I'll be home again to celebrate.

I hope you're having a good week, Em. I know it can't be easy covering all the bases while I'm stuck in here unable to lighten your load. By the way, have you gotten your oil changed yet? If that red light's still on, you don't want to risk blowing the engine. That's all you'd need! Well, anyway, Happy Halloween. I'm glad you're not going to take Maisie trick-or-treating. Safer this way.

Love you babe,
Corby

(440 days down, 655 to go)

———

Dear Corby,

Hi. I'm sorry I've been missing your calls. I've been wanting to write back since I got your last letter. It's 4:45 on Sunday afternoon and I finally have some time. My mother's taken Maisie to a performance of The Nutcracker and after that to supper. My schoolwork is done, I've paid some bills, vacuumed the house, and washed the kitchen floor. (Mom's made two remarks about it being sticky in spots.) The only thing left on my to-do list is getting the oil changed. I'm not even sure those lube places are open on Sunday, let alone after five. Don't worry. It will get done.

I'm glad you finally got those drawing supplies. I love your idea about the giraffe family. Maisie will, too. I hope you're still enjoying your outside crew work now that you're in charge of Solomon. That night he lost it and they made the rest of us leave early? His step-

mother, Adrienne, came up to me in the parking lot. She asked if I had a few minutes because she really needed someone to talk to. I just wanted to get home, but after what happened in there, how could I say no? So the two of us sat in my car for half an hour. Boy, did I get an earful! I hope he doesn't drive you crazy.

Corby, I want to respond to some of the things you wrote in your last letter, but I hear my mother's car in the driveway. They're home earlier than expected, so I have to go. I'll finish this letter after Maisie goes to bed.

Okay, I'm back. Mom said Maisie took a long nap during The Nutcracker, *so I couldn't get her to sleep until after nine. Like I said, I need to reply to some of the things you wrote in your last letter, and if I don't get it done tonight, there'll be no time to finish it during the week.*

First of all, I guess I forgot to tell you that my father and Ana broke up last year. Dad relocated to San Miguel de Allende in Mexico. There are a lot of wealthy expats from the US there so he gets plenty of carpentry jobs. He seems happy.

Corby, I'm not *selling the house. Moving back to California with you and Maisie is off the table. Niko's death would be with us in California, too. So would your record. You can't just drive away from that either. Sorry to be so blunt, but assuming otherwise is just magical thinking.*

You ask how my work with Dr. Patel is going. It's been worthwhile, but really challenging having to confront the fact that

Sorry, Corby, but I have to get to bed. I probably shouldn't have poured myself a glass of wine when I sat down to finish this. The next thing I knew, I woke up drooling with my head on the table. Not pretty!

Okay, it's Monday morning and I'm at school. My class has back-to-back specials—music and gym—so I have about ninety minutes.

I usually use this time to correct papers, but I really want to get this letter finished and off to you. The kids' journals and their quizzes on adding and subtracting fractions will have to wait.

As I started to say, my work with Dr. Patel hasn't been easy but it's been helpful. She's getting me to face a lot of things I might prefer to avoid. Can I find a way to let go of the anger that still lives beneath the grief I feel about losing Niko? Can I forgive you—for Maisie's sake, and for yours and mine? I don't know yet. That's what's so hard about this whole thing—so freaking confusing. Until the day you did what you did, you were a great dad. Warm and loving, the fun parent. It was obvious how crazy the twins were about their daddy and sometimes I envied that.

I need to be honest with you about something else. After you went to prison, I met with a divorce lawyer. Just one time. I decided to postpone making a decision until after you're released. Whether or not I eventually pursue it will depend on some of the things I mentioned that I'm working on. And I will need proof of your continuing sobriety. If you start using or drinking again, that will be a dealbreaker. But for now, and for the rest of your incarceration, you and I will stay married.

I want to address something else you said in your letter: that you've always needed me more than I've needed you. I don't think in those terms, Corby, but I feel your absence and sometimes it's painful. You're not in our bed (snoring), you're not in the kitchen making breakfast, you're not picking out something for us to watch on Netflix. Last week, after Maisie went to sleep, I was putting the photo album we'd been looking at back on the shelf when an envelope of loose pictures fell out—photos from that first summer when we started dating. One of those pictures has always been my favorite. We were at the beach near the end of the summer. You were standing at the water's edge, staring out at the waves. Just as you turned back and saw me, you broke into a beautiful smile and I snapped your picture.

You've told me more than once that you knew you loved me and wanted to marry me from that very first summer. If you had said that back then, it might have scared me off because I was falling in love with you, too, and it disoriented me. You were funny and cute and the sex was amazing. I had never felt like this with any other guy. But I was about to go back to the West Coast, so maybe this would just be a summer thing. Then, back at school in the middle of the semester, I opened the door and there you were. You had left school and driven all the way across the country because you needed me. And that was when I knew I needed you, too. Since those pictures from that first summer fell out of the album, I've looked at them a bunch. They draw me back to those people we used to be—just kids, really, with no idea how hard and complicated life can get.

With a hug,
Emily

CHAPTER TWENTY-FIVE

—

November 2018
Days 461–63 of 1,095

Solomon doesn't join the crew until halfway through my third week on the job. I brace myself, assuming he's going to be a defiant pain in the ass, but now he seems more sad than hostile. Maybe prison life's ground him down. November means sweatshirt weather, so I can't see whether that cut on his arm has left him with a nasty scar or whether he's carved any fresh ones. I don't bring it up. It's like Cavagnero said, I'm only expected to supervise his work, not be his shrink.

On the day Solomon joins us, Lieutenant Cavagnero has us raking leaves. He divvies up the property among us and hands out our rakes and work gloves. Solomon and I are assigned the north lawn, from the main building down to the security fence, probably the easiest job because it means raking a downward slope. I divide our section in two and ask Solomon whether he wants the right side or the left. He shrugs, so I tell him to rake the left side, and that we can take a five-minute break after the first half hour. "That sound all right to you?" He shrugs again.

His raking is slow and haphazard—he's being passive-aggressive, I guess. He refuses to wear his work gloves, even after I warn him about blisters. The section of lawn he's raked still has plenty of leaves on it when, after not even ten minutes of work, he throws down his rake and sits on the ground, his legs bent and his head resting against his knees. I'm not sure, but he might be crying. Rather than telling him to get back to work or asking whether he's okay, I just keep raking. He sits there for several more minutes. Then he stands, picks up his rake, and starts working again.

By the time Lieutenant Cavagnero comes by to check on us, I'm near the bottom of my section and Solomon isn't halfway down the slope yet. Cavagnero asks me how he's doing. "Let's just say he's a work in progress," I tell him. "No outbursts yet, so that's good. Right?" He nods, then reminds me that Solomon and I are a team, so if my teammate's work isn't up to par, we're both accountable. Before I can voice an objection, he climbs the slope and stops to talk to Solomon. Whatever he's saying to him, Solomon, staring down at the ground, is nodding in agreement.

By eleven or so, despite all the sanctioned and unsanctioned breaks he's taken, Solomon has managed to rake to the bottom of the hill. "Good job," I tell him. "But let's go back up to the top and take one more pass to catch the leaves we missed." When he protests, I tell him this round will go much faster. "So let's go." He stays put on the bottom of the hill while I climb to the top and start raking his side. "Hey!" he calls. "You're not my boss!" When I don't answer him, he starts up the hill, rake in hand, and joins me. By the time we've made it to the bottom again, the hill looks pretty good. "Gives you a sense of accomplishment, doesn't it?" I say.

"Not really."

At lunchtime, my charge sits apart with his back to the rest of us. "Hey, Solomon," I call over to him. "You want to join us?" He shakes his head. Takes his sandwich out of the bag, pulls it apart, and drops it back in. The only thing I see him eat is his cookie.

"What's up with him?" Ratchford asks. "He antisocial or something?"

"Solomon likes to keep his own counsel," I say.

"How old is he?" Harjeet wants to know. I tell him he's eighteen.

"Ain't that the kid who shot those dog-pound dogs?" Tito asks. The others wait for my answer, but I just shrug. "Woof woof," one of them says under his breath. I'm relieved when the conversation shifts to who'd be the better lay: Shakira or Nicki Minaj?

Cavagnero gives us thirty whole minutes to eat, talk, and relax—a luxury compared to the way we get shortchanged in the chow hall. When lunch is over, he hands each of us two clear plastic garbage bags. Our afternoon task is to finish raking our sections and bag the piles of leaves. I think about the time I swiped two of this same kind of bag when I was planning my suicide, and more recently, when Piccardy slashed the water-filled ones to remind me that he had the authority to harass my wife at the metal detector, and if I complained about it, he'd make me regret it. Asshole.

Solomon's afternoon productivity is even less than it was in the morning, but we manage to get the leaves bagged without any major problems. I remind myself that he's probably never had to do much physical work before and that I need to bring him along gradually. Confronting him like a foreman is not the way to go with this kid.

Just before quitting time, a dozen or so wild turkeys strut across the lawn, pecking away at grass and bugs. I give them a quick look, but Solomon stops and stares at them. I watch him watching. He's mostly focused on a mother hen and the four chicks who hurry behind her. What's going on in his brain right now? Does he think they're cute? Is he fantasizing about shooting them? Remembering his birth mother? It's impossible to know what's in that screwed-up head of his.

When the whistle blows, we drag our bagged leaves back to the barn, hand in our rakes, and start walking back to our buildings. I'm walking a little ahead of Solomon when he says, "Hey, wait up." I stop and he catches up. I ask him what he wants. "There's a library here, right?" I nod. "Where's it at? And don't try and bullshit me either."

"Main building, top floor. Why would I bullshit you?"

He says none of the guys on the other tier would give him a straight answer. "'It's in the building behind the chow hall,' they'd tell me. Or, 'It's in the basement of C Block.' But C Block doesn't *have* a basement and the only thing behind the chow hall is that brick thing where they burn garbage. When I got a pass and went looking for it out there, some lady CO yelled at me for not being where I was supposed to be. I tried to tell her that was where they said it was, but the bitch told me I was lying and gave me a ticket."

"Were you raising your voice when you tried to explain?"

"No." His bottom lip pokes out and his eyes go glassy. "Maybe."

"Look, I saw the way you lost it that time in the visiting room. You've got to get ahold of your temper. People shut down when you start yelling. And as for those clowns giving you bogus directions, they were just screwing with you because you're new. It's boring as hell around here and some guys will grab at anything to entertain themselves. And the more you show them they're getting to you, the worse they'll treat you." Despite what he's in here for, I feel bad for the kid. Still, I need to hold the line at being his work buddy.

"My new cellmate says there's a form where I can file a complaint against those guys for harassing me. Do you think I should report them?"

"For giving you bullshit directions?" I shake my head. "Choose your battles."

"But they did other stuff, too," he says. "Pissed on me in the shower. One guy stuck his hand in my mouth and tried to yank my braces off. And look at this." He lifts the back of his shirt to show me a purple bruise at the base of his spine. "I was out in the yard, minding my own business, and six or seven of those assholes put me in the middle of a circle and started shoving me back and forth. And the guard just stood there, not doing anything. Then I got kicked in the back and fell down. And now my fuckin' jaw clicks when I chew." He's in tears now. "And I didn't even do anything to deserve it."

You killed six defenseless dogs, is what I'm thinking. A lot of the guys in here have brutalized or killed their victims, but I'm willing to bet that even those guys have a sentimental attachment to their dogs.

"Well, you can write them up for assault, sure. You've got grounds. But if a captain or a deputy warden investigates your complaint, the first thing they'll do is go to the CO who was on duty when the incident happened. And he'll probably deny it or downplay it. Maybe now that you're on our tier, you should let it go. Daugherty's your bunkie, right? What does he say?"

"That I should sue the state for not protecting me. He knows a lot about prison law and can represent me. File court papers and shit, and he says my stepmother can pay him his fee by putting money in his commissary."

Manny gave me the scoop on Daugherty. His parents are in real estate, his sister's a corporate lawyer, and he's the family embarrassment. Got kicked out of UConn Law for dealing fentanyl, then got caught trying to bribe a witness who was going to testify against him. Around here, he comes off as the righteous defender of the wrongfully convicted, and since half the guys in here claim they're innocent, he's got a following. The families of whoever he's advising pay him by contributing to his account.

"Be careful about taking legal advice from Daugherty," I warn the kid.

"Why? He's a lawyer."

"He's not a lawyer. Went to law school but never finished. You know what a 'fish' is in here?" He shakes his head. "A new arrival who gets taken by a con man." The kid looks confused, but I need to end this conversation before I get sucked any further into the black hole of his neediness. "Don't quote me, but my guess is that Daugherty's more interested in getting your mom to feed his commissary account than he is in seeing you get justice."

"She's *not* my mother!" he protests.

Okay, whatever. I'm not getting into that with the kid. I tell him I'll see him on the crew tomorrow and start to walk away. But there must be a disconnect between my brain and my big mouth, because I look back and hear myself saying, "Tell you what. Our tier can get passes to the library every other Saturday from one to three. We can't go this coming Saturday, but if we both request passes for *next* Saturday, I'll walk you over there. Okay?"

"Okay. Thanks."

"You're a reader, huh? What kind of books do you like?"

"Fantasy and sci-fi, mostly. My favorite authors are Frank Herbert and George R. R. Martin. Did you ever read *Game of Thrones*?"

"Can't say that I have."

"What about *A Dance with Dragons*?"

"Nope. Didn't Frank Herbert write *Dune*? I read that one once."

"Everyone's read that one," he says. "I've read all the books in the Magnificent Dune Chronicles except *Heretics of Dune*. Do they have that in the library here?"

"Couldn't tell you. Hey, you were a few minutes late for work this morning. Try to get there the same time as everyone else. Because you don't want the other guys thinking you get special treatment. Okay?"

He doesn't answer.

The next day, we're raking again, but Solomon doesn't show up for work, on time or late. When I ask Lieutenant Cavagnero about it, he says Solomon told him he couldn't work because he's got bad blisters from the day before.

I throw up my hands in frustration. "Because he wouldn't wear his freakin' work gloves!"

"Patience is a virtue, Ledbetter. Give him time. How did you two get along yesterday?"

"Okay, I guess. He opened up to me a little at the end of the day. From what he was saying, he took some pretty rough abuse down there on tier two, but it went under the radar. Now that I've given it some thought, I'm not so sure putting him in with Daugherty was such a good idea either."

"No? Why's that?"

"He's giving the kid 'legal' advice and I don't necessarily think it's out of the goodness of his heart."

"Maybe I could get the room assignments switched. Have them put DellaVecchia in with Daugherty and the kid in with you."

I tell him I realize inmates don't get to make decisions about who rooms with whom. "But honestly, being Solomon's babysitter on the job is hard enough. Having to do it twenty-four seven would drive me nuts."

He tells me to relax—that he was just thinking out loud. "I guess we'll leave things the way they are for now. But I'll keep an eye on the situation."

Solomon's back on the job the day after that, but he's late again. When I call him on it, he says, "We live on the same floor. Why can't *you* get me up?"

"Because that's *your* responsibility, not mine. When the squawk box says it's twenty minutes until breakfast, you drag your ass out of bed like the rest of us. By the way, how are your blisters?" He says they still hurt. "Guess you should have listened to me about the work gloves, huh?" He shrugs. Under his breath, he calls me an asshole. Look who's talking, I feel like saying, but remind myself that I'm the adult.

The crew's job today is to spread grass seed. Each pair of workers is equipped with a wheelbarrow and five forty-pound bags of seed that we're expected to scatter by hand. Solomon and I are assigned to the stretch of lawn behind the medical building. I load four of the bags into the wheelbarrow, grab the handles, and tell the kid to pick up the last bag and follow me. I start wheeling toward our area, but when I look back, he's just standing there. "What's the matter?" I ask him.

"It's heavy," he says. "Why can't *I* use the wheelbarrow?"

Doesn't he realize there's a 160-pound load in there? "Be my guest," I tell him. I pick the bag off the ground and start walking. Behind me, I hear a couple of grunts, a few "motherfucker"s. When I look back, I see that he's tipped over the wheelbarrow. "Need some help?" I ask.

He says he guesses so. "Can we switch? These handles are hurting my blisters."

I look away so he doesn't see I'm grinning. "Sure. No problem."

When we get to where we're going, I rip open two of the bags and pour the seed into the wheelbarrow. Demonstrate how to scoop up a handful and scatter the seed with a flick of the wrist. He does a decent enough job at first, but then he starts getting lazy—pours handfuls of seed at his feet instead of scattering it. He tells me the wind will do it. "There is no wind,

Solomon. And it's supposed to rain tonight, so these little piles you're making are going to get wet and rot. You have to spread it."

"Get off my fucking case!" he shouts. But he complies. Does what he's supposed to for about six or seven handfuls, then stops. Asks how much longer before lunch. I look up at the sky and tell him that, from the sun's position, I'd say we've got another ninety minutes, give or take. He groans.

At noon, we head back to the barn. I suggest that Solomon join the rest of us and stop acting antisocial. He says it's not an act—that he *is* antisocial. Still, he doesn't turn his back on the crew this time. With this kid, every small gain is a win. The conversation with the other guys is lively—a lot of good-natured teasing and talk about football, but nobody speaks to Solomon and vice versa. I'm relieved that when lunch is over, nobody's made a crack about dead dogs.

Heading back to work, Solomon and I are stopped in our tracks by what we see in front of us: an amazing number of wild turkeys pecking away at the seed we'd put down. Two of the bolder ones are in the wheelbarrow, gorging themselves on the loose seed. "Let's count them," I tell him. "See if we get the same number." When I'm done, I tell him my number is sixty-eight. "How many did you count?" But he hasn't counted. When I follow his gaze, he's just been watching that same mother hen and her chicks from a few days ago. At least I think they're the same ones. Why is he so drawn to them?

CHAPTER TWENTY-SIX

November 2018
Day 469 of 1,095

This call originates from a Connecticut Department of Correction facility. If you wish to accept this call . . .

"Hey, Em. Thanks for picking up. How's your weekend going?"

"Okay." She reminds me about that math workshop she had to go to yesterday—the follow-up to the one back in September. "Maisie was ornery about having to go to Grammy's for the day," she says. "When we got there, she got out of the car and just stood there. So I had to pick her up and carry her inside with her whimpering and kicking my legs. But by the time I got back and picked her up, she was excited about the 'buberry' muffins she and Grammy had made."

"Yeah? How were they?"

"Raw in the middle and so salty, they were practically inedible. Mom said Maisie poured the salt in before they could measure it, but she just let it go."

"Really? Your mother let something go? Wow." I tell her I was talking to my mom yesterday, and she said she wished Em would call her more often to babysit—that she hasn't seen Maisie in almost a month.

"That's because the last time we visited Vicki, I smelled marijuana. I can't have her getting high if she's going to take care of my child."

Our child. "Did she know you were coming or did you just drop in? Because there's no way Mom would smoke weed if she was watching Maisie."

"I hope not," she says. "But maybe you can appreciate why I'd be a little sensitive about the possibility."

Ouch. It's fair, I guess, but it hurts. "Okay, I can address it next time I talk with her. Make it sound like it's coming from me, not you. All right?" I wait for her to answer and when she doesn't, I rush to change the subject. "So tell me about your conference. Was it worthwhile or a waste of time?"

"Fifty-fifty," she says.

"And you carpooled with that new guy again? How was that?"

"It was fun. I've gotten to know him a little better because we've both been 'test-driving' the new Eureka math program. He loves it; I have a few reservations, but I don't want to be unenthusiastic since the district's already bought into it."

"Yeah? What's his name again?"

"Evan. He's really a sweetheart."

But not your sweetheart, right? "And he's how old?"

"Twenty-five," she says.

"Didn't you say he's already divorced? Wow. What was that about?"

"I have no idea," she says. "What about you? Have you had any more trouble with that guard?"

I tell her no, unless I count dirty looks. Plus, he was off last week doing some kind of training.

"And what about your work crew? How's Solomon doing?"

"He's a challenge, but no meltdowns yet." I tell her about the wheelbarrow incident, his refusal to wear work gloves, how he doesn't interact with the other guys.

"Hey, by the way, remember how you said his mother gave you an earful that night when you and she talked in your car? What did she tell you? I'm trying to figure him out, but Solomon doesn't say much about his homelife."

"Well, first of all, Adrienne's his stepmother. His birth mother was an addict who had her parental rights revoked. When he was three, I think she said. Not long after that, she died of an overdose. There was no dad in the picture. Adrienne told me she and her husband had decided against children. Then the husband found out Solomon was going into foster care. He and the birth mother were both Wequonnoc, related somehow. So he felt like he needed to step in."

"Wait. Solomon's Wequonnoc?"

"Half anyway. Adrienne's husband wanted him to grow up with a consciousness of his Native identity. It was something he himself had been deprived of. I had never heard about this before, but until the seventies, it was fairly common for government agencies to separate Native kids from their families and put them in white boarding schools so they could be taught 'proper' values. Can you believe that?"

I tell her I heard something about that once. "So arrogant, huh? They assumed they were doing this for the Indigenous kids' benefit because the white way was the right way. Jesus! What else did the stepmother say?"

"That Solomon was difficult right from the start. Lying, stealing, violent tantrums. They felt way over their heads trying to deal with him. Had him in therapy since he was seven. And the older he got, the worse it became. She said his self-hatred was heartbreaking to witness, but it was hell being victimized by his rage. Then, two years ago, the husband, Gordon, had a heart attack on the golf course and died unexpectedly. Solomon told Adrienne he wished *she* was the one who had died. The husband's gun had been secured in a safe. She said she'd wanted to get it out of the house but hadn't done it yet. Solomon somehow got ahold of the combination. She says she still doesn't understand why he shot those dogs instead of her."

"He probably doesn't understand why he killed them either. Being inside that head of his must be a scary place. It must have been hard for you to have to hear all that. What did you say to her?"

"Not much. I pretty much just listened. Before she got out of the car, she suggested we exchange numbers, which we did. She's called twice, but I haven't had the strength to answer. Maybe that sounds selfish, but Dr. Patel tells me I need to respect my boundaries. Deal with my own challenges and let her deal with hers."

"That's good advice. And it's not selfish either. Hey, not to sound like a broken record, but did you get your oil changed yet?"

"Uh-huh."

"Where'd you take it? Jiffy Lube?"

"No, Evan changed it for me. He used to work at his uncle's service station when he was going to school. He knows a lot about cars."

Well, whoop-de-do. "What about the filter? If you change the oil but not the filter, it's like taking a shower and putting your dirty underwear back on." I don't mention that's something I heard once on *Car Talk*.

"Well, listen to you, Mr. Mechanic," she says, teasing me. "You can relax. Evan replaced that, too. I had bought the wrong kind, but he exchanged it for me." Jesus, this guy's like a superhero. Instead of saying anything, I bite at a hangnail on my left thumb. "He wouldn't take any money for the job, so I told him Maisie and I would take him out for pizza next weekend."

"Oh, yeah? Maisie met him?"

"Mm-hmm. She was shy around him at first, but after he finished with the car, he won her over. He had brought his dog, Jasper, with him. He showed Maisie how to make him sit for treats. She really got into bossing that poor dog around. 'Sit, Jasper! Sit! I said sit!' "

How many times had I suggested we get a dog for the twins to grow up with? But oh, no. They're too young for a dog. What if he bit one of them? Then Evan the Great brings *his* dog over and she's all yeah-rah-rah dogs! I'm suddenly aware that I've been biting the skin around my thumbnail and that it's bleeding.

"So he's what? Ten years younger than you?"

"Nine, actually. Why?"

"Nothing really. I just—"

The phone cuts off, which is probably a good thing. My point, Emily, is that he's too fucking young for you if that's where this is heading. I bang the phone back on the cradle and walk toward our cell. My thumb feels sore and it's still bleeding a little. Do I need to be worried about this guy? He services cars, charms little kids, even has a dog who doesn't bite. . . . I wonder whether she's told him about our situation—me being in prison and why. He'd better not be getting any ideas about the coast being clear. If he is, she'd better set him straight. No divorce for the rest of my time in here, she said. Or is that magical thinking, too?

"Door!" I call down the corridor. It pops and I enter our cell.

"Talk to your wife?" Manny asks. "How's she doing?"

"Good question," I tell him. "You got any small Band-Aids? I cut my thumb."

Later, after lights-out, I can't stop imagining him and Maisie playing with his dog. The three of them sharing a pizza at Tony's. Him sticking around after she puts Maisie to bed. The two of them having wine and one thing leads to another. . . .

But what's the point of working myself up? God, I miss her so much. Talking to her on the phone helps, but it makes it harder, too. And the times she's visited me, it's fucked-up having to hug her across a fucking table for a couple of seconds. I miss touching her, miss her touching me. . . . When the crew had lunch break the other day, I overheard Spence talking to Tito about how he and his girlfriend sometimes do phone sex when they talk. She gets him hot and bothered for ten minutes, then he goes back to his cell, finishes what she started, and gets a great night's sleep. There's no way Emily would do something like that—especially since I told her the goon squad can listen in on our conversations. . . .

I think back to that first summer when we couldn't get enough of it. When we were so hungry for each other's bodies that we fucked whenever and wherever we could, living in the moment without a clue about where this might be going. And when we were living out in California, too. Sometimes we'd make love twice in the same day. And then she got that call from her mother about her cancer. We drove back east and that was that.

In my dream tonight, she and I are on one of those mansion tours. I put my finger to my lips, take her by the hand, and we sneak away from the others. Wandering through an upstairs hallway, she's afraid we might get caught but I'm aroused. At the end of the hall, there's an unlocked bedroom. We go in, undress, and fall together on the bed. I kiss her breasts, her nipples, pass my fingers and then my tongue against her wetness. She's ready, I'm ready. When I mount her, she guides me inside and I move in and out of her, slowly at first, then faster, then slow again, then so fast that I'm right at the edge and . . .

I wake up ejaculating. Reach down and touch my stuff. I can't remember the last time I had a wet dream.

———

It's pouring out and it's supposed to last all day, so work gets canceled. Manny's got another migraine, his third since we've been cellies. I've learned from the other two times that there's nothing I can do for him other than not make noise. I'd take a nap but it's only midmorning and I'm not tired. I guess I'll read.

Slim pickings, though: one of my aunt Nancy's Holy Roller books or *Native American Genocide: The U.S. Government's Systematic Efforts to Eradicate Indigenous Populations.* I've renewed that one three different times now without even cracking it open. I'm not sure why I've been resisting it. But now that I know Solomon's part Wequonnoc, it gives me a little extra incentive to read what it says. Not that I think it can provide any answers to why he's so messed up, but at least I might be able to get a little historical context. What's that saying? The past is prologue? Well, whether it is or isn't, who could have predicted that that messed-up kid would shoot those defenseless dogs and wind up here?

I settle in as quietly as I can and open *Native American Genocide.* It says one of the authors, Dr. Aurora Eubanks, is a professor emerita of anthropology at Spelman College. "My fight for racial justice was activated on March the seventh, 1965, during the 'Bloody Sunday' march to Alabama's state capital. In the company of my parents, I was clubbed by a white police officer as we attempted to cross the Edmund Pettus Bridge in Selma. I was twelve years old."

The coauthor, Malinda Bravebird, describes herself as a naturopathic doctor, a writer and podcast host, and the Medicine Woman of the resurgent Wequonnoc Nation. "My ancestry is Indigenous, African, and Irish; of these three, my identity as a ninth-generation First Nation woman is the strongest. I am currently researching the discrepancies between Native American and European concepts about humans' relationship with the land. Guided by my totem animal, the blue heron, I practice stillness and patient observation as I investigate the deeper truths that are revealed to us in the natural world."

Her mention of the blue heron sends a shiver through me. Takes me back to that bird on the rock in the river that was staring me down as I tried to decide whether I should try to get my blood test results tossed or turn myself in. As much as I hate prison life, I've never felt that I was dealt an injustice when I had to come here.

The book says the original inhabitants of what later became known as North America arrived from Asia via a land bridge that existed between what is now Alaska and southern Siberia, and that by the time western Europeans landed on the shores of what they misnamed the "New World," the continent had been inhabited for thousands of years by Indigenous people. At the dawn of the seventeenth century, it says, an estimated seventy thousand to a hundred thousand First Nation people lived in what is now southern New England.

I skim the parts about the importance of the rivers, riverbanks, and the Atlantic's coastal shores in sustaining the Native communities, but slow down when I read about a battle between two brothers who belonged to the most powerful of the area's tribes, the Wequonnoc.

Following the death of Chief Matwau, his eldest son, Achak, was installed as the Wequonnoc Nation's new sachem, to the disgruntlement of Achak's younger brother, Samuel, whose skills as a warrior, a hunter, and a negotiator were considered superior. A group of about seventy warriors and their families who were loyal to Samuel split from the tribe with him. Calling themselves the Shetucket, they became the sworn enemies of the larger and more powerful parent tribe.

Same old same old, I think, all the way back to Cain and Abel. Growing up, I always wanted a brother, but maybe I was better off as an only child. . . . I feel a sudden pang thinking about Maisie, a twin who, because of me, is now an only child, too. I've read that her conscious memories of her brother will fade away, but what about her subconscious memories? Does she feel Niko's loss without being able to understand what it is? Does she remember him in some deep-seated way? There's no way to answer these questions, so I tell myself to get back to my book.

It says the influx of Europeans seeking religious freedom, known as the Great Puritan Migration, took place between 1620 and 1640. The new arrivals believed in the concept of God-given white supremacy, which they backed up with the power of the flintlock, the musket, and the blunderbuss. Was that the start of it? America's love affair with the almighty gun that's alive and well today?

The authors zero in on the Connecticut Colony, a splinter group from the Massachusetts Bay congregation, who began claiming land that the Wequonnoc tribe had hunted, fished, and cultivated for hundreds of years. The Colonists declared war on the tribe, aiming to annihilate them. To that end, they enlisted the help of the smaller Shetucket tribe, whose leader, Chief Samuel, calculated that there was more to be gained by aligning themselves with these "pale strangers" than by resisting them. Trained and armed with muskets, thirty Shetucket warriors joined ninety British soldiers in a surprise early morning attack on the fortified Wequonnoc village. They set fire to the community's wigwams and shot many of the tribesmen and women attempting to escape.

The leader of the Wequonnoc genocide was Captain John Woodruff, a British army officer who had crossed the Atlantic during the Great Puritan Migration. In the days that followed, Woodruff's men hunted down, captured, and enslaved many of the tribespeople who had escaped.

Wequonnoc women and girls were forced into service as domestics in the homes of British settlers in the Connecticut Colony. To guard against reprisals or revolts, the colonists shipped Wequonnoc men and boys to the West Indies, where they were exchanged for African slaves who were brought north to serve masters in New England.

So slavery didn't just happen in the American South during the eighteenth and nineteenth centuries. It began in New England as soon as white Christian settlers arrived. According to what I'm reading, these settlers thought of Native people as "savages" closer to animals in the wild than to women and men of Christian faith—this despite the reality that, like them, Indigenous tribes had a rich culture, a religion of their own, and a well-established language. The bottom line was that there was profit to be made, not only from the seizure of Indigenous land but also from the capture and selling of Native people or, later, by sequestering them on reservations.

I think about some of the shit I see here at Yates. The ratio of Black and Brown prisoners to Caucasians; the white supremacist assholes who try to recruit other whites for the race war they're sure is coming; the length of Lester Wiggins's sentence. Before they sent me here, I was aware that Blacks got a raw deal in the criminal justice system. That was something I knew but didn't think too much about. Now it's something I'm starting to feel. And it doesn't feel good.

Eubanks and Bravebird's book points out that, by the nineteenth century, as Wequonnoc descendants assimilated into white or Black families, the Connecticut Historical Society honored John Woodruff by commissioning and installing a bronze statue of him on what had once been the sacred burial ground of the Wequonnoc Nation. And that during the twentieth century's Great Depression, the WPA funded the building of a four-lane road that, upon completion in 1949, was dedicated as the John Woodruff Parkway.

How many hundreds of times had I driven on the Woodruff Parkway without ever knowing or caring who John Woodruff had been? He'd orchestrated a mass murder, enslaved the survivors, stolen Indian land with bullshit treaties he knew would hold up in white men's courts. That made him a hero? They parked a statue of him on top of the buried bones of his victims? Named a four-lane road after him? Jesus Christ.

In school they taught us that *we* were the good guys—the descendants of brave freedom seekers who had crossed the Atlantic and established their claim to the "New World." *Land where our fathers died, land of the pilgrims' pride, from every mountainside, let freedom ring.* But we *weren't* the good guys. That was just propaganda. I recall what Javier said when he checked out this book for me: that "the man" likes to rewrite history because the truth makes him look bad. And he's right. To us white victors had gone the spoils *and* the right to flip the narrative.

In my head there's a swirl of all I've been seeing and hearing and experiencing at this place: *You ain't turning me into your Uncle Remus or your magical Negro. . . . Hey there, handsome! I'm Jheri Curl. Like what you see? . . . You must have figured out by now that the spics, the spades, and the half-breeds outnumber us. Now that presents a clear and present danger. . . . I hate everyone at this place and when I get out of here, I'm going to get a gun and kill all of you* and *your dogs! Day by day by day by day by day . . .*

CHAPTER TWENTY-SEVEN

November 2018
Day 476 of 1,095

On Saturday afternoon, Solomon's waiting outside my cell. Through the tray trap, he calls in, "Library time!" Suddenly, he's Mr. Prompt.

A few minutes later, we're in the main building, climbing the stairs to the third floor. "What did you do anyway?" he asks. I know what he wants to know, but I don't respond. Make him say it, which he does. "What are you in prison for?"

"Yeah, look. That's one of the unspoken rules around here. You don't ask another inmate shit like that. Guys talk around here and everyone's charges are public record anyway. But it's not cool to confront someone face-to-face about what he's doing time for."

"Why not?"

"Well, I guess it's the trust thing. At this place, you don't want to volunteer too much about yourself because it could be used against you. And I guess because . . . if you've done something you're ashamed of, it's painful to have to verbalize it."

"Oh. Did you kill someone? Is that it?"

Jesus Christ! Did he not just fucking hear me? I start taking stairs two at a time. Put some space between me and this annoying little shit. Once I've shown him where the library is, I'm going to keep my distance. At the top of the stairs, I take a left and he follows me down the corridor. "Hey, wait up," he says. I walk faster.

The library is in chaos: empty metal bookshelves huddled together in the middle of the large room, books stacked all over the floor. Lester Wiggins is the only constant; he's sitting in his wheelchair by the window, reading as usual with his index finger and his moving lips. I don't see Mrs. Millman, but her right-hand man, Javier, is up on a stepladder repainting the side wall. "Library's closed!" he calls, not bothering to look over his shoulder. "You can check books out, but you can't stay."

I tell Solomon to have a quick look around. Then I walk over to Javier. "Hey, Picasso. What would you call that color? Caterpillar-gut green?"

Javi turns around, chuckling. "Hey there, hombre. How's it goin'?"

"It's going." Like most of the guys here, I've gotten good at saying something that says nothing. "How about you?"

"No complaints," he says. He comes down from the stepladder and walks toward me. We do the bro greeting: half handshake, half chest bump. "We ain't seen you at the Sunday meeting last couple of weeks. Why's that?"

"No good excuse," I tell him. "But I'll be there tomorrow."

"Gonna hold you to that. It's like they say, man. Meeting makers make it."

As we catch up a little, I scan the room, looking for Mrs. Millman. "Where's the Queen Mother?" I ask.

Her head pops up from behind the circulation desk. "The Queen Mother's over here on her hands and knees, trying to pry dried gum off the linoleum with a single-edge razor blade," she says. "Oh, hi, Corby. I didn't realize that was you. What have you been up to?"

"Just livin' the dream," I tell her. "This place get hit by a tornado or something?"

"Looks like it, doesn't it?" she says. "Give me a hand, will you?" She's not exactly a featherweight, but I manage to pull her up onto her feet. She tosses the razor blade she's been using onto the counter and pulls me in for a hug.

"Wow, initiating physical contact with an inmate? That's the kind of infraction that could land you in seg."

She gives me a "pfft" and surveys her pulled-apart domain. "We got a memo that there was going to be an extended lockdown this week—no movement around the compound for five to seven days. So I said to myself, rather than just sitting around here twiddling my thumbs, I'll do some housecleaning. Freshen things up. Rearrange the shelves, weed out the collection, take down those old posters and have Javier repaint the walls."

"I just hope you put those posters back," I tell her. "Because having Yoda, Weird Al, and the Dukes of Hazzard encourage convicted felons to read is truly inspirational."

"Such a wise guy," she says. "And for the record, that *Dukes of Hazzard* poster wasn't for you guys. It was for me. Luke and Bo could squeeze into tight jeans like nobody's business."

I laugh. "Your husband know you've got a thing for those two?"

"What Howie doesn't know won't hurt him," she says. "Anyway, right after I had pulled everything apart in here, they sent out a second memo about the lockdown being postponed because of the lieutenant governor's visit. When the VIP entourage came through with Warden Rickerby, I could see she wasn't happy with the condition of this place, but tough titty. I've outlasted eight other wardens and I'll probably wave goodbye to her before very long, too."

It's amazing, really: Mrs. Millman's ability to stay upbeat. I see she's wearing a cheap-looking wig now, but her color's come back and so has her energy. Cancer hasn't defeated her and neither has the system. Last time I was here, she was in the middle of a dustup with Deputy Warden Zabrowski. He wanted her to take down the Buddhist prayer flags she'd tacked up behind the circulation desk, but those flags are still up there.

Solomon appears out of nowhere. Ignoring Mrs. Millman, he tells me he can't find it. Mrs. M introduces herself and asks what he's looking for.

"*Heretics of Dune*," he says.

"Frank Herbert? We have a few of them in that series, but I'm not sure about that one. You see those big hardcover books on the floor beneath the back window—the law books? Our science fiction and fantasy collections are stacked just to the left of them. You can go look there if you'd like or if you'd rather—"

Without waiting for her to finish, he makes a beeline toward where she's directed him. "Friend of yours, Corby? How old is he, anyway?" Mrs. M asks.

"Eighteen, but he looks and acts a lot younger. And he's my assignment, not my friend."

"Oh?"

"We're both on the grounds crew and I'm supposed to watch out for him. Make sure he does his work and that nobody antagonizes him. His name's Solomon."

She repeats the name and her eyes widen as it dawns on her. "Is he the one who . . . the dogs?" When I nod, she winces. Mrs. M and her husband foster greyhounds that travel up here from Florida. "Well, no matter what he did, he's still a kid," she says. "Why in the world would they put him at Yates?" She shakes her head. Says he's lucky he has me looking out for him.

"Only on the work crew," I tell her.

"And at the library, apparently."

"Yeah, well, this visit is a one-off."

"Uh-huh." Why's she smiling?

When Solomon returns to the desk with a couple of books, Mrs. M asks him whether he found what he was looking for. "Nah. You've only got *Dune, Dune Messiah,* and *Children of Dune.* You should order *Heretics of Dune.*"

She hands him paper and pencil and says he should write down the title—that her budget for the year's been spent, but sometimes she sees things at yard sales or buys them used at the Book Barn. "Looks like you've found a few things to check out, though. What have you got there? Ah, a George R. R. Martin and *Eragon.* Did you know that the author started writing *Eragon* when he was only—"

"Fifteen. Yeah, I know. I already read it. They made a movie of it, but it sucked. The book's better." When she asks him whether he's already read the George Martin book, too, he says yes.

Turning to me, Mrs. M says she heard some good news yesterday: DOC has finally okayed the library's request for a computer. "It's a repurposed IBM Aptiva, they told me, and it comes with a keyboard, a mouse, and one of those old dot-matrix printers. Javier says that, technology-wise, it's an antique from the 1990s. But at least it will have word processing, so you fellas won't have to submit your court letters in longhand."

I tell her I already know the answer to this question, but any chance there will be internet access? She laughs and says I'm right, I already know the answer.

"Does it have games?" Solomon asks. I'm pretty sure he has no idea how primitive computer games were back in the day. Mrs. M tells him she might be able to install a few games—"the old standbys like solitaire and . . . what's the one my sons always used to play on our first computer? The object was to aim a bouncing ball at a brick wall and destroy the rows of bricks until—"

I blurt it out. "*Breakout!*"

"Oh, yes. *Breakout.* I played it myself a few times, but I was terrible at it."

Solomon says, "Yeah, but I mean *good* games like *Sniper Elite* or *Mortal Kombat: Deadly Alliance* or *Mortal Kombat: Armageddon.*"

"I don't think those would pass inspection around here, my friend," she says.

"And the amount of storage space those games would need would probably make that poor old IBM Aptiva explode," I joke. Solomon doesn't seem to think this is funny.

Mrs. M puts Solomon in the system, checks out his books, and places a Milky Way mini on the top one. I tell her I'm going to say hello to Lester before we take off. But when I go over there, his book's fallen to the floor and he's asleep. His breath is whistling in and out.

Back at the desk, Mrs. M says, "He's sleeping, right? He does a lot of that now. He's really slipped lately." Leaning in, she whispers, "Some of us are working on getting him a compassionate release. Not me, officially, because employees can't get involved with such things. But when has that ever stopped me?" I give her a thumbs-up and ask her whether Lester's son, Cornell, ever visits him here. "Oh yes. They're in different buildings, so that's not supposed to happen, but the officers look the other way. They mostly just sit together, hold hands, and pray or sing hymns. Cornell does most of the praying and singing and Lester joins in here and there." She tears up telling me about it.

Shifting gears, she says, "Oh, Corby, I almost forgot. I saw Beena Patel the other day. She said to say hello and wonders how you're doing." I nod. Smile. Now *I'm* getting a little teary-eyed.

"Well, come on," I tell Solomon. "Let's not wear out our welcome."

"Okay, don't be strangers, you two," Mrs. Millman says. "Hopefully, the next time you come in, this place will be put back together again." She tells Solomon he's always welcome.

Javier's off the stepladder now, using a roller on the middle of the wall. "See you later, Javi," I say.

"Later, brah," he says. "See you tomorrow at the meeting."

Just inside the doorway, I stop before a big pile of discarded books. A sign made from a manila folder says, *Help yourself.* Mrs. Millman said she was weeding the collection, so I guess these are the weeds. Solomon's already out the door, but I call to him to wait up. Two of the books near the top of the pile grab my attention. The first is a Collier's yearbook covering the events of my birth year. The second is a damaged but beautifully illustrated volume about Greek mythology. Several of its pages are loose and the binding's broken, but the color plates depict scenes from the ancient stories by several of the artists I've studied and admired: Botticelli, Rubens, Bruegel, Caravaggio. No matter the condition of the book, these plates are a real find!

A third book catches my eye, too: a pocket-sized collection of Buddhist quotes. I don't know much about Buddhism, but the book's free and Buddha's serene smile reminds me of Dr. Patel's. Mrs. Millman is spraying the circulation desk with Fantastik. "Okay if I take three of these?" I ask.

She rolls her eyes and smiles. "What does the sign say?"

Solomon and I are halfway down the corridor, headed for the stairs, when Javier calls to us. I stop but Solomon keeps going. "Hey, hold up," I tell him.

When Javi catches up, he says, "Where is it?" He's talking to Solomon. "Where's what?" Solomon says.

Javier grabs the books he's checked out. Shakes them and fans the pages. Mrs. M's razor blade falls out of *Eragon*. Javi picks it up and hands the book back to Solomon. "She said to tell you you're suspended from the library for the rest of this month. After that you'll be on probation for three months. That means you can check out books, but you're not allowed to stay and read. Or use the computer. Got it?"

Solomon shrugs. Says it's a shit library anyway.

"Knock it off!" I tell him.

"Don't tell me what to do. You're not my father."

"Thank God for that!"

Javi shakes his head, then turns and heads back up to the library. Solomon and I go down the stairs and out of the building. I'm so pissed at him that we're halfway back to our block and I still don't trust myself to speak.

"Do you think I'm gonna get another ticket?" he asks.

"I have no idea. You should. Of all the stupid . . . Why the fuck would you want to pull a stunt like that to someone who was nice to you? Can't wait to cut yourself again? Is that it? Or were you planning to slit the throats of those turkeys you keep staring at?"

He starts to cry. "What makes you think I'd do something like that?"

"Hey, why not? Maybe you've got it in for all kinds of animals."

"Fuck you!" he screams. "At least I didn't kill my own kid."

Lucky for him, he runs ahead after he says it. Lucky for me, too, because I don't trust what I might have done to him if he was in reach.

Back in my cell, I flop down on my bunk and try to make sense of what happened. Why, if he wanted to get to the library so badly, would he risk burning his bridges once he got there? . . . Why did he ask me the reason I'm in prison when he already knew? . . . What would he have done with that razor blade? . . . I shouldn't have said that about the turkeys, but why had it made him cry? . . .

There's a saying in AA: too much analysis can lead to paralysis. I need to chase that kid out of my head before he drives me nuts. I do some deep breathing to calm myself down. Then I take out Dr. Patel's letter and read it again: live in the present; the mind-body connection; stay engaged with work and other people. Well, I'm *dis*engaging from Solomon and if Lieutenant Cavagnero kicks me off the crew because of it, then tough shit. . . . *At least I didn't kill my own kid.* . . . I'm done working with that little monster.

I put Dr. Patel's letter back in the envelope and look at the books I grabbed off the throwaway pile. Start leafing through the little book on Buddhism. Read a random page. *In truth will I speak, not in falsehood. Gently will I speak, not harshly. To his profit will I speak, not to his loss. With kindly intent will I speak, not in anger.* Easy for Buddha to say; he never had to deal with a kid like Solomon. Still, I shouldn't have lost my shit and gone off on him like that. He's not a monster; he's just a fucked-up, badly damaged boy trying to survive in a place where he doesn't belong.

Next I look through that yearbook and read about stuff that happened the year I was born. Someone was killing people by lacing Tylenol with cyanide. . . . *Time* magazine's Man of the Year was the Computer. . . . Prince Charles's wife, Diana, gave birth to the future king on the same day Mom had me, something I'd been told but had forgotten. . . . The CDC announced that the general public needn't worry about the mysterious new immune system virus; the disease was "mostly confined to drug addicts and homosexual men." . . . And this: seventeen months after he'd tried to assassinate Ronald Reagan, John Hinckley was acquitted by reason of insanity and sent to a psych hospital instead of prison. I shake my head when I read that. Most of those state hospitals have closed. Prison is where they send a lot of the mental cases now. That's got to be why Solomon's here instead of someplace where he might get decent treatment. And why, thanks to Reagan's policy of beefing up the sentences of drug offenders, two-thirds of the guys in here are Black or Brown. . . . *Mostly confined to drug addicts and homosexual men.* So neither of those groups count? That pisses me off on behalf of Manny and the majority of the guys doing time here. One thing about having to come to prison: it gives you twenty-twenty vision about who wins and who loses in the good old USA.

Most of the stuff in the mythology book is familiar: Pandora's box, the Minotaur, the one-eyed Cyclops. I was really into all those gods and mortals when we studied ancient Greece in sixth grade. But now I'm taken with the artists' depictions of human suffering on the faces of the characters: Sisyphus's torment as the boulder begins its backward roll; Orpheus's despair as he realizes his mistake and sees Eurydice fading back into the shadows; the fear in Icarus's eyes as the wings his father constructed for him fall apart and he begins his fatal descent.

The book includes two renderings of the Icarus myth. In *Landscape with the Fall of Icarus*, Bruegel the Elder's painting, it's business as usual in a seaside village: a farmer plows his field, a ship sails along the coast, a man fishes, a shepherd boy minds his flock, and Icarus plunges headfirst into the sea, unnoticed by the villagers. It reminds me of being in here versus being on the outside, where life goes on at a busy pace. In here, our lives—and sometimes our deaths—mostly go unnoticed. Notorious inmates get ink and prison suicides sometimes make the news, but an inmate with no name recognition who dies of natural causes gets the quiet "back-door parole" and that's that. No service, no obituary in the paper. Within a week, a new arrival is sleeping in the dead guy's bunk.

In Jacob Peter Gowy's dramatic *The Fall of Icarus*, father and son are aloft in close proximity at the moment the wings of the impetuous boy begin to fall apart. When I was younger, I identified with Icarus, whose father's warnings not to fly too close to the sun fell on deaf ears. What do parents know about anything? Now, studying Gowy's painting, my sympathies are with Daedalus, powerless to save the boy. And as the inventor of the wings, he realizes he's the unintentional orchestrator of his son's death.

CHAPTER TWENTY-EIGHT

November 2018
Days 477–80 of 1,095

Hoo hoo hoo-hooo . . .

   Hoo hoo hoo-hooo . . .

There they go, calling to each other. You only hear them in the quiet of early morning before the clamor and white noise of another prison day gets going. *You hear that, Corby? Those are great horned owls. The male calls, the female answers. Snowy owls, grays, pygmies, great horneds: they've all got their own mating calls. Hoots, most of them, except for barn owls. They don't hoot. They scream.*

Like he did the time he came home from campus and saw that Mom had taken his framed Roger Tory Peterson lithographs off the living room wall and replaced them with the macramé God's eye she'd made on her loom. Or the day he arrived home early and caught Mom smoking weed in the backyard with two of her Wiccan friends. After he kicked out her company, she was so mortified that she screamed back at him for once. That was the first time he hit her—the first time I witnessed him doing it, anyway. Too afraid to get between them—to get him angry enough to hurt me, too—I escaped to the brook and tried to unsee what I'd just seen by focusing on the way the water moved. Letting it soothe me. Hypnotize me, almost. I stayed out there until the mosquitos started biting.

When I got back to the house, everything was quiet. The God's eye was gone; the lithographs were back. I grabbed the waxed paper–wrapped sandwich Mom had left for me on the kitchen counter and headed toward my bedroom. The TV in the living room was on and he was sitting in his chair watching television with the volume turned low. "G'night," his silhouette said. "Night," I answered.

When I closed my bedroom door, I flopped on my bed and fell asleep in the middle of eating my sandwich. I woke up, startled. His red face was screaming at me because of the mud I'd tracked through the house. When he came closer, I thought I was about to get hit. Instead, he pushed a wet dish towel against my face. "Clean it up!" he ordered. "If your mother and you think I'm going to live in a pigsty, you're both sadly mistaken." It was the summer I turned ten.

I've been incarcerated for a year and a half and in that time, I've waited for a visit or a letter from my father. Nothing. Instead, it's his sister who writes, my aunt Nancy, who lives in Utah and whose faith in God seems as strong as my father's faith in God's nonexistence. "Our congregation is praying for you, Corbin Junior, and prayer is powerful! I hope you got the book I ordered for you last month." Yes, I'd gotten it: *Christian Awakenings to the Glory of God.* I'd thrown it, unread, on top of the other one she'd sent me that I'd never cracked: *When Jesus Speaks, Are You Listening?* "I know your father can be difficult sometimes, but you can rest assured that he loves you and hopes you are abiding." Seriously? Who told her that? Jesus?

Okay, Corby, shake it off. *Mind-body. Mind-body. Mind-body. . . .*

Sixty sit-ups, sixty push-ups, five reps each of squats, curls, lunges, and side bends daily. When I get out of here in another year, I'll probably be in the best physical shape of my life. And my anxiety level's much more under control now, too. Some nights, I hit the mattress at lights-out and don't wake up until the sun's come up. Doesn't always happen but I'm grateful when it does. Last time my mom visited me, she said I looked better-rested and noted that my physique had changed. "You're starting to look like the muscle-bound good guy on that cartoon show you watched when you were a kid. You had his action figure and carried it around with you all the time. Remember?"

Of course I remembered. The show was *ThunderCats*, the character was Lion-O. With his team, he used to vanquish bad guys like Mumm-Ra and Vultureman. What Mom didn't know was that as I sat there watching that show, I'd secretly imagine the bad guy *I* would vanquish, the villain I both loved and hated: my father, the esteemed professor, noted zoologist, and avowed atheist, Dr. Corbin Ledbetter.

Hoo hoo hoo-hooo . . .

Hoo hoo hoo-hooo . . .

"Fucking birds! Shaddup!"

On the bunk above me, Sleeping Beauty has awakened. His skinny legs hang over the side. Then he jumps down and shuffles groggily to the toilet.

"Good morning, Manny. Did the owls interrupt your beauty sleep?" He mumbles something, but I can't hear it over his loud morning piss.

Okay, now that he's awake, I can start my morning workout. I do some stretches. Drop to the floor for push-ups and sit-ups. Manny walks around me, sighing. "You exhaust me," he says. Climbing back up to his bed, he pushes his face into his pillow and groans.

After morning chow, I head over to the Sunday morning AA meeting in D Block. I've perfected my arrival, getting there right after the makeshift Catholic Mass instead of in the middle of it.

I fill my lungs with the crisp midmorning air and think about one of the quotes from that book of Buddhist sayings I grabbed from the library's giveaway pile that day. If you focus on what's harmonious and beautiful in your present surroundings, harmony and beauty will follow you. Or something like that.

Entering the meeting, I fist-bump with Javier and take a seat. Lenny, an ex-offender who got out, stayed clean, and has been making good money flipping houses, is chairing today. The topic he's chosen is how to handle the challenges after we're released: avoiding the traps that will send us back here; finding an employer willing to take a chance on a recovering addict with a felony conviction; accepting the reality that the people we love won't necessarily want us back. Lenny's a stickler for the rules: no cross-talking, no political opinions, no shares longer than three minutes. He enforces that last rule with a stove timer that dings when someone's time is up.

There are fourteen or fifteen of us at today's meeting: Tyrone, Dusty, "Meth Mouth" Freddie, Durnell, Javier, the crew from C Building, and me. At Lenny's meetings, everyone's expected to share. The person to his left begins and we move clockwise around the circle until we get back to Lenny. When it's Meth Mouth's turn, he retells the same old sob story about how he began using the day he saw his cat get killed by a car. Lenny stops him when the timer dings.

Dusty's up next. He's been stuck in here since 2002 and is due to be released in a few months. He says as much as he can't wait to get out, part of him wants to stay put because he's scared to death about walking back into an unrecognizable world of streaming, online betting, phishing, and swiping right or left. "And what the hell is Bitcoin, anyway?" he says. Smiles and shrugs all around.

I'm next and would just as soon pass, but not sharing is like "coming empty-handed to a potluck supper and expecting to eat for free," according to Lenny.

"I'm Corby, cross-addicted," I say. Everyone hellos me back. Before I can say anything else, the door bangs open and a new guy strolls in. Beefy face, hanging gut, ponytail, Semper Fi tattoo. He's maybe in his midfifties. "Sorry I'm late," he says. "I had trouble finding you." He crash-lands on the empty seat next to me. Lenny welcomes him and tells him the topic we're dealing with is the challenges of freedom.

"Oh, I can talk a blue streak about that," the new guy says.

"When it's your turn, and as long as you keep it to three minutes," Lenny says. "Go ahead, Corby."

I tell the group I can relate to what Dusty said. "I've got plenty of time left in here, but I get nervous when I think about what happens when I leave. *Crazy* nervous sometimes. I mean, the cravings have pretty much left me since I've been here, but once I'm out, who knows? And as far as employment? After the company I was working for laid me off, I couldn't find another job, not even some stopgap thing. And that was *before* my arrest got covered on TV and in the papers. If someone who was considering hiring me Googled my name, I'm sure that's the stuff that would come up first. So who the hell's going to hire me now? Fuck, I'm not even sure *I'd* hire me."

A few of the guys chuckle, but most just look down at the floor and nod.

"And as for my marriage, my being a dad, I'm hoping she'll forgive me and let me come back home so that we can be a family again. But what if, by the time I'm out of here, she's moved on? Met someone else and . . . I mean, I try to hold out hope, you know? I just don't want hope to sucker punch me. Okay, that's it. I'll share the time."

Next up is the new guy. "Frank," he says. "Addict, alcoholic."

"Hi, Frank" all around.

Turning and looking directly at me, he says, "I've been where you're at, brother. My love affair with booze and blow cost me two careers, two wives, and now my second extended 'vacation' at this resort. So my advice to you is—"

Lenny puts up his hand like a traffic cop. "Hey, Frank? We don't allow cross-talking in this group. Whatever you have to say, say it to everyone."

"Oh, yeah. Okay." When he changes course, it becomes obvious that Frank is one of those guys who wants everyone to know how smart he is compared to the rest of us dumb fucks. Within a three-minute ramble, he refers to Carl Jung, the *I Ching*, and an episode from the original Star Trek TV series called "Tomorrow Is Yesterday." Unable to follow what his point is, or even whether there is a point to this word salad, I write him off as a blowhard and stop listening.

But later, after we all stand, say the Serenity Prayer, and start back to our units, Frank latches on to my shoulder and says, "What I was going to tell you before I got cut off is that hope is never going to sucker punch you."

"No?"

"Uh-uh. If you give up hope, you become bitter. Cynical. You start saying to yourself, what's the point? Next thing you know, you're using again. So you want to keep *hope* alive. Just be careful about *expectations*. If you *expect* things to happen a certain way and they don't, it can clobber you like a Mike Tyson left hook. Knock you right on your ass. My first wife? Bettina? Nice little Italian gal, sweet as anything. And true blue, or so I thought. But when I got out of here after my first bid, expecting us to pick up where we left off, the *last* thing I expected was that she would have gotten herself a new man and had him change the locks."

"Wow, that must have sucked," I say. "Okay then. See you around."

"What's your name again, buddy? Sorry. I'm terrible with names."

"It's Corby," I tell him, over my shoulder. I'm walking fast.

"Got it. You believe in God, Corey?"

I stop. What business is it of his? I tell him I'm on the fence.

"Okay. Agnostic then. Maybe yes, maybe no. You want both bases covered just in case, right?"

"Something like that," I say. Who does he think he is? My spiritual guru?

"Think of it this way, Corey."

"Corby," I said.

"What?"

"My name's Corby with a *b*, not Corey."

"Okay, yeah. Like I said, when it comes to names . . . But think of it this way. Having hope is kind of like *praying*. Like *asking* God for something and hoping He'll hear you. But if you have an expectation, it's more like a *demand* than a prayer. Like you're saying, here's what I expect, God, so make it happen for me. See? Like you're the one who gets to give the orders."

"All right," I tell him. "Thanks. See you." It annoys me that someone I've already decided I don't like has just given me something useful to think about.

Back inside B Block, I'm trudging up the stairs to our tier when I'm hit with a memory of my father, my mother, and me at the dinner table. I guess I was about twelve. He was going on as usual about how organized religion is a scam perpetrated on the gullible when Mom, who may or may not have been stoned, interrupted him to announce that she'd decided she's agnostic.

"What's that?" I asked, but neither of them answered me.

Snickering, Dad wanted to know where *that* had come from. "Agnostic, huh? You hedging your bets, Vicki? In case, after you die, you find yourself standing at the pearly gates instead of under the ground being worm food?" I remember him making finger quotes when he said "pearly gates."

Mom said no, that wasn't it at all. As far as an afterlife was concerned, her feeling was *que será, será.* I'd sometimes hear her sing that song while she was dusting or making supper. She was agnostic, she said, because it was hard for her to accept that everything in life happened randomly— maybe some higher presence was ordering our lives by a design no human could understand.

Dad stood and said he'd lost his appetite. On his way out of the kitchen, he turned back to me. "Don't listen to this, Corbin Junior," he said. "It's bullshit."

I was, at the time, already a nonbeliever like my father, but emotionally I was on my mother's side. "You and I are simpatico, Corby," I remember her telling me one muggy summer day when she opened the freezer, took out a pair of Creamsicles, and handed me mine. When I asked her what "simpatico" meant, she said we were like two peas in a pod. "Same hazel eyes and chestnut-colored hair, same temperament. We both like to read and listen to music." I reminded her that we both had won spelling bees in elementary school, too. Her prize had been a half-dollar-sized medal, mine a paperback copy of *Treasure Island.* "That, too," she said. "See? Simpatico."

"Do you hate Dad?" I asked her.

She took a bite of her Creamsicle and shook her head. "Why? Do you?"

"No," I said. "But sometimes yes."

Shortly after that, my parents' divorce was finalized and Mom turned Wiccan. Whenever she'd try to tell me about her new beliefs, I wouldn't listen. But the one thing I still remember is her explanation of something called the Law of Threefold Return. The gist of this was: whatever things you did in your life, good or bad, they would return to you with triple force. "When that happens to your father, he's not going to know what hit him," she said. I remember her looking genuinely worried for the ex-husband who had verbally and physically abused her. To lighten the mood, and maybe to mock her a little, I began singing that old John Lennon song. *Instant karma's gonna get you! Gonna knock you right on the head!* She gave me a disappointed look and walked out of the room.

———

On Monday morning, I'm heading over to the barn when I hear, "Hey! Wait up!" I ignore him. My anger has diminished since Saturday, but I'm still determined to tell Cavagnero to find someone else to be Solomon's work-time babysitter.

When he catches up, he asks me whether I'm going to the library this week. I remind him that, whether I am or not, he's suspended. He says he knows, but he's finished the books he checked out. Can I bring them back and check out some other ones for him? He reminds me he likes sci-fi. I don't respond.

"Did you notice I'm on time today?" he asks.

I turn and face him. "Are you expecting me to congratulate you for something you should have been doing all along? Get more books for you? Instead of asking for favors and attaboys, how about an apology instead?"

"For what? I didn't even do anything." Instead of saying what I'd like to, I break into a jog to get ahead of him. "What's your problem anyway?" he calls to me. When I don't answer, he says, "Well, you won't see me tomorrow. I got court. The lawyer told my stepmother he's asking for a continuance. So you can think about me having a day off while you're stuck here working all day."

The little shit has no idea how tough court runs are. If I wasn't so fed up, I'd warn him. I'm still going to press my case with the boss, tell him it's someone else's turn to work with Solomon, but maybe at lunchtime, I can give the kid a heads-up about court so he doesn't freak out. Whatever the hell is wrong with him, he's as fragile as glass underneath that bravado. Better if he's forewarned. When I don't hear his footsteps behind me, I look over my shoulder to see what's up. He's just standing there, kicking at the dirt and looking pathetic. Putting up with Solomon isn't easy, but it can't be easy *being* him either.

When I get to the barn, I'm stopped in my tracks. Cavagnero's not there. In his place are Piccardy and his lacky, Goolsby. They're chatting with each other, ignoring the rest of us. Ratchford and Harjeet are whispering something about Cavagnero, but I can't make out what they're saying. What the hell is going on?

"Okay, listen up!" Piccardy says. "Officer Goolsby and I are supervising this crew from now on, so—"

"Where's Cavagnero at?" Tito asks for all of us.

Piccardy ignores the question. "We expect a decent day's work out of all of you, and as long as you comply, we'll get along fine." He looks at me when he says the next. "We know how to deal with slackers and rule breakers and, trust me, you won't like it. Now, Officer Goolsby's going to call the roll."

Goolsby calls Solomon's name last. There's no answer. "That's the kid," Tito volunteers. "Sometimes he's late."

I see Solomon coming over the rise. "Here he is."

As he approaches, Piccardy says, "Glad you could make it. Someone from the crew said you *used to be* late, emphasis on the 'used to be.' Get it?" Solomon looks confused. I wonder if he realizes Piccardy was the one who grabbed him from the back and dragged him out of the visiting room. "I just asked you a question, Clapp. Do you get my point when I say you *used to be* late?" When Solomon looks over at me, I mouth the answer. He looks back at Piccardy and says, "Yes, sir."

Piccardy nods and turns back to the rest of us. "Before we give you guys your assignments for today, are there any questions?"

Ratchford asks whether what someone told him is true: that Cavagnero fell off a ladder while he was cleaning out his gutters and broke his hip.

"Fractured his pelvis," Harjeet adds. "That's what I heard."

Piccardy frowns. "What happens to staff is none of your business," he says. "Anyone have a question that's work-related?"

"I do," Tito says. "Is Culinary Arts still gonna make our lunches?"

Piccardy smiles and turns to Goolsby. "We've got our work cut out for us, Officer Goolsby," he says. "These fools have been spoiled rotten."

Piccardy announces our work assignments. Israel and Harjeet get the plum job: weeding and tending to the fall beds of asters, mums, and flowering kale that decorate the front yard, then washing and waxing the warden's and deputy warden's cars. Solomon, Ratchford, and Tito are handed push brooms and told they'll be sweeping the walkways and the parking lots. When Solomon tells Officer Goolsby that Cavagnero always has him work with me, Goolsby says, "Oh, yeah? Gee, thanks for letting us know. Now get over to the parking lots and start sweeping." This earns Goolsby a thumbs-up from his mentor but leaves Solomon looking shaken. The poor kid may still be within earshot when Piccardy asks Goolsby whether he knows who he is. When Goolsby shakes his head, Piccardy makes his finger a gun. "Woof, woof. Bang! Bang! Bang!" Goolsby says Solomon's nothing like he pictured him.

Piccardy saves the last assignment for me and, just as I guessed, it's the crappiest job. Handing me a rake, a short-handled shovel, and a bucket, he tells me to clean out the decaying leaf sludge beneath the long row of barberry bushes that separates the back lawn from the woods. I nod, denying him the satisfaction of seeing that I'm pissed to be singled out for this work detail. As I start off toward the job, he catches up and walks alongside me. "Too bad about Cavagnero, huh?" he says. "I bet you're going to miss him. I understand you two were pretty tight."

"Tight? I wouldn't say that. We get along okay. He gets along with everyone."

"Ain't that sweet," he says. "From what I hear, he's probably not coming back. He'd be out for months anyway, so he's looking into early retirement."

"Well, like you said, Officer. What happens to staff is none of my business."

He smiles at the "gotcha" I just landed, but then he retaliates. "So how's your wife, Ledbetter? It's Emily, right? How's Emily?"

Rather than whacking him in the face with this shovel I'm carrying, I keep walking toward those barberry bushes. "Enjoy," he says, then turns and walks back toward the barn. Fuck him and fuck his boot-licking assistant, too. If Piccardy doesn't let up, I'll quit rather than put up with his bullshit.

It rained most of the night before, so the ground where I'm working is saturated. Within the first hour, my work boots and socks are soaked. Worse than that, the muck I'm scooping up is mice- and bug-infested and they're not happy that I'm screwing with their domain. There hasn't been a frost yet, so I'm spending half my time swatting away flies and mosquitos. By midmorning, I've pulled two ticks off me. The one on the back of my neck had already begun to embed itself. It's warm for October—Indian summer, the TV weather guy said last night—so I dressed in just my scrubs this morning, no jacket. Now I'm covered in bites. The only good thing about this shitty work detail is that it's closer to the river, which I can hear loud and clear after all that rain. I wish I could see it, too.

At noon, the crew reconvenes at the barn, but there's no sign of Solomon. Has he freaked out and made matters worse for himself? Walked off the job? I remind myself that, whatever happened, I'm not responsible for him. I just hope that short fuse of his hasn't gotten him in trouble. Well, Piccardy isn't here either, so at least that's a win.

Goolsby passes out our lunches and tells us we have twenty minutes. "That's ten minutes less than what Cavagnero gives us," Harjeet points out.

"*Gave* you," Goolsby says. "Who are you—the union rep? Like I said, twenty minutes." Piccardy's star pupil is coming right along.

I open my bag lunch—a thin gray slice of bologna between two slices of white bread, two bendable carrot sticks, a stale mini-doughnut, and an eight-ounce plastic bottle of water. The bologna's a launching pad for bacteria so I pull it out and just eat the bread. Goolsby's nearby, so the guys are keeping their voices down, but I tune in to the chatter. "You know who she is, right? Works in the office, blond hair, nice rack. She's got to be pushing fifty, but I'd still tap it." . . . "He's Zabrowski's nephew. Got into some kind of trouble at the women's prison. They transferred him here so that Unk can keep an eye on him." . . . "How come they want to impeach him but not her? What about Benghazi? What about her fucking emails?" . . . "Houston's had home-field advantage and the Nats were running out of gas. That's why it was the Astros in six."

Solomon hasn't done anything stupid, has he? He was working with Ratchford and Tito. "Hey, where's the kid?" I ask Ratch.

He rolls his eyes. "We were busting his chops a little, nothing serious, but he started yelling at us, calling us lowlifes. Then he sat down, puts his face against his knees, and starts wailing. When we told him it was lunchtime, he didn't move. Kid's a real wacko, huh?"

I nod. "DOC never should have put him here. Cavagnero was kind of looking out for him, but now . . . Okay, here he comes. Hey, Solomon!"

As he walks toward me, I get up and move away from the others so that I can talk to him in private. He's red-eyed, red-faced. I ask him how the parking lot detail's going. "Terrible!" he says. "They keep making fun of me."

"Yeah? What did they say?"

"I made one honest mistake when we were walking over there, okay? Called it brooming instead of sweeping and they started laughing at me. And I was like 'Hey, it makes sense. What did we use when we raked leaves? *Rakes.*' Or when someone plays baseball, what does he bat with? A *bat!*' And Ratchford goes, 'Yeah, but when some guy in the outfield makes a catch, he uses his glove, not his catch.' Then Tito grabs his crotch and says that when he fucks a woman, he uses his cock, not his fuck. Ratchford said he couldn't believe I got to be my age without knowing not to call it brooming. So I said maybe he and Tito had to do lowlife jobs like sweeping where they came from, but I didn't because we have a cleaning lady. Then they started calling me Richie Rich and shit and they wouldn't let it go."

I tell him he's got to be careful about knocking where people came from because that could hit a nerve. "So they can make fun of *me* all they want, but I have to be careful about what *I* say? I hate this stupid crew and this stupid job. At least I'm getting away from here tomorrow."

"Yeah, about that, Solomon. Court runs are tough. Don't think of it as a day off. They'll wake you before the sun's come up, shackle and belly-chain you, load you into the van, and chain you to whoever else has court that day. Then they'll drive around the state for hours picking up cons from other facilities. It gets hot and stagnant in the back of that van. If you start feeling nauseous, put your head down and take some deep breaths so you don't vomit."

For once in his life, he shuts up and listens instead of giving me an argument.

"When you get to the courthouse where your case is being heard, they'll put you in a holding cell with a bunch of other guys. Some of them may be mean, some of them sick or smelly. Just keep your mouth shut. And when you and your lawyer finally get in front of the judge, it'll take maybe five minutes to get your continuance. Then it'll be back to the holding cell, then back in the van for several hours while they drop off everyone they picked up before. By the time you get back here, it'll be after dark and you'll be hungry and thirsty. But don't drink anything during the day. They might not let you out of the cell to pee. You don't want to end up peeing your pants."

"Why are you telling me all this? To scare me?"

"Why would I want to scare you, Solomon?"

"Because you hate me after what happened in the library."

His bottom lip pokes out and he looks close to tears. God, the poor kid is so maddening but so vulnerable. "I was pissed at you for that, yeah, but I don't hate you. I just don't want you to expect tomorrow's going to be a vacation day because it's not."

"When do you think Lieutenant Cavagnero's coming back?" he asks.

Doubtful that he *is* coming back, but rather than telling him that, I just shrug.

"I just want to work with *you*," he says. "You're the only one who understands me." He's wrong; there's no way I'll ever be able to fathom that damaged psyche of his. But seeing him in pain like this makes me feel guilty about how intent I was to get him off my back. Like it or not, he's mine.

I put my hand on his shoulder and tell him that, for the time being, the work assignments aren't in our control. "But when you get teased, you have to try to laugh it off or give it back a little. Just don't say anything more like you had a cleaning lady and they didn't."

"But we *did* have one," he insists.

"That's not the point, Solomon. What you don't want to do is push your privilege in people's faces. Make them feel like you think you're better than they are."

"But you just said that when they make fun of me, I should give it back! Now you're saying the opposite!"

"No, I'm not. And lower your voice or this conversation's over." But it's over anyway when Goolsby announces that it's time for us to get back to work.

I haven't seen Piccardy, but who's complaining? Okay, speak of the devil. Here they come, up over the rise and heading toward the barn: Piccardy and his best buddy. But what's Anselmo doing here? He worked third shift last night. Doesn't he have anything better to do than hang around at Yates with his bro? He's carrying a pizza box and a liter of Coke and it looks like Piccardy's gotten himself a salad and a bottle of water. No soda or mozzarella for him. The jerk's always bragging about his low body fat percentage, like anyone but him gives a shit. Goolsby's eaten with us, but not these two. Piccardy apparently gets as much time as he wants. Your tax dollars at work, Connecticut.

Before heading back to my assignment, I sidle up to Ratchford and

Tito. Tell them I realize they were just horsing around with Solomon, but maybe they should ease up a little. "He's pretty fragile."

"Yeah, fragile like an egg," Tito says. "Cracked."

"Okay, Dad. We'll cool our jets," Ratchford promises.

Back at my post, I rake a pile of muck out from under a barberry bush, scoop it up with my hands, and drop it in the bucket. Pick up the bucket, carry it over to the woods, and empty it. Standing there, I listen to the siren song of the Wequonnoc. *Come and I'll cleanse you of this place*, it seems almost to be promising.

Should I risk it? Is it worth getting a ticket to wander off for a few minutes if they catch me? But why would they know when they're back at the barn having their pizza party? Fuck it, I tell myself. Go for it!

I can feel my heart jackhammering as I run past pines and sycamores and scampering squirrels, dodging brambles and boulders embedded in the soft dirt.

Then there it is!

I move closer and stand there, savoring the thunder of it in my ears, the sun diamonds sparkling on its surface. Thanks to a jagged rock embedded in the river's path, I feel its spray on my face, the taste of it on my lips and tongue. It's exactly what I need—just a minute or two to take it in after all these months of cement and sensory deprivation.

I look across the river to the sheer rock ledge on the other side. It's maybe seventy or eighty feet high, unscalable by someone attempting an escape, like that guy back in the seventies who's something of a legend at Yates—and a cautionary tale. He got halfway up, then lost his footing and fell to his death, bashing his brains against a boulder at the bottom.

Escaping's not even something I fantasize about. With almost half of my sentenced served, I'm not about to screw *that* up. Seeing the river in motion and hearing it up close is all I need. At my feet is a fallen maple leaf. I pick it up, toss it into the river, and watch the current carry it south. It's the same direction I'll be traveling when I get out of here—hopefully heading home to Emily and Maisie.

I have to get back before my absence is noticed, but I need to carry some of this hope with me. Something tangible. At the river's edge, I reach into the water halfway up to my forearm and scoop up a handful of mud and gravel. Sitting on my palm, half-hidden, is an oval stone about the size of a quarter. With my other hand, I pull it out and finger it between my thumb and index finger. It's milky quartz, white and translucent, smooth to the touch. I fling the rest of the mud back into the water but hold on to the stone. Tighten my fist around it and run back toward the clearing, hoping my defiance hasn't been detected.

It hasn't. I'm safe, but it's a close one. I hear Piccardy before I see him. "Okay, I got one," he says. "Drunk walks into a saloon and orders a shot and a beer. He sees a jar full of twenties and asks what that's all about. Bartender tells him whoever completes three tasks successfully gets the money." I try my best to tune him out by listening to the river.

Then I see them. Anselmo's still hanging around but Goolsby's not with them. "So the drunk says, okay now where's the old lady with the bad tooth?" That must be the punch line because Anselmo guffaws on cue.

"Two more bushes and I'm done," I tell Piccardy. "What do I do after that?"

"Grab a push broom and sweep out the barn."

Okay, asshole.

"Hey, Ledbetter," Anselmo says. "That cell of yours ever dry out after we visited you?"

It did, dickhead. Thanks for asking. "Yes, sir."

———

It rains most of the next day, so work is canceled. I keep wondering how Solomon's doing. Maybe I shouldn't have tried to warn him about court runs. One thing I've noticed is his tendency to lash out when he gets scared or overwhelmed. I just hope he's able to hold it together because if not, he'll get the worst end of it.

Midway through the morning, I'm stretched out on my bunk, reading another Easy Rawlins book, *Charcoal Joe*. Manny's writing to his sister, something he does every week. When the intercom clicks on, the officer at the desk says, "Ledbetter?" I'm told Ms. Jackson, the new counselor supervisor for our block, would like to meet with me in her office. Am I free this afternoon at two? I tell the squawk box I guess I can fit her into my busy schedule. The intercom clicks off.

"What do you think this is about?" I ask Manny.

He says he got called into her office last week. "It's just a meet-and-greet. She wants to put names to faces. I guess she hasn't gotten the memo yet about staff needing to show their indifference. I liked her."

I like her, too. Firm handshake, warm smile, close to six feet tall. Her hair's in cornrows with a braided bun on top. She's already read my file, so I'm spared the pain of having to talk about my conviction. "I'm more focused on the here and now," she tells me. "How are things going?" Before I can answer, her phone rings. "Excuse me," she says.

I scan the room while I'm waiting. Two stacks of inmate files on her desk, a bookshelf that holds sociology and criminology texts and family pictures. She's hung her framed MSW degree on the wall behind her. Aliyah Brooks Jackson, it says. Awarded two years ago—the year I entered this place. I look back at the photos. In one, a framed newspaper clipping, she's wearing a number and leading a pack of other runners. The headline says, "Aliyah 'Tubby' Jackson Breaks State Record." Tubby? Did that nickname survive early childhood or were they being ironic? In another photo, she's a bride with her new husband. Three smaller pictures chart the growth of a little girl from infant to toddler to schoolkid with missing front teeth. Her daughter, I presume. That must be the daughter's artwork on the bulletin board. I smile, wondering how those giant people are supposed to live in that much smaller house. Makes me think of that book *Clifford the Big Red Dog*. And, of course, the giraffe family that lives next door to Maisie in the book I'm doing for her.

When Ms. Jackson hangs up, she asks me again how things are going. I tell her about how hard it is not seeing my daughter and she commiserates, but I end up talking mostly about Solomon—his crying jags and temper tantrums, the self-abuse, his vulnerability in this hostile environment. "An adult men's prison is the last place where this kid should have been placed. Lieutenant Cavagnero thought it might be good to put him outside on the grounds crew, so we had an arrangement that Solomon would only work with me and I'd kind of look out for him. That worked okay, more or less, until the lieutenant left. Now that we've got a new supervisor, all bets are off."

She cocks her head. "Why is that?"

She and I have only just met, but because she seems genuine and hasn't been here long enough to have gotten jaded, I decide to risk it. "Best-case scenario? Officer Piccardy doesn't give a crap about Solomon or any of the rest of us, so me looking out for the kid isn't something that interests him. Worst case? He's a bully with a sadistic streak."

Her forehead wrinkles. "That's a bad combination," she says. "I'll look into it."

She writes something down. Whatever her "looking into it" means, I hope it doesn't come back and bite me in the ass. She says she hasn't met Solomon yet but she'll read his file and call him in. I tell her he's at court today. "It's just for a continuance, but court days can be hard."

"And you're worried about him?" When I nod, she smiles and says, "Well, I think it's great that you're stepping up. Taking on the role of his prison dad."

"No, no," I tell her, shaking my head. "It's just situational because of what got set up when Cavagnero was the crew chief."

"No need to be defensive," she says. "Attachment can be a *good* thing. For *both* of you." Since she's read my file, she knows why I'm here. But if she's jumping to the conclusion that Solomon's a stand-in for Niko, she's way off base.

"Good talking with you, Ledbetter," she says. "I'll be in touch."

She stands; I stand. She gives me that vise grip handshake again and I'm out of there, worrying that I've said too much. I could have said a lot more, but I stopped short of telling her how Piccardy is training Goolsby to follow his lead or that his best bro, Anselmo, has been coming off the night shift and hanging around in the daytime, too. It was probably stupid of me to say anything. Counselor Jackson is a wild card. Bottom line: if you don't know whom you can trust, don't trust anyone, staff especially.

———

There's no sign of Solomon at supper chow. When our cell doors pop at eight for our last five-on-the-floor before lights-out, Manny and I leave our cell. "They never get back *this* late," I say. "This isn't good. Something must have happened. "

"Look," Manny says. I follow his gaze to the end of the corridor and there's Solomon. He's walking, zombielike, past his and Daugherty's cell and heading toward me. As he comes closer, I see that his face is puffy on one side. He's got a shiner. When he leans his forehead against my chest, I put my arm around him. "Rough, huh? You want to tell me about it?"

His head moves side to side. "I might as well just kill myself," he says.

I break from him and make him look me in the eye. His bottom lip is trembling and tears are spilling down his cheeks. "No, you're not going to do that, Solomon. Whatever happened today, you're not going to harm yourself or let it defeat you. You hungry?" He says he hasn't eaten anything all day. "Okay, stay put and I'll get you something." I reenter our cell and grab a package of cheese crackers with peanut butter and an Almond Joy. Go back out and hand him the food. The buzzer sounds, signaling the end of five-on-the-floor.

"Get some sleep," I tell him. "I'll see you tomorrow morning. Get yourself up in time so you don't get hassled for being late. We can walk over together."

He shakes his head. "I'm not going."

"Yes you are, Solomon. What you're *not* going to do is sit in your cell all day tomorrow and replay today. You're going to get up on time, walk over to the barn with me, and keep busy." What do they call this? Tough love?

I have no idea whether that's what he needs, but I know that wallowing in self-pity was what made *me* think suicide was the answer. "Here, take this," I tell him. "It's not a gift. It's a loan. Don't lose it." I hand him my river stone.

He glances at it, then looks up at me. "I don't get it," he says.

"It's from the river back there. It's powerful."

He rolls the stone between his thumb and index finger, studying it. When he looks back up at me, I can tell he's skeptical.

The following morning, Solomon is up in time but withdrawn. He sits across from me at breakfast chow. The swelling on the side of his face has gone down and his black eye's begun to change color. When the guard calls time, we dump our trays, leave the hall, and walk toward the barn in silence. "Here," Solomon says. He hands me back the river stone. I tell him he can keep it for a while—that I don't need it back this soon. "I don't want to lose it on you," he says.

I tell him to suit himself and take the stone back.

CHAPTER TWENTY-NINE

—

November 2018
Days 484–86 of 1,095

Piccardy is doing push-ups while he waits for the crew to assemble. He's been in a good mood the last couple of days because he was in a weight-lifting competition last weekend and won in his weight category. "What was his prize?" Ratchford wondered. "A mirror so that he can kiss it?" We all laughed at that one.

"Everyone here, Officer Goolsby?" Piccardy asks. Goolsby gives him a thumbs-up. "Okay, listen up, ladies!" he says. "We're starting a project today that's probably going to take a couple of days to finish."

"What's that, boss?" Tito asks.

"The maintenance department's planning to repaint the barn before the really cold weather gets here, but as you can see, it's peeling pretty bad." As if on cue, Spence comes out of the barn pushing a wheelbarrow full of scrapers, wire brushes, wooden blocks, sheets of sandpaper, and face masks. "You're working in pairs. Two to a side, one of you up on a ladder, the other on the ground. Tito and Israel, you're scraping the east side, Ratchford and Harjeet the west. Ledbetter and Clapp, you do the back. Spence, you and Officer Goolsby can tackle the front." This seems to take Goolsby by surprise, but he recovers quickly from the demotion. "That all right with you, Officer Goolsby?" Piccardy asks. Goolsby gives him a nod and a half-smile.

I can tell from Solomon's face that he's relieved we're working together again and I guess I am, too. Has Aliyah Jackson worked some kind of counselor's magic or is this just a coincidence? Probably the latter; nothing gets done this quickly at DOC. But if she did intervene, I'm sure Piccardy didn't like it.

"Where are the ladders at?" Harjeet asks.

Goolsby points to the pickup rumbling toward us on the dirt road. One of the maintenance guys is at the wheel and four extension ladders stick out from the back of the truck bed. "Okay, girls. Grab your equipment and get started!" Piccardy says. "Chop chop!"

Goolsby drops the tailgate down and Tito, Harjeet, Spence, and I slide the ladders out. Israel says he has trouble with heights and wants to be on the ground. "Me, too," Solomon says. I tell him sure, but that he should grab the other end of the ladder. Of course, he objects. Tells me Spence and Tito are carrying their ladders by themselves. Why can't I? When I give him a look, he cooperates.

Things go okay for the first hour, although Solomon's no more enthusiastic about scraping than he was about leaf-raking or "brooming." When he complains that the paint I'm scraping off overhead is getting chips and dust in his hair and eyes, I ask him how he might solve that problem. "Oh," he says, and moves to the other side. Like I told Cavagnero: he's a work in progress.

When Goolsby shouts that it's lunchtime, I tell Solomon to go ahead. I have one more little section in the corner to scrape and then I'll be right down. He disappears around the corner, but here comes Piccardy. He stops at the base of the ladder and when I get off the bottom rung, he latches on to my shoulder and says, "I met your new friend yesterday afternoon."

I know who he means, but I play dumb. "Which new friend is that?"

He lets go of my shoulder and pulls down my face mask. "Jackson. You really gave her an earful, didn't you? Talking about how you and Clapp have a father-and-son bond or some such horseshit."

I clarify that I didn't say that; she did.

"Guess she doesn't know about your history as a father then, huh?"

He's goading me, but I stand there, blank-faced, waiting for this to be over.

"Or maybe that's not the kind of bond we're talking about. You and that little geek got a man-boy love thing going on? Is that why you want to be his daddy?"

I feel my right hand make a fist. "No, sir. Is that all, Officer Piccardy?"

"Not quite." He gets a foot from my face. "You fuck with my authority again, Ledbetter, so that a counselor tells me who's working with who on *my* crew, you better remember that payback is a bitch. Got it?"

"Yes, sir. I understand. May I grab some lunch now?"

"Sure thing. Maybe Clapp's saved Daddy a seat."

———

After work, I tell Manny about the exchange. "I know you care about that kid, Corby," he says. "But be careful. Piccardy has a ten-pound chip on his shoulder where you're concerned. Plus he's insecure as fuck, so he's going to feel threatened by a supervisor pulling rank, especially a self-confident Black woman. The last thing you want to do is get in the middle of a pissing contest between Custody and Counseling."

I know he's right.

On our second day of scraping, the work assignments get juggled—everyone's but mine and Solomon's. Piccardy isn't going to buck authority, but Manny's right: I need to watch my back. Things go without incident all morning.

At lunchtime, Piccardy leaves Goolsby in charge and takes off over the hill toward the facility. Later, when we get back to work, I can see from my vantage point on the ladder that he's coming not from the prison but from the woods. Anselmo's with him and his voice is the one that carries. "I thought you said this shit was mellow, but I'm fuckin' *baked*, man. I gotta sit." When he plops down on the grass, Piccardy sits, too. Whatever he just said makes the two of them giggle.

I look down at Solomon to see whether he's heard or seen any of this, but his attention is elsewhere. A turkey hen and her young are pecking and circling at the crest of the hill. If those are the same ones he's watched so closely before, the chicks have grown. They must have started molting, because their birth fluff is mostly gone. When Solomon takes five or six steps toward them, the mother hisses and ruffles her feathers and her young scurry in different directions, then freeze in place. Solomon stops in his tracks and Momma somehow gives the all-clear. The poults unfreeze and rejoin her, resuming their scavenging for bugs and seeds. They're about halfway between Solomon and the two stoned COs.

"Ten bucks says you won't do it," I hear Anselmo say. Do what, I wonder.

"The fuck I won't," Piccardy says. "One of those stupid birds put little dents in the door of my Mustang last week, right after I'd washed and waxed it. Saw its reflection and attacked it like it was an enemy. How dumb is that? Sanborn seen it when he was coming on shift and chased her away."

He gets up off the ground and draws his canister of pepper spray out of its holster. Arms extended like he's holding a Glock, he says, "This is for you, bitch!" and shoots. The mother hen takes a direct hit. She screams in ear-piercing agony, then falls over, beating her wings against the ground. Her panic-stricken young run around her in frenzied circles.

Laughing, Anselmo calls his buddy "one crazy motherfucker" and says he hopes no one comes across the injured bird and starts asking questions. Piccardy tells him he worries too much. Then he walks over to her and stomps her head. Picking her up by her feet, he rears back and flings her into the woods. "Don't forget my ten bucks," he reminds his bud.

It doesn't dawn on me that Solomon's just witnessed what I have until I see him charging Piccardy, his paint scraper raised like a weapon.

"No, Solomon! Stop!"

Alerted by my shouting, Anselmo and Piccardy turn and short-circuit his kamikaze assault. Anselmo grabs his wrist and twists it until Solomon cries out in pain and drops the scraper. Piccardy picks him up from behind, then slams him down against the ground. Solomon's screaming, "You murdered her! You murdered their mother!" As Piccardy comes at him, Solomon curls into a fetal position.

I scramble down the ladder fast as I can to stop what's happening. Piccardy presses his boot against Solomon's neck, eases up, then kicks him in the head and in his side—once, twice. "Cut it out!" I yell.

Reeling around, he faces me, red-faced and furious. "Stay the fuck out of this, Ledbetter, or I'll have you down on the ground next!"

Anselmo tells his buddy to calm down. "They're not worth it," he says. He looks scared, but Piccardy is still seething.

When a voice behind me asks what happened, I turn around and see Officer Goolsby. Lured by the commotion, the other crew members are standing behind him. "Stop dogging it and get back to work!" Piccardy screams at them.

"Nothing to see here," Anselmo says.

Some of the guys look from Solomon to me, their faces asking what's just gone down. I shake my head. Not now, maybe later. I can tell from the look on Goolsby's face that he can't figure out what's happened either.

After the onlookers have been dispersed, I approach Solomon to see how badly he's hurt, but Piccardy steps in front of me. "Weren't you supposed to control this little psycho?" he says. "Isn't that why I had to make sure you two worked together?"

I stand there, glaring back at him, saying nothing.

"You saw him try to attack an officer without provocation. And you had better corroborate that if there's an investigation," Piccardy says.

"But there *was* provocation. He saw you pepper-spray an innocent animal."

His pupils are still dilated from the weed, but his eyes flash with hatred. He gets right up in my face. "You didn't see a thing. Understand?" When I don't respond, he says, "You saw nothing except this batshit-crazy little freak try to attack me out of the blue." Spittle flies from his mouth and lands on my face. "And if you claim otherwise, I'll make your life a living hell. Got that? Now get back up on that ladder, Daddy, so that we can haul your twink out of here." I stand there, hand in my pocket, fingering my river stone. "That's an order," he says. "Unless you want me to write you up for insubordination."

"Yeah, go ahead," I finally say. "You write me up for not following an order and I'll write you up for what I saw you do."

"Keep it up, big shot," he says. "And I'll fuckin' *break* you."

"He means it," Anselmo adds. "You better play it smart."

Climbing the ladder as ordered, I look over my shoulder to see them pulling Solomon up on his feet. Piccardy shouts to Goolsby that they've got to take care of something, but they'll be back before quitting time.

"Okay, boss," Goolsby shouts back.

I climb higher and watch the three of them head off. Anselmo's and Piccardy's upper arms are hooked under Solomon's armpits and they're walking him backward. Half walking and half dragging him. The way Piccardy slammed him down on the ground, he might have injured him, and those kicks he delivered could have broken one or more of his ribs. From my vantage point, I watch them lead Solomon not toward the facility but into the woods. My better judgment says to stay put and scrape paint—that I can't help him—but I climb down anyway.

Entering the woods where I saw them go in, I follow Piccardy's voice. From behind the trunk of a good-sized oak tree, I watch what's going on. They've got the kid down on his hands and knees. When Piccardy orders him to do it again, louder this time, Solomon barks like a dog. "I can't *hear* you," Piccardy keeps saying. He makes him repeat himself until the sound coming from Solomon is part barking, part sobbing. Seeing what those motherfuckers are doing makes me lightheaded. I have to lean against the tree to steady myself.

Anselmo asks him why he got so bent out of shape about some stupid turkey when he's in prison for killing a bunch of defenseless dogs. "I don't know!" Solomon cries. "I don't know!"

Piccardy says he wants to hear what those poor dogs sounded like as they were being executed. When Solomon tells him he doesn't remember, Piccardy pulls out his pepper spray. "Well, you better remember quick or you're gonna get 'the turkey treatment.'" Broken and terrified, Solomon begins to howl. Sickened by what I'm witnessing, I have to stop it no matter what it costs me.

I step out from behind the tree and shout, "Hey!" Solomon and his two tormentors look up and see me. I turn and run.

Almost out of the woods, I spot the dead, mangled turkey. Without knowing why, I grab it, cradle it, and keep running. Reaching the clearing, I look back at the barn. Goolsby's standing there, staring at me. I turn and run in the opposite direction toward Block B. Is this really happening? Have I gone this far out on a limb? Yes! So fuck Piccardy and his threats! They're not getting away with this. . . . And fuck counseling protocol, too. I'm not waiting around for an appointment. She's going to see me *now*! I enter the building and head toward Jackson's first-floor office.

She jumps when I barge in. "Ledbetter?" She looks at the dead hen I'm holding, then up at me. Out of breath and realizing from her face that I'm scaring her, I try to explain but can't get the words out. Can't catch my breath.

"Calm down," she says. But I can't. My heart is revving. I begin to shake. Hyperventilate. I'm just barely able to squeeze out the words: "Panic . . . attack."

"Okay, sit down and take some deep breaths." I do what she says. Drop the dead bird on the floor beside me. I hear something Dr. Patel once said. *Panic attacks aren't fatal.*

When I'm a little calmer, she unscrews her thermos, pours some water into a paper cup, and tells me to drink it. Swilling it, I begin to choke. "Easy," she says. "Slow down. Sip it slowly." Wiping away my tears, my left eye begins to sting and I realize I have some of the bird's pepper residue on my hand. When I tell her why I'm screaming, she pours more water and has me hold the cup to my eye and keep blinking. I follow her instructions until it stops stinging.

When I'm finally able to tell her what happened, she's measured and professional. "But if he was rushing at him with a weapon, didn't Officer Piccardy have a right to defend himself?"

"Yeah, but he already had him down on the ground. Why would he start kicking him in his side, kicking in his head, stepping on his neck?"

"Did anyone else witness this?"

"Just Anselmo, but he's not going to throw his buddy under the bus."

"What about when they took him into the woods? Can anyone corroborate your account of what they made him do?"

I shake my head. "No one except Solomon."

Deep sigh. She shakes her head. "Okay, let me explain how the grievance system works. First of all, an offender can't file a grievance on another offender's behalf. It would have to be Clapp who made the complaint by submitting an Administrative Remedy form, requesting a formal review of what happened. Then the Administrative Remedy Coordinator for your unit would either let the complaint proceed or dismiss it."

"So who would this coordinator be? A captain? The unit manager?"

"Not at this stage. It would be another of the custody officers in your building. Typically, that person will side with the officer being grieved, not the complainant. It doesn't always happen, but that's the way it usually goes."

"In other words, the deck is stacked. If it gets dismissed, can he appeal?"

"Yes, but in this case, it's unlikely to go anywhere. If, as you say, CO Anselmo backs up CO Piccardy's account, it would be one offender's claim against two officers."

"But I'd corroborate what Solomon says, so it would be two against two."

"And whose version do you think would prevail?"

She has me there, but I'm not ready to give up. "Kicking the kid? Making him bark like a dog? Piccardy's been pulling all kinds of shit around here and gotten away with it, but this was flagrant. The guy's a sadist. The problem is, he's more or less untouchable because of his uncle."

"Who's his uncle?" she asks.

"Deputy Warden Zabrowski."

She winces. Says she didn't know that.

I get up off my chair and go to pick up the dead bird. "Leave that," she says. With my hand on the knob, I stop and turn back to her. "Do you believe me? That all this happened?"

"I do, as a matter of fact, just by seeing your condition when you came in here. She tells me to sit back down. Look, it's a slippery slope when Counseling tries to challenge Custody's authority. I know a counselor in Enfield who lost his job for daring to do that. Ledbetter, I have a husband out of work and a daughter to support, a mortgage, car payments. So if you're planning to take this to the mat, I can't afford to get down there with you. And before you decide to pursue this, think about the possible repercussions for both you *and* Clapp. You're not in a position to fix this, no matter how justified you'd be for trying. And if Solomon's just been on the receiving end of an ugly, traumatizing episode, do you want to set him up for more of the same?"

I shake my head. "He'd probably be too scared to blow the whistle on them anyway. And I don't think that turkey's going to file one of those Administrative Remedy things either." Either she doesn't appreciate my gallows humor or she's thinking about something.

"That's actually something you *could* file a grievance about. I'm not suggesting you do it, but it's the one thing that's not about Clapp. Not directly anyway." I wait. "Inappropriate use of a state-issued weapon against a defenseless animal. But I doubt that would go anywhere either. It would still be your word against theirs."

"Not if there's evidence. Do you have a cell phone? Maybe you could take a few pictures that I could use."

She says the first thing they'd want to know is how you *got* those pictures.

"And you've got a daughter, a mortgage, and a car payment. Okay, I get it."

"There is one thing I *can* do," Jackson says. "Get Clapp to the hospital and have his injuries looked at, have some X-rays taken. I'll request a psych eval while he's there, too. I'll flag it as an emergency so they don't just walk him over to the med unit and give him a couple of Tylenol. The state shouldn't be housing Clapp here when he clearly needs to be in a psychiatric facility. I might not be able to get him transferred by myself, but a report from the hospital couldn't hurt."

I thank her for listening to me and taking it seriously. She thanks me for caring about Solomon. "But I'm worried about you, too," she says. "You need to take care of yourself. Do you know anything about black holes, Ledbetter?"

"I know that whatever gets sucked into one never gets out."

"Exactly," she says.

Standing up, I tell her I'd better get back to the job we're doing. I ask her what she wants me to do with the dead turkey. She tells me to leave it, that she'll get it disposed of. "Somehow," she says.

After I leave her office, I head back to the worksite to face the music. I start chastising myself for being too emotionally involved in Solomon's problems. Sure, I feel sorry for the kid and want to help him, but he's not really my responsibility. Jackson's got a daughter to support and so do I. The best way for me to support Maisie is to keep my nose clean until I can get out of this place and be back in her life. Solomon's not my kid; she is. Still, I'm *not* as powerless as Jackson thinks. Getting Anselmo and Piccardy fired is a long shot, but it *could* happen. Inappropriate use of a state-issued weapon against a poor, dumb animal. Somebody's got to do something to expose those two and the shit they're pulling.

When I get back to the barn, the sun's on the descent. I can hear the other crew members scraping. I'm guessing about an hour to go until quitting time. I grab my scraper and start climbing the ladder when someone grabs my foot. "Hey!" I yell. "What the fuck?" Looking over my shoulder and down, I see it's Piccardy and, behind him, Goolsby.

"Tell him, Officer Goolsby," Piccardy says.

"Go back to your block, Ledbetter," he says. "You're off the crew."

"You had a good thing going here, but you blew it," Piccardy adds.

I'm tempted to say what I'm thinking: you COs have a better thing out here than we do. Pizza parties, pot parties, no one watching you. That would wipe that smug expression off Piccardy's face, but I'd end up paying for it in spades.

Walking back to B Block, I decide that if I get the third degree from any of the other crew members, I'll keep my mouth shut. The less said, the better. I enter the block, climb the stairs to our tier, and stop at the control desk. "What's up?" CO McGreavy asks. I tell him I need an Administrative Remedy form. McGreavy and I have never had any issues, but he gives me a suspicious look as he hands it to me. When I ask him where it goes after I fill it out, he points to the locked box at the far end of the desk.

"Who reads these?" I ask.

"The unit officer who handles grievances for this block," he tells me.

"Officer as in a regular CO?" He nods. "Who is it?" He says I'm not privy to that information. "It's not Piccardy, is it? Or Anselmo?"

He looks around to see whether anyone's watching. Then he shakes his head.

"So I write up the complaint and drop it in the box. Then what happens?"

"Depends. The grievance officer either dismisses the complaint or passes it up the chain to the unit supervisor, or sometimes to a captain or a lieutenant."

"But not to the warden?"

"Jesus, Ledbetter, what is this? Twenty Questions? Maybe one time out of a hundred it goes as high as the warden's office, but it's usually dealt with before it gets that far. You sure you and whoever you got a problem with can't talk it out instead of putting it in writing? Settle it that way?" I tell him yes, I'm sure.

On the way back to our cell, I try to second-guess which CO would be reading my complaint. Kratt? Hernandez? Maybe even McGreavy himself.

Whoever it is, I get the feeling a lot of the other guards think Piccardy's a douche, so it might make it to the next round. And Captain Graham's our unit supervisor; she's no-nonsense but she strikes me as fair. If it gets to her, she might follow up, ask questions, pass it up the chain. It's worth a shot.

Back in our cell, when Manny asks me about my day, I can't help but laugh, though nothing's remotely funny. I tell him I got kicked off the crew.

"What for?" he says.

"Piccardy and Anselmo were abusing Solomon, so I walked off the job and reported them to Jackson."

"Wow, that was either ballsy or stupid. Abusing him how?"

"Threw him on the ground and started kicking him." I feel my anger bubbling up again just thinking about it. "Then they took him into the woods, made him get down on all fours and bark like a fucking dog!"

"Jesus, that's bad. But I've seen worse, Corbs."

I make him promise not to say anything about what I just told him—to let me handle it. "Jackson's going to have him checked out at the hospital," I tell him. "Get some X-rays taken and have him talk to a shrink, although who knows how that's going to go? But seriously, Manny. Don't discuss this with anyone."

"Okay, okay. I get the message. Sheesh."

"I'm worried about him, you know? He's just a fucked-up kid."

"You know who I'm worried about, Corby?" he says. "*You*. You've gotten too involved with that kid. Yeah, he needs help and yeah, he doesn't belong here. But you can't fight his battles for him."

"Okay, Manny. Thanks for the unsolicited advice."

I put the big mythology book on my lap, grab a pencil, and start filling out the grievance form. "What's that?" he asks.

I read him the heading. "CTDOC Form 16-E, Administrative Remedy Regarding Alleged Staff Misconduct. Don't you love all the bullshit euphemisms they have at this place? Administrative Remedy? The real remedy will be if I can get Piccardy and Anselmo fired over this."

"For bullying the kid? Roughing him up a little?"

"No. You can't file a grievance on another inmate's behalf. This is about what they did to the turkey."

Looking bewildered, he lets go a laugh. "The turkey? What turkey?"

"Never mind. I want to get this done. You can read it after I finish."

But the day has taken its toll and I'm too emotional and too exhausted to phrase it right. I stop after the first three or four sentences. I'll write the rest of it tomorrow. I don't have work anymore, so I'll have plenty of time.

I flop down on my bunk, face to the wall, and close my eyes. It plays in my head like a movie: the way they hurt him, humiliated him. I'm just starting to doze when I hear, "I wouldn't if I were you." I turn my head and there's Manny, standing next to my bunk. He's holding the grievance form.

"Except you're *not* me."

"Come on, Corby. You *know* how these things go. Anselmo and Piccardy will back each other up and you'll end up standing in dog shit. Then they'll want to get even. And frankly, I don't want to get caught in the middle of it."

"This isn't about *you*, Manny."

"The *fuck* it isn't! What if they shake down our cell again and go through *my* stuff, too? See what I've got stashed away? I don't want to get a ticket for contraband because of your grandstanding."

He climbs up to his bunk, crosses his arms across his chest, and pouts.

"I'm not grandstanding! I'm standing up to a couple of bullies."

He jumps down again and goes to the back window. With his back to me, he says, "And if you think you're gonna get those two goons fired over a turkey, you're fuckin' delusional. You planning to take on their union, too? And Piccardy's uncle?"

"No, but if my complaint travels a few links up the food chain, at least it will put the administration on notice that these two need to be watched."

He pivots, facing me again. "Okay, man, if you want to stick your neck out, you better watch out for the ax. And keep me out of it."

I snatch the grievance form away from him and tell him to chill out. "I fucking know what I'm doing, Manny."

"Ha!" he says. Goes back up to his bed and pulls the sheet over his head.

—

The next morning on the way to breakfast chow, I catch up to Solomon's cellmate, Daugherty. "How's the kid doing?" I ask. He shrugs. Says he hasn't come back from the hospital yet. What does it mean if they kept him overnight? Is he that badly injured? Has he had a breakdown?

After I eat, I go back and start in again on the grievance. I go back and forth about including the part about them smoking weed while they were on the job, but decide against it. Too hard to prove so I stick to the animal abuse. *They made a ten-dollar bet. . . . Piccardy was the one who pepper-sprayed her. . . . She was suffering but still alive when he stomped her head and threw her into the woods. . . . Her chicks can't fly yet, so without her protection, they'll be easy prey.* I probably should not have added the flourish at the end of the complaint. *If the matter is not taken seriously and dealt with appropriately, I will have no choice but to notify the SPCA about Officers Piccardy and Anselmo's cruelty toward a defenseless animal and her young.*

The instructions say to limit your complaint to the back of the form and one extra page. By writing smaller on the last half page, I just make it. When our cell doors pop for our five-on-the-floor break, I walk down to the desk to drop my grievance into the box, but I stand there, hesitating. Maybe Manny's right. Maybe sticking my neck out is a mistake. But if I'm called in to talk about the pepper spraying, then maybe I can mention what they did to Solomon. The trouble with thinking like Manny is that it's defeatist. Jackson said she didn't think I'd have a shot either. They both assume inmates are powerless, but maybe we're not. I'm starting to lose my nerve a little, but I'm in it now and I'm doing it for Solomon and whoever else they've been bullying—myself included. I drop the form through the slot.

On my way back to our cell, Daugherty stops me. "Couple of the guards just came in and packed up Solomon's stuff. Said he's been transferred out of here, but they wouldn't tell me where." Hopefully, Counselor Jackson performed some kind of miracle and got the poor kid into a psych facility. I'm relieved that he's out of this place, but I wish I'd had the chance to tell him goodbye and good luck. He drove me nuts, but I'm already feeling his absence. One day he's here, the next day he's gone.

CHAPTER THIRTY

December 2018
Days 508–13 of 1,095

I've waited three weeks for a response to my grievance but have gotten zilch, so on Saturday I get a pass and head over to the library. I have to get an address for the SPCA. When I threatened to notify them, I wasn't really going to do it, but by not responding to my complaint, they're calling my bluff. I figure I'd better follow through. Mrs. Millman's not there, so I have Javi look up the address on the computer in her office.

I write the agency a three-page letter, stamp it, and drop it in the slot for outgoing mail. Midmorning the following day, Manny's at work and I'm giving the cell a cleaning. A new CO who looks like he's about eighteen unlocks our door and comes in. "Room search," he says.

Nothing of Manny's is touched, but my stuff—mattress, bedsheets, pillow, books, art supplies, toiletries—is thrown in a pile in the middle of the floor. "You looking for anything in particular, Officer?" I ask.

He says he's just following orders. Then he grabs my plastic bottle of shampoo and squeezes its contents all over my stuff. "Orders from who?" I ask. When he doesn't answer, I tell him that's okay—I know it was Piccardy.

"Don't know anything about it," he says. "Oh, yeah, and I'm supposed to say, 'Gobble, gobble, gobble.' Okay, you're clear. Sorry about the mess."

In the middle of the next night, I wake up to someone tapping my shoulder. Startled, I jump up in bed, blinded by a flashlight beam being held a few inches from my face. When the beam is turned around, it lights up the contours of Piccardy's face. "Hey there," he whispers. "Just thought I'd bed-check you to make sure you're okay." I feel his breath on my face but say nothing. Do nothing. After he leaves, I squint over at Manny's digital clock. Two forty-seven. I'm awake for the rest of the night.

Over the next few days, I remain clenched and vigilant. Anselmo and Piccardy are both working third shift, which isn't helping my sleep any. Someone's slipped me a folded note through our tray trap; when I open it, it says, "You're going to be sorry." Each time I go to the chow hall, I hear some random gobble-gobbling. I don't know who's doing it and I'm not giving anyone the satisfaction of looking around to see who it is, but I'm pretty sure it's coming from one or more of us inmates. Whoever they are, they must be doing Piccardy and Anselmo a favor to see what they get in return. Manny and I haven't been saying much to each other, but every time someone gobble-gobbles, he looks at me. He was right about me getting pushback, but I don't want to admit that the harassment is messing with my head.

Back on the tier, I try calling Emily, hoping to get a sympathetic ear. I'm grateful there's no one else using the phones. Usually there's a line at all three of them, so it's kind of a miracle.

This call originates from a Connecticut Correctional facility. If you wish to accept a collect call from . . . "Corby."

I hold my breath and wait for her to hit the "accept" number. She doesn't. Either she's out or she's standing there, staring at nothing. She hasn't accepted my calls in a couple of weeks now or visited me in almost two months. I recall that conversation we had about her work in therapy—how she was being encouraged to respect her boundaries and take care of her own needs ahead of others'. Meaning *my* needs, no doubt. But what does taking care of her own needs entail? Taking a spa day? Getting a manicure? Spending more time with her new "friend," Mr. Wonderful? Too bad her needs don't include driving down here to see her husband.

I hang up and dial the number of my second line of defense: Mom.

Less than a minute into our conversation, she says, "You sound upset, honey. Are you okay?" She always knows.

"Yeah, just feeling a little down." Why bother going into it about the intimidation campaign when she can't do anything about it except get upset?

"Well, I know something that will cheer you up. Maisie, honey, you know who's on the phone? Your daddy! Come say hello to him." Emily almost never asks Mom to babysit. Where did she go that she didn't ask her mother? "Maisie?"

There's an awkward silence, then Mom's voice again. "Sorry, Corby. She's very focused right now on her Play-Doh project. I showed her how to roll out snakes and—"

"That's okay, Mom. Don't pressure her. How's she doing?"

"Oh, she's fine, Corby. And smart as a whip! Knows all her colors and letters and the entire alphabet. And she's artistic, too, just like you. Even has some of your gestures when you were her age."

Unable to speak because of the lump in my throat, I say nothing.

"Emily says she's going to hold her back another year before she en-rolls her in kindergarten. I think she's more than ready. By next year, she'll probably be correcting the teacher! Of course, I don't say anything. It's Emily's decision, not mine."

"Not mine either, apparently," I say. "But then again, why should I have input when I haven't seen her since I got here?"

Mom tries one of her cheer-me-up comments. "Everyone thinks Maisie resembles Emily. And sure, she's got her coloring and her dark eyes. But when I look at that daughter of yours, Corby, I can see a lot of you at this age."

"Where did she go?"

"What?"

"Emily. Where did she go that she didn't ask Betsy to babysit?"

"I'm not sure, honey. Maybe Christmas shopping? I don't get to see

Maisie that much, so I wasn't about to rock the boat by asking a lot of questions."

"Not even about where she was going? What if something happened and you needed to get ahold of her?"

"She said she'd leave her cell phone on and I could call or text her."

I scoff. "Like you know how to text, right?"

"Honey, I've been texting for quite a while now." As in: *you* may be stuck in neutral, Corby, but none of the rest of us are.

"Did she say if, wherever the hell she was going, it was with someone else?"

"No. Why?"

"Because I'm starting to think there's another guy in the picture—that she may be getting ready to unload her loser husband for a new model."

"Come on, honey. It doesn't do you any good to think like that. It's like we say in NA: you can *look back* at the past, just don't keep *staring* at it."

"I know you mean well, Mom, but the last thing I need right now is one of your twelve-step slogans."

From the time I was a kid, my mother smoked weed—a consequence of having to put up with my father, I figured. By the time he finally left, she'd become a confirmed pothead. She'd tried to give it up a couple of times, but she only started going to NA after they sentenced me. Told me that the first time she visited me here. She said she needed to face her grief about Niko and the terrible repercussions for me instead of escaping from them by getting high. "I keep thinking that maybe, if I hadn't been so casual about smoking marijuana when you were growing up, what happened to Niko might not have—"

I stopped her right there. "Mom, I have to manage my own guilt about Niko every single day, sometimes hour by hour. Plus, my guilt about the pain and suffering I've caused Emily, you and Dad, her family. But I'm not taking on your guilt, too. Niko's death is about what *I* did that day. It has nothing to do with the fact that you used to smoke weed. Okay?"

"Yes, okay. I'm sorry, Corby. The last thing I want to do is upset you.

It's just that the program has helped *me* so much, I can't help but share the wisdom it's—"

"Mom!"

"All right, I get it. You called me for a little TLC and I'm making you feel worse. And no, I doubt Emily is seeing someone else. Her mother told me she's worried that Emily's been isolating herself again and dropping weight. Betsy says it's a pattern—that she gets this way around the holidays and closer to the anniversary of Niko's . . . Well, you know. I told her that's a rough anniversary for you, too. For all of us. I'm just thankful Maisie doesn't seem to remember anything about that day."

"Unless it's a buried memory that will surface later. Give her another reason to hate me besides disappearing from her life."

You have one minute remaining.

"Okay, Mom. Sorry I'm in a bad mood. Kiss Maisie for me and tell her Daddy loves her."

"Why don't you tell her yourself?"

"Better not. I'm sure Emily would want to prepare her for—"

"Maisie, sweetheart! Stop what you're doing and come say goodbye! . . . Right now, young lady. . . . *Maisie!*"

"It's okay, Mom. Don't force her."

"No, wait! Here she comes. Now you speak into the phone and tell your daddy hello."

I wait. Hear their whispered consultation. Then, my daughter's on the line! "You know what? Gammy Vicki and I are making snakes. And later on, we're gonna make pudding." Hearing her small, shy voice brings tears to my eyes.

"You are? Wow, that sounds like fun. What kind of pudding?"

"Chawkit."

"Oh man, that's my favorite. Hey, do those snakes you're making bite?" She giggles at the thought of it. "Do you remember who I am?"

The silence on the other end is agonizing. Is she confused? Afraid? Have her memories of me faded away?

"I'm Daddy. Do you remember when I used to give you piggyback rides and push you on the swings at the park? And read you stories at night-night?" My heart is pumping hard. My hand clutching the receiver goes sweaty. "*Good Night, Moon* and *Pat the Bunny* and . . . and . . . I haven't seen you in a long, long time, but pretty soon—"

We get cut off at that point: conversation terminated by Securus Technologies.

I slam the phone down. Kick a plastic chair and send it clattering. "Hey!" CO Wierzbicki shouts from halfway down the corridor. "Pick up that chair and get back to your cell!"

"You got it, Officer," I call back. "Sorry." I try not to let him see I'm in tears.

Yeah, Emily, we lost him because of me, but I'm losing her, too. It's not right for you to withhold her from me because of . . . because . . . So fuck you, Emily, and fuck your new boyfriend, too, if that's what he is. Self-care? Is this how you're taking care of yourself, Em? Not visiting me? Not picking up the phone and accepting my call? We *both* lost him, not just you. And now I'm losing her, too, because you never let her see me. What's that about, huh? Payback for the pain I've put you through? The humiliation I've caused you and your mother because you married the guy who got addicted, killed his son, and went to prison?

I'm awake for a good part of that night, my emotions swinging back and forth between resentment of Emily and sympathy for what I've put her through. Why *shouldn't* she start seeing someone while I'm stuck in here? File for divorce and move on? But if she and this Evan dude start playing house and Maisie grows up thinking of *him* as Daddy, I won't be able to take it. Not after I will have been in here for three years, unable to see her. Hold her. Play with her and put her to bed at night.

I get a couple of hours' sleep before waking up with an acid stomach and a sour attitude. I consider skipping morning chow because I'm in no mood to put up with anyone's bullshit. Then again, if they're serving something bland, maybe it'll calm down my gut.

Okay, it's reconstituted scrambled eggs, two slices of white bread, and dishwater coffee. Could be worse. On the walkway heading back to B Block, I see Warden Rickerby coming toward me accompanied by a trio of suits—politicians, probably, getting the PR tour, which explains why they were scrubbing down the block after hours yesterday. This is about the only time you see Rickerby on the grounds: when she's making the place seem like it's run better than it is. The expectation when she's in the company of visiting VIPs is that you give them a polite nod and keep moving. But I decide to risk being seen, being heard. "Warden? Sorry to interrupt, but can I speak with you about something?"

The entourage stops. "Not now," she says. "Can't you see I'm busy?" The metal button pinned to her coat says, *Ho, ho, ho!*

"Please. It's urgent."

"Excuse me for a moment, gentlemen," Rickerby says. "All right. What is it?" Her back is to her guests, so they can't see how pissed she looks. I tell her about having filed a grievance against two of her officers because of an incident I observed and that I've gotten no response. She glances down at my ID. "Look, Ledbetter," she says. "There's a procedure to follow and a chain of command. You can't just jump the line because you feel your complaint is more important than everyone else's."

"Warden, I *don't* think that, but I wanted you to know that two of your COs have been bullying some of us. And that one of them pepper-sprayed a—"

"Stop right there, Inmate Ledbetter. I'm not having you litigate whatever problem you're having with my officers. Let the grievance process take its course and consider it an opportunity for you to practice patience. And in the future, don't interrupt me when you can see I'm busy with guests."

"Yes, ma'am. I apologize." And screw you, Your Highness. Maybe if you got off your throne and looked around, you'd see what's going on around here.

Two days later, my complaint comes back to me in inmate mail. Stamped across it diagonally in red, it says "Dismissed." The following day, my letter to the SPCA is slipped through the tray trap of our cell door. It's been opened but there's no postmark. Those fuckers! It never even left the compound.

I pace, kick stuff, stop to look at the calendar. Tomorrow's the twenty-fifth. Merry fucking Christmas!

CHAPTER THIRTY-ONE

March 2019
Day 600 of 1,095

A red-haired boy, age eight or nine, and I are fishing from a rowboat. The boat drifts among flowering lily pads on that pond where a kid in my fourth-grade class named Eddie Elrod tried to swim from one side to the other but drowned halfway across. The boy might be Eddie or he might be Niko; I'm not sure. Whichever one he is, his bob plunges underwater. "Got something!" he says, and begins to reel it in. But what comes to the surface isn't a fish. It's a large bird—a great blue heron. Flapping the water off its wings, it skids across the pond's surface and takes flight. The fishing pole dangles beneath the heron until it's shaken loose and falls back into the pond. I watch the bird, unburdened now, fly farther and farther away from us. Us? I'm alone now. The boy is gone.

I smile, remembering that Eddie Elrod had blond hair, not red. The boy in the boat must have been Niko.

"Hi, Ledbetter."

"What? Who's there?" The tapping on my shoulder stops. "Did I wake you? Sorry about that." I know the voice. In the darkness, his whispering against my ear makes me flinch. "Just wanted you to know that Emily's been looking for it online. She's using a different name, but I recognize her. Hope nothing bad happens to her, because some of the guys on those websites are dangerous. Well, nighty-night, Ledbetter. Get some sleep."

After I hear him leave, I start to shake. My breathing is fast and shallow. That's bullshit about Emily, but it's jarred me. Hasn't he made his point? When the fuck is this going to stop? Deep breaths, deep breaths.

From the top bunk, Manny asks what's going on.

"Nothing. Go back to sleep."

"Was someone in here? I thought I heard someone."

"You must have been dreaming."

"Oh. Okay then. G'night."

"Night." A couple of minutes later, he's snoring.

When my shaking subsides, I roll off my cot and walk to the back of the cell. Look through the narrow sliver of window to the outside. Not much to see. The empty visitors' parking lot, the tipped-over garbage bin. It's probably been raided by that fat raccoon I've seen on other sleepless nights. The lamppost light is flickering, getting ready to die. Above it, the moon's waxing or waning, I'm not sure which.

Back in bed, I keep shifting positions but can't get comfortable, can't settle down. I'm furious with myself for thinking I could take on those two sons of bitches and win. I should have known better. I *did* know better, but I became so intent on making them pay for what they did to Solomon that a kind of temporary insanity took over. The insanity of ego maybe.

My father sometimes woke me out of a sound sleep, too, but he didn't whisper; he yelled. *What goes on in this house stays in this house*, he was fond of reminding me so that I wouldn't blow his cover. At his college, he was the well-respected professor. At home he was the tyrant whose specialty was verbal abuse. *You know who brings home report cards like this, Corbin? Losers! People who are never going to amount to anything. . . . You want to know why I never ask you to come with me to university parties, Vicki? Because you're an embarrassment, that's why! . . .* Maybe taking on Solomon's tormentors was a belated attempt to take on the illustrious Professor Ledbetter, the bully who demeaned and humiliated Mom and me and then made his escape.

I was never going to win that fight either. Justice would *not* be served.

Three fifteen according to Manny's clock radio. Goddammit! How can I be exhausted and wired up at the same time? . . . In that fishing dream, Niko was older than he was the day he died. School-age, third or fourth grade maybe. So, at least in my dream state, he lives on and grows. I didn't end his life after all. Desperate to shut off my mind and get back to sleep, I do something I haven't done in a long time. "Hey, Niko? Are you there? It's Daddy." I'm mouthing the words but not speaking them out loud. "I think I saw you tonight in a dream. Was that you?

"I'm still here in prison. Still doing my time for having taken you out of the world. Out of *this* world, anyway. I'm still clean and sober and I try every day to be a better person than I was the day you died. You've been my North Star in this effort, buddy. Do you know that?

"In AA, there's a prayer where we ask for the wisdom to know the difference between what we can change and what we can't. I'm in a tough situation right now because I *wasn't* wise enough. See, I saw something bad happening to this kid I was kind of looking out for, and my ego convinced me I could take on the system and stop it. But doing the right thing in here isn't the same as doing the *safe* thing, and there's been these two guards who are out to get me. The good news is that that kid, Solomon, got transferred out of here. How much do you see, Niko? Do you know how he's doing? I worry about him.

"I worry about your sister, too. First *you* disappeared from her life and then *I* did. Do you think this might have screwed her up—made her feel abandoned or whatever? Your mom sends photos of Maisie and writes me sometimes about the things she's into: Disney princesses, tea parties, swimming lessons—she's in the Guppies class. In return, I send her notes and drawings, stories I write and illustrate to try to keep her memory of me alive. Her favorites are the one about her and her best friend, Jeremy, who's a giraffe. I was into writing and drawing their third caper when I realized Jeremy Giraffe was a stand-in for you.

"I have trouble accepting that your mother keeps your sister away from this place, and maybe from me. I thought she'd change her mind after a while, but she's stayed firm on that. The last time we talked, she said Maisie's had to sit in time-out a couple of times at her nursery school for hitting other kids. Boys, not girls. Your mother says it's just normal kid stuff, but is it? Where's that anger coming from? And how might this affect her down the line? There was such a strong bond between you two. Is that somehow still intact? Do you watch over her, Niko? Even if she can't see or hear you, can she feel you're still there?

"With over half of my sentence served here, I have a lot of anxiety about what happens when I get out. I have two versions in my head about the day I walk out of here. In the first, the gate opens and your mother and sister are there, waiting. In the other, I walk through the gate and look around. No one's there.

"Well, I'm getting sleepy now, so I guess I'll say good night. Please look after Maisie for me and keep her safe. I love you, Niko. Thank you for listening."

I drift off, smiling and wondering whether I've finally discovered what, until now, has eluded me. Is my dead son the one who can remove my defects of character and restore me to sanity in this place where insanity reigns? Is Niko my spiritual touchstone?

———

The shouting wakes me up. "Goddamn it, Corby! I just stepped on that fucking thing! I think it bit me! Get it the hell out of here!"

I'm confused. What's he yelling about? I follow his pointing finger, but all I can see in the dim light is that it's a snake. Jesus, is it a copperhead? Those things are poisonous.

Climbing to the safety of his upper bunk, Manny continues his rant. "You had to file that stupid grievance, didn't you? 'I know what I'm doing, Manny. This isn't about you.' The fuck it isn't! I *knew* I heard someone in here last night!"

I swing my feet onto the floor, walk cautiously toward it. "False alarm, Manny. It's a milk snake. They're harmless. You're all right."

"I *knew* I'd get caught in the middle because of that grievance. Such a stupid move! You see them kill a fucking *turkey* and you get so bent out of shape that . . . Well, your space is my space, too, asshole, and if this shit continues, I'm putting in for a cell change so I don't have to step on a fuckin' snake when I get up to take a piss! Now get that fucking thing out of here!"

I make a grab for it, but it's fast. Try again. And again. Get ahold of it on the fourth try when it slithers into the corner. Holding it so that its head pops out from the top of my loose fist, I take a couple of steps toward Manny. "Look at him. He's kind of cute, isn't he? What are you afraid of?"

"Get that thing away from me! I mean it, Corby! It's not funny!"

I hold it until they call us for morning chow, then carry the snake with me and let it go once we're outside. It pauses for a second or two, lifts its head, then slithers off the walkway and toward the woods. Probably hears the river out there. *How can snakes hear if they don't have ears?* I remember asking my father when I was a kid.

They don't have outer ears, but they have inner ears. They hear vibrations.

———

Later that day, I apologize to Manny about the snake and he says he's sorry he lost his shit. In the time I've known him, he's never said much about his childhood, but he opens up about how kids in his Staten Island neighborhood used to chase after him with toads and snakes and call him a "sissy pants." And that by middle school, "sissy pants" became "pansy," "faggot," "fairy," "flit."

I tell him one of the things I admire about him is that he's comfortable about who he is and doesn't seem to get pushback from the homophobic assholes here.

He says that's because straight guys enjoy a good blow job just as much as gay guys do. "And believe me, I give a great one."

I smile. Tell him I'll take his word on that.

"But I tell you, Corby, when I stepped on that snake this morning, I went flying back to Willoughby Avenue with those punks tormenting me, and Bobby Costello, who I had a secret crush on, putting his pet snake a few inches from my face and me staring at its flicking forked tongue."

Talking to Manny gets me thinking about how most of us must carry our bruised childhoods on our backs when we come here. Solomon was the most obvious example. No matter how well-intentioned his adoptive parents might have been, or how unfit his birth mother was, she was still his mother. Maybe getting separated from her is at the root of his troubles. For a lot of the other guys here, the bruises might not show, but they haven't necessarily healed. My conflicted feelings about my father take center stage whenever I think about my childhood. Dad was the guy who taught me my love of nature when I was a little kid. Taught me the names of the constellations in the nighttime sky and the stories that went with them. *Those three bright stars make up Orion's Belt. Above them and to the right is his shield. He was a warrior and a great hunter. . . . There's Pegasus, the winged horse, who emerged from the sea to help Perseus rescue the beautiful princess, Andromeda, from being devoured by the sea monster, Cetus. That cluster of stars tells their story. . . .* I can still pick out those stars in the sky and I have vivid recall of those ancient tales.

But Dad was also the guy who, as I got a little older, began to chip away at my self-confidence and sense of worth. *You acted like you were afraid of the ball out there. And you didn't show the coaches any hustle whatsoever. That's why you were one of the last ones picked. What did you expect?*

I blurt it out. "Manny, you were right. I wish I had listened to you. I never should have taken on those two. Piccardy's been sneaking in here in the middle of the night, waking me up and whispering shit to scare me. And that had to have been him who dropped the snake in here. I mean, Anselmo's a thug, too, but he takes his marching orders from Piccardy. He's the ringleader and, for all I know, a fucking sociopath. I'm sure they're planning to make the time I have left as miserable as possible." Manny sighs but doesn't say anything. "So have you requested that cell change yet? Because if you haven't—"

"I changed my mind about that," he says. "You're a pain in the ass, Corby, and I'm still sort of pissed at you, but we're friends. I'm not going to bail on you now."

What he says brings tears to my eyes, which I try my best to hide from him.

CHAPTER THIRTY-TWO

August and September 2019
Days 734–79 of 1,095

I remember a folk song my mother used to play and sing along with on one of her albums—a Joan Baez record, I think. *Yesterday's dead and tomorrow is blind.* . . . Live in the present, Dr. Patel's letter advised. Day at a time, the Big Book says. But with two-thirds of my sentence completed, it's hard not to get preoccupied about the future. Twelve more months to go. But then what?

The squawk box clicks on. "Hey, Ledbetter? The library just called. They need to see you about something. You want a pass?"

"Sure. I'll be right there. Thanks."

Truth is, my attendance at the library dropped way off after that incident with Solomon. It wasn't my fault, but I was the one who brought him over there. A missing razor blade could have turned into a big headache for Mrs. Millman if she hadn't caught it right away. Wonder what she wants. Has a job finally opened up? I could use one. I've been going a little stir-crazy here in the cell.

That time I brought Solomon here, everything was in chaos. Now when I walk in, the books are off the floor and back on the shelves. The freshly painted walls have brightened the place up a little. The computer station's up and running now; some guy's hunting and pecking on the keyboard of that refurbished IBM.

Mrs. Millman sees me, smiles, and walks toward me. "Hello, stranger," she says. I tell her the place looks great. She nods and thanks me. When I ask her what's new, she says she supposes I've heard that the library's lost its most faithful patron. I glance over at the table where Lester Wiggins used to sit. Empty chair. I shake my head. Tell her I didn't know.

"He died in his sleep a little over a week ago. Poor man was suffering terribly toward the end. He wanted so badly not to have to die in prison, but the warden denied the merciful discharge we were trying to get for him. At least they let his son visit him in hospice and pray with him before he passed. Lester wasn't religious, but it must have been a comfort for him to have Cornell there."

She says she wanted to organize a celebration of life for Lester here in the library. "But Deputy Warden Zabrowski put the kibosh on it. So we made a little tribute to him instead." She points to a small display halfway down the room. "Zabrowski says we can keep it up for a week. Then it has to come down and Lester's wheelchair has to be returned to the med unit."

"A whole week, huh? What a guy."

She shrugs. Asks why she hasn't seen me over here in so long.

"I'd like to say it's because I've been busy," I tell her. "But the truth is, I've had nothing but time on my hands since I got booted off the main-tenance crew."

She says she heard about that. Didn't it have something to do with that boy Solomon I was helping?

"Yeah. I mean, the kid's got major psychological problems so they sent him *here*? What genius made *that* decision? By the way, I'm sorry about the stuff with the razor blade."

"No, that was my own fault for being careless. Leaving it on the counter where he could be tempted. I should have known better."

"At least they finally transferred him to a psych facility."

"Is he doing any better now?"

I shrug. "I asked my counselor for a progress report. She was his counselor, too. But she says she can't access that information without written permission from him. I asked for the address of the place where he's at, but she says she's not authorized to give me that either."

"Well, he was lucky you were helping him while he was here. You're a good man, my friend."

"That's debatable," I tell her. But I like that she said it and called me her friend.

Her smile becomes a frown. "Now what's this I hear about some of the custody officers giving you a hard time?"

Taken by surprise, I mumble that I'm fine, it's just a few of them. But how the hell does she know? I solve *that* little mystery when I glance over at Javier, who's across the room shelving books. At the last AA meeting, I spilled my guts about some of the shit Piccardy and Anselmo keep pulling. So much for *Who you see in here and what's said in here stays here.* I don't mind so much that he leaked what I said to Mrs. Millman, but who the hell else did he tell? At least I didn't mention those goons by name. Good thing I didn't. If it got back to them, who knows what they'd do? Should I go over there and remind Javi that it's Alcoholics *Anonymous* or just let it go? Well, first things first.

"So what did you want to see me about?" I ask Mrs. M. "Don't tell me I've made it to the top of the waiting list for a library job." Before she can answer me, the phone in her office starts ringing. "Hold on, Corby. Let me get this first."

Rather than stand there waiting, I wander down to check out Lester's tribute. The sign on the little table next to his wheelchair says LESTER HERBERT WIGGINS 1941–2019. Four photos are displayed on the table. In one, Lester's a member of a high school baseball team, the Wilby Wildcats; in the middle of the back row, he towers over his teammates.

In the second photo, a formal wedding portrait, Lester's the groom in a sharp-looking three-piece suit. He and his pretty bride look to be in their early twenties. Their faces reveal their innocence about the bad things to come.

The third photo's a family picture: Lester's grown his hair out into a misshapen Afro and he's starting to go gray. His wife, maybe in her mid-to-late forties now, smiles at her husband as if he's *not* wearing scrubs—as if the family is *not* standing in the prison yard with guards and security fencing looming in the background. The couple's kids are dressed like they're going to church. Cornell's maybe thirteen or fourteen, his two sisters a few years younger than that; the three of them are wearing matching expressions somewhere between solemn and glum.

The fourth, more recent photo was taken here at the library. Lester is a gray-haired great-grandpa now, decades into his fifty-year sentence. He's at his regular table, reading a book and ignoring the camera. I recall when I first met him. No, I could *not* draw him, he said, because he wasn't my Uncle Remus. I smile, thinking about how firmly I'd been put in my place for being so condescending.

There's a folded newspaper on the table, too—the *Prison Times*, dated April 1989. What? They had an inmate newspaper? Under a front-page headline, "Wiggins Wins Fishing Derby," there's a picture of a beaming Lester holding a good-sized rainbow trout. *Back then we was treated like more than just our crime,* I still hear him saying.

Two columns of books, stacked on the seat of Lester's wheelchair, bear witness to his love of reading. The spines face out, so the titles are—

I flinch when I feel a hand reach from behind and cup my shoulder. "Jesus, Javier!" I snap.

"Sorry, hombre," he says. "Kind of jumpy today, ain't you?" It's more amusing to him than it is to me. I'm always jumpy now; it's the Piccardy-and-Anselmo effect. "So you like this thing we put up for the old guy?" I nod. "Mrs. M and I were going to give him a bigger send-off, but Zabrowski said no. So we came up with this idea. She told me her and Lester came to Yates the same year, so they've known each other forever."

I tell him I like looking at the photos—being reminded that there was more to Lester's life than his incarceration. "How did you guys get them?"

"Cornell put the word out to one of his sisters and she sent them to us. And *Mami* wanted to show what a big reader he was, so she had me look up what books he took out over the years and pull some of them off the shelves."

"Nice," I say. "Hey, speaking of 'Mami,' how did she know I've been getting hassled by a couple of the guards in my building? Who would have told her that?" He looks down at the floor, says nothing. "Because the only ones I talked to about that were the guys at last Sunday's meeting. And I'd hate to think I can't say what I need to in AA because I can't trust that it won't get repeated."

"*I* told her," he says. "The day after that meeting, she asked me if I seen you lately and it just came out. I'm sorry, man."

"You tell anyone else?"

He shakes his head. Says he owes me an amends. "I'll bring it up at the next meeting and apologize to you for breaking a confidence. It won't happen again, bro. I promise. We good?"

"Yeah, we're good," I tell him. "And you can skip the public apology. Your promise is good enough."

When he thanks me and walks away, I glance at the titles of the books Lester's read. There're a number of Walter Mosley novels, of course, and baseball biographies of everyone from Smokey Joe Williams to Mookie Betts. He was into political books, too: *Soul on Ice, Between the World and Me, Notes on a Native Son*. So many of the men who come to prison spend their time stewing in resentment and letting their minds rot. Not Lester. I guess being a reader and a thinker was the way he found to survive his lengthy sentence.

"Corby!" Mrs. M calls. "I'm off the phone now. Let's talk."

Approaching her, I ask again what she wanted to see me about. "Well, you finally made it to the top of the waiting list, but in order to be a library assistant, you have to have more than a year left on your sentence. I checked on your release date and it disqualifies you."

"Bad timing's one of my specialties," I tell her.

"But I have an idea for a special assignment I hope you'll consider."

"Yeah? What's that?"

"Follow me," she says, and takes me over to the wall where those dated posters of celebrities promoting reading used to hang. "We have this big blank wall now."

I pretend-gasp. "Don't tell me you're retiring Yoda and Penny Hardaway and the Duke boys."

"I just hope the American Library Association will forgive me," she says. "At first, I was thinking I'd buy some inexpensive art at Home Goods or TJ Maxx to fill up the space. Then I remembered when Beena Patel mentioned you were an artist and I asked to see some of your work."

"Yeah, well, those drawings I showed you were just rough—"

"Stop being so modest. How would you like to make this wall your canvas?"

"What do you mean? Paint you a mural?" She nods. I shake my head. "Why not?"

"I've never done anything this large. I'd screw up the perspective. Too much pressure. Plus, I'm not even that good."

"Nice try, but I've seen your work. You've already passed the audition."

"Yeah, well, that's flattering, but there's a big difference between doing pencil drawings in an eight-by-twelve sketch pad and painting an entire wall." I hand her the book I'm borrowing and she checks it out. "Thanks for thinking of me, though."

"Well, I'm disappointed," she says. "I guess it's back to Home Goods."

"Not necessarily. There's got to be a lot of guys doing time here who have artistic talent. I'll ask around, see if I can come up with a couple of names for you. Okay, I better get back. See you next time."

I'm out the door and halfway down the stairs when I stop and go back in.

"What subject are you thinking of?"

She says she doesn't have anything specific in mind—that it would be up to me. I remind her that I've passed on the offer, but she says, "Maybe you can come up with a few ideas, work up some sketches. Nothing too controversial that the powers that be could object to."

"Okay then. How about a scene out in the yard with cons pole-vaulting over the fence? Or a seascape with Warden Rickerby playing beach volleyball with her custody officers? Do you think she'd pose for me in a bikini?"

She laughs and tells me not to be naughty. "But seriously, Corby, I suppose it should be something uplifting. Hopefully, something colorful."

"I think colorful would be a tall order since the only color palette they seem to have here is drab gray, drab pink, and drab green."

"Oh, you don't know how resourceful I can be. I have contacts I can hit up at Sonalysts, Sherwin-Williams, and the Art Department at Connecticut College. I can get you all the colors of the rainbow, whatever you need. What do you say?"

I tell her I'll think about it. Work on some ideas.

"So that's a yes?"

"It's a probably not but maybe." She taps her finger against the blank wall and waits. "Okay, it's a maybe unless you hate what I come up with."

When she reaches over and kisses my cheek, I mockingly remind her that staff-inmate contact is against the rules. She says she doesn't think she'd have lasted six months here if she didn't break rules.

"Which is why you're a badass," I tell her. She grins and says she'll take that as a compliment.

As I walk back to B Block, I get a little choked up by the faith she's just shown me. The challenge of that blank wall begins to excite me and ideas for the mural are already spinning by the time I'm back in the building and climbing the stairs. Colorful, she says. Tropical birds in a rainforest? Monarch butterflies against a blue sky winging their way back to Mexico? She says she'd like it to be uplifting. A sky filled with hot-air balloons would be uplifting *and* colorful. Okay then. Problem solved. . . . Except how would that be different from the kind of art she'd buy at Home Goods? And more important, why would hot-air balloons speak to the guys in this place?

Sports heroes? I imagine it like the *Sgt. Pepper* album cover. Jordan, Jesse Owens, Muhammad Ali, and Babe Ruth in the front row. Behind them Jackie Robinson, Ted Williams, Jim Brown, and Larry Bird. But what about Clemente, Gretzky, Tiger, Serena? And what about Olympic athletes? Carl Lewis, Usain Bolt, Jackie Joyner-Kersee. Would anyone besides me know my sentimental favorite, Steve Prefontaine? Nah, I can just hear everyone bitching about who I included and who got left out. And I'd probably have trouble getting all those likenesses right. *That's supposed to be Magic Johnson?* Nope. Way too complicated.

How about something historic? Maybe a battle scene between the Wequonnocs and the Connecticut colonists? Uh-uh. Nothing uplifting about war. . . . Historic moments in the Civil Rights movement? MLK, John Lewis, and the freedom fighters at the Pettus Bridge? I'd love to stick it to the white supremacists around here, including some of the COs, but I don't want it to come back at me or land in Mrs. Millman's lap. . . . Famous American writers? . . . Rock stars and rappers? . . . The Apollo 11 moon landing? *That's one small step for a man . . .*

I spend most of the rest of the day thinking up ideas that seem promising, then scrapping them. By lights-out, I still haven't come up with anything I want to go with, but it dawns on me that I've been so engaged by this project, I've barely given a thought to those two a-holes who are out to get me and what they might pull next.

The next day, same thing. Ideas keep sparking in my head, but nothing catches fire. By day three, I have a sketchbook filled with notes and drawings that turn into dead ends. I'll give it another day or two. If I still can't come up with anything that excites me, I'll throw in the towel.

On the fifth day of driving myself nuts, I start thinking about mythology. I open up that book I grabbed from the library when they were throwing shit out and thumb through those color plates by the masters. I flip past Bruegel the Elder's *Landscape with the Fall of Icarus*, then pause and turn back to it.

I study the painting's composition—the unconventional choices

Bruegel made. The farmer in the foreground plowing a patch of land is the most prominent figure. His size and his bright red shirt grab the viewer's attention before anything else. Yet, he's insignificant to the Icarus story. So are the shepherd minding his flock, the man fishing at the water's edge, and the sailors aboard the cargo ship on the pale green sea. These ordinary people going about their day's work are oblivious or indifferent to Icarus's headfirst crash into the Aegean and what I imagine came next: his flailing and fighting against a watery death. Again, I wonder why the artist chose to make the story's doomed hero the least significant figure in the composition—render him as a small detail rather than the central figure. What's Bruegel saying? The Icarus myth is usually understood as a cautionary tale against the recklessness of youth. But maybe that lowly shepherd one tier down from the farmer provides a subtle clue about the artist's intent. He stares up at the sky, his attention focused on something the viewer doesn't see. Could he be staring at Icarus's father, Daedalus, who invented the makeshift wings that led to his and his son's escape from prison but also the son's fatal fall? Is the painting about Daedalus's fate: having to bear witness to his son's untimely death while he remains alive and aloft himself? Having to outlive his boy, suffering with the knowledge that he's the unintentional orchestrator of his demise?

I tear the color plate of *Landscape with the Fall of Icarus* from the mythology book, walk it over to the library, and run my idea past Mrs. Millman. "So clarify something for me, Corby," she says. "Does this mean you've decided to paint the mural?" I tell her it must because it's all I've been able to think about for days now. She applauds my answer. Then she takes the Bruegel print from me and studies it. "I know this painting," she says. "It's in a museum in Brussels. I saw it when my husband and I were traveling in Europe. So you're envisioning a landscape painting then. Any place in particular?"

"Yeah, *this* place. The land, not the prison. You ever see that ledge on the other side of the river?"

She nods. Mentions the inmate who tried to escape by scaling that ledge, but lost his footing and died from the fall.

"I was thinking about that guy. But what if he had made it to the top, then turned around and looked down at the view. The woods, the fields, the river, but not these ugly buildings and the ugly stuff that goes on here?"

"So you want to show what the property looked like before they built Yates?"

"Or after they tear it down. Or both."

She looks confused. "Well, work up some drawings that we can show the deputy warden," she says. "He'll need to sign off on what you're planning."

"Do you think that will be a problem?"

She looks at me intently. "Nothing too controversial or he'll take the easy way out and say no. And think about what you'll say if he asks why you've omitted the institution."

"Okay. Got it."

Back in our cell, I draw a rough layout of the composition on paper. Make a tentative list of who and what I might want to place in this past-and-future landscape: Lester Wiggins on the riverbank reading a book, Wequonnoc people hunting and tending to their crops before the white settlers arrived, a deer and her fawn grazing in a meadow, a blue heron flying up from the river. I've borrowed a set of colored pencils from Mrs. M, so I add blue sky, green vegetation, brown for the river. If Zabrowski asks where the buildings are, I'll make up some bullshit answer. Try to talk over his head so that, hopefully, he won't be able to come up with any reason to object.

Four days after I submit my design, I'm called to the library. The deputy warden is there and so is Warden Rickerby. Mrs. Millman tells them how excited she is that, pending their approval, the library will soon display original inmate-generated art. Then she knocks me for a loop. "Mr. Ledbetter and I have discussed the importance of making sure the mural makes no political statements that some could find offensive. Now, of course it's his right to exercise his freedom of speech through his art, but he's agreed to eliminate the Pride flag and the phrase 'End Police Violence' from the mural. To his credit, he was happy to comply."

What? I never even thought to include those things, but I'm following Mrs. M's lead. "Good," Zabrowski says. "We don't want to promote any of *that* stuff."

Mrs. Millman asks whether either of them has any questions for the artist. "I do," Zabrowski says. "If this is supposed to be Yates CI property, where are the buildings?"

"Well, I suppose you've heard about the space-time continuum," I say. "The three dimensions of space—length, width, and height—plus time, the fourth dimension? Physics 101, right?" The warden looks hesitantly at her deputy and nods. Zabrowski nods back. "So if you've studied Einstein's theory of relativity, you probably remember that he thought time travel might be possible, okay? That's kind of what I'm getting at. Assuming it would be possible to travel both back to the past *and* forward into the future, my intention is to illustrate that there was a time when the buildings here hadn't yet existed and there will most likely be a time in the distant future when they no longer exist. Get it?"

There's a long five seconds of uncomfortable silence. "Brilliant!" Warden Rickerby suddenly declares. Zabrowski nods in agreement. When Mrs. M asks whether we can assume my design has their approval, the warden says, "Absolutely! And maybe when the mural is finished, we can get the press to do a story on it. It would be nice to get some *positive* publicity for a change." With that, she claims she and her deputy have another meeting to get to and they exit the library as quickly as possible.

"You jolted me for a minute, Mrs. M, when you started talking about Pride flags and 'End police violence.' What was that about?"

"It's an old trick I learned from my community service days back in the seventies. When you're negotiating with the opposition, you start off by making a concession, real or imagined. It puts them at ease so that they think you're being totally reasonable. But what about you? The space-time continuum? Einstein's theory of relativity?" She chuckles. "How in the world did you come up with that stuff?"

"There's a new guy on our tier," I tell her. "A physics professor who's here for embezzling from his college. I just asked him if he thought time travel could be a thing and let him ramble. I didn't really understand much of what I was saying just now, but I think they bought it."

"Oh, they definitely did. They think it's a big secret that they're dumb as rocks, the two of them. Don't quote me." I tell her my lips are sealed. "Now then," she says. "When I got up this morning, Howie was already downstairs in the kitchen baking cookies. Could I interest you in a snickerdoodle?"

I'm feeling pretty lifted when I head back to B Block. The design's been approved and I'm brainstorming all kinds of ideas about the mural. But halfway to our building, I see two shadows approaching from behind. "No big surprise. That kid was more fucked-up than a soup sandwich." I recognize the voice; it's Piccardy. "Hey, Ledbetter. You hear the news about your little buddy?"

I keep walking; I'm not taking the bait.

"He hung himself."

I turn and face him. Them. The two of them. "Solomon?"

"Bingo!" Piccardy says. "You gonna be the next hang-up?" They're both smiling. I ask them where they heard this.

"Where'd we hear this, Officer Anselmo?" Piccardy asks. "Do you remember?"

"Can't say that I do, Officer Piccardy. We heard it somewhere, though."

"Yeah, somewhere. What a shame, huh? RIP Psycho Boy."

They stop once they've delivered the message, but I keep walking. I'm short of breath, choked up and fighting tears. That poor kid never had a chance.

Counselor Jackson's coming out of the building as I enter. "Corby? You look upset," she says. "Are you all right?" I ask her whether she's heard about Solomon. When she shakes her head, I tell her what I've just heard. "Oh my God," she says. She turns around and reenters the building with me. "I have the number of the facility where he's been in my office. Let me see if I can find out what happened. Who told you about this?" When

I say it was Anselmo and Piccardy, she gives me a skeptical look and tells me to check in on my tier. She'll let me know what she finds out.

I do what she says. Back in our cell, I'm relieved to find myself alone. I sit on my bunk, put my head down, and sob. Ten minutes later, I'm called up to the control desk. Jackson's standing there, waiting. "False alarm," she says. "It didn't happen."

I stare at her for several seconds, floored by the depth of their cruelty. Then I wipe my eyes, thank her, and walk back down the corridor. Those sick fucks have the upper hand for now, but I've got less than a year to go in here. Maybe after I get out, I can find a way to blow the whistle. Expose the kind of shit they've been pulling. That would wipe the smiles off their faces.

———

With the mural project approved, I get to work in earnest. First, I superimpose a grid over the drawing I showed them, figuring it will be less overwhelming for me to think in terms of smaller squares than the mural's overall expanse. Mrs. Millman provides me with a stack of printer paper so that I can draw detailed studies of the humans and animals I want to include in the painting. From there, I move on to the library's blank wall and take a deep breath. The wall is eight feet high and fifty-six feet wide. It takes me a couple of hours to re-create the grid. After that, I begin penciling in the details in each square. That takes the rest of the week. I'm nervous just thinking about it, but on Monday, I'll begin committing color to the wall.

———

When Emily accepts my call on Friday evening, I spend most of our ten minutes describing what the mural's going to look like when it's finished. "You sound so upbeat," she says. "I'm happy for you, Corby." When I ask her what her weekend plans are, she says just the usual chores. "Oh, and I have company coming for dinner tomorrow night."

"Oh yeah? What are you making?"

She says she'll keep it simple: chicken parmesan, salad, garlic bread. "And I'll probably pick up cannoli at Romano's for dessert."

"God, that sounds so good. Who's coming over? Evan?"

"Yes. And Amber."

"The one who teaches with you? Got jilted at the altar?"

"It didn't exactly happen that way, but yes. I told Evan he should ask her out and so far, so good. This will be their third date."

Does her voice sound a little sad or am I just imagining it does? I tell myself not to say it, but then I do. "You know, for a while, I wondered if you and Evan might be . . ."

There's a pause on her end. Then she says, "Well, to tell you the truth, it was headed that way. But it wasn't going to work, so . . ."

"So you fixed Amber up with him instead. Wow, that was nice of you." I put my hand over the receiver so that my sigh of relief won't be audible. "So what about Maisie? Is she going over to your mother's?"

"No, she's going to *your* mother's," Emily says. "Vicki's taking her to see *Frozen Two*. Then Maisie's sleeping over and they're going to breakfast in the morning."

"Nice," I say. "Mom must be thrilled."

Securus gives us the one-minute warning. "Well, good luck with your mural, Corby," Emily says.

"And good luck with your dinner party. I wish *I* was having chicken parmesan and cannoli tomorrow. Put some in the freezer, will you? I'll eat it after I get out." She doesn't respond. "It was a joke, Em. Okay, love you."

"I love you, too," she says. It sounds like she means it, but I tell myself not to read too much into it.

Walking back to our cell, I can't help but wonder what "it was headed that way" means. Were they sleeping together? Had they talked about him moving in? And who pulled the plug, him or her? I know better than to ever ask these things. I have to let it go. I'm just relieved that, whatever might have been happening, it's not happening anymore. Amber hasn't been teaching that long, so she's probably still in her twenties. So good for you, Evan. You're finally interested in someone your own age.

———

Mrs. Millman's scavenger hunt for supplies has yielded a bonanza of paints, brushes, thinner, and other materials. On Monday morning, I take a deep breath, squeeze an inch of acrylic paint out of a tube of cerulean, combine it with matte gel medium, and dip my brush into the mixture. I start with the sky.

Thirty-one days later, another month of my sentence has been served and the mural is finished. Like the plowman in Bruegel's painting, I'm in the foreground, wearing a red shirt and standing at the top of the steep rock ledge on the opposite side of the Wequonnoc river. My back is to the viewer as I gaze at the scene below. Yates prison no longer exists; I've banished the buildings and the security fencing that contains us. The land has returned to its natural state of woods, fields, and streams that feed into the tea-colored river. Cedars and sycamores, maples and elms grow in abundance. In the crotch of a ginkgo tree at the river's edge, a great blue heron tends to her nestlings as her mate flies toward them, a fish in his beak. A mother turkey crosses an open field, her brood following behind her. They're unaware they're being stalked by a pair of predators—two copperheads ready to pounce.

In my mural, a number of people have come to the river and its banks. On one side, Lester Wiggins sits on a rock, fishing, perhaps about to catch that prize-winning rainbow trout. On the opposite side, three Wequonnoc women till the soil as a hunter from their tribe emerges from the woods, carrying the bow he's used to kill the young deer draped around his shoulders. Mrs. Millman and Dr. Patel, both barefoot, wade into the water. Dr. Patel holds up the bottom of her sari so that it won't get wet. Mrs. M waves to the men floating downriver on inner tubes. Manny is one of them, Javier's another, Angel's a third. Farther down from them, three young men skip stones that bounce along the river's surface. One boy wears a fedora, the other a hoodie. Emmett Till and Trayvon Martin are alive again, two friends having fun. The third boy is Solomon, no longer a loner but a buddy of theirs, too. Near those three but farther back, Emily and Maisie stand on a path that travels alongside the Wequonnoc. They gaze across the river and up, looking at me, seeing that I'm free but on the other side, atop the unscalable ledge. And on the far-right side of the mural, as insignificantly placed as Icarus in the Bruegel painting, Niko, my butterfly boy, stands alone, an easy-to-miss figure with chrysalis-green skin. From the top of his head, just-hatched monarchs rise to join the others in a kaleidoscope journeying south, a hundred orange and black wings against a cloudless blue sky.

CHAPTER THIRTY-THREE

—

October 2019
Day 802 of 1,095

It's Warden Rickerby's idea to hold a reception to celebrate my artistic achievement, but the last thing I want is attention of any kind. I ask Mrs. Millman to explain this to the warden, but Rickerby's opportunity for favorable press trumps any consideration of the artist's comfort level. Our law-and-order governor is invited, as are several state and local politicians, the corrections commissioner and some of his staff, prominent members of the community, and the local media. Mrs. Millman asks me to play along; the reception will give her the opportunity to make a pitch for more funding for the library. Reluctantly, I agree but lose a lot of sleep thinking about the last time I was on TV and in the papers, worrying that everything might get dredged up again and stoke the outrage of the hard-liners on Facebook or whatever. *He's there to be punished, not paint la-di-da pictures on the walls.*

Governor Witham sends his regrets but issues a statement assuring voters that while he expects full accountability for crimes committed, he supports inmate rehabilitation. Some of the other politicians promise to make appearances—probably just long enough to get their pictures taken for the newspaper. Mrs. Millman tells me that Food Services will provide a carafe of fruit punch and an urn of coffee with setups. Her husband, Howie, has volunteered to bake a tray of cookies. "Three kinds, a dozen and a half each," she says. "Chocolate chip, oatmeal raisin, and frosted lemon. He's thrilled to have the assignment." She promises she'll squirrel away some of the goodies so that I can take them back to "the fellas" on my tier. "Are there any people you'd like to invite?" she asks. "Write down their names and I'll see what I can do."

Here's who I put on my list: Emily, Dr. Patel, Lieutenant Cavagnero, and for moral support, Manny and a couple of my other buddies on the tier. I would have put Mom on the list, but she's going in for knee surgery. Dad? No way. He still hasn't visited me here and he never wanted me to go to art school in the first place.

Manny and the other guys get denied; the warden's office notifies Mrs. Millman that it would be inappropriate for offenders to mingle among the dignitaries. Emily and I haven't spoken for a couple of weeks, so I have no idea whether she's planning to come. Mrs. Millman says she tried to invite Dr. Patel personally, but her husband said she was in London, visiting her son and their grandkids.

On D-Day, shortly before the reception is due to begin, Manny says my pacing the cell is driving him crazy. "Relax, man. This is a *good* thing."

"Painting the mural was the good thing, not this yea-rah-rah bullshit."

"It's not like you're going to your execution." But that's what it feels like when Zabrowski arrives to escort me to the library. How many movies have I seen where the con who's about to fry in the chair is flanked by a couple of guards?

"So how does it feel to be the man of the hour?" Zabrowski asks me.

Feels terrible, but I know I'm supposed to voice my gratitude. "Quite an honor," I mumble. He's wearing his full-dress uniform and, per usual, I'm in my tan scrubs. He tells me to take off the ID that, on a normal day, I could get a ticket for *not* wearing. As we walk along the walkway in silence, we pass Goolsby and Piccardy out in the yard supervising the crew on their break. Piccardy is giving his uncle and me the once-over and he doesn't look happy. I fantasize about using my "man of the hour" status to blow the whistle on Zabrowski's sick fuck of a nephew—tell him about some of the shit he and Anselmo have been pulling. But getting through the next hour is going to be challenging enough.

The library's been rearranged for company: rows of plastic chairs, a tablecloth on the counter where the refreshments are, red carnations in a vase. The mural's covered with three large blue tarps taped together. Like Zabrowski, Commissioner Knox and Warden Rickerby are wearing their dress uniforms. The commish's handshake is limp but Rickerby's is a firm grip. When Mrs. Millman sees me, she walks over and hugs me in front of them—a brazen disregard of the rules! "This will be over before you know it," she whispers. "Just keep smiling." This close to her, I get a whiff of lavender, a fragrance that Emily used to wear. I haven't smelled lavender in a long time. I ask Mrs. M if she knows whether my wife's coming today. She says she made sure she was invited but doesn't know whether the warden's office heard back. "Now come with me. I want you to meet my husband. He's hiding out in my office. Loves to bake, hates to schmooze."

Howie Millman and I shake hands. I thank him for making the cookies. He makes a joke I don't quite catch. They're a matched set, the Millmans. She's not much over five feet tall and he's maybe five-four or not even. They're both wearing T-shirts. His says, "I Read Banned Books" and hers says, "I'm a Librarian. What's YOUR Superpower?" Mrs. Millman tells me to go out and mingle a little. "Under ten minutes," she promises. "Then I'll start the program."

Mrs. M's right-hand man, Javier, is the only other con in tans at this shindig. He congratulates me and hands me a coffee and one of Mr. Millman's bakery-sized cookies. I'm so jittery that the coffee jumps over the top of the cup, and when I take a bite of the cookie, it gets stuck going down. I have to clear my throat three or four times to dislodge it, drawing the attention of the dignitaries nearby. When I take another slug of coffee, it finally goes down, but everyone's still looking at me. My face feels hot and I know I'm turning red. "Sorry," I say to no one in particular. The commissioner jokes that he was getting ready to give me the Heimlich maneuver, ha ha ha.

After ten minutes go by—I've been watching the wall clock—Mrs. Millman invites everyone to take their seats for the unveiling. She begins by thanking the administrators for green-lighting the mural project and today's celebration. Looks like they're eating it up, too, especially when they get a round of polite applause. Mrs. M's not a kiss-ass; she's playing politics because she wants more money for her library. It's fun to watch the way she operates. She invites the warden to speak.

I tune out most of Rickerby's blah-blah-blah but catch the end of her spiel: "My team and I *always* do our best to accentuate the positive at this institution." Really? I hadn't noticed.

Rickerby and Zabrowski are the designated unveilers. As they walk toward the mural, I feel my stomach muscles clench. Sit on my hands so that no one will see how badly they're shaking. To make things worse, the warden starts counting backward from ten. I'm glad *she's* enjoying herself in the midst of my panic. What if everyone hates it? What if all the political protests I've embedded in the work—anti–white supremacy, antiracism, antiprison—are blatantly obvious? Embarrassing the powers that be around here could cost me big-time. Rickerby reaches the end of her countdown and, from opposite ends, she and Zabrowski yank down the tarps, exposing the mural. And me.

I hear a couple of "wow"s, a "fantastic." A few people applaud at first, then more, then many more. All I can see are the flaws: some of the trees are hastily rendered; the sky's too blue. Most of all, I wish to hell that I'd kept Emily and the kids out of the mural; I shouldn't have tampered with their privacy like that. Our story is too personal for public art. What was I thinking?

When Javier stands, clapping loudly, most of the others follow suit. I look down at the floor until Mrs. Millman, seated next to me, leans in and says, "Enjoy your moment, Corby. Look at your audience." Facing them, I put my hand over my heart, bow my head, and wait for the applause to stop. When it does, I say, "Not sure I deserve all this, but thank you."

Mrs. Millman retakes the floor. She tells the audience that she'd invited me to share some remarks about my work, but that, being a bit shy, I asked whether she would speak on my behalf. (Truthfully, it was more like begging her than asking.) "Howie?" she says. "You want to do the honors?" From behind the circulation desk, her husband props up a poster-sized enlargement of *Landscape with the Fall of Icarus*. Mrs. M explains that Bruegel the Elder's sixteenth-century masterpiece was the inspiration for my mural. She says how exciting it was for her to witness the day-by-day coming together of my vision, first sketched out in detail, then painted. "I'm telling you, folks, I couldn't wait to come to work so I could see what was going to happen next!" Polite laughter, people looking between the mural and me. I look away.

Mrs. M picks up some index cards, looks over her notes, and begins her prepared remarks. I'm moved that she's spent so much time and effort on this. She says she believes that painters and writers are magicians of a sort—that they invite us to lose ourselves in their work and, in doing so, *find* ourselves. "As you take in Corby Ledbetter's mural, you most likely see and feel something different from what the person standing next to you sees and feels; we bring our own lives, our personal histories, and our values to art and literature. Yet somehow, simultaneously, art and literature connect us to one another. That's the magic! So I feel it is entirely fitting that this mural now resides in a library filled with books and ideas—a *prison* library where incarcerated men arrive feeling remorseful or resentful or defiant, perhaps wondering how their lives went so far off track from what they imagined. And if they are brave enough to face themselves without looking away, then this is a place where they can gain the valuable insights that will help send them on a better path." She ends with a quote from Supreme Court Justice Thurgood Marshall: something about how an inmate who comes to prison does not have to lose his humanity or end his quest for self-realization and growth.

"And now, Corby, I'd like to say something to you personally," she says. "Long after you leave Yates and go on your way, your evocative work will remain here, inviting the incarcerated men who enter this library to linger over your mural's mysteries and meaning and puzzle through whatever it says to them. Thank you for your gift. We are grateful." More applause. More blushing from me. I scan the room, looking for Emily, but she's not here.

Up from their seats now, the audience mills around, chatting and enjoying refreshments, studying the mural up close, pointing out details to one another. People keep coming up to me, complimenting and congratulating me, and it's so nerve-racking that I take refuge in the stacks. Having grown up in my father's house, I feel more comfortable with criticism than praise. And has everyone conveniently forgotten what I did? Why I had to come here?

"Corby?" Mrs. Millman calls. "Some of the media people are looking for you."

I try to beg off being interviewed by a reporter from the local TV station, but thankfully it only lasts for thirty seconds and the camera lingers on the mural, not me, as I speak. No mention is made of why I'm doing time.

The *Hartford Courant* reporter tells me she and her photographer are on a tight schedule. "Let him get his picture first. Then I need to ask you some questions before we have to take off." The photographer says he wants to shoot me in front of the mural. Remembering the only other time my face appeared in the *Courant* and why, I think fast and point out that the figure in the painting closest to the front with his back to the viewer is supposed to be me. "How about if I stand facing the painting rather than looking at the camera and you can photograph me from the back?" To my great relief, he says he likes the idea and obliges me.

But I'm not so lucky with the eager young reporter. She looks like she just arrived from some journalism school and is angling for a big story. "Do you feel the rehabilitative services at Yates have helped to prepare you for a successful return to life on the outside?"

The commissioner, his media relations officer, the warden, and Mrs.

Millman are standing close by, so I give her a pallid version of what they want to hear.

Next she asks me a series of softball questions. Was I trained as an artist or am I self-taught? What drew me to the Bruegel painting? How long did I work on the mural from start to finish? Then she leans close. "You were sentenced to prison after being convicted of negligent homicide in the death of your son, right?" I nod. "There's rehabilitation, sure, but is there any getting over a tragedy like that?"

None of her goddamn business! "Can we please just talk about the mural?"

"Okay, sure," she says. "Would you care to comment on the subversive nature of the work, Mr. Ledbetter?"

It's a "gotcha" question, the kind I was dreading during my bouts of insomnia. When I glance over at Corrections' PR person, it looks like she's gone on high alert. I figure I'd better play dumb. "Subversive? What do you mean?"

"Well, you've painted the prison property without the prison. Why?"

"Because I'm imagining the area centuries before there *was* a prison— way back before the white European settlers came and it was Wequonnoc land."

"Right. I get that. But that guy over there tells me *he's* in the mural." She nods toward Javier, who's chatting with one of the local politicians. "He says that's him floating downriver with two other prisoners. Prisoners but no prison? Emmett Till and Trayvon Martin resurrected? An Indigenous tribe living again on the land? Correct me if I'm wrong, Mr. Ledbetter, but isn't your painting a protest of sorts? Aren't you arguing against white oppression? And wouldn't some consider *that* subversive?"

Although she's right, all I can think of to say is that all art is open to interpretation. She smirks as she jots down something on her pad. The photographer approaches, tapping the face of his wristwatch. "Come on, Abby," he tells her. "We're running late and I've got to get a shot of that ribbon-cutting."

"Okay, last question then, Mr. Ledbetter," she says. "Tell me about the little boy with the butterflies who's way in the background. Is that your son? Your Icarus?"

Mrs. Millman runs interference for me before I can respond. "Corby, look who's here!" Thinking it's Emily—that maybe she got here in time to see the standing ovation they gave me—I see, instead, Lieutenant Cavagnero.

"Excuse me," I tell the reporter. "There's someone I need to talk to." As I pass by Mrs. M, she gives me a wink.

Cavagnero's face looks pale and drawn; he's using a walker. "Good to see you, Ledbetter," he says, limping slowly toward me. "If I'd have known you were an *artiste*, I would have exchanged your rake for a paintbrush." I thank him for coming and ask how he's doing. "Better than I was right after I took that spill," he says. "A fractured pelvis is no joke, believe me. But anyway, congratulations. How've you been?"

I have the urge to tell him about getting kicked off the work crew and why. Instead, I say things are okay and that I'm looking forward to getting out in another ten months. "Oh, and that kid Solomon? He got transferred to a psych facility."

"Good," he says. "Never should have put him here in the first place. Now tell me about this mural of yours. What's it mean?"

"Whatever you want it to mean," I tell him.

I stick pretty close to Cavagnero for the rest of the reception, avoiding as best I can any more questions or compliments. The commissioner and his gang leave shortly after the *Courant* folks, followed by most of the others. When it's only Javi, the Millmans, and me, Mrs. M tells me that several of the people she spoke with said how impressed they were with my work and that she thinks things went well. "I just hope all that praise wasn't too painful for you." She smiles.

"Excruciating," I tell her. "Nah, just kidding. It was okay. Thanks for doing all this and for the kind words you spoke. Did you get a chance to lobby for more funding?"

"I did," she says. "I spoke with Dr. Spears, the Unified School District superintendent, about beefing up the literacy materials for our new readers and maybe updating the law books in our collection. He's invited me to call his office and make an appointment."

"Sounds like a good sign. And by the way, thanks for rescuing me from that eager-beaver reporter."

"You know, Corby, every time I stand in front of your mural, I see some detail I hadn't noticed before. And when I discovered the little boy in the distance, I never presumed to ask you about him. Interacting with art is about being *immersed* in its mysteries, not *solving* them—getting to the bottom of what they mean. That's like asking Picasso why he misplaced Dora Maar's eyes in the portraits he did of her. That reporter had no right to grill you like that, but she's young; she didn't know any better. Maybe she'll learn."

"Yeah, maybe. But anyway, thanks for rescuing me from her detective work. I appreciate it. Let me give Javier a hand with the chairs. Then I'm going to take off. I'm exhausted and I'm starting to get a headache."

"It's okay, hombre," Javi says. "I got this. Now that you're a celebrity, you don't have to stack no chairs." I start stacking anyway and tell him to knock off the celebrity shit. "Oh yeah, that's right," he says. "You only *made* the mural, but I'm *in* it. Guess that makes *me* the celebrity."

"Yeah, you'll probably have people start asking you for your autograph." He grins and says he's going to charge five bucks a pop.

When I start to leave, Mrs. M tells me to hold on. Says she has something for me. She hurries into her office and comes out carrying a plastic bag bulging with leftover cookies. "As promised," she says. "And this. It's a printout of a poem that might interest you. Do you like poetry, Corby?"

"Not so much. My seventh-grade English teacher kind of killed that off when she made us memorize these corny poems she loved. 'Flower in the crannied wall, I pluck you out of the crannies.' "

"Not a fan of Tennyson then," she says.

"Nope. Or Vachel Lindsay either. We had to perform this poem of his called 'The Potatoes' Dance' at an assembly. I had to do a solo: 'There was just one sweet potato / He was golden brown and slim / The ladies loved his dancing / They danced all night with him.' A couple of us tried to convince her that rap was poetry so maybe we could recite something by LL Cool J or Coolio, but she wasn't buying it."

She laughs. Says the poem she wants to share is by her favorite poet, W. H. Auden, and that it references the Bruegel painting that guided me as I created the mural. "I promise you don't have to memorize it, but Auden might be more to your liking. If not, just toss it. Okay then. Get some rest. Don't be a stranger." She reaches over for another hug and I hug her back. The lavender scent is gone. I wonder why Emily was a no-show. Would she have been mad that I painted her and the kids in the mural? Would she have resented having to witness all that praise being heaped on the husband who had taken the life of her child?

Just outside the library entrance, a thin, elderly man who was at the program says he's been waiting to speak to me. He's well-dressed and soft-spoken—a retired-professor type, except for the skinny John Waters mustache above his top lip. "I won't hold you up," he says. "I just wanted to tell you I think your mural is exceptional. May I ask how much longer you have on your sentence?" When I tell him, he says, "That's splendid. Not much more time at all." For him, maybe.

He tells me he's an art agent in New York but has been in Stonington Village for the past few days, doing some appraisals for an antiques dealer. "She was invited to your celebration but couldn't go, so she had me put on the list in her place. I'm so glad she did. I wonder if you realize how talented you are."

I shrug. "For a prisoner maybe."

"No, no. That's irrelevant. Look, here's my card. My client list includes several muralists. If you want to get in touch with me after your release, I may be able to get you some work. If it's corporate, we could negotiate a nice price—something to start you off on the right track once you're out of here." I stuff the card in my pocket, thank him, and tell him I'm expected back at my building. "Of course," he says. When we exit the building, he goes one way, I go the other. He seems harmless enough, but you never know. He represents muralists and he might be able to get me work? Seems a little too perfect to be real, so I'm not getting my hopes up.

At the entrance to our block, I'm stopped by one of the newer COs. "What you got there?" he asks, pointing to the bag of cookies. I explain about the library, the reception, the fact that they're leftovers. He makes me hand them over. "You want cookies, order them from commissary like everyone else. Where's your ID at?" I take it out and hand it to him, explaining that the deputy warden told me to take it off for the program I was going to. "Oh yeah? What program was that?" I explain it to him again, adding that I was kind of like the guest of honor at this library thing. He smirks the way a lot of the guards do when they think they've caught you in a lie. He writes down my name and inmate number and says, "Okay, Ledbetter. Put your ID back on. To be continued if I find out you're bullshitting me."

Climbing the stairs to our tier, I remind myself that if I was "the man of the hour" over in the library, my hour's up.

Back in our cell, when Manny asks how it went, I give him a thumbs-up. "See? I *told* you you'd enjoy it," he says.

He's blasting his music and I ask him to turn it down. The day's taken its toll and my headache's getting worse.

When it's quieter, I lie down on my mattress and turn onto my side. Closing my eyes, I try for a nap, but I'm both exhausted *and* overstimulated. In my mind's eye, I see all the things in the mural I'd like to fix. See that standing ovation. Hear that reporter: *Is that your son? Is he your Icarus?* I hope to God that whatever she writes isn't going to dredge everything up again. I can just imagine the Facebook outrage. *This is how they're "punishing" a guy who killed his own child? . . .*

When I roll over onto my stomach, I hear the crinkle of paper. Pull out that poem Mrs. M gave me and, with it, that guy's business card. I pick it up and read that first. *John-Michael Chesley, Art Agent International,*

New York, San Francisco, London. Specializing in the commissioning of new works of public art. Well, okay, I guess he's legit. Maybe there *is* a job in this for me down the line. And even if not, it feels good to be validated by someone who knows art.

That poem she gave me is titled "Musée des Beaux Arts," whatever that means.

> *About suffering they were never wrong,*
> *The Old Masters: how well they understood*
> *Its human position: how it takes place*
> *While someone else is eating or opening a window*

What's the deal, Mrs. M? Why did you think I might like this or even know what the hell it means? And what's it got to do with the Icarus painting? I'll read it again tomorrow, but for now I'm just going to try to sleep my way past this headache.

As I start to doze, I invent reasons why Emily didn't come today. Maybe she's having car trouble. Maybe Maisie's sick. Maybe she just didn't care enough to come. And if that last one's true, what's going to happen when I get out? Okay, come on, Corby. Deep breaths. The present, not the past or the future. Go to sleep.

CHAPTER THIRTY-FOUR

—

October 2019
Day 809 of 1,095

A week after the reception, I get a letter from Emily.

Hi, Corby—I hope you're doing well. I'm sorry I wasn't there for your reception. I was planning to go, but at the last minute, I got called in for an emergency meeting at Maisie's school. She had gone to the girls' bathroom and scribbled in crayon all over the walls. She also took a boy's Spider-Man action figure out of his cubby and tried to flush it down the toilet. She denied she'd done these things at first, but the principal, Mrs. Sotzing, finally broke her down and got her to admit it. For her consequence, her teacher, Ms. Demko, made an example of her with her classmates, then moved her desk to the back of the room by herself. At the meeting, I said I thought there were better ways to make her accountable than by shaming and separating her from the others, especially since during the last meeting, she'd voiced concern about Maisie not socializing with her classmates. They barely listened to my objection.

If I'd been at that meeting, I would have *made* them listen.

The school social worker suggested Maisie may still be showing signs of grief about the significant losses in her life. I'm not so sure. The tantrums have stopped. She never talks in that weird language anymore or freaks out about having her poops go down the toilet. I don't think she has any memory of Niko at this point. She understands that you're "away" but that you're coming back. (We still have to figure out how that's going to work.) I left that meeting with the names of two child psychologists and the distinct impression that my parenting was being judged. I cried all the way to my mother's house when I went to pick up Maisie. When we got home, I sat her down and asked her why she had done those naughty things. She said it was because she was sad, but she didn't know what she was sad about. To me, her actions seemed more angry than sad. She can be so hard to read sometimes. I should probably call one of those psychologists, but when I took her to that last one, it didn't seem to make any difference. I'm not sure my insurance will cover it. I think what upset me the most at that meeting was their arrogance. I've been a teacher for twelve years and know a thing or two about child psychology myself.

But it's not about you, Em. It's about Maisie.

Congratulations on your mural! I wish I'd been there to see it in person. I know your Creative Strategies job was more about the paycheck than about doing what you loved, but it sounds like you were able to go where you wanted to with this project. Artistic freedom in prison? That's pretty ironic. The write-up in the <u>Courant</u> was great and, from the little I could see in the photo, the painting looks amazing. It must feel good to get such a positive reaction. You've probably already seen the article, but I thought you might want this extra copy.

Maisie and I visited your mom at the hospital. Her surgery went well and they've already got her up and walking. We brought her flowers and Maisie drew her a get-well card. For some reason, it had these weird potato-shaped people with toothpick arms and legs that she's been drawing lately. Of course, Vicki fawned over it and said what a great artist she was, just like her daddy.

Love,
Emily

I had *not* seen that article but was relieved to read that the reporter didn't go into my conviction or include any of the "gotcha" stuff from her interview. Warden Rickerby must have loved the piece, too; it praises her for her progressive leadership and her encouragement of innovative rehabilitative activities for inmates. Please. Mrs. Millman didn't even get a mention, but that probably bothers me more than it does her. She's just happy that she may be getting more funding for books.

According to Mrs. M, the response to the mural from people coming into the library has been positive, and this includes staff as well as inmates. "Ledbetter's one of the decent ones over there in B Block," Captain Graham told Mrs. Millman. "But I didn't know he could do something like this." A few of the guys on our tier got passes and went over there to see it. Manny and Angel both got a kick out of seeing themselves floating down the river past this place. Lobo was with them and Manny said he stared at the mural for so long, it was like he was hypnotized.

Despite all these pats on the back, I haven't gotten away unscathed. During the weeks I was working on the mural, Piccardy and Anselmo pretty much left me alone. Out of sight, out of mind, I guess. I figured they'd maybe gotten their fill of harassing me and gone on to some other con who'd challenged their authority. But no.

I'm walking back from D Block after an AA meeting that Sunday morning. As I enter our building and start up the stairs, I hear footsteps behind me. I look back and there they are, the two of them, their voices echoing in the stairwell.

"Paints some stupid pictures on a wall, gets in the paper, and now he thinks his shit don't stink."

"Thinks he's Rickerby's fair-haired boy. Forgets that he's here because he killed his kid."

"Harry in Maintenance told me they got orders to paint over Baby Killer's pretty picture as soon as he's out of here."

"Hey, you hear that, Ledbetter? Guess you're not such a hero after all!"

Two more flights to go. I tell myself to hold on and not react to their goading. Assaulting two COs is a luxury I can't afford. Instead, to drown them out, I start singing, loud as I can, that old R.E.M. song I used to play in my bedroom with the volume jacked up. *"What's the frequency, Kenneth? Is your Benzedrine, uh-huh . . ."*

It works. They get off on the tier below ours. When I reach our floor, I head to the control desk to check back in. I'm flustered by what just happened, something McGreavy evidently picks up on. "What's the matter?" he asks. I shrug, tell him I'm okay, and start down the corridor.

It's the five-on-the-floor break, so everyone's out of their cells, chatting and laughing, lining up at the hot pot. The bored ones are leaning over the railing to check out the comings and goings on the tier below. There's a lot of bitching about the latest stupid rule administration's come up with: the buddy system. Going to and coming back from chow, we now have to march in line with a partner, all of us keeping the same pace. No gaps, no pileups, no talking to anyone besides our partner. Prison's supposed to get us ready for life on the outside, so I guess when we're released, we'll be all set for kindergarten.

"Break's over!" Goolsby bellows, herding us back to our cells.

"Yo, Corby," Angel calls. "Look who couldn't stay away from us." Following his pointing finger, I see that Boudreaux's back.

Manny, of course, has the scoop on the Ragin' Cajun's return. Before Parole would let him leave the state and head home to Louisiana, Boudreaux got mixed up in a carjacking that won him a return ticket here.

"Claims it was a setup and that he's innocent," Manny tells me. We say it in unison: "Uh-huh."

That evening, I can't get Piccardy and Anselmo out of my head. . . . *Thinks his shit don't stink. . . . Thinks he's Rickerby's fair-haired boy. . . . They've got orders to paint over Baby Killer's pretty picture.* I doubt that last is true, but it landed like a kick in the balls. To distract myself from hearing their voices, I grab a pen and a couple of sheets of notebook paper and write back to Emily.

Hi, Em—

Thanks for your letter and the congrats. Being able to design and paint the mural was the best thing that's happened to me here. I wasn't all that comfortable with the attention I got at the reception, but I survived and was grateful, most of all to Fagie Millman, the Yates librarian. She's been my champion. I was hoping I'd see you, introduce you two, but I understand. Thanks for sending the clipping. I hadn't seen it and was sweating out what that reporter was going to write, but she went easy on me. Jesus, what's going on with Maisie?

I've never really accepted Emily's reason for keeping her away from here. What's more traumatic: seeing me in prison or not seeing me at all?

That school meeting sounded awful. When I get out of here, we can go to meetings like that together unless you'd rather I don't go. If you think they were judging your parenting, I'd hate to imagine what they'd think about mine.

I talked to my mom earlier today and she says she's making good progress since her surgery. Wants to get back to work ASAP so she can see her "breakfast regulars." I doubt that gang of retirees she waits on are big tippers, but I'm pretty sure she loves the job more for the social interaction than anything else. Thanks, by the way, for visiting her at the hospital and for bringing Maisie. She told me she really appreciated it and that seeing Maisie and you was the bright spot of her day.

Oh, by the way, at the reception? Some art agent who was there told me he was impressed by the mural and that he might have some work for me after I'm out of here. Probably won't amount to anything, but he gave me his card. Okay, it's lights-out in a couple of minutes, so I'll end here.

I love you, Emily

I fall asleep pretty easily, but an hour later I'm wide-awake and worrying about the future: not only what's going to happen when they let me out but also what happens between now and then. The attention I've gotten because of the mural has fanned the flames of Piccardy and Anselmo's hatred of me. My pulse starts racing and I move every which way trying to get comfortable. I'm up for an hour or more before I can get back to sleep.

———

I sleep past breakfast, so I miss the first walk to the chow hall under the new buddy system. Manny reports that things went fairly well; only two guys got tickets for noncompliance. His "buddy" was a new arrival on our tier, a young guy named Austin. "What a hunk," he tells me. "Green eyes, curly brown hair, and you can tell he's put in some serious time at the gym. I think I'm in love."

"Yeah? Sounds to me like you're in lust."

He puts his hand on his hip and bats his eyes. "Is there a difference?"

When I ask how old this guy is, Manny says early to midtwenties. Although he doesn't admit to it, my cellie is fifty-four. What's that saying? Hope springs eternal? He brags a lot about the hookups he's had, but come to think of it, I've never heard Manny talk about being in any long-term relationships. Kind of sad, really. The only constant in his life seems to be his sister, Gloria.

Later, when we line up for our ten-thirty lunch, Manny pushes past me and some of the other guys so he can buddy up with his new heartthrob. I'm at the tail end of the line. They must have run out of buddies, because I'm solo, which is fine with me.

God, what a day: sky-blue sky, the sun shining on the vivid oranges and yellows of the dying leaves. It's a "five-out-of-five" fall day, as they say on the TV weather.

Up front, leading the parade, Officer Anselmo yells, "Get the lead out, ladies! The longer you take to get there, the less time I'm giving you to eat." Behind me, his lackey, Goolsby, claps his hands and imitates his mentor. "Come on, gentlemen! Let's see some hustle!" Piccardy usually works the same shift as these two, but he hasn't been around this week. I'm enjoying the respite.

Halfway between our block and the chow hall, my eyes land on that ginkgo tree I've noticed before. Its scalloped leaves have turned a brilliant royal yellow. It looks spectacular and carries me back to an October memory during the twins' first year.

Maisie, Niko, and I were out at the reservoir where I took them sometimes for midmorning weekend strolls while Emily stayed home, doing her schoolwork. She and I were just a normal couple still, unmarked by tragedy and prison. We both had jobs; we were doing okay financially. Monday through Thursday, we dropped the kids off at a daycare we liked and Emily's mom took them every Friday. I drank a little too much on the weekends, maybe, and enjoyed the occasional recreational drug, but neither was a problem yet. We were happily unaware of the bad shit that was about a year away from happening.

It was breezy that morning out at the reservoir but warm still. Maisie had fallen asleep in their double stroller, but Niko was awake and alert, his arms reaching up toward all those dancing colors in the trees. "Come here, buddy," I said, and lifted him out of the stroller. Held him up to a low-hanging branch of a majestic red maple. Just as he was reaching out to touch a leaf, a strong gust came up. Fluttering vermilion leaves fell down around us. When I managed to grab one and give it to Niko, he squealed with delight at his treasure. On our way back to the car, I stooped to pick up others for his collection: a yellow elm leaf; the coral, burnt orange, and scarlet yield from a row of oaks and sugar maples. He clutched, studied, and babbled to his bouquet on the drive back to our house. He was responding emotionally to the palette of colors he was holding. Of the two of them, Niko was the one who was already showing an artistic sense. Had the artistic temperament, too. When Maisie, awake by then, reached over and grabbed at his leaves, he howled in protest and swatted her. "No!" I yelled, and they both froze. Then Niko handed his sister two of his treasures.

"What are you smiling at?" someone asks, yanking me out of my reverie.

"Hmm? What?" It feels like I've just been caught doing something wrong.

Boudreaux's walking beside me. "Where did you come from?" I ask him.

"I was walking up there with Daugherty, but Anselmo sent him back on account of he got a bloody nose. Told me to buddy up with you instead."

"How did he get a bloody nose?" I ask. "You pop him one?"

"Nah, he was picking it too hard. Didn't mean to spook you just now, but man, you was someplace else. And from that shit-eatin' grin, I bet you was thinkin' 'bout some nice piece of ass. Am I right or am I right?"

"Guilty," I say. And I *do* feel guilty, but not in the way he thinks. Do I have any right to enjoy a *happy* memory of my little boy? Do I need to tamp down recollections like the one I just had to atone for what I did? For the pain I caused?

"I *knew* it, brother," Boudreaux says. "I can read people's minds by reading their faces. And your face was saying loud and clear that you was having yo'self a poontang memory." Yeah, right, I think. The Amazing

Kreskin must be shaking in his boots knowing what a powerful mind reader Boudreaux is.

Entering the chow hall, Boudreaux and I get in line behind Lobo, Angel, Manny, and the new guy he's crushing on. Rashan, the head server, ladles creamed chipped beef onto my tray—slop on Styrofoam. One-Eye adds a watery scoop of canned peas. The third server—he's not familiar—tops things off with two slices of white bread and a powdered-sugar doughnut, cellophane-wrapped. As we get off the line, Goolsby points to an empty table like he's the fucking maître d'.

The six of us take our seats, lean forward, and start eating as fast as we can—everyone, that is, except Manny, who can't ever keep his mouth shut, and his new friend, who doesn't know speed-eating is advised. "Hey, you guys, this is Austin," Manny says. "He was telling me he used to compete in motocross races when he lived in Florida."

"Cool," Angel says. "What did you ride?"

"A Kawasaki KX Two-Fifty."

Lobo wants to know where in Florida he lived. "Grew up in Ocala," he says. "Raced in Tampa before I screwed up my leg during a practice run."

"He came up here to go to the business school at URI," Manny tells us. "And get this. He worked part-time for a caterer who did parties at Taylor Swift's beach house in Watch Hill. This past summer, he was a waiter at this big Fourth of July party she had. And guess who some of the guests were?"

No one guesses. We'd rather eat.

"Give up? Nick Jonas, Ryan Reynolds and Blake Lively, Miranda Lambert, Lorde!" Manny, a teenybopper in his fifties, is way more excited about the guest list than the rest of us, Austin included.

Anticipating Anselmo will cut our mealtime short as usual, I shovel it in as fast as I can. It weirds me out that every time I look over at him, he's watching me. Meanwhile, Manny keeps talking a blue streak. I feel sorry for this Austin guy. I remember when I first got here how Manny overwhelmed me with his advice and mentoring.

"Chow's over!" Anselmo shouts, maybe eleven or twelve minutes into what's supposed to be our twenty-minute meal. All around me, guys stand to obey, stuffing sopped-up bread into their mouths and packaged dough-nuts under their shirts. Austin, whose meal is only half-eaten, looks shocked that lunch is over.

I spend the afternoon reading another one of the Easy Rawlins titles Lester Wiggins recommended. During five-on-the-floor, I see Austin stand-ing by himself, looking a little lost. "About Manny," I tell him. "Don't be afraid to tell him to back off. He enjoys taking new guys under his wing, but you don't want to suffocate under there, right?" He nods but doesn't smile. Then, speak of the devil, Manny approaches us carrying two Styrofoam cups. "Coffee, Austin?" he says. "I got instant in these. Come on. I'll show you where the hot pot is."

A few minutes later, they're back, neither of them talking or holding coffee. There's a red mark under Manny's eye that looks like it's starting to swell. I don't know for sure what happened, but I think I can guess. When we're locked back in our cell, I ask Manny whether his eye's okay. He says it's fine. Changes the subject by telling me about a rumor he's heard: Piccardy's wife asked him for a divorce. "Maybe that's why we haven't seen him for several days," I say. "He must be taking time off to do some soul-searching." We both laugh at that.

A hundred and fifty pages of Easy Rawlins later, Goolsby yells that it's chow time again. When the doors pop, I see Anselmo at the other end of the corridor. These two must both be doing double shifts. "Grab a buddy and line up!" Anselmo shouts.

Subdued by what's turned into one hell of a shiner, Manny hangs back and partners up with Lobo. Once again, my buddy is Boudreaux. As we head off, he says, "Hey, Ledbetter, the post office is open." What's he talking about? "The *post* office, man. It's *open*." He points down at my unbuttoned fly. When I close it up, he nods and says, "Ça c'est bon." I tell him half the time I don't know whether he's speaking English or Swamp. He says it's not his fault if we people "up the bayou" don't talk right.

Our four o'clock supper is meat loaf, mashed potatoes, canned carrots, bread, and cake: enough carbs to bloat us up and a sodium level so high we could all have strokes. Austin's at the far end of our table, eating fast and talking to no one. Manny's at the other end. For once in his life, he's not saying much either. An argument breaks out at a table on the other side of the room, but Anselmo shuts it down before fists fly. I find an undissolved protein pellet in my meat loaf, which means there's more cereal than meat in there. I concentrate on the potatoes, bread, and carrots instead, thinking my mom would probably faint if she saw me eating carrots without making a fuss. Boudreaux, seated across from me, keeps eyeing my cake. "Jesus Christ, just take it," I tell him. He makes the grab.

When Goolsby yells that time's up, I look at the clock on the wall. He and Anselmo have given us seventeen of our twenty minutes to eat. Not bad.

Manny, Boudreaux, and I are walking side by side out of the hall when Anselmo tells me to hold up. The other two stop, too. "There's a salt shaker missing from the table where you guys were at," he says. "You swipe that, Ledbetter?" I tell him no, that there was only an empty pepper shaker where we sat down.

"But this wouldn't be the first thing you ever lied about, would it? You know the drill. Let's go."

"Hey, come on, brother. He didn't take nothing," Boudreaux says.

Anselmo gets in his face. "I'm not your brother, brother. Keep moving." The Ragin' Cajun shakes his head and does what he's told.

I'm about to be patted down and there's nothing for me to do but comply, so I stare up at the ceiling as Goolsby does the honors. His hands move from my shoulders down my outstretched arms, then up and down the rest of my torso. "Step aside, Officer Goolsby," Anselmo says. He pats down the outsides, then the insides of my legs. When he's up around my groin, he clasps his hands together and knuckles me in the nuts. I wince and cough but force myself not to cry out or double over from the pain. I'll be damned if I'll give him the reaction he wants.

"I'm thinking he might have stuck it up his butt," he tells Goolsby. "A lot of these artist types are into that kinky shit. Drop trou, Ledbetter."

Some of my peers are still filing past on their way back to the cellblock. "Full strip searches are supposed to be done in private," I remind him.

"There he goes again," Anselmo says. "Telling officers what they should and shouldn't be doing. He got his picture in the paper, so now he thinks he's buddy-buddy with the warden and the deputy warden. Maybe you should write me up then, Picasso. Make sure you spell my name right. It's F-U-C-K-Y-O-U." He pulls out a pair of latex gloves and snaps them on.

"Officer? Excuse me."

I look around and realize that Manny's still here. "I was at that table, too. There was no salt shaker when we sat down."

"Is that right?" Anselmo says. "Ain't that sweet, Officer Goolsby? Twinkle Toes is sticking up for his cellie or his boyfriend or whatever they are to each other. How'd you get that black eye, Twinkle Toes? Someone's dick slap you in the face?"

Goolsby orders Manny to get back to his tier before he writes him up for interference. He looks to Anselmo for approval.

"Or we could always go over there and shake his cell down," Anselmo says. He hits the jackpot with that threat.

"Sorry, Officer," Manny mumbles. Walking away, he turns back and shouts, "But there was no stinking salt shaker on that table!"

I appreciate Manny's effort, but he could have saved his energy. To get this over with, I open my mouth wide so Goolsby can check inside— make sure there's no missing salt shaker pouched in my cheek or hiding under my tongue.

"Why don't you head back, Officer Goolsby?" Anselmo says. "I got this. I'll see you over there." His sidekick does what he's told. Now it's just Anselmo and me. "Okay, Ledbetter. You want some privacy? Follow me."

He leads me to the door of the walk-in storage room adjacent to the kitchen. Unlocks the door and swings it open. "After you," he says. I know in my gut that I shouldn't go in there, but it's not like I have a choice.

Anselmo steps in and yanks the pull chain hanging from a bare bulb. The room is cold and reeks of onions; bushel bags of them are piled on the floor. Towers of cartons are lined up against the wall, labeled: cooking oil, powdered eggs, canned tomatoes. Anselmo closes the door behind him. I'd better think fast.

"Could you leave the door open a crack, Officer? I get claustrophobic when—"

"Oh, sure," he says. Opens the door a foot or so, then slams it shut again. "That better? Okay, you know the drill. Drop your pants and underwear, then turn around and put your hands on the wall." I do what he says. "Now bend over, spread, and cough." I comply. Relieved that this is over, I start to stand up. "Hold on there, Picasso. We ain't through yet. Bend over again, spread your ass wider, and cough again. Louder this time."

I break out in a sweat and can feel my heart pounding. This isn't just harassment. It's torture, pure and simple. I half expect him to order me to bark like a dog. But the sooner I can get out of this room, the better. I bend over again, pull my cheeks apart, and cough once, twice, three times. "Satisfied?"

"As a matter of fact, I'm not," he says. "And if we have to keep doing this until I *am* satisfied, then that's what we're going to do. Now get in position again, spread that hairy ass wide enough so I can see the pink inside your butthole, and cough until I tell you to stop." Furious, I do what he says. I'm goddamned if I'm going to give him a reason to ticket me for noncompliance.

As I bend over this time, I feel something poking and jabbing around back there. "Hey! What the hell are you—"

I scream out in pain as something is shoved up my rectum, withdrawn, and plunged back in again. Overcome with nausea, I lose my balance and stumble forward, hitting my forehead against the wall as I go down on my knees. I might have passed out for a few seconds, I'm not sure.

Dazed, I struggle back onto my feet, and as I do, my eyes move from those bags of onions to the weapon he's used: one of those expandable aluminum batons they swing at inmates when a fight turns into a free-for-all. I stare at that thing as he collapses it, picks my shirt off the floor, and uses it to wipe off his weapon before he slides it back into the holster on his belt.

"Well, looky there, Officer Anselmo. The baby killer's got himself a boner." There, suddenly, stands Piccardy, in street clothes instead of his uniform. He must have been here all the time. "You enjoy that, Ledbetter? You want some more? Maybe enough to get you to a happy ending?"

I shake my head, struggling to speak. "You two are going to lose your jobs over this," I finally manage to say. My voice is a croak.

Piccardy shrugs. "I'm not even here," he says. "I'm off until next week." He brings his face so close to mine that I can smell his hair gel. Whispers, "Better not make threats you can't prove, baby killer. You see anyone who can back up your bullshit? Who do you think they'd believe: a whiny little bitch like you or an Officer of the Month who was just doing his job?"

Anselmo joins in. "Good thing I checked, too, Officer Piccardy, because look what fell out of his asshole." He reaches into his pants pocket and tosses something onto the floor. It rolls toward me and stops against my shoe: one of the chow hall's cylindrical cardboard salt shakers.

Piccardy shakes his head and clucks his tongue. "Stolen contraband, Ledbetter. Exhibit A. Now if I were you, I'd get the fuck back to my unit and keep my mouth shut unless I want more of the same. Or worse. And from now on, try to remember who's in charge around here and who isn't." With that, he pivots, opens the door, and disappears around the corner.

"Is that clear what he said?" Anselmo asks. His hand is on the pull chain. He watches my involuntary trembling.

"Yes, sir."

"Good." He pulls the chain and the room goes dark.

Hobbling in pain along the walkway, I don't know why all those fall colors have turned monochromatic gray. I'm confused by the numbness that's overtaken me as I walk back toward B Block. Where's my outrage about what they've done to me? I flash back to Emily's behavior the night of Niko's death and most of the next day. Picture the way she sat slumped on the couch for hours, hugging a pillow to her chest and paying attention to no one, not even Maisie. Her pupils were saucers and her complexion was ashen. When I sat beside her and reached for her hand, it felt clammy and cold. Later, a counselor we talked to said she'd probably been in shock. Is that why I'm feeling detached from what they just did? Am I in shock? If not for the pain back there, I might almost be able to convince myself that it didn't really happen. That it was just some perverse dream I was relieved to wake up from.

But it *did* happen. They raped me with a state-issued defensive weapon to punish me. Silence me. And they must have planned it ahead of time. Why else would Piccardy have shown up on his day off?

Nearing the cellblock, I approach two guards chatting with each other. Neither looks familiar. As I come closer, their conversation stops. Why are they staring at me? Is this something Anselmo and Piccardy would keep to themselves or brag about to other officers? Has word already gotten out? Walking past them, I glimpse their batons and shudder. *Better not make threats you can't prove. . . . Who do you think they'd believe: a whiny little bitch like you or an Officer of the Month?* Challenging their two-bit authority put me in their crosshairs. That was how it had started. Then, to make matters worse, I got noticed and praised by their superiors. They had to punish me for that, and if I don't want more of the same or worse, I'd better keep my mouth shut.

Inside the building, I climb the stairs in pain. Walk down the hall and stand in front of our cell door for longer than usual. Mullins is at the control desk. He and I don't have a problem. Why isn't he letting me in? Is he fucking with me, too? Has he joined the campaign against me? "Sorry, Ledbetter. Didn't see you there," he finally calls. He buzzes me in.

Manny looks up from the TV. "Hey," he says.

"Hey."

"You okay?"

"Yeah."

"They're still hassling you over those turkeys? Why they keeping that alive?"

I shrug.

"Well, don't let it bother you, Corbs. They're just idiots. I mean, a missing salt shaker? Give me a break. Those shakers always go missing. If it's not salt, it's pepper."

I say nothing, hoping he'll stop.

"Hey, what's that bump on your forehead from? Those goons didn't rough you up over there, did they?"

Instead of answering him, I ask whether he has any aspirin or ibuprofen.

"I got both," he says. Opens his lockbox and reaches in. Pulls out two small plastic bottles and shakes them at me like maracas. "Chills and headache or achy muscles and minor injuries?" I point to the second one. When he tosses the bottle to me, I shake out three tablets and swallow them dry. "How hard did you hit your head?" he asks. "No concussion, I hope."

Without answering him, I ease myself down onto my mattress and shift onto my side, facing the wall.

"Can I just say one more thing?" he asks. "If they *did* rough you up, you might feel better if you talk about it."

"Yeah, thanks, Dr. Phil. I'll keep that in mind."

He doesn't deserve the snark, but I'm not telling anyone what happened, especially Manny. Gay guys are into that anal stuff—tops and bottoms, butt plugs. And sure, he'd understand the difference between a good time and a sexual assault, but Manny's a talker. The last thing I need to do is second-guess who has or hasn't found out what those sick fucks did to me. And what if it gets back to Anselmo or Piccardy that I *didn't* keep my mouth shut? What kind of fresh hell would they dole out then?

Still, I *wish* I could tell him. Maybe it *would* make me feel better to let it out. But telling him doesn't feel safe. . . . *Well, looky there. The baby killer's got himself a boner.* Why had *that* happened? Why was I participating in my own humiliation? So no, I need to just keep it to myself. Keep crossing off the days on my calendar until I'm out of this place and can pretend it never happened.

I skip five-on-the-floor. Don't want to be around anybody, guards or inmates. What I *do* want—what I need—is to stop the nausea and clean myself up. Later, when I hear Mullins whistling as he lopes down the corridor, I call to him. Ask whether I can grab a quick shower. "I missed shower time yesterday and I'm starting to stink." He unlocks the cell door. "*Real* quick," he says. "In and out. I don't want to hear 'Well, how come you let Ledbetter take one?'" I thank him and grab my soap, washcloth, and towel. It hurts like hell to hurry down the corridor toward the shower room, but I want to respect his kindness.

When I step out of my clothes, the sight of my bloodstained underpants triggers a flash of revulsion. I turn on the shower and step beneath it. The warm water sluicing down my back and between my cheeks feels soothing, but when I try to clean down there with a soapy washcloth, it hurts too much. I have to stop. Watching a string of blood wash down the drain rockets me back to the day I saw Niko's spilt blood on our driveway. Despair hits me so hard that I double over and wait for the vertigo to pass. . . .

If there *was* a god, here's what I'd want to know. Can a man who caused the death of his child *ever* atone enough to be forgiven? Is absolution even possible?

CHAPTER THIRTY-FIVE

—

October and November 2019
Days 818–31 of 1,095

"Hot dogs tonight," Manny reports when he gets back from chow. "I was going to sneak a couple out for you, but they were watching us like hawks."

I tell him I still don't have much of an appetite anyway. "But thanks for the thought." He sits down on my bunk, says he's worried about me, and asks whether we can talk. Bracing for the pep talk that's coming, I give him an indifferent shrug.

"I know something's the matter with you, Corby. You've been staying in here, skipping meals. Why don't you go over to Medical and get checked out?"

"Why would I do that?"

"I don't know, but when I was bagging up the laundry this morning, I noticed there was blood in your underpants."

I cover my fear of exposure with an angry retort. "How do you figure that's *your* fucking business? Do me a favor, will you? Keep your hands off my underwear."

"Then put them in the laundry bag rather than leaving them under your bunk, douchebag!" Other than that time with the snake, this is the closest he's ever come to yelling at me and, in a way, I'm proud of him. Most cellies just ride it out in close proximity, but Manny and I have come to care about each other. He shows it more than I do, but the friendship is mutual. I'm grateful for it, as annoying as he can get.

"If it's hemorrhoids, they can give you some suppositories, Corbs." Groaning, I tell him I don't have hemorrhoids. "Jeez, I hope it's not an ulcer. My friend Finley had a bleeding ulcer and when he took a shit, there was this blackish blood."

"Stop it, Manny. I don't need to see a doctor because there's nothing physically wrong with me. Those bloodstains were from weeks ago and never came out. Okay?"

"Maybe it's emotional then. I know something's up with you. If you don't want to talk to me about it, maybe you should put in a request to see one of the shrinks who come here."

I consider his suggestion. There are two psychologists at this place. I've heard that the younger one is pretty good, but seeing Blankenship would be a waste of time. He's the one who interviewed me when I was on suicide watch and he was pretty much dialing it in. Their schedules rotate, so you can't make a specific request. Maybe I'll give the psych wheel a spin anyway. Telling either one what they did to me would be brutal, but at least it would be confidential. Keeping it to myself is driving me nuts. Still, even if I get the new shrink, how useful will a sympathetic ear and some coping strategies be when what I really want is to figure out how to make those fuckers pay?

"Hey, you're right," I tell Manny. "I have been acting douchey lately. Sorry. Maybe I *should* go talk to one of those shrinks." He says it couldn't hurt. "Oh, by the way, do you mind if I hold on to those ibuprofens?" I ask him. It's been a little over a week since the assault and it doesn't hurt as much, except when I take a dump, which is when there's a little blood. I promise him I'll order him a replacement bottle on my next commissary sheet.

"Don't worry about it," he says. "Hey, by the way, you got any more of those Jolly Ranchers?" I remind him that he ate the last of them. "Did I? Oh, yeah. My bad. Mind if I watch TV?"

"Go for it," I tell him. I lie on my bunk, face to the wall as usual, half listening to Alex Trebek and then Pat Sajak. Start dozing when one of those lame-ass sitcoms with the phony laugh track comes on. . . .

I must have slept for a couple of hours at least, because when I wake up, it's already lights-out. Needing to take a leak but not trusting my aim in the dark, I sit on the seat. My butt is still sore, so back in bed I grope around in the dark for the ibuprofen. Instead, my fingers touch the smooth, cool surface of my river stone. I pick it up and clutch it in one hand, fumble around for those tablets with the other. I swallow three more, then flop back down and try to deep-breathe my way back to sleep. No go. The night demons are taunting me. . . .

Maybe after I get out of here, I can contact one of those investigative reporters on TV or in the paper. See whether I can get someone to do an exposé about the kind of shit Piccardy and Anselmo are getting away with in here—not just what they've done to me. What about what they did to Solomon? And others. I didn't witness it myself, but it's gone around the compound about how they amused themselves that time by convincing Billy, a Down syndrome inmate, to imitate a bunch of farm animals. And how Piccardy got transferred here because his uncle, Zabrowski, pulled some strings after Lover Boy knocked up that female inmate. Maybe if the public gets wind of this shit, the commissioner might have to fire them both. That's the thing DOC is most afraid of: negative publicity, complaints from the public. . . .

Maisie understands that you're "away" but that you're coming back. We still have to figure out how that's going to work. Yeah, well, maybe if you'd brought her down here to see me, they wouldn't be telling you she needs a shrink. Tell the truth, Emily. Isn't keeping her from me another way to punish me because of Niko? Having to be caged in here for three years isn't punishment enough? And what do you mean when you say we have to figure out how that's going to work after I'm out? How much are you going to try to restrict access to my daughter?

When that judge came out of her chambers with her decision, she said some sentences were easy to decide, others kept her up at night, and mine was one of the latter ones. *My decision is that you are to be incarcerated for a period of five years, suspended after three, and another three years.* Then she pounded her gavel and left the courtroom. I bet she hasn't thought of me once since then. . . . And why had Dad sobbed when he heard her decision? Who was he crying for: the grandson he'd only bothered to see once? For himself because he'd fathered a loser for a son? It's doubtful Professor Ledbetter was crying for me. If that had been the case, he probably would have answered the one letter I'd written him two or three weeks into my bid here. Or maybe even shown up here and sat down across from me to see how I was doing. . . .

I have months, not years, left to go before I get out. No matter what's going to happen between Emily and me, I'll fight her tooth and nail if she's going to try to screw with my parental rights. I was a *good* dad before it happened. She *knows* that. Doesn't that count for anything? Does it all just come down to that one worst thing I did? I guess I know the answer to that one. . . .

Piccardy and Anselmo better watch their backs once I'm out of here. If I can't get the media to do anything, I'll find some other way to make them pay. At the library, I'd found an article in the staff newsletter about the pair. They'd played football for competing high schools. After graduation, they both enlisted in the army. Both went to Fort Benning for basic training and they bonded there. Piccardy fought in Afghanistan, Anselmo in Iraq. After they both got out, the article said, they commuted to the police academy for their training to become correctional officers. They've run 5Ks together, been each other's best man, and competed together in one of those Tough Mudder challenges. The article included two photos of them. In one, they're at a game at Yankee Stadium, both of them wearing US Army caps, one of them with an embroidered eagle, the other camo with a stars-and-stripes patch. In the second picture, they're caked with mud and baring their teeth for the camera—a couple of self-congratulating "tough mudders." . . . Lying here, I imagine the two of them jogging along some country road, unaware that I'm tailing them in a car—something heavy like a Ford Expedition or a Chevy Suburban. When I'm sure no one's coming, I gun it, passing close enough to scare them both. Then I turn the car around. When I get close enough for them to recognize me, I floor it, aiming right at them. It's a sick fantasy, but a satisfying one. They deserve it. Then I'm stopped cold, realizing who *didn't* deserve it: my little boy. I was at the wheel when he died, too. Nausea overtakes me. I get off my bunk, rush to the bowl, and heave. Lying back down, I break out in a cold sweat. You see what kind of a sick bastard prison's turned me into, Emily? And half the time, you can't be bothered to pick up the phone and accept the charges? You can't manage more than a couple of letters a month, sometimes one a month? How long has it been since you visited? Two months. Right, Em? Eight weeks. Fifty-six days.

Clock says twelve forty-seven . . .

One sixteen . . .

Two thirty-nine.

Fuck all this lying awake thinking. What I need is sleep. . . . The river is loud tonight. After all that rain we've had, it sounds urgent as it rushes past, heading south. Rubbing my thumb against the stone, I begin to relax. Start to doze. Wake up, doze some more, then fall into a deep sleep.

When I crack my eyes open, I glimpse, through the slit of the cell's back window, the drab gray of another morning getting ready for the sun to break through on the horizon. Lying there, I recall the dream I've just woken up from. Emily and the twins are in a paddleboat on some lake. I'm happy that Niko's alive again or wasn't dead after all. For some reason, I'm not in the boat; I'm swimming after them, trying to catch up. When I hear something behind me and look back, I see a bear, dog-paddling after me. I swim faster, but the paddleboat has gotten far ahead. The bear is gaining on me. I can hear it chuffing and growling. When I look back, its eyes meet mine.

———

"But it's baked chicken leg night," Manny says. "You don't want to miss chicken leg night, do you?" He's up on his bunk in just his skivvies, his scrawny legs dangling over the side. I'm sitting on my storage box, my face in the book I'm pretending to read so he'll shut up. It's not working. "Last week you skipped Jamaican meat pies and now this? I wish you'd just tell me what's bothering you, Corby. Maybe if you talk it out, you'll feel better."

Without looking up, I tell him I've been on this same freaking page for ten minutes now and I'm wondering whether he's going to shut up anytime soon.

"Is it about your wife? Or—"

"Leave it alone, Manny."

"Are Piccardy and his wingman still bothering you? I thought that had died down, but has it?" Now he's really pissing me off because he's getting too close to the truth. And yes, their harassment seems to have stopped, but the assault served its purpose. The toy cops must be so proud of themselves now that they've shut me up and shut me down.

Out in the corridor, CO Sullivan shouts five minutes till chow call. Manny jumps down from his bunk, pulls on his pants, and slips his feet into the frayed checkerboard Vans I wear as slippers. He used to ask me whether he could wear them. Now he just assumes they're his.

"Is it about your daughter? The custody thing?"

"Stop it, Manny! You're not my shrink."

"No, I'm your friend."

When I look over at him, the compassion in his eyes hurts so much that I have to look away. He's my *only* real friend in this place. Well, he and Javi over at the library. "Look, I'm sorry I've been so surly lately, but I've got less than ten months left in here. All I want to do is lie low and keep crossing off those days on my calendar. Okay?"

"I still think you should put in a request to talk to someone."

"I already did, okay?"

———

I'm disappointed to see I've drawn the short straw. It's Blankenship again. He's on the wall phone, talking to someone he's calling "sweetheart." He holds up his be-with-you-in-a-minute finger and gestures that I should take a seat.

I don't. I just stand there, looking around the room where I was told to meet him. Pink cinder-block walls, dirty blue plastic chairs on either side of a chipped metal table, bulletin board with nothing much posted on it, an almost empty bookshelf. This is nobody's office; it's just a room where you're sent when you put in a request to see someone, which I did two weeks ago.

Why am I even here? I just need to keep my head down, keep my mouth shut, and keep counting the days until I'm out of here. That documentary I saw last week about "the Greatest Generation" talked about how those guys who had survived the brutality of war came home and kept their memories to themselves. Compared to what those soldiers and sailors suffered, what happened to me is nothing.

Blankenship looks different. Better than I remember him looking. Nice suit, matching necktie and pocket square. Looks like he lost some weight. New wife maybe? Some younger woman who's given him a makeover? Didn't he used to be bald? "No, don't book it yet, sweetheart. I know it's a good deal, but the flight's not going to fill up between now and when I get home tonight." This is ridiculous. I signal to him that I'm leaving. "Hold on," he says. He tells Sweetheart he's got a patient waiting and he'll see her shortly after five. Adds that he loves her, too.

As he hangs up the phone, he checks his watch. "Sorry to keep you waiting," he says. "I'm Dr. Blankenship. And you're . . ." He looks down at the pass I just gave him. "Corbin Ledbetter." No recognition of our earlier exchange, not that I should have expected it. It was almost three years ago. "So what can I do for you, Corbin? Tell me what's happening." He may look different, but he still has that high-pitched voice.

I scan the room. Feel the fingernails of my one hand digging into the flesh of the other. Squint to read the spine of that paperback on the bookshelf; it's Stephen King's *The Stand*. When I look back at him, I tell him that someone did something to me and it's messing with my head.

"Go on," he says. Waits. "If you want me to help you, Corbin, you're going to have to be more specific."

My right foot's tapping against the floor like crazy. I should have walked the fuck out of here while I had the chance. "Hey, can I ask you something? Before I got sentenced, I was seeing this doctor. Dr. Patel. Didn't she used to work here?"

"Yes, part-time. Lovely woman. You saw her at her private practice?"

"Yeah. . . . Yup."

"So what did that person do to you?"

I take a deep breath and let it out, but give him an edited version. Tell him I got butt-raped but don't correct his assumption that my assailant was another inmate.

"Did you go to the medical unit? Get tested for HIV and any other STDs?"

I lie. Say I did. "Everything came back negative."

"Well, that's a relief. Right?" I nod. "Have you reported this? Filed a complaint? Talked to your counselor?" I shake my head. "What about privately? Have you told anyone in confidence? A friend or a custody officer who you can trust?"

"An officer I can trust? Where would I find one of those?" He doesn't respond. "No, you're the first person I've told."

"And this incident happened when?"

"About three weeks ago."

He glances again at his watch. "How have things been going for you since?"

"Not so good."

"And what are the specifics of 'not so good'?"

"I feel nervous a lot. Scared that it might happen again. And just so freakin' angry, you know? I've been having fantasies about payback."

"But they're just fantasies? Nothing you're planning to act on?" I shake my head. "You having problems sleeping? Depression? Loss of appetite?"

"All of the above, actually."

"Anything triggering you? Making you relive the memory?"

I shake my head. "No, wait," I tell him. "The assault happened in a storage room outside the chow hall, okay? And there's these big sacks of onions piled up in there. Last week, someone left the door to that room open, and on my way into the hall to eat, I got a whiff of those onions and . . . It didn't last long, but for a couple of seconds, I started breathing hard and it felt like it was going to happen again."

"Like a flashback?"

"More like a mini panic attack or something."

"You've experienced panic attacks before?"

"Yeah. Dr. Patel? When I was seeing her, she gave me these strategies to help me short-circuit them when they're starting. Breathing exercises, grounding exercises. And then, after I came here, she wrote me this letter, which, you know, she didn't have to do, but it was really helpful."

"And what did the letter say?"

"Said a lot of things. Useful suggestions to let me hold on to hope and not get sucked into the black hole of being here."

He nods. I don't tell him about the timing of the letter: that I got it right after he sprang me from the observation cell. "She was really pushing the mind-body thing. Said if I was isolating—which I was—I needed to fight against it. So I forced myself to go to chow instead of skipping meals. Started exercising, playing cards in the dayroom with other guys on my tier. Later on, I got a job on the grounds crew, which was great at first. Fresh air, sunshine, physical work. Pulled me out of my funk, you know? Our supervisor was a good guy, but then they switched supervisors and there were issues."

Another check of the wristwatch. He says our time is limited and suggests we focus on the present. "Now, since this incident, I take it you've been isolating again."

Interesting that he's calling what happened to me an "incident." I tell him I just don't want to be around people—that I feel on edge about everything. "Am I going to get attacked again? What's going to happen when I get out of here? How much of my life am I going to get back?"

"When *do* you get out?" I tell him I have less than ten months. "Okay, well, let's see if we can take away some of that stress you're feeling. I'm not sure you're aware of this, but there are protocols available to someone in your situation. Do you know about PREA? The Prison Rape Elimination Act?"

I shrug.

"It's a zero-tolerance policy against sexual assault—a protection for people in confinement facilities: prisons, jails, lockups. Basically, it says that if you report to PREA that you've been sexually abused, the allegation gets investigated promptly and thoroughly. Theoretically, that's what happens anyway. It's been around for a while and there are mixed reviews about how effective it is. But if you wanted to go that route, it might make you feel more in control than just staying in your cell and stewing about things. You think you might want to look into that?" When I shake my head, he asks why not.

"Well, besides the obvious: that I'm pretty goddamned ashamed that it happened, I'm afraid they . . . *he* might retaliate if there's an investigation. And maybe I'm cynical, but I doubt anything would happen if I *did* report it. When I filed a complaint about something else a while back, it went nowhere."

He nods. "A second ago, you said '*they* might retaliate' and then you corrected yourself—said *he*. Were you assaulted by one person or more than one?"

"You mean, was I gang-raped? No. It was just a slip of the tongue. . . . There were two of them there, though. One of them did it and the other one watched. He was the one who probably orchestrated it."

"Got it," he says. To refresh his memory about what my name is, he glances down at the call slip I handed him when I walked in. "Well, Corbin, unfortunately, you're not the first guy at this place that this has happened to. Comes up from time to time with the men I see in here. And maybe you're right to be cautious about who you tell. It's not a bad thing to be self-protective in here. And to tell you the truth, it didn't end well for one guy I counseled when he decided to file a PREA complaint. That said, think about that option, and if you change your mind—"

I tell him I won't.

"Okay then. Let's get back to the symptoms you're experiencing. Anxiety, insomnia, loss of appetite, lack of motivation."

Jesus Christ, *another* check of the watch. How many times is that? Four?

"I'm going to call Dr. Beller, who does some consulting here, and get you a prescription for antianxiety medication. Benzodiazepines aren't magic, but they can help to take the edge off, and the effect kicks in pretty quickly. There's a bunch of them out there: Xanax, Ativan, Halcion, Klonopin. Klonopin's used to treat panic attacks and seizures, and a couple of my patients with anxiety and sleep-disorder issues have had good results taking it, too. How much longer did you say you have in here?"

"About eight and a half months."

"Okay, that'll work. I'm going to have you take a half milligram twice a day to start with, then once a day as you get closer to your release date, and then every other day. With benzos, you don't want to go off them cold turkey. You have to taper off. So let's go with the Klonopin then. Sound good?"

Here's where I should come clean. Instead, I hear myself saying, "Sounds good."

"So let's see how that works for you. We can always adjust the dosage up or down as needed. Okay?"

"Okay." A benzo's a benzo and an addict is an addict. But this time it will be monitored. Controlled. It's not like when I get to the front of the med line, they're going to give me more than what's prescribed. Half a milligram's not much, but if it lifts me out of the hell my mind's putting me through, that's all I'm looking for. And a plan's in place so that I will have stopped taking it before I get out of here. So that will work. All bets would be off with Emily if I don't walk out of here clean.

"All right, my friend. Anything else you want to ask me before you go?"

Should I say it or not? No. Forget it. I start to get up from my chair.

"Yes? No? Looks like you've got *something* on your mind."

Too embarrassed to face him, I look down at the floor. "Just that, while it was happening . . . the assault? . . . This doesn't make any sense but . . . there's one thing I'm confused about."

"And what is that?" I struggle to come out with it. "Did you get an erection? Have an orgasm? Is that what's confusing you?"

My face goes hot. "An erection, not . . . it just happened."

He tells me to sit back down. Says I don't need to worry about it or feel guilty—that the nerve endings in the anal canal were only reacting autonomically to a stimulus. When I shrug, he says, "Think about the difference between a blink and a wink. Winking's a conscious act, right? But blinking's autonomic. You do it without thinking about it."

"Uh . . ."

"Okay, let me put it this way. An enjoyable sexual experience results from the body and the brain working in concert to give pleasure. Female rape victims sometimes feel guilty or confused when, during an assault, they become wet the way they would with a lover. But there's no shame in that. It's just their body having an autonomic response. You see?"

I tell him I do.

"All right then, my friend. Go forth and prosper." Quick handshake. Big, straight teeth. He's one of those people who look creepy when they smile.

"Yeah, okay. Thanks."

I'm guessing neither one of us can wait for me to get out of there, but I can't chalk this up to being a total waste of time. He's put me at ease about the hard-on. And more important, he's going to get me that prescription, which, this time, I'll be taking under controlled circumstances, not because I'm craving it. Thank God that obsession has left me. And I'm not really breaking the promise I made to Emily before I came here. Well, I am and I'm not. It's just a port in the storm—a way to survive the last months of my bid here before, for better or worse, I'm free. I'm never going to tell her that I was sexually assaulted and she doesn't need to know that I'm going to get past it with the help of a low-dose benzo either. It's all good.

CHAPTER THIRTY-SIX

December 2019 to January 2020
Days 872–901 of 1,095

I'm surprised when Aliyah Jackson, the counselor-supervisor who got Solomon transferred, calls me into her office. I like the orange and blue beads she's decorated her dreads with. At this place, I'm always grateful for color. "Two things," she says. "First of all, I'd been hearing so much about your mural that I went over to the library to check it out. Awesome job, Corby. Congratulations."

I thank her. Ask her what the other thing is.

"It's good news," she says. "The governor's going to be rolling out a new initiative after the holidays. He wants to bring down the numbers at state prisons, so they're releasing some inmates earlier than scheduled—fifty or so of the guys here. Merry Christmas, Corby. It looks like you'll be going home in February."

I'm stunned. "What? Six months early?"

"I don't have a date yet, but your name is on the list. What did the judge give you? I haven't looked it up yet."

"Five years suspended after three, plus three years' probation, as long as I don't screw up."

"I don't see that happening. You've done well in here, and because of the hiring freeze, the caseloads for probation officers have gotten ridiculous.

You'll probably just have to report once or twice a month. . . . I'm having trouble reading you, Corby. What are you thinking?"

"Well, I'm glad. But when you say I'm going home, I'm not sure where home is going to be. Back with my wife and our daughter is what I'm hoping for, but it's up in the air. She went to see a divorce lawyer the first year I was in here, but she never followed through."

"So that's a hopeful sign, right?"

"Maybe." And then there's the Klonopin. I'll need to wean myself off it earlier now. Not really a problem.

"Either way, your residence postprison has to be established before they let you out. So this early release will have to set something in motion. Maybe a reconciliation."

"I hope so."

Later that day, when I call Mom with the news, she starts to cry. Says she's just as happy for Maisie as she is for me.

"And if Emily lets me come back home, we'll be able to avoid all that visitation stuff. What do you think the chances of that happening are?"

Silence on her end for three or four seconds. Then she says she doesn't know. "Just don't count your chickens before they hatch, sweetheart."

Why's she saying that? "Do you know something I don't?"

"No, no. Emily and I don't discuss what happened in the past or what's going to happen. That's up to you two to figure out. The most important thing is that you'll finally be out of there and that you and Maisie will—"

Securus cuts us off.

I try Emily's number, which is stupid because she's going to still be at work.

"Hello?"

Oh. She *is* home.

The canned spiel kicks in: *This call originates from a Connecticut Correctional facility. Press one to accept the charges. . . .*

Which she does. "No, Maisie's not sick," she says. "She's still at school.

The water heater sprung a leak and I had to be here when they came to replace it. They're working on it now."

I give her the news that I'm getting out six months earlier than I thought, and that my residency has to be established before they release me. "I don't want to pressure you, Em, but it's more urgent now." When she asks me what the exact date is, I tell her I don't know yet. Sometime in February. "My counselor's going to let me know, but at the rate things happen around here, it could be—"

"Use your mother's address," she says. "I assume she'd be okay with that."

"Yeah, but wouldn't it make more sense if I moved back in with you and Maisie? I could take her to school and pick her up. Bring her to her after-school stuff. Make dinner. Make your life easier."

"No. That's not happening."

"It would just be for convenience's sake. I can sleep on the couch."

"No."

One two-letter word and that's it? "Because?"

"Because you can't expect to walk out of there and pick up where we left off before . . . everything happened. You've been in prison for two and a half years, Corby. You've changed, I've changed, and it would be too overwhelming for Maisie. Don't get me wrong. I want you back in her life and she's going to want that, too, but it has to happen more gradually."

"You're going to file those divorce papers, aren't you?"

"I didn't say that."

"I mean, there was no rush before. But now that I'm getting out—"

"Look, Corby," she says. "You're an addict and your substance abuse has cost us all a hell of a lot." She's saying it without saying it: it cost her Niko. "And to tell you the truth, when Maisie needs to go someplace, I can drive her myself like I've *been* doing." Meaning she won't risk our daughter's safety if I'm at the wheel. I go someplace else for a couple of seconds because it hurts to listen to how my offer has scared her. Triggered her.

When I tune back in, she's saying she believes me when I say I've stayed clean and sober since I've been in prison, but—

"For the record, I got clean *before* I got here, and, except when we were in lockdown, I've hauled my ass to meetings once or twice a week."

"Which is really good and I'm sure it hasn't been easy. But once you get out, you're going to have a lot more access to drugs and alcohol."

"I'm past all that. The obsession has left me."

"Then I'm happy for you. Happy for Maisie, too. All I'm saying is that you're going to have to prove to me that you're committed to maintaining your sobriety before we can talk about driving her places or living arrangements."

"Prove it for how long?"

"Well, let's say a year. Which doesn't mean that you and Maisie can't—"

"You shopping around for someone else, Em? Swiping right to find my replacement?" I can hear myself being an asshole, but I'm not yet sorry I said it. Still, why am I arguing *against* the case I'm trying to make?

"No, that's *not* it," she says. "I'm going to end this conversation now before we both say things we're going to regret. I'm glad you're getting out early. Take care."

What's it been—less than an hour since I received the news from Ms. Jackson? And in that time, my emotions have ricocheted like a pinball: relieved, excited, afraid, hopeful, hopes dashed. But that's no excuse for going off on her like that. Hasn't my time in here—all of it *sober* time— taught me anything about restraining myself? Being humble enough to resist running off at the mouth? It says in the Big Book that humility is the bedrock of recovery.

———

Manny says, "I'm going to miss you, but I'm happy for you, Corbs. Can I give you a hug?"

"Probably not," I tell him. He gets that hurt look of his, so I tell him that when I leave, I'm not going to want to take a lot of the shit I've accumulated.

"Like what?" he says.

I know what answer he's looking for. "Well, for one thing, my TV." He breaks out in a big grin. It's taken me a while to figure out that Manny's commissary account, which his sister, Gloria, funds, doesn't allow for many extras. She can't make much as a nighttime cleaner in a couple of office buildings, but Manny seems to think his and his sister's ship is going to come in once that uncle kicks the bucket and they inherit his motel. That's probably wishful thinking since it's on some secondary road in Jersey close to where Palisades Amusement Park used to be. From time to time, I hear him singing their old radio jingle: *Palisades has the rides, Palisades has the fun. Come on over!* I hope I'm wrong, but I can't imagine a motel on the way to where a tourist attraction *used to be* is going to be much of a moneymaker.

I've done my best to avoid Anselmo and Piccardy, but even when I can't, they ignore me—look past me as if I don't exist. The only exception was the time out in the yard when Piccardy put his finger to his lips and smiled. Even his silent threat didn't intimidate me that much, thanks to the Klonopin. It's really helped me to stay calmer during the day, sleep better at night, and quiet the violent fantasies I'd been having about how I'd make him and Anselmo pay for what they did. The only problem is that when Blankenship prescribed it for me, I told him I was getting out next August. After that changed, I put in a request for an appointment to discuss getting off it sooner. I heard back yesterday, but the appointment's not for another week and a half and it's with the other shrink. What I'll do is start tapering down six weeks before my release. I'll start going over to the med line every *other* time I'm due for a dose. Then, for the last couple of weeks, I'll stop taking it altogether. Wean myself off it that way. It's just a crutch, and the closer I get to leaving, the less I'll need it.

Hey, Em—

I'm writing for two reasons. First, and most important, I want to apologize for the stupid things I said on the phone last week. I had just found out about my earlier release and my head was all over the place emotionally. Still, that's no excuse for me acting like a dick. I should have let the news sink in before I called you. I'm sorry.

I've been thinking a lot about the things you said and realize they make sense. You're right. I need to prove myself once I'm out. Addicts get to be really good liars and I was no exception when I was drinking and drugging. I get it that I have to win back your trust over time. My probation officer will drug-test me regularly and will have the power to send me back here if I test positive, but that's not going to happen! Once I'm out of here, I'm never coming back.

There's this saying in the program—"meeting makers make it"— and it's true. I've heard people in AA and NA say they were five, ten, even twenty years sober, but then they got complacent, stopped going to meetings, and started drinking or using again. I've promised myself that I'll get to meetings four or five times a week <u>minimum</u>. With my counselor's help, I've just recently gotten my sponsor's address and written to him. Dale was who I was working with before I got sentenced. He and I were doing the Twelve Steps, but that got cut short when I had to come here. We were getting ready to start Step Nine, which is about making amends to the people we've hurt. I'm hoping to hear back from him so I can finish the last four steps. I know promises can sound empty, but I mean it when I say I'm going to work consistently on my sobriety, for you, for Maisie, and most of all for myself.

The second reason I'm writing is to update you on a couple of things. I've found out my release date. It's Tuesday, February fourth. My mom says I can stay at her place for as long as I need to. I'm hoping to get some kind of a job ASAP so that I can begin to contribute toward your expenses, plus give my mom a little something every week. She's not charging me rent, but I want to chip in. I have the number of an agency that helps ex-cons find employment, so I'll contact them. Meanwhile, Mom says one of her regulars at the diner

hires ex-prisoners at his scrap metal business and that her boss, Skip,
is always looking for dishwashers. And I can always mow lawns and
shovel snow or whatever. Start small and stay humble. Right?

Take care, Em. Kiss Maisie for me and tell her Daddy will see
her soon.

Love you two,
Corby

For some reason, writing that letter takes it out of me. I address the
envelope and put the letter inside, but instead of sealing it, I decide I'll read
it over tomorrow before I put it in outgoing mail on the way to breakfast.

In the morning, the one part of my letter that makes me a little uncomfortable is when I wrote, *Addicts get to be really good liars and I was*
no exception when I was drinking and drugging. I get it that I have to win
back your trust over time. When I *was* drinking and drugging: past tense.
But I'm taking a benzo again. Should I rewrite the letter and leave that
sentence out? . . .

Nah. It's low-dose, I'm taking it medicinally under supervision, and
I've got a plan to start tapering off it as my release date gets closer. That's
a whole different thing than abusing it. It's just a crutch, that's all. When
someone breaks an ankle, no one expects them to get around without
using crutches. Same difference. She might not understand the difference
between how I was using it then and now—decide it's a deal-breaker
when it's not even a problem. And anyway, if I told her I'm taking it in
here, I might have to tell her why—because I was anally raped by one
guard while another one watched. There's no way in hell I'm doing that.
It's just a crutch, Emily. After they sodomized me, I was losing it. It calms
my nerves and helps me get to sleep. Taking it is just temporary. I know
what I'm doing.

So the letter is fine as is. I seal the envelope and, when they call us for
morning chow, hand it to the desk sergeant. "Outgoing?" he asks.

"Yes."

The following Saturday morning, Manny and I are cleaning up the cell when the squawk box clicks on. "Hey, DellaVecchia. You've got a visitor."

Must be Manny's sister. He said she was driving up from Jersey to visit him.

"Ledbetter, you there?"

"Yes."

"You've got visitors, too."

Visitors? Plural? Emily and my mother? No, it can't be Mom. Not at ten thirty on a Saturday morning when the diner gets its biggest crowd of the week. Could be just Emily, though. Singular not plural, a slip of the tongue? Maybe my letter apologizing to her has put us back on track.

It can't be Em and Maisie, can it? No, don't even go there. . . .

Dad and his wife? Uh-uh. I don't remember putting Natalie's name on my visitors' list. The first year I was here, whenever they said I had a visitor, I'd brace myself, thinking it might be my father. I'd walk over there feeling dread that I had to face him and, at the same time, relief that he'd cared enough to come. But it never *was* him, so by the third year, I hid my disappointment with a fuck-him attitude. Fake it 'til you make it, as they say. But at this point, I really couldn't care less whether he shows up. In fact, I hope it's *not* him. Too little, too late. My complicated feelings about Dear Old Dad have gone to sleep and I'd just as soon not poke the bear.

"Who's your company?" Manny asks me.

"I'm not sure. Maybe Melania and the Donald?" He pretends he's gagging.

Entering the visiting room, I recognize the pair of guards up there on the platform—the same two who were on duty the day Solomon had that meltdown and they pulled him out kicking and screaming and made the rest of us leave. Goatee Guard looks like he's put on a little weight; Butch has grown her crew cut out into a modified Afro. Per the usual protocol, we have to be seated before they let the visitors in. Goatee goes over the rules: a brief embrace and a quick kiss, no tongues; everyone's hands up on the table where the guards can see them; no exchanges of any kind or we'll get a ticket and our visitor will be banned from coming here.

Here come the troops, passing by the sally port window. Then the steel door grinds open and they're in. I recognize Cornell's wife and grandson from earlier visits. That's got to be Manny's sister behind them; she's a Manny look-alike in a Hawaiian shirt, crop pants, and a thick gray braid. Watching them hug each other makes me wish I had a sister.

Hey, I was wrong; it *is* Mom. What's she doing here on a . . . Oh my God, it's Maisie! She's brought Maisie! As they walk toward me, hand in hand, I'm hungry to take her in. Dark eyes, dark hair; she's got her mother's coloring. As I watch her scan the room, taking in the noisy reunions of families, friends, and cons, I have an unwelcome flashback to that morning, me turning and looking in the back seat, seeing her strapped in safely next to Niko's empty car seat. I refocus on who she is now, a kindergartener in a pretty plaid dress with a white collar, white anklets, and those little-girl shoes with the straps. Is she tall for her age? She looks tall. When Mom directs Maisie's attention to me, I wave. She stares at me without waving back.

As they reach my table, I swipe the tears from my cheeks and get down on one knee, my arms outstretched. Instead of stepping forward for a hug, she hides behind her grandmother. "Easy does it," Mom tells me. "She's feeling a little shy. Why don't we all sit down?" Given the choice of a chair of her own or her grandmother's lap, she opts for Grandma Vicki.

"Well, hi, Maisie," I say. "I haven't seen you in a long, long time and I'm so happy you came to see me. Do you know who I am?" She shakes her head.

"Sure you do," Mom tells her. "Who did I say we were coming to see?"

She reaches up and whispers in Mom's ear. "That's right. And here he is." Maisie shakes her head and tells her grandma that her daddy doesn't have a beard. "Not in the pictures you have of him at home, but he's grown one since he's been here. Right, Daddy?"

"Yes, that's right. Do you like it, Maisie, or do you think I should shave it off?"

"Shave it off." She says it to Mom, not me.

Manny calls to me from one table over. "Hey, Corby! Is that your kid?"

I nod. "And my mother."

"Pleased to meet you," Manny says. "This is my sister, Gloria." We all say hello and Gloria tells me my daughter's adorable and asks me how old she is. Before I can answer, Butch yells to us from the guards' platform that we need to limit our conversations to our own visitors. Everyone nods. Okay, we get it.

"Maisie, pretty soon, you and I are going to see a lot more of each other," I tell her. "And we can do fun things—maybe go to Wequonnoc Park so you can swing on the swings and climb on the monkey bars."

"Can Grandma Vicki come?" she asks.

"If she wants to. Would you like to come with us, Grandma?" She says she would.

"What about my mommy?"

"Oh, sure, she can come, too. And maybe after the park, we can get ice cream or go to McDonald's. Do you like Happy Meals?"

Ignoring my question, she says, "That man is a pirate." Confused, I follow her pointing finger to the end of the table. She means Mick, a guy on the tier below ours who, for the sake of his visitors, is wearing a patch over his dead, milky eye. When Mom reminds her it's not polite to point, Maisie takes ahold of one of her braids and starts twisting it around her finger—a nervous habit, I suspect. Am I making her nervous? "Grammy, are we going soon?" she asks. Mom tells her they just got here.

For close to three years, I've imagined this reunion with my daughter. From across the room, she would see me and run to me. We'd hug, not wanting to let each other go. All those drawings I'd been sending her would have worked their magic, keeping her memory of me alive and intact. But this is nothing like that. She's wary of me. It's understandable; I've been gone from her life for so long. But it's painful, too, and it's hard not to resent Emily for keeping her from me. Does she have any memory of me at all? "Hey, Maisie, do you remember the song we used to sing at bath time? *The wheels on the bus go round and round. . . ."* She says she knows that song from school. "Oh, okay. So how's Mr. Zebra? Is he still your favorite stuffed animal?"

"Who's that?" she says. "My favorite is Monk Monk."

Mom is saying something to me in silence, but I'm unable to read her lips. I decide to go for broke. "Maisie, don't you remember me?" Without looking at me, she shakes her head and starts that braid twisting again. I look up at my mother. This time I can read her lips. "Don't pressure her," she's saying.

Patrolling the room, Butch—in fairness, she's Officer Stickley—stops at our table and asks Maisie whether she likes books. Maisie nods. "Well, you see Bert and Ernie on the wall over there?" She directs Maisie's attention to a badly done version of the *Sesame Street* characters. "Over there is where the books are. I bet if you pick one out, your daddy will read it to you." Maisie looks at her grandmother, who tells her to go ahead, so she slides off Mom's lap and heads for the books. "You *are* her father, right?" Stickley asks me. I tell her yes, but after she walks away, I say to my mother, "I used to be."

"Now stop that, Corby," Mom says. "This is a lot for her to process. Be patient. She'll come around."

"Yeah, okay. But I wish you'd have given me a heads-up that she was coming. Kind of a shock to see her walk in here when I wasn't expecting it."

"Well, this got put together very quickly, and you and I haven't spoken since when? Tuesday? It's not like *I* can call *you.*"

"No, you're right. I apologize. Thanks so much for bringing her here. How the hell did you pull it off? Is this visit clandestine or is it Emily-approved?"

"Corby, I never would have brought her here without permission," she says. "Emily had planned a weekend getaway in Boston with some of her teacher girlfriends. Betsy was going to babysit, but she came down with a bad cold, so I volunteered. I got one of the other girls to take my weekend shifts. I have Maisie until tomorrow night. I figured it was a long shot when I asked Emily about bringing her here to see you, but she surprised me and said it was probably a good idea. She told me the child psychologist she's taking Maisie to has urged her to let you and your daughter see each other again to prepare for your getting out. To tell you the truth, I think Emily was relieved when *I* offered to bring her. She told me she feels guilty she hasn't come to see you more often herself, but she finds this place so intimidating, she gets nauseous."

"You sure it's the *place*?" I ask, half kidding, half not.

Mom assures me that it's the place. "But having you back in her life is going to take getting used to for Maisie. Today is just the first baby step. Okay?"

"Okay. Hey, were you always this wise or is it something new?"

She laughs and says she doesn't know how wise she is; she's just trying to make things easier for everyone, Emily included.

All the time we've been talking, I've been keeping an eye on Maisie. I know most of the other guys who are here—we're all from B Block—and I haven't had a problem with any of them. But I know Jorge was a gang-banger; Lou's doing time for "doing" his girlfriend's underage daughter; Sal's here for human trafficking; Gallagher scammed two different widows out of their life savings. Nobody's bothering Maisie, and most of my peers, absorbed with their company, don't even notice her. But watching her pass within five or six feet of these guys puts me on alert. I'm not their peer right now; I'm Maisie's father. In all the time she's been kept away from me, I've only been able to see through the lens of my own selfish need— to look at her, talk to her, touch her, observe from visit to visit how she's doing, how she's changing. But this is the first time I'm able to see things through Emily's eyes. To consider that she may not have been withholding my daughter to punish me, but to make sure her only living child stays away from a potentially dangerous place that houses dangerous people.

Maisie returns with two books, *Curious George Goes to the Zoo* and something called *Pinkalicious*. She's also carrying a tattered and stained stuffed bunny. Emily would shudder at the thought of Maisie holding the thing, but I take my cue from Mom and let it go. "Which book do you want me to read first, Maisie?" I ask. She chooses *Pinkalicious* but says Grammy has to read it, not me.

"All right," Mom tells her. "I'll read this one and your daddy can read you *Curious George*." Maisie doesn't look thrilled with this plan, but she doesn't object.

When it's my turn to read, I reprise my performance as the funny daddy the twins used to love, hamming it up with over-the-top animal sounds and exaggerated responses to Curious George's hijinks. Maisie is poker-faced during the first few pages, but by the end, she's giggling in spite of herself. After that, and for the rest of our hour together, she's a little more friendly and talkative. At one point, she says, directly to me, "You know what?"

"No. What?"

"I'm going to a princess party at Michaela's house." I tell her that sounds like fun. Ask her whether she's going to dress up like a princess. "Yup. And guess what else?"

"What else?"

"I have a pet monkey. A *real* one." Mom gives me a discreet head shake.

"Wow, that's cool," I say. "What's its name? Curious George?"

"No! She's a *girl* monkey."

"Hmm, is her name Betsy?" Mom tries to suppress a smile.

"No, silly. That's my *gramma's* name."

"Your grandma? I thought your grandma's name was Vicki."

She widens her eyes and slaps her forehead. "My *other* gramma, dumb-head!"

"What? Your other grandma's name is Dumbhead?"

Mom reminds us both that it's not nice to call someone that.

When Officer Goatee gives visitors the five-minute warning, Mom tells Maisie she'd better put the books and the bunny back where she got them. She tells her no, she can't keep the bunny because other children will want to play with it, too.

As we watch her walk across the room, my protective-parent instinct kicks in again. Mom says she thinks Maisie and I made some good headway today. "They used to love it when I read to them and got silly," I tell her. "Came back like riding a bike."

"But please don't say things like that about Betsy. That's not going to help."

"Point taken," I tell her.

Mom says it broke her heart when Maisie told me she's going to that princess party. "It already happened and Maisie was the only girl in her class who wasn't invited. Apparently, when she asked that girl Michaela why, she told her it was because she's 'a weirdo.' Emily said poor Maisie was devastated."

Hearing this breaks my heart, too, but once I'm out of here . . . And here she comes, back to the table. For whatever reason she's an outcast at school, we're going to help her fix that.

"Visits are now over, people!" Officer Stickley announces. Most of the others in the room stand and embrace.

Mom and I share a quick hug and I get a peck on the cheek. "Not too much longer before I'm out of here," I tell her. She puts her hands together as if in prayer. Turning to Maisie, Mom asks her whether she'd like to give me a hug or a kiss goodbye. Maisie shakes her head. "Okay then, see you soon," I tell her.

I watch them walk with the other visitors to the steel door and wait for it to open. Mom and Manny's sister are saying something to each other. As they stand there, Maisie suddenly pivots, looks back at me, and gives me a timid wave. I wave back. For the time being, this little exchange is all I need. The door begins its noisy opening, the visitors walk through, the door reverses direction, and they're gone.

Dismissed from the visiting room, we line up to be strip-searched. Thinking about what Anselmo and Piccardy had planned when I was led into that storage room for a strip search, I break out in a sweat. Begin to shake. I'm desperate to hold on to my daughter's visit—the sound of her giggling, her braids, the joy of that surprise wave—but it's being snatched away from me as the ugliness comes back. I smell the onions, feel the surprise pain of it, the humiliation. When I'm next in line to be searched, I walk toward the CO. A few minutes later, I'm outside, walking back to B with Manny. I can't recall bending and coughing just now, any of that. When I began flashing back, I must have checked out until it was over.

I started weaning myself off the Klonopin two weeks ago and quit it altogether the day before yesterday. That's it, I told myself. No more. But I'm feeling so rattled by that strip search that, after chow, I get the okay from the CO at the control desk, head over to the medical unit, and get in line. I'll just take it this one last time so that, after that flashback I had, I can calm my nerves and get some sleep tonight. Then that will be it.

Dear Emily,

I'm writing to thank you for giving the okay to let Maisie visit me with my mom. For the past almost-three years, I've appreciated the pictures and updates you've sent me, but seeing her in person was magical. Sometimes when I think about that hour she and I had together last Saturday, I almost wonder if it really happened. I love her so much, Em.

Maisie's visit has gotten me thinking about our future—yours and mine—and the difference between the fantasy of what I've imagined happening and the reality of our situation. My gut tells me you're leaning toward going forward with the divorce. It kills me to write this, please know that, but I think I can admit to myself now that, other than legally, our marriage ended a while ago. That day on the phone when I was pushing for a reconciliation, you said that whatever was going to happen, you wanted me to still be in Maisie's life. I've done a lot of thinking about that and, especially since her visit, I realize that's the most important thing. And you're right that my reentry into her life should be gradual until she feels comfortable with me and you're comfortable that my recovery is rock-solid.

There's a skinny little window at the back of my cell that looks out onto the visitors' parking lot. In the time I've been here, I've sometimes witnessed through this window the reunions between some guy who's just been released and the families and friends who meet him and drive him away. For the past almost-three years, I've imagined the day when I walk out of here and now it's close to happening. My mom is going to pick me up and if it's okay with you, before we go back to her place, I'd love to see you and Maisie, either at the house or someplace where we can go for lunch or whatever. I hope that's not too much to ask and, if it is, I'll understand. You can let my mother know if it's okay with you. Thanks for considering it. Love you, Corby

CHAPTER THIRTY-SEVEN

—

January and February 2020
Days 914–17 of 920

It's Friday, January thirty-first, four days until my release. To make sure everything goes smoothly, I'm spending most of the day with a new CO, Officer Whiteley, who looks like she's just out of middle school, never mind the police academy. She's assigned to escort me to the offices where various personnel will help me do everything I need to do and sign everything I need to sign to ensure smooth sailing when I'm processed out of here on Tuesday.

Our first stop is the Inmate Trust Fund office. My account was frozen a week ago and I'm told I have eighty-seven dollars and forty-two cents left on the books. From that, fifty bucks will be subtracted and handed to me in cash as "gate money" just before I leave. The remaining thirty-eight dollars and change will be issued in a check forwarded to me at my mom's address.

Next, I have my picture taken for the ID card I'll exchange for my prison ID. This new identification will substitute for the driver's license I surrendered when I was indicted three years ago. I've been warned by my case manager that getting my license reinstated won't be easy, given the nature of my conviction. The DMV fees will be steep and I'll probably have a better shot at it if I hire a lawyer. I make a mental note to call Rachel Dixon's office later, but there's a part of me that dreads the thought of getting behind the wheel of a car again.

On our way to the property office, I ask CO Whiteley what drew her to this kind of work. "My last job was checking members in at a fitness center and saying 'Have a good workout!' a hundred times a shift. Plus, it's kind of in the family. My dad's a state cop and one of my brothers is a CO."

"Which prison is your brother at?"

That's when her training kicks in, I guess. Her face turns expressionless and she says, "Never mind. No more questions."

At the property window, I refuse the personal effects I came in here with. The last thing I want to be reminded of is the courtroom clothes I was wearing the day I was processed in here. "Donate them or throw them out," I tell the property manager. And so he issues me a thermal undershirt, a pair of khakis with an elastic waistband, and a hooded sweatshirt. "I ain't got any winter jackets at the moment. You can't walk out of here with the winter coat they issued you because it's state property. They'll make you surrender it before you leave. When you leaving?" This coming Tuesday, I tell him. "Supposed to snow," he says. "You need socks or skivvies? They'll let you leave here with those." I tell him I just got laundry back so I'm good. Last time I talked to my mother, I asked her to buy me some underwear and socks so I could throw out the used shit they issue us here. "Any excuse to go to TJ Maxx," she said.

More offices, more signatures. At Medical, a nurse tells me I still have some left on my Klonopin. Do I want them to send the rest of my prescription over to Discharge? I tell her no—that I've gotten myself off them. Haven't taken any for about a week and a half. "Any negative effects?" she asks.

Palpitations, some on-and-off twitching, a little more irritability. Nothing I can't manage. "None that I've noticed," I tell her.

"Okay then," she says. "If you're sure."

Our last stop is Counselor Jackson's office. "Okay, this is it for me," CO Whiteley says. "Good luck."

"Same to you," I tell her. "Hey, do me a favor, will you?" She says officers don't do favors for offenders. "Okay. I was just going to ask that you don't let this place make you cynical." I put my hand out to shake hers, but she refuses the gesture and walks away. I figure she could go either way after she's here awhile: become one of the decent ones who remember we're human beings or one of the ballbusters who has to keep reinforcing the message that we're scum and they're in charge. Something I've observed in the time I've been here is that a lot of the female officers are chameleons. They'll treat you reasonably one shift and go hard-ass on you the next, depending on who their shift partner is. For whatever reason they chose this work, women have to manage two groups of men: the prisoners and their fellow guards, including the ones who try to test them by making sexual remarks and the ones who assume this is no job a woman should be doing.

Counselor Jackson wants to know how I'm feeling. I shrug. Tell her my head's all over the place but I'm mostly happy to get out of here. "Understandable," she says. "Is someone picking you up on Tuesday?" I tell her yes, my mother. "Good old Mom, huh? Let her know she should be here no later than eight thirty, but that she'll probably have to wait awhile. Depends on how many others are getting processed out. And as you've probably noticed, nothing at this place moves too fast."

"Believe me, I've noticed. See if you can speed things up when they make you warden here."

She laughs and says, "Oh God, don't wish *that* on me. Here. Don't lose this." She hands me a card with the name and contact info of my probation officer and tells me I need to check in at his office within forty-eight hours of my release. I'm given a CT DOC discharge packet that contains information about transitional services and how to access medical insurance. I ask her to describe what happens on D-Day.

"Sure," she says. "They'll get you up early, probably have you take a shower and get dressed. They will already have issued you a couple of garbage bags for the stuff you're taking home, so you should pack the night before. Make a list of everything. Then an officer will escort you over to A&D and put you in a holding cell with whoever else is leaving that day. They'll call you up one by one, check the stuff in your bags against the list you made, give you a pee test to make sure you're leaving here clean, and ask you a bunch of questions to make sure you're really you, not someone who's trying to sneak out of here *instead of* you."

"Seriously? Did that ever happen?"

"Once, I heard. I guess it was all over the news, so they're super careful not to let it happen again. Anyway, just before they discharge you, you hand in all your paperwork and they give you your release documents. You'll get your new ID and your gate money. Then an officer will unlock three or four doors. When you pass through the last one, you're on the outside, a free man again."

"A free man. Wow. Is it really going to happen?"

"It is," she says. "You ready for it?" I tell her I'm *more* than ready, but the truth is, I'm on edge, too. The routines at this place can be mind-numbing, but what happens after I'm out and my days are unstructured? What if I can't get a job or get my license back? I ask Jackson whether I can use her office phone to call my attorney about having my driver's license reinstated. She nods, gets me an outside line, and hands me the phone.

"Attorney Dixon is no longer practicing here," the receptionist says. "Would you like to make an appointment with Attorney Stives? She's taken over the practice and has all of Ms. Dixon's files."

"No, that's all right. Thanks anyway."

———

It's February the first, late Saturday morning, and the final countdown to Tuesday has begun. Manny's sitting on my bunk and I'm kneeling in front of my open storage box, conducting the great cellmate giveaway. I've already promised my sweats to Pacheco, my Timberlands to Angel, and my blanket and knit hat to Lobo, who's always bitching about how cold he is. But to Manny go the rest of the spoils—whatever he wants to claim. He's already taken possession of my TV, writing with a Sharpie "Property of M. DellaVecchia" on both sides of the thing.

"How about these?" I ask, holding up my checkerboard Vans. "They're kind of frayed and there's a hole in the toe." Manny gives me a thumbs-up. He's probably worn them more than I have.

"Earphones?"

"I can always use an extra pair."

"Plastic bowls?"

"Fuck yes. One of mine's got a crack in it."

"Stamped envelopes?"

"Sure. I ran out last week and I owe my sister a letter."

"What about a half-empty tube of toenail fungus cream?"

"Why not?"

Giving away all the commissary shit I've accumulated is against the rules, officially; you're supposed to haul it all out of here whether someone else could use it or not. But for me, part of the joy of getting out of here is giving it to him and, really, who's going to check and say, "Hey, isn't that Ledbetter's antifungus cream?" It's one of the stupid rules here that begs to be broken, and I'm just seventy-two hours away from saying so long to all the stupid regulations at Yates fucking CI.

"Zatarain's?"

"Which kind? Blackened or Creole?"

"Creole."

"All right then. Yeah." Like *he's* doing *me* the favor.

He also says yes to two rolls of toilet paper, half a bottle of shampoo, a three-pack of Slim Jims, a barely used deodorant stick, my rubber shower shoes, an unopened package of smoked almonds, and a fingernail clipper. The only things he declines to take possession of are the come-to-Jesus books my aunt Nancy has sent me. It's not that I don't appreciate her thoughtfulness; it's just not the kind of reading I'm drawn to. Guess that's my father's influence, but at least I'm not as judgmental as he is about religion. It still strikes me as weird that one sibling becomes a Holy Roller, the other an avowed atheist who thinks believers have been duped.

I take the six books out of the box, spread them end to end on my bunk, and read the titles: *The Sacred Soul, Find Your Way Back to God, When Jesus Speaks, Are You Listening?, Chicken Soup for the Prisoner's Soul, Christian Awakenings to the Glory of God,* and *The Whole World in His Hands.* At first, I consider just tossing them, but then I decide I'll donate them to the library. They're still brand-new and some of the born-again dudes in here might want to read them. I want to say my goodbyes to Mrs. M and Javier anyway and return that book I've had forever, *Native American Genocide.*

Goolsby's at the control desk. Rather than giving me a hassle because I hadn't already put in a library request, he okays my going over there. "You're out of here pretty soon, aren't you?" he asks. I tell him yes, Tuesday. "Good luck then. Go to the door and I'll buzz you out."

I'm halfway down the corridor when Goolsby calls me back. Hanging up the phone, he says the mail room just called, wanting to know whether I was still in custody. "I told them you were here until Tuesday, so they asked me to send you over there before they close for the day. Go see what they want before you go to the library."

The system here is that inmate mail gets sorted, inspected, and sometimes opened and examined before it's sent to the blocks, where it's distributed to each tier's control desk, then shoved through the traps of our cell doors. So I have to ask Goolsby where the mail room is. "Same building you're going to," he says. "In the basement."

It's a happy surprise when I get to the mail room and a familiar face appears at the window. "Lieutenant Cavagnero? Wow, I didn't expect to see you here."

"Didn't expect to be back until a month ago," he says. "I can't get around like I used to and was filling out my paperwork to retire. But then Rafferty left and this position became available. Less wear and tear on the body and no second or third shift, so I decided to stick around a little longer and max out my pension. How are you doing? Painting any more pictures since that one on the wall?" I tell him no, that was it. "You're getting out soon, huh? Well, I'm happy for you."

I thank him. Tell him what my plan is, as much as I know at this point. Ask him why he wanted to see me. "Oh, yeah. Just a sec," he says, and hobbles to the back of the room. It's good to see him again. Reminds me that some of the COs around here are good people just doing their job.

When Cavagnero comes back, he's shaking his head. He's holding a bent-up envelope. "Gotta apologize for getting this to you so late," he says. "Rafferty? The guy I replaced? Nice enough guy, but he left this place a mess. Me and my workers took some time reorganizing things, moving the shelving and tables, and this showed up jammed behind that cabinet over there." When he hands it to me, I read the return address. It's from my father. The cancellation stamp says August 31, 2017. That would have been my fourth or fifth week here, around the time when I was thinking about how I could end my life. It would be too heavy-duty to open and read it now, so I thank Cavagnero, stick the letter in one of the books I'm donating, and head toward the stairs. I'm curious about what he had to say back then, but I'm not sure I want to find out. A part of me wishes his lost letter had stayed lost. Climbing to the top floor, I recall what he looked like when the judge sentenced me—the way he, of all people, was the one in tears.

At the library, I say goodbye to Javier first. We shake hands and when he pulls me in, we share one of those quick, back-patting embraces that even the macho men in here find acceptable. "Stay strong out there, hombre," he says. I tell him to do the same in here. We make a promise to reconnect after he gets out, maybe grab a meal and go to a meeting together.

Mrs. Millman is in her office. While I wait for her to come out, I place my book donations on the circulation desk and read the sign she's posted: *Beginning February 18, the hours when inmates may use this library will be limited and may fluctuate.* "What's up with this?" I ask when she comes out to the desk. She shakes her head and says it's about cost-cutting. The librarian at McFarland is leaving and they're not replacing him. "I'm told I now have to divide my time between *two* libraries and cut the hours at each by fifty percent. Oh, and the new materials the superintendent promised us? They've cut his budget, too, so that's kaput. Sometimes I don't know why I bother."

I tell her it's because we need her. Ask her whether she's going to take on the other library plus this one.

"I'll try it for a couple of months," she says. "And if it's too much, I'll retire so that Howie and I can hang around the house together and drive each other crazy. But that's enough of my tale of woe. I want to hear about *you*."

I tell her I'll be living at my mother's place and spending as much time as I can with my daughter. And that I'm hoping to get a job, maybe two, so that I can contribute toward Maisie's childcare and pay my mom a little toward expenses. "I may be able to get my driver's license back eventually, but for now I'll have to figure out the bus schedule and get ahold of a used bike."

She says her son's old Schwinn is just taking up space in their garage and I'd be doing her and Howie a favor by taking it off their hands. She jots her address and phone number on a slip of paper, folds it, and hands it to me. "We're not supposed to share our personal information with you guys, so don't let the officers see this when they discharge you," she says. I smile and tell her I'll swallow it if I have to.

Noticing the books I've brought, she picks them up and looks them over. I ask her whether they're anything she could use. "Oh, sure," she says. "Our spiritual books are always in circulation. We have a couple of these, but we can always use extras, and we're happy to get new titles. Thank you."

"Yeah, and sorry to be returning this one so late," I tell her, pointing to *Native American Genocide*. "Took me forever to get through it. It was a tough read."

"How so?" she asks.

"It was hard reading about how badly we screwed the Indigenous populations—'we' being the white man, of course. I mean, I knew about the Trail of Tears and Wounded Knee and all that, but this assumption of white supremacy went all the way back to the holier-than-thou Puritans. They tried to wipe out the tribes—attacked and slaughtered them, enslaved the survivors. You wouldn't believe the cruelty."

"Oh, yes I would, my dear," she says, smiling sadly. "I'm a Jew."

We lock eyes for a couple of seconds. "Yeah," I say. "Right."

We share a long goodbye hug. "So now you know how to get ahold of me," she says. "Stay in touch. And Corby . . ." She whispers the next in my ear. "Promise me you won't get too busy to practice your art. Don't squander your gift." Without a clue about what will happen after I'm out of here, I promise.

On my way out, I stop at my mural. My eyes wander over the various figures and come to rest on Niko. "So long, kiddo," I whisper. "I love you always."

Then I'm out the door. I'm halfway down the stairs when Mrs. M calls to me. "Forget something? This was stuck in one of the books you dropped off."

Had I forgotten it? Or had I subconsciously tried to get away from it? I'm not sure. Why had Dad's letter been hiding behind that metal cabinet in the mail room for years, waiting to boomerang back at me today when I'm feeling a hundred different emotions already? I spent the better part of three years hoping he might reach out in some way—be a real father instead of just the checkbook dad who paid for my lawyer and kicked in toward my commissary account. I concluded that he wouldn't or couldn't reach out in any personal way because he was too ashamed of me. My crime and conviction, my status as a prisoner, reflected poorly on him. Tarnished his sterling reputation. Receiving his letter now, three years after he sent it, leaves me bewildered. Having finally convinced myself that his rejection no longer matters—that I've become impervious to his disapproval—I realize I'm as vulnerable as ever.

When I get back to our cell, Manny's not there, so I take a deep breath and, with trembling hands, open the envelope and take out the handwritten four-page letter.

Dear Corbin,

I'm writing in response to your note thanking me for paying your legal fees and coming to your sentencing. You're my son; no thanks necessary. I just wish your lawyer had been able to keep you out of prison. There are some rough characters in there, so I hope you're holding your own.

I've been doing a good deal of soul-searching since that day in the courtroom when I watched them handcuff you and take you away. At first, I assigned most of the blame for your addiction to your mother. I told myself that if she had been less casual about her use of marijuana, you might not have come to rely on the addictive substances that led to such a terrible outcome. More recently I've admitted to myself that blaming Vicki left me off the hook. As I became more and more unhappy with your mother's and my married life, my drinking increased and I made no effort to conceal this from you. Added to that was how my moving out may have impacted you. Of course, there had to have been other variables at play. Children weather their parents' divorces all the time without there being such dire consequences later in their lives.

I'm so angry, I have to stop reading and catch my breath. Par for the course that he was blaming Mom, his favorite scapegoat. Her smoking weed had nothing to do with it. . . . His abandonment "may" have impacted me? Most kids from broken homes *don't* grow up and cause "dire consequences"? So which is it, Dad? Are you still trying to wiggle off the hook or is your big ego telling you that your defection had such a big influence that . . . And his name was Niko, Dad. He was a beautiful little boy, not just a "terrible outcome." You might have gotten a kick out of him, maybe even loved him, if you'd bothered to see him and his sister more than once. Your loss, Dad. Maybe I should rip up the rest and throw his bullshit letter in the trash. Instead, I keep reading.

Thinking back, I recall how we used to enjoy our nature walks when you were a little guy. You seemed so fascinated by all the creatures we'd spot in the woods, the ponds and streams, the fields, and I felt so proud to be able to share my knowledge of the natural world with you. My expectation back then was that you would follow in my footsteps and become a man of science, perhaps in the field of zoology. It was no secret that I was unhappy with you when you went in a different direction and chose to study art in college. I've come to realize only lately that my disapproval was based on my own ego. You had every right to pursue what you were interested in, instead of creating a life in my image. This is late in coming, Corbin, but I apologize for having devalued your artistic impulses.

Though this does not come easily, Corbin, I need to admit something to you. Despite the circumstances that led to your little boy's death, you were a far better father than I was. That became crystal-clear to me the time Natalie and I visited you, Emily, and the twins. I'm ashamed to say this, but seeing the loving way you interacted with your wife and children made me feel jealous of you. I had to admit to myself that I did not have the capacity to love the way you did, so I took the coward's way out. I made no further effort to visit you and your family.

Corbin, I don't know how you'll react to the things I've shared in this letter. I have no idea if they might bring us closer together or drive us further apart. I'll leave it to you to decide. If you write back and tell me you want me to visit you, I'll contact your mother and ask her what the procedures are. If I don't hear back from you, I'll understand that you don't want me to come. As you know, I am

*not someone who can pray to a nonexistent god, so instead of prayers
I offer you my deepest hope that you will remain safe and that your
time in there will pass as quickly as possible. I love you and look
forward to the day when you walk out of there a free man.*

Sincerely,
Dad

It's too much to take in all at once—too overwhelming and confusing—
so I put his letter down and pace the cell. Take deep breaths. Then I sit back
on my bunk, pick it up again, and read it a second time.

"If I had been a better father . . ." Is he actually owning up to his
flaws? . . . And Jesus, I didn't see *this* coming: his giving me belated permission to be myself. Are you actually humbling yourself, Dad? I didn't
realize you were capable of doing that. And you're saying you only came to
see the twins once not because you were indifferent to them but because
you were envious of *me*?

His letter is such a total mindfuck that I sit here, stunned. How do I
feel? How am I *supposed* to feel? What's my relationship with him supposed
to be like now? When Manny enters our cell, I barely notice him until he
speaks to me. "Hey, man, did you forget you're getting out of here? What
the hell are you crying for?"

CHAPTER THIRTY-EIGHT

—

February 2020
Days 918–20 of 920

After supper chow on Sunday, I head over to my last jailhouse AA meeting. They changed the time a few months ago, from late morning to early evening. The membership has changed some, too, since I started coming. Santiago and Red Sox Danny have been good additions. Durnell's gotten released and I hear he's doing great. Meth Mouth died in his sleep last Thanksgiving. That was a sad one, but Dusty's death was even sadder. I remember him talking about how scared he was when his discharge was coming up. Didn't take him long before he was back here again, telling us he'd been rejected as a candidate for a liver transplant and reacted to the news by going on an extended bender that he funded by pickpocketing shoppers outside Walmart. There was a yellow cast to his skin now and nobody wanted to sit next to him because he had "keto breath." He ended up in the hospice here and died last month without any of the inmate tributes that the more popular "back-door parolees" get.

Frank is chairing today's meeting. I think back to when he first came in and what a know-it-all he acted like. He's still not one of my favorites, but he works a good program and his shares are usually worth listening to. Of all the things I've heard in here, something Frank said that first day he showed up has been the most useful: that having hope was never going to hurt me, but having unreasonable expectations could clobber me and start me drinking and drugging again. I remember trying to get away from him because I was like, who was *he* to give *me* advice? But what he said stuck with me and the more I thought about it, the more I realized that what he said was true. Knowing the difference between hope and expectations has helped me ever since.

At the end of the meeting, I say goodbye and thank everyone for keeping me sober. "Same," someone says. "We'll miss you, man." "Have a ginger ale on me." When we hold hands and say the Serenity Prayer, I'm standing next to Frank. At the end, he gives my hand a squeeze and says, "Good luck out there in the Wild West."

Walking back to my housing unit, I think about how I've spent two and a half years romanticizing what freedom was going to feel like. One of the emotions I hadn't expected to feel was survivor guilt. How many times had Lester Wiggins been denied a sentence modification? Why had they even refused to grant him a merciful release when he was close to the end? Why do I deserve to walk out of here and move on when I ended Niko's life when he was only two? . . .

Back in B, I'm glad to see that it's Captain Graham and CO McGreavy working this shift. Both have always been decent to me. I tell them that tomorrow's the day I get out of here, and the captain says, "So we heard. Some of your friends are waiting for you in the rec room. You guys got one hour, that's it, so go on. Get."

I do what she says and walk into what turns out to be my farewell party, organized by Manny and okayed by Graham and McGreavy. Most of the guys on our end of the tier are here. Pacheco, Angel, Daugherty, Boudreaux, and the new kid, Jesse. They give me an embarrassing round of applause and, to stop them, I put up my hand like a traffic cop. Refreshments-wise, they've pooled their commissary resources: teriyaki beef jerky, chocolate chip Pop-Tarts, buffalo chicken nuggets, spicy pork rinds, mini Hershey bars, Gatorade, and Royal Crown Cola. With the help of a hair dryer and a paper bag, Boudreaux's made string-cheese-and-chili-with-beans nachos. It's a frickin' feast!

And what's a party without music? Angel has his radio dialed to an old-school R & B station and when Marvin Gaye's "Let's Get It On" comes on, a couple of the guys break out their slow-dance moves as if they're grinding against their women. Manny's moves flirt with being X-rated, so who knows where *his* fantasies are taking him. Luckily, the song ends before CO McGreavy pops his head in. "Ledbetter's leaving tomorrow," Angel tells him. "Captain Graham gave us the okay."

"I know, I know. Just keep the music down." But when James Brown's "I Feel Good" comes on, McGreavy starts doing a little two-step and joins the sing-along.

An hour later, as the party wraps up, I make an attempt to thank everyone and say how much the effort means to me, but it sounds so sappy, I cut it off midsentence and just tell them I'm going to miss them. "Stick around then," someone quips.

"Nope. Not a chance," I tell them, and they answer with a cheer.

Back in our cell, I thank Manny for his loyalty to me and for organizing the party. "Hug?" he says. I tell him okay and hold him tight, then tighter. He's already given me the address of the motel he and his sister will inherit, but he writes it down again in case I lose the first. I promise him that when he gets out in a few more years, I'll go down to see him and Gloria. "You fucking better," he says.

Before I go to bed, I make that list of what I'm walking out of here with—signed legal paperwork, the letters I've saved, my sketchbooks and art supplies, the photos of Maisie that Emily sent, and my lucky river stone. Because I gave away most of my shit, I only have to use one of the two plastic bags they gave me. At lights-out, I get into bed, then remember I forgot to pack the river stone. No sense in groping around in the dark for it. I'll drop it in the bag first thing in the morning.

I drift in and out of restless sleep all night, my mind going in a hundred different directions. *And let's not forget the individual who may end up paying the highest price of all—Niko's twin sister, Maisie . . . You ain't turning me* into *your Uncle Remus or your magical Negro! . . . You're the baby killer, right? . . . Code Purple! Building B, first floor! . . . Seeing the loving way you interacted with your wife and children made me feel jealous of you. . . . Mind-body. Mind-body. Mind-body. . . . You've gotten too involved with that kid. . . . There's a salt shaker missing. You swipe that, Ledbetter? . . . So let's go with the Klonopin then. Sound good? . . . We have this big blank wall now. How would you like to make it your canvas? . . . This call originates from a Connecticut Correctional facility. . . . Seek the light, dear Corby. Move toward the light. . . . She's not coming here, Corby. End of subject.* But then Maisie did come, thanks to Mom. She seemed uncomfortable at first, then warmed up a little, then gave me that unexpected wave goodbye. As I think about what a gift that was, my restlessness subsides and I finally fall into a deeper sleep.

I wake up a little before four on Tuesday. The day is finally here and I feel happy, sure, but not what you'd call joyous. My stomach's clenched and my hands are a little shaky. I've been told it could be a long morning before I'm able to get in Mom's car and look at this place in the rearview mirror.

Manny's snoring away up top. When I get out of bed, I go to the back window. I can see from the lamppost light that it's started snowing. The visitors' lot has about an inch already. This isn't going to screw things up, is it? I haven't heard anything about accumulation.

McGreavy must be doing a double shift, because at four thirty, he unlocks our door and enters the cell. He gives me my instructions: shower, get dressed, strip my mattress, and leave the laundry on the floor. At five, I should go over to morning chow as usual. At around seven, he says, a first-shift officer will escort me over to Discharge. "Hey, nice party they gave you last night," he says. "Not everyone gets one of those."

"Can't believe I'm saying this, but I'm going to miss some of the guys here, even a few of you COs," I tell him. He nods, then points up at Manny, still asleep on the top bunk. He says he bets I won't miss that snoring though. I laugh and tell him no, I won't miss that. "I just hope he lucks out with whoever they move in here next."

McGreavy says he's going off shift pretty soon. Do I have any questions?

"Yeah. Do you know how many of us are getting out today?"

"Not a clue," he says. "Anything else?"

"How much snow are we supposed to get?"

"I heard six inches, but I doubt it. It's never as much as they forecast. Okay, if there's nothing else, good luck. We don't want to see you back here."

"Hey, one more question," I tell him. "Who's on duty first shift?"

"This morning? Dang, I read it on the schedule, but I can't remember."

"It's not Anselmo and Piccardy, is it?"

He cocks his head. "Why you asking about those two? You hear something?" I tell him no, I was just wondering. "They're both on administrative leave," he says. "And don't ask me why because I'm not discussing it."

Administrative leave means they're in trouble for something, doesn't it? Have those two motherfuckers finally gotten nailed?

Morning chow is sparsely attended. Just as well. I'm too jumpy to keep up my end of a conversation. I eat with my head down, grateful that this will be the last gummy-oatmeal-and-powdered-egg breakfast I'll have to swallow—reason enough not to screw up and have to come back here. Maybe one day this week, I'll go into work with Mom and order one of those California omelets with the avocado and bacon. Maybe ask Skip about a dishwashing job while I'm at it. Gotta start somewhere.

Leaving the chow hall, I try to listen in on a conversation two guys in front of me are having. I miss a lot of it, but one of them says he heard three female guards filed a joint complaint. The other one says he heard the whistleblower was keeping track of all kinds of shit. They've got to be talking about Piccardy and Anselmo.

Manny's awake when I get back, but for once he doesn't have any intel about why those two are in trouble. "Could be a hundred different things," he says. "Including whatever happened that night Anselmo gave you shit about stealing the salt shaker."

He's fishing, but I don't take the bait. All I'll tell him is that Piccardy showed up unexpectedly that night. "So they double-teamed me." He stands there, waiting for me to say more, but I don't. I'm taking my humiliation with me when I walk out of here and never saying anything to anybody. Whatever those two have gotten nabbed for, I hope they both get shitcanned, but it's not going to have anything to do with me.

At quarter of seven, Manny puts me through another of his sentimental goodbyes, then leaves for his job at data processing. Fifteen minutes later, my escort arrives, right on time. It's Pawlikowski, one of the older guards. "Ready?" he asks. I grab my plastic bag of stuff but tell him to hold on a second. Go to the back window and look out. It's stupid; Mom's not supposed to get here until eight thirty, but maybe she's come early because of the snow. Nope. No cars, no tracks. When Pawlikowski unlocks the door, I leave the cell without looking back.

But we're only about ten steps down the corridor when an announcement comes over the PA. Because the morning count hasn't cleared, all movement throughout the compound is suspended until further notice. "But that doesn't mean me if I'm getting discharged, does it?" I ask Pawlikowski. I'm starting to panic.

"Sure it does," he says. "I've got to lock you back in, but take it easy. It should clear pretty soon."

It doesn't. Half an hour goes by. Then three-quarters of an hour. My nerves are electric and I can't stop pacing. Can't stop checking the empty lot. Why does it have to snow today of all days?

Then there she is. And my God, here comes Emily, too. The doors of both cars swing open and they get out, hug, talk. Maisie's running circles around her mother and grandmother, catching snowflakes on her tongue. It's real now! I'm getting out of here and Emily and Maisie have come to meet me. My eyes are stinging as I blink back tears. I think I've done more crying in this place than I've done in my whole life before I got here.

The count clears a few minutes later, but the walk over to the main building where I'll be discharged is so slow, it's torture. "Bad knees," Pawlikowski says. "All that jogging I used to do back in the seventies. And this snow is slippery so I gotta move slow. Could have retired two years ago, but me and the wife are raising our grandson and my retirement won't cover all the things he needs." He doesn't say why the kid's parents aren't raising him and I know not to ask.

When we enter the building, Pawlikowski leads me to the holding cell and locks me in with two other guys who are getting out. Then, with a weary sigh, he plops down on a metal folding chair by a door marked DISCHARGE. Coincidentally, I recognize one of the guys I'm waiting with; he and I rode to Yates chained to each other on that hot August afternoon back in 2017 when we both were processed in. He has no recollection of me. Good. That ride's not something I feel like reminiscing about. The other guy keeps letting them rip and it's stinking up the cell. Where the fuck's the Febreze when you need it? . . .

Jesus, how long have we been waiting here? Fifteen minutes? Twenty? Why's nothing happening? The other two don't seem like they're in any particular hurry to get out of here, but my mind is racing and I can't sit still. When I call over to Pawlikowski and ask him what's taking so long, he shrugs and tells me to just relax. Relax? I've been putting up with DOC's hurry-up-and-wait shit for two and a half years and I'm champing at the bit to get free of it. So fuck you, Pawlikowski, and fuck the fucking Department of Correction, too.

Finally, from the other side of the door, someone shouts, "Abraham!" Pawlikowski struggles himself off his chair and unlocks the holding cell door. Luckily, Abraham's the farter. Pawlikowski lets him out and unlocks the discharge door, and whoever's processing us out asks Abraham for his full name and date of birth. Maybe I'll be next.

Fifteen minutes later, I hear, "Holloway!" Shit! I'm number three out of three. Figures. I feel bad for Emily, Mom, and Maisie. They've already had a long wait and it's not over yet.

I have no idea how much more time has passed when they finally call my name. Pawlikowski delivers me to the two COs working the discharge counter. One of them's a young bodybuilder type like Piccardy, Officer Ostertag according to his name tag. I've never seen him before. The other is Stickley, aka Butch, the guard from the visiting room. When I hand over my bag, she dumps everything onto the counter and starts checking items against my list. Ostertag third-degrees me to make sure I'm the real me, not someone who's trying to bust out of here. In the middle of answering his questions, I spot a folded newspaper at the end of the counter. One of the headlines says, "Yates Correctional Officers Under Investigation." When Ostertag catches me looking at it, he grabs the paper and shoves it under the counter. Then he hands me the exit clothes and laceless sneakers they sent over from Property. Pointing to the bathroom door, he tells me to take off my uniform and that when I'm down to my underwear, he'll search me. After that, I can change into the civvies they've provided. "And you know the drill," he says, handing me a pee cup. "Leave it on the top of the tank when you're done. And don't fill it to overflow like the last dingleberry." He nods toward a small puddle on the bathroom floor. Then he stands at the open bathroom door as I do what he says.

Once all that's accomplished, I figure there can't be much more to this rigmarole. I emerge from the bathroom wearing what feel like clown clothes. The shirt's too small, the elastic waistband on the khakis has had it, and the sneakers fit me like Bozo shoes. Stickley says everything on my list checks out except for one thing. "Lucky stone," she says. "What's that?"

Oh, shit. All that time waiting around during the lockdown and I didn't remember to put it in the bag. "It's just a stone I picked up at the river out back when I was working on the grounds crew. It's kind of like my good-luck charm, I guess you could say. I forgot to pack it, but maybe if you let me—"

She cuts me off, shakes her head, and crosses the item off my list. "Lucky stone," she mumbles. "You men are more superstitious than a bunch of old ladies."

I smile at that. Ask her what time it is.

She checks her watch. Says it's twenty past ten.

"Oh, wow. Is there much more you have to do before I get out?"

Ostertag's the one who answers. "You're not getting out, Ledbetter. Not today anyway. Your urine's dirty."

I shake my head. "No, it's not. It can't be. I swear to God I'm clean!"

He shrugs. "Well, what can I tell you? You say one thing, your test says something different."

"Then test me again. Because either you didn't do it right or the one you used is flawed. And don't tell me I'm not getting out today because that's bullshit!" He tells me to lower my voice and watch my tone when speaking to an officer.

I turn my attention to Stickley. "Look, I've got family waiting out there in the snow, including my little girl. Remember her from the visiting room? You told her where the kids' books were? They've been waiting here since eight o'clock. Just, please, retest me. You'll get a different result and I can go."

Her face goes DOC-neutral. "That's not how it works, Ledbetter. You're right. These instant-result tests aren't foolproof; you can get a false positive once in a while, so you will be retested. But there are procedures we have to follow. The second specimen has to be sent to the lab, where the results are going to be more accurate."

"The lab? How long would that take?"

"A couple of days, three at most."

"No! That's fucking unacceptable!"

"Watch your mouth," Ostertag warns.

"You two in cahoots with Piccardy? You one of his weight-lifting pals?"

He and Stickley look at each other like I'm nuts. "We're not in cahoots with anyone," Stickley says. "We're just following procedure."

"Whether you find that 'unacceptable' or not," Ostertag adds.

His sarcasm infuriates me. "You don't even give a shit that I'm telling the truth, do you? My wife and kid can freeze to death out there for all you care!"

Stickley says she understands I'm upset but I need to calm down *right now.*

"Oh, I'm way more than upset! I'm fucking furious!" I'm shouting at them, at Anselmo and Piccardy for what they did to me, and at everyone else in this place who treats us like we're subhuman. And I'm not taking it anymore! My adrenaline's in charge now and I'm finally fighting back.

Ostertag comes out from behind the counter, stands next to me, and talks into his radio. "Ostertag in Discharge. We've got a Code Two here. Guy who's being sent back to his block and—"

"No, I'm not!" I scream. "I'm clean! I'll fucking fight my way out if I have to!"

Stickley comes out from behind the counter, too, and stands next to him. "Yeah, he's pretty agitated," Ostertag says. "All right, thanks."

"Mother*fucker*!"

I take a swing at him, but it misses and clips Stickley instead. I'm grabbed and slammed to the floor on my back, Ostertag's breath blasting in my face. Wrenching my left arm, he flips me onto my stomach and pins me to the floor, his knee pressing hard against my back. Less than a minute later, three of his fellow goons arrive. I'm yanked up onto my feet, shackled, and belly-chained. Two of them grab me under the arms and drag me backward while the third one videotapes us. As I'm pulled out of Discharge, the last thing I see is Officer Stickley holding her hand against her nose, blood dripping in the spaces between her fingers. "I'm clean," I keep insisting. I'm not shouting anymore; I'm mumbling. The fight's gone out of me. Is this really happening? How can it be when today's the day I'm getting out?

CHAPTER THIRTY-NINE

—

February 2020
Day 923 of 1,095

The door to my cell in the segregation unit is unlocked. From the doorway, the guard says, "Let's go, Ledbetter."

I'm groggy. Sleep-deprived. My balance is off. Unable to eat, I've been dry-heaving whenever the nausea overtakes me. "How long have I been in here?"

"You got questions, ask your counselor. And you'd better not pull any stunts like you did in Discharge. You're in enough trouble around here. Come on, get moving." It dawns on me who he is: Officer Garcia. When he worked at B Block, he was one of the more affable guards. Not now. Not with me, anyway. His contempt is coming through loud and clear. And I get it. That swing I took missed one of his fellow officers and hit the other one—a female guard, no less. From now on, I'll be on the shit list of just about everyone who works in custody.

Outside, the sun against the snow is blinding. I'm a little unsteady on my feet and my back still hurts from being slammed against the floor. I'd ask him whether we could slow down a little, but I know what the answer would be, so I force myself to keep up. Inside B Block, instead of leading me up to the third floor, he walks down the hallway of the first. I ask whether they're moving me. "No idea," he says. "Your counselor wants to see you. That's where we're going."

When I enter her office, Jackson gives me the once-over and tells me I look like hell. "Yeah, I'm pretty sure I stink, too. How long was I in seg?"

"Seventy-two hours," she says.

"So it's Friday?"

"That's right. Friday, February the seventh. You know, Ledbetter, I still can't wrap my head around it. Why would you sabotage yourself when you already had one foot out the door?"

Shame and fury rip through me again. "Because in my head, I already had *both* feet out the door. My family was waiting for me in the parking lot. *Had* been waiting for a couple of hours by then. I'd jumped through every hoop, signed everything they told me to, answered all their questions. All that had to happen was for them to open the gate and let me walk out. So when they said they *weren't* letting me out because I had a dirty urine, I thought they were fucking with me and I lost my shit. Because I knew I was clean."

"Except you weren't, Corby. Your test results came back from the lab yesterday afternoon and confirmed that you had benzodiazepine in your system."

I shake my head. "Not possible. I hadn't taken anything in two weeks. Fourteen days. I kept track."

"Okay, back up," she says. "You have a history with benzos. Why were you taking them?"

I can't tell her the real reason: because of what those two did to me in that storage room. "I'd been feeling anxious, okay? Having trouble sleeping. So I saw Doctor What's-His-Name and he gave me a prescription for Klonopin."

"Dr. Blankenship," she says. "When I spoke with him yesterday, he didn't seem to know you had a drug problem. Why didn't you tell him?"

"Because he didn't ask." I look away from her disapproval, then look back.

"The circumstances were totally different than before. I was taking them temporarily under regulated conditions. Standing in the med line twice a day, then once a day, then every other day. Then I stopped taking them. It was all under control."

"There are other kinds of medications that address those symptoms, Corby. Why didn't you request something nonaddictive?"

"I don't know. Klonopin was the first one he suggested so I just went with it. And the way it was going to be dispensed, it's not like I'd be able to abuse it. There's plenty of opportunity around here to go that route if you want, which I *didn't*. I just needed to deal with my anxiety and get some sleep. . . . What? Why are you looking at me like that?"

"I can't decide if you're trying to convince me or yourself." We stare at each other for the next several seconds, no words between us.

"Okay, moving on," she says. "Blankenship checked his notes and said you and he had made a plan so that you'd be totally clean prior to your release, and that that was a priority for you. But his notes also said you weren't scheduled to be discharged until August. Didn't you get back to him when you found out you were being released six months earlier?"

I explain that I tried to make an appointment with him but got the other shrink instead. "I didn't want to go over the whole thing with him, too, so I just began tapering off myself. You can ask them over at med line. I had a lot left on that prescription when I stopped taking them. . . . And okay, full disclosure: when I said I hadn't taken anything for fourteen days? I took a couple of pills during that time because my symptoms were coming back a little."

"A couple? How many is that?"

"Three, I think. Maybe four. But not right near the end. And not enough for me to have tested positive."

When she asks whether Blankenship told me about the "half-life" of drugs in the benzodiazepine family, I shake my head. "I'm guessing that's why you tested positive. You rolled the dice and the Klonopin was taking its sweet time leaving your system. I think you need to own up to it, Corby. This is on you."

I turn away from her. "Which makes me a fucking loser, doesn't it? For almost three years I've tried so hard in here to get better. To *be* better. And now, because there might have been a trace of something in my system, I'm staying stuck in here on a technicality and everyone's going to assume the worst."

"Well, Corby, the thing is—"

"My wife's probably saying to herself, 'Our son's death wasn't incentive enough for him to stay clean?' And now I'm probably going to lose my daughter, too, because I flunked a fucking pee test."

"It's not about the pee test," she says. "That could have been straightened out in a few days. This is about assault and battery. You took a swing at one officer and broke the nose of another."

"Jesus, her nose got broken?"

"In two places. She needed realignment surgery and will be on medical leave for a couple of weeks."

"Oh, man. She didn't deserve that. She's actually pretty decent."

"Okay, so it's a given that they're revoking those six months they gave you for early release. You have to serve the rest of your sentence. The warden might have taken into account the stressful circumstances that made you lose control. But Custody's up in arms about Officer Stickley's injury, so they're demanding that the department press charges. That will most likely mean you'll be sentenced to more time in here."

I'm afraid to ask, but I need to know. "How much more time?"

She shrugs. "Six more months? A year? I don't really know. If you're represented by a lawyer, they might negotiate. Reduce a year down to nine months, say. I'll do what I can, but it's out of my hands. I'm really sorry, Corby."

I shrug. "Well, like you said, it's on me."

She says she has a few pieces of good news for me. "They were going to move you to D Block, but I checked and your bunk in B hasn't been reassigned yet, so I made a call and you'll be going back there. You've told me you and your bunkie get along, and I assume some of the others on your tier will be sympathetic about what happened. At least you won't have to deal with strangers in a different building."

"Yeah, good," I tell her. "Thanks. What's the other news?"

She says she knows I had issues with Officers Anselmo and Piccardy. "But you won't have to deal with them anymore. They've both been fired."

"Fired or suspended?" I ask.

"Suspended at first, fired yesterday. Another officer blew the whistle on them for abusive treatment of some of the inmates and sexual harassment of some of the women who work here. The whistleblower was smart enough to collect evidence and get statements. I've heard arrests may be coming, too."

When her phone rings, she answers it and, while she's talking, it hits me that what's happened this week is the opposite of what was supposed to happen: Piccardy and Anselmo are out of here but I'm not. Win the battle, lose the war. But if those two sociopaths get arrested, I could probably help get them convicted if I opened my mouth about what they did to me. But there's no way in hell I can talk about that.

When she's off the phone, Jackson says, "You look exhausted. Come on. Let's get you back to your block."

I see Angel on the stairs, heading down while I'm going up. He's wearing the Timberlands I gave him when I thought I was getting out of here. As we pass each other, he says, "Tough break, brah." I nod without managing to look him in the eye. I guess the word is out. When we pass three guards chatting on the landing, I hear one of them say, "Someone ought to break *his* nose."

"Don't listen to that stuff," Jackson says. "You're probably going to get a lot of it for a while, but don't react. Just tune it out."

"Easier said than done," I tell her. Climbing the next flight of stairs in silence, I imagine the *other* me, the Corby who *didn't* sabotage himself. He's been out of Yates since Tuesday, enjoying his freedom. Maybe taking a hike out by the reservoir or catching a movie on Netflix.

When we get to the third floor I see Pawlikowski, the CO who escorted me to Discharge four days ago, sitting behind the control desk. "Boy, you really stepped in it, didn't you?" he says. I don't respond. Officers Sullivan and Kratt are there, too, and I feel the chill from both of them. Jackson says goodbye and promises she'll check in with me soon. Officer Sullivan says nothing when he walks me down to my cell, unlocks the door, then locks me back in.

Manny's up on his bunk, looking so sorry for me, I feel like punching him in the head. "Hey," he says.

"Hey."

"I heard you were in seg. How you doing?"

"I'm great, Manny. Just great." How the fuck does he *think* I'm doing? "What else have you heard?"

"That when they said you weren't getting out, you flipped out and assaulted an officer. Why wouldn't they discharge you?"

I have to look away from his pity. "Dirty urine."

"You?" He shakes his head. "That's bullshit."

It's not, but let him think whatever the fuck he wants to. *Why didn't you tell him? There are other kinds of medications. This is on you.* The truth fills me with such self-loathing that I grab the one chair in our cell and whack it, hard as I can, against the locked door. Do it again and again and again until the plastic cracks down the middle.

Manny's down from his bunk, pulling at me and shouting for me to stop it. "You just got out of seg! If they hear this racket down at the desk, they could come down here and haul your ass back there!" When I throw the chair against the wall, it ricochets back at me, clipping my left ear. Manny puts a hand on my shoulder and tells me to calm down. "Don't fucking touch me!" I warn him. Pulling away, I grab the wastebasket and hurl it at the back window, sending crap all over the place. Spotting the empty storage box under my bunk, I yank it out and kick it so hard that I twist my ankle, screaming out in pain. Manny stands there and says nothing.

As soon as my adrenaline spike subsides and my breathing slows down, the exhaustion kicks back in. I flop face-first onto my sour-smelling, sheetless mattress and fall asleep. . . .

When I open my eyes again and lift my head, I ask Manny how long I was out. "A few hours," he says. "You were flailing around at first and arguing with someone, but it came out like gibberish. I figured you might be cold so I covered you up. You calmed down after that."

"Thanks. Isn't this the blanket your sister sent you?"

"Well, Amazon sent it, but she ordered it. Yeah, last Christmas."

I notice that the shit I'd strewn all over the floor is back in the wastebasket and the cracked chair is upright. I apologize about the tantrum and for wrecking the chair.

"Three days in the hole when you thought you were getting out of here? No wonder you went nuts."

Pitching that fit wasn't about being in seg; it was about how my selfsabotage has landed me back here with him for who knows how long. But let him assume what he wants. I stand, fold his blanket, and put it back on his bunk.

"Thanks for the loan," I tell him. "Sorry about the chair."

"That's okay. You can still sit on it if you're careful, Corbs. Leans to the side a little but it should be okay for a while. Hey, did you hear about Anselmo and Piccardy?"

I tell him I heard they got fired but I don't know the details.

"They were being investigated for months by a CO from another facility who was working undercover."

"No shit. I'm surprised the dep warden didn't intervene and save his nephew's ass like before."

"I heard he tried to, but the warden wasn't having it. The mole had uncovered too much of their shit: physical abuse, psychological abuse. They'd target the weak ones and threaten them with what would happen if they said anything. Like when they found out you'd complained about Piccardy pepper-spraying those turkeys. They gave you a hard time, too, but you got off easy."

I flash back to what happened in that storage room. *You enjoy that, Ledbetter? You want some more? . . . Better not make threats you can't prove, baby killer. You see anyone who can back up your bullshit?* And what happened because of that assault and the threats they made if I were to say anything. *Benzodiazepines aren't magic, but they can help to take the edge off, and the effect kicks in pretty quickly. . . .*

"They got hit with sexual harassment charges, too," Manny says. "Making comments to the female guards about their sex lives, posting dick pics inside one woman's locker." When I ask him whether anyone knows who the mole was, he says, "Yeah. It was Goolsby."

"Seriously? Man, he had me fooled. Fooled those two dumb fucks, too. They treated him like he was their newbie-in-training."

"I heard Goolsby wasn't even his real name. They transferred him the hell out of here as soon as he blew the whistle in case there was retaliation. You know what happens to snitches at this place."

"Yeah, but I have the feeling there was no love lost between them and most of the other guards." *And from now on, try to remember who's in charge around here and who isn't.* "I tell you one thing, though. If those two get convicted and end up having to do time, I hope they send them here. They'll get what's coming to them, compliments of all the guys they've fucked with in one way or another. I'd join that team myself."

I get up and hobble over to the toilet to take a leak. My ankle's aching and swollen from when I was kicking my storage box. Manny notices and gets me a couple of Tylenol from his stash. I tell him I lucked out when it comes to cellmates and it makes him smile. "Fuck, yeah," he says. He opens his mouth to say something else, then closes it again. I tell him to spit it out, whatever it is. "No, I'm just really sorry about what happened to you, Corbs."

"It didn't happen *to* me. I *made* it happen. When they told me I wasn't getting out, I shouldn't have started swinging."

"Yeah, well, don't beat yourself up too much. Half the guys here would have reacted the same way if they had the rug pulled out from under them like you did."

"But how many would have broken a CO's nose?"

"Well, there's that," he says.

"I just wish I knew how my family's going to react when I try to explain what happened." Pointing to our back window, I tell him I saw them standing in the snowy lot, waiting for me. "I don't know if someone went out in the cold to tell them I wasn't getting released or if they finally just gave up and left."

"They? I thought just your mom was picking you up. Who else was there?"

"Emily and our daughter. I guess they planned it as a surprise."

"Oh Jesus, Corby," he says. He goes to the back window and looks out, shaking his head. Then he pivots. "Hey, before I forget, I got something of yours." He opens his storage box, rummages around in there, and takes out a piece of paper folded up like a packet. "I didn't know if you meant to take these when you packed your stuff. They were both under your bunk. I figured I wasn't going to see you anytime soon, but I didn't want to just throw them out."

When I unfold the paper, my river stone falls out. He'd wrapped it in the other thing I'd left behind: the printout of that poem Mrs. M gave me—the one about the Bruegel painting that had triggered my idea for my mural. I don't care about the poem, but I thank him for not tossing out the stone.

"No problem," he says. "I figured from the way you were always holding it that it meant something to you."

I wrap my hand around the stone and squeeze. "Means hope," I tell him. "Back when I was on the grounds crew? I left my post one time and snuck down to the river out back. I used to listen to it on nights when it got quiet in here, but I wanted to *see* it, too. Watch it flow *past* this place. And before I snuck back, I pulled this little stone out of the water as a keepsake or whatever—a promise that one day I'd move past this place, too."

As he looks at me and listens, I can see that something's just dawned on him. "Hey, wait a minute," he says. "You know how, in your mural, you painted some of us floating down the river? Was that supposed to be like an escape or something?"

"More like a liberation," I tell him. "I set you guys free."

From the corridor, CO Kratt calls us to supper chow. My stomach's growling, but I can't handle going over there, being glared at by the guards and getting the third degree from whoever's at my table. Not to mention having to choke down the prison slop I thought I was done with. Meanwhile, that other Corby is probably sitting down to a steak right now, medium rare, with sauteed mushrooms and my mom's scalloped potatoes. I need to call her tonight to let her know I haven't had a full-blown relapse if that's what she thinks. I also want her to know that I'm owning up to my mistake. *Mistakes*, plural. Letting that doc prescribe me Klonopin and throwing that punch. Poor Mom. This has got to be hard on her. And Emily, too. I wonder how she explained it to Maisie when I was a no-show. I need to assure her that even though I let my guard down about the benzos, I'm committed to my recovery and plan on keeping that commitment when I'm finally out of here.

When Manny gets back from eating, he asks whether I mind him turning on the TV so he can catch the news. "Have you heard about that virus that's going around?"

"The one in China? I heard something about it last week, but it's not like you can watch TV in seg. Why? What's going on?"

"It's spreading and it's killing people," he says. "A thousand deaths worldwide and now there's a big breakout in Italy and another one on some cruise ship."

"But nothing here in the States, right?"

"Wrong. There are fifteen confirmed cases, mostly out on the West Coast."

The TV's all staticky, but when Manny fiddles with the coat hanger antenna, a press conference comes into focus. Some old guy in a lab coat is at the podium. Trump, Pence, and several sober-looking expert types are standing behind him. I ask Manny to turn up the volume.

When Trump takes the mic, he says the coronavirus is very much under control in the USA. "Looks like by April, you know, in theory, when it gets a little warmer, it miraculously goes away." He looks over his shoulder, acknowledging the guys behind him, then continues. "The scientists in charge have been working hard and they are very smart. When you have fifteen people infected and the fifteen within a couple of days is going to be down close to zero, that's a pretty good job we've done."

"Did he just congratulate himself for accomplishing something that hasn't happened yet?" I ask. "Doesn't exactly inspire confidence, does it?"

Manny looks worried. He says he lived through it once and can't believe it's happening again.

"You were around back in 1918? Jesus, you're even older than I thought."

"Not funny," he says. "I'm talking about HIV."

For all his gabbing about everything else, Manny's never said much about his life during the AIDS crisis and I've never asked. But now I want to know.

He says he was seventeen, a busboy at a pizzeria, when he began having sex with a closeted assistant manager at a Sherwin-Williams store in the same plaza. "Billy was thirty-one and he had his own apartment. My pop kept threatening to kick me out for being a 'homo,' so I told him I'd save him the trouble and moved in with Billy.

"He was sweet to me and he didn't charge me for rent or food and beer, but he started saying how he loved me and how I was his boyfriend, and it kind of freaked me out. I was young and horny and more into dancing, drugs, and the pickup sex available at the clubs. I was basically just using Billy. He'd go clubbing with me sometimes, but he didn't like the way I'd go off with other boys. And I didn't like him telling me what I should and shouldn't be doing. We broke up at about the time HIV started being a thing on the news. Reminds me of what's happening now with Covid: older people waking up to how scary it might get and younger ones thinking keep the party going because nothing's going to happen to them."

Tears are welling in his eyes. He folds his arms across his chest and looks out the back window. I can tell his memories are hitting him hard.

"I was young, you know? So I figured I was immortal. This 'gay disease' I kept trying not to hear about was affecting older queers. Wear a condom? No thanks. That would be like eating a candy bar with the wrapper still on. Me and my fake ID were looking for pleasure, so safety could go fuck itself.

He grabs some toilet paper and wipes his eyes, blows his nose.

"This one guy, Hamish, who used to make the rounds at the clubs? Midtwenties, built like a god. Everyone wanted to fuck Hamish. Then he kind of dropped out of the scene. But one night while I was delivering pizzas, I passed him on the street and got a reality check about what AIDS could do to a person. He had these purple blotches on his neck and he'd lost maybe fifty pounds. The virus had turned him from a god to a walking skeleton. That scared me enough to start being more careful. Getting tested, making sure I had Trojans on me. I'd still take risks once in a while, but for the most part, I got way more cautious. And then I started having to go to the funerals—guys who were maybe four or five years older than me.

"But to this day, Corby, it doesn't make sense that Billy became infected and I didn't. I had heard he was sick, but when he started calling and leaving messages, I wouldn't call him back. The last time he tried to get ahold of me, I answered thinking it was someone else. He said he was in the hospital with pneumonia. He told me in this whispery voice that he was scared. Could I come see him, sit with him, and maybe just hold his hand? There was still a lot of confusion about how, besides sex, you could catch it. I promised him I'd come, but I didn't. And then he died. And to this day, I haven't forgiven myself for that. And for surviving when *I* was the one who should have died, not Billy. I don't know. Maybe I loved him, too, in a way or maybe I didn't. But he was the closest I ever got to a guy I was fucking loving me."

I don't say anything for a while. Can't think of what I *could* say.

He turns off the TV and says he's scared that this new virus is going to spread like HIV. "If it comes here, we'll be sitting ducks the way they pack us in. I don't think I can go through it again."

I thank him for telling me about Billy. "Thanks for listening," he says. He climbs up to his bunk. Neither of us says anything more.

On evening break, I go down to the phones, intending to call Mom. Instead, I push the buttons for Emily's number. She picks up on the third ring. I wait out the recorded spiel about where the call originates from and blah blah blah. If she hits "1" and decides to talk to me, I have a chance that she might listen to my explanation.

"Hello, Corby," she says.

"Oh, hey. Thanks for taking the call. I wasn't sure you would."

"I only picked up because I need to tell you something. I'm through. I can't do this anymore. Don't call here again."

"Yeah, but if you'll just let me explain, I think I can—"

"You can what? Give me more excuses? Tell me more lies? I mean it, Corby. I'm done. If you call me again, I'll change my number."

"Listen, you can't just cut me off. She's my daughter."

"And he was my son, you bastard! You killed my son!"

Click.

What she's just said and the way she said it—the hatred in her voice—knocks the wind out of me. Her inability to forgive me has always been there, under the surface, since the day he died. And now she thinks I didn't get out because I'm using again. I put my hand out and grab the wall to regain my balance. My other hand's still clutching the receiver. "Hey, dude, you through yet? Someone else might want to make a call, too." I turn and face a new arrival on the tier, an acne-scarred punk who's begging for an attitude adjustment. I'm tempted to smash the receiver against his pockmarked face. Instead, I slam the phone back on its cradle. "It's all yours, loser," I tell him.

As I walk away, he challenges me. "Loser? Why am I a loser?"

"You're here, aren't you? We're all losers here."

When I get back to our cell, Manny's asleep. I keep trying to *un*hear Emily telling me she's done with me. That she'll change her number if she has to. Am I going to have to fight her to get visits with my daughter? I will if I have to. If they'll even grant them to me.

How has everything gone so wrong so quickly? I'm pissed, sure, but more than that, I'm scared. What's the point of sobriety if this is where you end up?

Lying on my bunk, I keep shifting around because I can't get comfortable. When I hear the crinkle of paper, I reach down and grab that poem, the one about Bruegel's painting of Icarus. It didn't make sense before, but I try reading it again.

"Musée des Beaux Arts" by W. H. Auden

About suffering they were never wrong,
The Old Masters: how well they understood
Its human position: how it takes place
While someone else is eating or opening a window or . . .

I still don't get it, but instead of crumpling it up and aiming for the waste-basket, I skip to the second part.

In Breughel's Icarus, for instance: how everything turns away
Quite leisurely from the disaster; the ploughman may
Have heard the splash, the forsaken cry,
But for him it was not an important failure; the sun shone
As it had to on the white legs disappearing into the green
Water, and the expensive delicate ship that must have seen
Something amazing, a boy falling out of the sky,
Had somewhere to get to and sailed calmly on.

So maybe I *do* get it. The plowman, the sailors, the townspeople: everyone goes about their business, unfazed about a boy's falling from the sky into the sea and drowning. Maybe the poem's about dying alone. . . . It makes me think of that guy Billy, whispering into the phone and waiting for Manny to come. And about all the other gay men taken by that disease. And about the victims of this new plague that's on its way. . . .

I think about Lester Wiggins, who died alone in prison because he was denied the compassionate release that would have returned him to his family. And about that prisoner, Hogan, who committed suicide during my first year here—how he made a noose out of ripped bedsheets and jumped into the stairwell. And about how, in desperation, I might have suffocated myself with my head inside a plastic bag if those two COs hadn't caught on and stopped me. . . .

Finally, I think about Niko, my precious boy, suffering and dying alone in the back of an ambulance as it sped toward the hospital. How could I ever have expected her forgiveness when I can never forgive myself?

At lights-out, I lie on my bare mattress, twisting and writhing from the sad truth that Bruegel painted and Auden wrote about: that to live means to suffer, then to die alone. At first, I don't know where the strange sound I hear is coming from. But then I feel it traveling up from my gut to my diaphragm, moving past my throat and out my mouth. I'm wailing and I can't stifle or stop it. From the top bunk, Manny tells me to let it out, to release the suffering inside of me. Then he's down off his bunk and standing next to mine. His hand cups my shoulder. "Let it out, Corbs," he keeps saying. "Let it go."

"I've lost everything! She's finished with me and she's going to keep Maisie from me, too! . . . I didn't tell that doctor I was a benzo addict because I wanted those pills! Needed them! They warned me that if I said anything, they'd do it again. . . . And I was weak and scared and I just needed a way to block what they did from my mind and get some sleep! And now I've lost everything! Everything! It was a setup. Anselmo rammed that aluminum baton into me and Piccardy came out of nowhere and laughed. They raped me, Manny! They fucking raped me!"

He tells me to push over, and when I do, he gets on my bunk with me, pushing up against me. Puts his arms around me and begins rocking me like I'm his child. "You're not alone, Corby," he says. "I'm here. You're not alone."

PART FOUR:

Butterfly Boy

CHAPTER FORTY

Dr. Patel
June 2020

"Beena? Beena, darling? Time to wake up, sleepyhead."

"Oh." I open my eyes and there's Vikram, already up and dressed. I am back in the living world.

"What would you like for breakfast? I'll make it for you before I go."

"Just tea and toast, please."

"With ghee and lemon curd?"

"Yes, that would be lovely."

When he leaves our bedroom, I try to bring back the strange dream I just had, but the details are leaving quickly. I reach over to Vikram's night table for the cover of the DVD we watched last night. "*Monster's Ball,*" it says. "Billy Bob Thornton, Halle Berry, Heath Ledger." Before Vikram started the film, he said the actor who played the tragic son died before he was thirty from an accidental overdose of prescription medicines. I was struck by his resemblance to Corby Ledbetter. Perhaps that's why I dreamed about Corby. Of course he'd be on my mind. I learned just yesterday that he died in prison, a victim of the coronavirus.

When I join Vikram at the breakfast table, I tell him about my odd dream. "I was dead, but I was alive, advising the newly arrived in the afterworld about reincarnation." His smile says he is more amused than intrigued. He goes over to the counter to check on my toast.

I'm still pondering the dream and my former patient's appearance in it. Corby was one of the first inmates at Yates to succumb to the coronavirus. "Fagie Millman told me yesterday there have been four more deaths at the prison since then," I tell Vikram. "The men there live in such close proximity that, until the vaccines they're developing become available, they're terribly vulnerable."

"As we all are," Vikram says. He looks at the clock, eats his last spoonful of egg, then stands and says he'd better get going. His university students are all on Zoom now, but he still likes to go to his office. He kisses my forehead and says he'll return the DVD to the library and take out another on his way to work. "Any requests?" he asks.

"These are such sad times. Maybe a comedy."

"I'll look for one," he says. "Wear your mask if you're going out. Don't forget."

After I hear him drive off, I pour myself another cup of tea and go to the back window. One of my favorite things about our house is the view from here—the way our yard slopes down to the tall grass and then to the marsh where all manner of animals and birds gather. Last year when our grandson Rajesh came to stay with us, it was springtime. He scooped up tadpoles from the water and caught frogs. It took some time to convince him that they are the same—that one becomes the other.

A large bird in flight catches my eye. Ah, a great blue heron—a male, I think, perhaps the father of the family we watched last year. He's carrying a stick in his bill, probably preparing a nest for his mate and their young that, later in the season, will hatch, be fed and defended against predators, then fledge and fly away. Vikram likes to observe these creatures' habits with his binoculars. Last season, he saw one of the chicks fall from the nest, presumably to its death. The others, parent and siblings, were focused on feeding. Vikram says he was the only one who seemed to notice.

Well, enough bird-watching for now. Time for me to get dressed and ready for my nine o'clock Zoom appointment, then put on my mask and go out into the world.

CHAPTER FORTY-ONE

—

Emily
June 2023

The letter arrives in a stack of other mail: a J.Jill catalog, the electric bill, pleas for donations to politicians and the Red Cross, and Maisie's *Highlights* magazine. The envelope is addressed in pencil and the sender lives at a place called Phoenix House in New Britain. The cancellation stamp across the face of Chief Standing Bear says it was mailed the day before yesterday. The letter, also written in pencil, is littered with cross-outs and smudges.

Dear Emily,

I hope its okay to call you by your first name. I'm a better talker then a writer so sorry if this letter has alot of mistakes. My name is Manuel DellaVecchia (Manny for short). Corby and me were bunkies at Yates CI for almost three years. Maybe he mentioned me. First of all, I'm sorry for your loss. I know it's late to say that but I didn't know how to reach you while I was on the inside. I hope you and your daughter are doing good. I saw her in the visiting room once when she came with Corby's mother. She looked so cute.

I'm living at a halfway house until Parole says I can leave the state. They have a computer in the office here that we can use. I got your address off of Google. I hope we can meet somewhere and talk.

Corby's death hit me hard. I have things I need to tell you about
that you might not know. I feel like I owe it to him. I also have a
few things of his that I would like you to have.

We could meet here where I live. Or I might be able to get a
ride to your house if that's ~~more conveniant~~ easier. Or I could meet
you at the Westfarms mall. I work at Cinnabon there and get off at
4 p.m. If you want to get together and talk, the main number at
Phoenix House is 860-229-5240. Have them ring the second floor.
The phone's in the hallway, so it might be a while before someone
picks up. Say you want to speak to Manny in room 4. I hope to
hear from you soon.

Yours ~~truly~~ truely,
Manny D

My first thought is: there's no way I'm letting him come here! I don't want
to meet him at his group home either. Or drive to Westfarms for that matter, although I could do a little shopping, something I haven't done since
before the pandemic. Do I even want to hear what this guy has to say or see
what he wants to give me? I've struggled for more than two years to move
on from Corby's death, and things have been going so well with Bryan
that I've accepted his proposal. Bryan's easygoing, owns his own business,
doesn't drink more than a beer now and then. No children of his own, but
he and Maisie have really hit it off. And because his wife died unexpectedly,
he understands about grief and the complicated feelings about moving
on. Meeting with Corby's cellmate at this point might be like reopening
a wound that's finally begun to heal. I'm leaning toward not calling him.
Still, when I reread this letter, I'm touched by it. Manny says he's not much
of a writer, which I can tell from all the mistakes, cross-outs, and smudges
where he's erased things and written over them. That effort is what moves
me. What does he need to tell me?

How many times in the past two years have I thought about our final conversation when I told Corby not to call me again? By the following week, my anger and disappointment had subsided and I was ready to talk again. But he *didn't* call; he took me at my word. And then he got sick and died, no more words exchanged between us. So maybe I should meet with this Manny guy. Who better than his cellmate to fill in the gaps about what happened between the day I hung up on Corby and the day he died?

Over the next few days, I go back and forth. My mother is against my getting in contact with him; why upset the applecart? But Bryan says that hearing him out might be better than wondering what he was going to tell me. So I phone the number he gave me and ask them to ring the second floor. When someone picks up, I ask to speak to Manny. "You're talking to him," he says.

We agree to meet at the mall on Saturday after his shift is over. I'm nervous driving to Farmington, wondering now whether I should have taken Bryan up on his offer to come with me. When I get there, I pull into the Nordstrom garage where I've parked before. Unlike the other times I've come here, there are plenty of spaces to pick from—partly due to online shopping, no doubt, but partly, I'm guessing, the result of people's coronavirus hangovers. I have a mask in my purse in case I need to put it on, but if Manny's not wearing one, I won't either.

Our plan is to meet at the central court's seating area on the lower level. I see several shoppers chatting with one another, and one middle-aged man sitting by himself at a small table. "Emily?" He's short, rounded, wearing his work clothes: tan cap, tan apron over an aqua golf shirt. He says he recognized me from the pictures Corby had. "Thanks for coming," he says. "Hug?" His arms are extended so it would be awkward to refuse. He smells like cinnamon.

"Have a seat," he says. There are two paper cups on the table and a large manila envelope. "Are you a tea drinker?" he asks. "I drink tea in the afternoon. I got you one, too. Is chai okay?" He seems nervous and I am, too.

I tell him chai is perfect. We sip our tea and exchange pleasantries. When he asks how Maisie's doing, I show him a recent cell phone picture. "Getting big," he says. His thin hair, strawberry-blondish, looks dyed. He's wearing clear fingernail polish and a stud in one ear. "Do you want something to eat? A scone or something? A muffin?" I shake my head. What I want is for us to cut to the chase.

"What's in the envelope?" I ask.

He pulls out a pencil sketch on legal-sized paper. "Corby drew this," he says. "When he was getting ready to paint his mural." In the drawing, three boys—two of them Black, one white—are tossing stones in the water. All three are smiling. The boy in the hoodie looks like that innocent kid down in Florida who was shot and killed by the neighborhood vigilante. "He did a bunch of those practice drawings, fifteen or twenty of them. I forget what he called them."

"Studies," I tell him.

"Yeah, studies. After he finished his mural, he started tossing them in the trash. I grabbed this one and another one that had me in it, floating down the river in an inner tube. I kept that one for myself, but I thought you should have this one. I don't know who the other two are supposed to be, but the white kid was at Yates for a while. He had killed some dogs at a dog pound."

"Solomon," I say. "I saw him once when I visited. He was giving his stepmother a hard time, causing such a ruckus that the COs pulled him out kicking and screaming. Then they made the rest of us leave."

"Yeah, that kid was mental. And he was a real pain in the ass, too. Excuse me. Pain in the butt. But I had to hand it to Corby. He took him under his wing because the kid was getting bullied. But then the bullies started messing with Corby, too. I used to tell him, 'Corbs, don't stick your neck out too far over that kid or it's gonna get whacked. It's not like you're his father.' But it went in one ear and out the other. Anyway, I don't know how he did it, but Corby got the kid transferred to a mental hospital so he didn't have to stay stuck at Yates."

It's news to me that Corby went out on a limb for Solomon, but it doesn't surprise me. He hated bullies. I've always suspected his motivation in trying to stop people from being picked on was connected to his father's treatment of him when he was a kid. And who knows why, as Manny says, he stuck out his neck to defend Solomon? Maybe he was trying to atone in some way for Niko's death.

I thank Manny for the drawing, slip it back in the envelope, and remind him that in his letter he'd said he needed to tell me things I didn't know.

His face turns serious. "Well, first of all, Corby talked about you all the time. He loved you very much."

"I loved him, too, Manny. Still do. But things got very complicated."

"You mean after your son died," he says. "Corby never talked much about it, but I could tell the guilt he felt never let up. I'd hear him crying down there on the bottom bunk, sometimes even when he was asleep. He told me once that he was never going to forgive himself for the pain he caused you."

I look away from him. Look back. "We were having problems before Niko's death, too." For whatever reason I'm sharing this with someone I've just met, I keep going. "When he lost his job and became a full-time dad, he assumed it would be temporary. We both did. But when he couldn't find another job in his field, he became depressed. Anxious. He had trouble sleeping. It was my idea that he should see a doctor and get something for his anxiety, but I didn't know the medication he was taking was addictive, or that he was overdoing it. And drinking during the day when he was watching the kids. He kept it from me so I had no idea."

Manny gives me a skeptical look. "Huh," he says.

"What?"

"No, nothing. It's just that I've known a lot of addicts. Been in relationships with a couple of them. And even if they hide what they're doing, they usually give themselves away in one way or another."

What is he implying? That I wasn't being vigilant? That I was looking the other way? "Well, Manny, I bet you have no idea how hectic a full-time teacher's life can get—especially if she's got two toddlers waiting for her when she gets home. Corby had had them all day, but they wanted Mommy as soon as I walked in the door. And then, after supper and bath time, when we finally got them in bed, I had school work I needed to get to. So maybe I did miss some of the signs, but . . ." I trail off, not bothering to finish my thought. I don't need to defend myself to him.

"Or maybe Corby was better at covering his tracks than the guys I knew. Those were just *my* experiences. Every addict is different. Right?"

"Right."

I make a point of checking my watch and tell him I'm a little pressed for time—that I have to get back for Maisie. It's a lie. Bryan's taking her to see that new Pixar movie, so there's no rush. But I hear myself telling Manny I have to leave in about twenty minutes. "So what else did you need to tell me?"

Momentary loss of eye contact. Fidgeting. Then he looks straight at me and says, "I can see how you'd assume that flunking the piss test meant he'd started using again. And when he tried to explain why his urine was dirty, I can understand why you'd think he was bullshitting you. Addicts lie; there's no arguing that. But he was clean and sober the whole time we were bunkies, I swear to God. He went to meetings a couple times a week and he was always reading that Big Book that's, like, their bible.

"When he went ballistic because they wouldn't let him out? And got carted off to seg? As soon as they let him back to the tier, he said he needed to call you and explain why he flunked that test. And when he came back to our cell, he told me how your conversation had gone south. It wiped him out, Emily. It was tough to see how much pain he was in after he made that call. But don't get me wrong. I can appreciate why you'd had it. Why, if you thought he was using again, you told him not to bother you anymore. But he had a *prescription* for the medication he was taking. If they had let him out when they said they were going to, he wouldn't have lost it so bad. And if that hadn't happened, he'd be alive today. I really believe that."

We're both in tears now. Manny excuses himself, gets up, and walks over to the Starbucks counter. He's right. It was a horrible misunderstanding and I'd give anything to be able to take back that last conversation we had. Every time I think about it, I'm filled with regret and shame. But still, prescription or not, with his history of misusing them, why did he start taking benzodiazepines? If he loved us so much, why would he risk that? I can feel the anger rising in me, an emotion I thought I'd gotten past. So maybe my mother was right that I shouldn't have come here today. Why upset the applecart? I use my hand to swipe away my tears, then look around to see whether anyone else is watching or listening, but no. Two teenage girls are the only ones close enough to have heard and they're deep in conversation about whatever girls that age talk about.

Manny comes back with a fistful of napkins. Takes a couple and slides the rest across the table for me. He wipes his eyes, blows his nose, and continues.

"Me and Corby got Covid at the same time," he says.

"What? You had it, too?"

"Yeah. I'm pretty sure we both caught it from a transfer from Rikers—a barber who was doing time for running a sports bookmaking operation. He was offering haircuts to the guys on our tier. He had a cough, I remember, but nobody thought much about it at the time. But less than a week after he got here, they sent him to the hospital and he never came back.

"Me and Corby both started feeling like crap: headaches, body aches, coughing fits. He had it worse than me. Lying down made his coughing worse, but he was getting so weak, he had a hard time sitting up. Sometimes after lights-out, I'd hear him gasping for air. Then he'd get quiet. *Too* quiet, you know? So I'd climb down from my bunk to make sure he hadn't . . . well, you know. And I could hear other guys on the tier coughing, too. Three or four of us had gotten haircuts from that guy. I guess he was one of those superspreaders."

When he asks me whether he should stop, I shake my head. This is why I came here.

"So after some of us got sick, they put the whole place on lockdown. They closed the chow hall and staff started delivering meals through our tray traps. If you asked them if there were any breakouts on the other block, they wouldn't answer you. Everything was hush-hush, which made it harder. I didn't have any taste or smell, but I ate a little to try and keep my strength up. Corby was too sick to eat. He was crying out a lot from the pain, but he kept trying to tell me something. I couldn't understand much of it, but I caught something about the river out back. After a while, he got so frustrated that I couldn't get what he was trying to say that he just closed his eyes and stopped talking.

"That night, he got worse. I had to do *something*, so I started shouting through the tray trap, '*Ledbetter needs to go to the hospital! Get Ledbetter to the hospital!*' I guess they got the message, but it was two in the morning when the ambulance finally got there. That was the last I saw of him. I heard later that the hospital was so jammed up with Covid patients that he had to wait in the hall on a stretcher until they could get him a bed. And by the time he finally got hooked up to a ventilator, it was too late. He didn't make it."

In tears, I watch him pick up the envelope he's brought. When he overturns it, something falls out: a little stone. "Corby pulled this out of the river once when he was on the grounds crew. He told me that whenever he felt like giving up, he'd hold it and it would give him hope. I thought you might want to have it."

When he hands it to me, I examine it. It's just a simple stone, white and gray, oval-shaped, smooth to the touch. Mostly quartz, I think. I clutch it, imagining Corby holding it. I thank Manny and drop it back in the envelope. "I'm grateful to you for being such a good friend," I tell him. "And I'm glad *you* survived. How many Covid deaths have there been at Yates?"

"About a dozen by the time I left, maybe more now," he says. "The department tries to keep those numbers on the QT."

"But they must have put protocols in place. Right?"

"Oh, sure. Corrections came up with all kinds of rules and regulations about how to prevent spreading the virus. The problem was, nobody in charge did much checking to make sure they were being followed. A lot of the COs thought it wasn't macho to wear masks, so you'd see them dangling off one ear or poking out of their pocket. And when the vaccines became available, some of the guards refused to get shots because they didn't trust the government, especially once Biden got in. So yeah, there were deaths. And a lot of emotional problems from being quarantined for so long. No visits, no phone calls, no chow hall, no library. It was the same as being stuck in seg for weeks and weeks. And you know how staff helped us deal with the isolation? They passed out coloring books and puzzle books that were supposed to keep our minds occupied." Anger creeps into his voice. "Like, if you got busy coloring some stupid picture, you'd fucking forget about guys around you getting sick and dying!"

He apologizes for swearing. Says after you've been in prison for a while, using the f-word becomes about as natural as breathing. "Not a problem," I tell him. But I've heard about all I can take, so I thank him and tell him I have to be going.

"Yeah, but can you hold on a minute?" he says. "There's one more thing I think I should tell you about, even though Corby probably wouldn't want me to."

I sit back down.

"He had a hard time at the beginning of his bid. Got called names. Had shit smeared on his sheets. It's sick what some cons will do to a new guy, especially if his crime involved the death of a kid."

Oh my God, poor Corby! I tell Manny I had no idea that kind of thing was going on—that he kept it from me.

"Wanted to spare you, I guess. I kind of helped him out. Showed him the ropes, promised him it was going to get better. I felt sorry for the guy, you know? Plus, he was cute. I kind of had a crush on him, not that he was interested. With some guys in prison, it's gay for the stay and straight at the gate. But Corby made it clear we weren't going there and I was cool with that."

Is *this* what he wanted to tell me? I'm not sure it's something I need to know.

"Anyways, after he got more used to prison life, things went better for him. Guys on our tier got to know him and like him, so they backed off. Me and him were already friends, but then we became cellmates. I did two bids and had a bunch of different cellies, but none as good as Corby. We had opposite personalities and I think I drove him crazy sometimes, but all in all we got along good. He was a stand-up guy. Don't take this the wrong way, Emily, but I loved him. And respected him. Pretty much everyone did. We even threw him a party when we thought he was getting out. And he *would* have if it wasn't for those two motherfuckers who were out to get him. And again, excuse my language."

"What do you mean? Who was out to get him?"

"Two of the guards on our tier. They went out of their way to make Corby's life a living hell."

"Why? What had he done?"

Manny looks away. Sighs and looks back. "He stood up to them. Called them on their shit. Now that I think about it, the whole thing started over you."

"Over me? What do you mean?"

"You came to see Corby. It might have been your first visit. And one of those clowns hassled you about something. The metal detector maybe?"

I nod, recalling the incident. "He was harassing me. I forget his name but—"

"Piccardy. And when he finally let you into the visiting room, you were pretty shaken is what Corby told me. The next day, he got on Piccardy about it. Told him he'd better not ever treat you like that again, and that was all it took. See, Piccardy and his wingman, Anselmo, were bullies. And when Corby stood up to one of them, that made him their enemy."

I tell Manny I remember asking Corby to just let it go.

"Well, he wasn't able to do that. He had to defend your honor, I guess. But that was just the first thing. See, Anselmo and Piccardy were doing all kinds of shit but keeping it under the radar—or so they thought. When Corby was on that work crew, he caught them abusing some wild turkeys that were roaming nearby. Pepper-spraying them for fun. And he tried to blow the whistle on them about that. And about Solomon, too. Like I said, those two liked to bully the weakest ones in the herd. And because the kid was too screwed up to defend himself, Corby defended him. They hated him for that, so things went from bad to worse. They kept needling him. Goading him. Waking him up in the middle of the night to scare him. One time they put a snake in our cell, but that bothered me a lot more than it did Corby."

"It sounds cruel but so childish."

"Yeah, but then they went way over the line. Did something really bad to him."

"What?"

"Maybe I shouldn't . . . I mean, it explains why he started taking those benzos. Are you sure you want to know?"

I'm *not* sure, but I tell him I am. This is why I've driven here.

"Well, okay then. We were leaving chow one night and Anselmo stopped him. Accused him of swiping a salt shaker off the table. Everyone knew it was bogus, but it gave Anselmo an excuse to strip-search him. In private. Piccardy was off that day, but he was in on it. He was there."

"Did they beat him up?" I ask.

"Not so anyone would be able to see," he says. "They wouldn't risk that. But they found a way to humiliate him and shut him up. And it changed Corby. The poor guy was nervous, depressed, couldn't sleep. He became afraid of them, so he'd stay in our cell if they were on duty together. That was why he started taking those meds. Which is why, when he was due to get out, he failed the drug test."

"What are you saying, Manny? Why was he afraid?"

He bows his head. Doesn't look at me. "At Yates, the COs carry defensive weapons. Pepper spray, batons. So that they can stop fights, control a crowd if a riot breaks out. And—"

"Batons?"

"You know, like the billy clubs cops used to carry, except these are metal rods that extend to about two, two and a half feet. In case they need to start swinging."

"What? I don't . . . Did they beat him with one of those?"

"No. They strip-searched him. Then they made him bend over, and raped him with it. Sodomized him."

My stomach heaves. I have to get away before I lose it. "Excuse me," I tell Manny, standing abruptly.

"Are you all right? You said you needed to know, but—"

I rush past stores and kiosks until I find a restroom. Lock myself in a stall, put my head down, and cry long and hard for Corby. When I'm finally able to stop, I go to the sink and splash cold water on the puffy red face in the mirror. I leave and Manny's standing there, waiting for me. "You forgot this," he says, handing me the envelope. I manage a thank-you, but I need to get in my car and drive away from here.

"It caught up with them eventually, Emily," he says. "Not what they did to Corby, but they were pulling stuff with other guys, too. They both got fired. Then they got arrested. Corby knew about that at least. I just wish he had lived long enough to know they're both doing time now, one in upstate New York and the other in Massachusetts. And if word's gotten out about the crap they were pulling at Yates, they better watch their backs twenty-four seven."

It's spontaneous. I reach out and touch his cheek, and he puts his hand over my hand. I tell him I really have to go.

"Yeah. Hey, listen. After they let me leave Connecticut, I'm moving back to Jersey. Me and my sister inherited a motel from our uncle. It's just over the GW Bridge in Fort Lee. If you're passing through and you want a place to stay, you're welcome anytime. Free of charge."

"Okay. Thanks."

I start walking fast toward the Nordstrom exit.

"It's on Route Nine, close to where Palisades Park used to be."

"Oh. Okay."

"There's a pool! And free continental breakfast! Anytime, Emily."

Driving home, I can't unhear the things I heard. *Metal rods that extend to about two, two and a half feet. Raped him with it. Sodomized him. . . . Whenever he felt like giving up, he'd hold it and it would give him hope. . . . I'd hear him crying down there, sometimes even when he was asleep. . . . Addicts usually give themselves away in one way or another.*

I might have smelled alcohol on Corby's breath once when I got home from school. And when I counted his Ativan that time, I wondered why he was going to run out before he could get a refill. But he was so touchy about everything by then, I figured I'd monitor the situation instead of saying something and getting into another fight. So maybe there *were* signs. Maybe he *was* giving himself away, waiting for me to notice.

——

When Corby's remains came back from the crematorium, his mother and I agreed to divide his ashes: half to her, half to me. Vicki bought a plot at the Sheltering Arms Cemetery. To memorialize her son, she had a flat stone carved and installed. Her portion of Corby's remains were buried at the foot of it so she could have a place to visit and a grave to decorate. This all happened a year and a half ago. Meanwhile, my canister of his remains has sat on a shelf in my bedroom closet since I received them, but it's time for me to stop procrastinating.

Given Corby's love of nature, I decide I'll release the ashes I have into the Wequonnoc river. There's a boat launch at the river's approach to Three Rivers. I pick a date, imagine a small early morning service, and jot down whom to invite: Corby's parents, of course; Manny; Dr. Patel; Mrs. Millman. I'd invite Solomon if he was well enough to come, but I wouldn't know how to contact him. Should I include Maisie? I'm undecided. The concept of her birth father having been transformed into dust and bone fragments might be difficult for her to handle. Maybe I'll have her stay home with Bryan.

That evening, thinking about my plans for the memorial, I remember that Solomon's stepmother, Adrienne, and I exchanged phone numbers that night at the prison. I find her in my contacts and call her the next morning. She says she's sorry for my loss and sorry that she's late in acknowledging it. "I found out how much your husband advocated for Solomon when he was at Yates, and that he paid a price for doing that." She doesn't say how she knows this and I don't ask.

"So how is Solomon doing?" I ask.

"*Much* better," she says. I tell her I'm calling to invite him to join us when we scatter Corby's ashes. Give her the date and the time and ask if she could let him know. "But please tell him not to feel obligated."

She says she and Solomon have very limited contact these days, but she'll make sure he gets the message. "A couple from the tribe, Ron and Bev Bramlett, have taken him under their wing and he lives with them on the reservation now. I'll call Bev and let her know. Solomon works at the casino in food service. I didn't imagine he'd ever be able to hold down a job, but he's done very well. The medication he's on has helped. There are side effects but the gains he's made have been worth it."

I tell her that's wonderful to hear and would have made Corby very happy.

When I call Manny's halfway house, I learn that he has left the state.

Dr. Patel says she wishes she could come but will be in Europe. While I have her on the phone, I ask her whether I should bring Maisie to the service. "Well, Emily, you've told me more than once that you came to regret having withheld Maisie from her father while he was in prison. Why would you withhold her from an opportunity to tell him goodbye?"

"Because if I try to explain cremation to her, it might scare her."

"Then don't dwell on that. Maybe you could give her a task—something she can focus on so that she feels she has an important part in what's happening. That's my suggestion, but of course it's up to you."

"Oh, dear, we have a commitment that morning," Mrs. Millman says. "But that will be over by midmorning. Hey, I have an idea. Since you're going to be in that area anyway, how would you like to see your husband's mural? I'm retired now and the library hasn't reopened since Covid, but I'm sure I can arrange a visit. Maybe we could meet there after Corby's service."

My desire to see Corby's work competes with my dread of returning to that awful place, but I tell her I'd like that very much. "I'll have my daughter with me. Will I be able to bring her, too?"

"Of course!"

Corby's mom and dad have already attended their son's graveside memorial, and with the others unable to be there, I scrap my plan. It will just be Maisie and me at the boat launch. Then we'll drive over there and meet Mrs. Millman.

8:00 a.m., Saturday, October 21, 2023

It's a beautiful, breezy fall morning. The sky is blue, the air is crisp, and the foliage, late this year, is at its peak. Maisie and I walk down the leaf-strewn path to the dock. It's fitting, I think, that the sound of the river flowing under our feet provides an accompaniment to what we're about to do.

I pry the lid off the canister of ashes. With the cup I've put in there, I scoop up half, hold the cup at arm's length, and overturn it. The breeze carries most of Corby's remains into the flowing river, but some of the dust settles onto our jackets and the tops of our shoes. For a few seconds, Maisie and I are wearing Corby. Then a gust sends his dust on its way.

"Hi."

I turn around to see a lanky young man with a goatee. Who is this? What's he doing here? And then, oh my God, it hits me. I'd invited him but never called his stepmother back to cancel. I only saw him that one time in the visiting room. He seems taller and more filled out now, more a man than a boy. "Thank you for coming," I tell him. He gives me a curt nod.

"Who's he?" Maisie asks me.

It's Solomon who answers. "Corby was my friend."

When I hand him the canister, I notice that his hands are shaking. Either he's nervous or tremors are a side effect of the medications he's on. *But the gains have been worth it,* I hear Adrienne say. He removes the cup and puts it down on the dock. Then he pours ashes onto the palm of his hand, takes a deep breath, and blows them into the river.

I reach into my pocket, take out Corby's stone, and hand it to my daughter. "Maisie's father once pulled this little stone out of this river," I explain to Solomon. "There's nothing distinctive about it that I can see, but when his friend Manny gave it to me, he told me that Corby thought of it as his lucky stone. Whenever he was feeling sad or upset, he would place it on his palm and wrap his hand around it. And like magic, holding it would make him feel better."

Solomon says Corby lent it to him once. "But I gave it back."

I tell him Maisie and I discussed whether we should keep the stone or return it to the river. "And we decided that Corby would want us to let it go back home." Solomon nods in agreement. I ask Maisie whether she's ready. With a face that's solemn and purposeful, she says yes and walks to the end of the dock. "Bye-bye, stone," she says. She leans back, then throws it about six feet into the water, where it makes a soft plunk and sinks.

Walking off the dock toward the parking lot, I ask Solomon whether he needs a ride. He says no, his "Wequonnoc parents" are waiting for him in their car. "Okay," I tell him. "Thank you so much for coming." I hold out my hand.

"No problem," he says, sounding like every other young person these days. But as we shake, I feel those tremors in his jumpy hand.

I wave to the couple who've been waiting for him. They wave back. Now it's on to the last of the unfinished business.

During our final session before Dr. Patel's trip abroad, she urged me to accept Mrs. Millman's offer to come to see the mural. Engaged now to Bryan and pregnant with his child, I still haven't been able to let go of the guilt I feel about the way I treated Corby when he was in prison. "Maybe standing before his mural and saying what you need to say to him will free you to move on," she said.

So I drive along the John Mason Parkway, then take a deep breath, put on my blinker, and turn into the long driveway that leads to the visitors' parking lot. It's been three years since that snowy morning when Vicki, Maisie, and I waited for hours, expecting Corby to walk out a free man. Maisie's in the back seat on her box, probably watching some YouTube video about dinosaurs. She's become obsessed with them ever since Corby's father and his wife, Natalie, took her to Dinosaur State Park. Since Corby's death, his dad has made a conscientious effort to spend time with his granddaughter. Corby's relationship with him had been so damaged and difficult, I wasn't sure about these visits at first. But they've been good for Maisie. I wish Corby had lived to see how his father is making amends to him through her.

"Hey, Maisie, does this place look familiar?" I ask her. No response. I raise my voice and ask again. She looks out the window at the imposing brick buildings behind the surrounding fence and shakes her head.

"Oh, wait," she says. "This is where my first daddy used to live. It's a prison, right?"

"That's right." I hold my breath, worried that she might ask me *why* he lived here. I'll tell her when she's a little older—when she wants to know, but not now. I'm relieved when, instead of asking that, she says, "I came here once with Grandma Vicki to visit him."

"You remember that, huh?"

"Yeah. I was kind of scared at first."

"Scared because it's a prison?"

"No. Scared because he had a really bushy beard. But after a while, I *wasn't* scared. He was nice. He read me a story."

"And he *wrote* you a story, remember?"

"Uh-huh. About the giraffe family. He drew the pictures, too. And I'm in it."

"That's right. You're the girl who lives next door."

"Tell me again why we're here," she says.

"To see the big wall painting your daddy painted when he lived here."

"The one in that library?"

"That's right. Your father was friends with Mrs. Millman, the librarian. It was her idea that he should paint the mural because he was such a good artist. She's going to meet us inside and show us where to go."

"Oh. My now-daddy has a beard, too, but his is neat."

"Uh-huh. He keeps his trimmed."

"But sometimes he leaves whiskers in the sink. Yuck."

"Well, sweetie, you can't have everything."

I park. We get out of the car. Walk toward the building and climb the long set of cement stairs to the prison's main entrance. I recall the earlier times I'd do this, my nervousness increasing with each step.

Mrs. Millman has beaten us here; she's waiting for us just inside the building. She smiles and tells Maisie she's pleased to meet her. "I'm excited to share your father's mural with you and your mother. Would you like to see it?" Maisie says she does. "Well, come on then. Follow me. I've gotten us VIP clearances, so we can avoid the usual rigmarole. Having worked here for over three decades has gotten me *that* much clout at least." She waves to the guard behind the counter and he waves back. Apparently as VIPs, we get to sidestep the metal detector. Thank God for that! I recall that bleak room where I waited my turn to pass through the metal detector, my panic when I couldn't figure out what kept triggering it.

Halfway up the stairs, I ask Mrs. Millman how long she's been retired. "Since the start of the pandemic," she says. "They've been dragging their feet about hiring my replacement and reopening the library, but I'm going to keep bugging them until they do. It's a crime that these fellas don't have access to reading materials."

As we reach the second-floor landing, the baby gives me a sharp kick and my "oof" gets Mrs. Millman's attention. "Someone's very active today," I tell her. When she asks how far along I am, I tell her seven and a half months.

Turning to Maisie, Mrs. Millman asks whether she's hoping for a little brother or a little sister. "I wanted a brother, but it's going to be a girl," Maisie tells her.

"And I bet you're going to be a *great* big sister," Mrs. Millman says. Maisie shrugs and says she doesn't know yet.

I worry less about my daughter than I did before, when I was getting calls from school about her disturbing behavior; Bryan has had a stabilizing influence on her and they're genuinely fond of each other. But she's the odd girl out with the kids in her class and the girls across the street whose parents bought the McNallys' house. Bryan says he thinks it bothers me more than it does Maisie—that some kids are content not to run with the herd. She has made one friend at school this year, a boy named Rory, but he's pretty eccentric, too.

When we enter the library, Mrs. Millman turns on the lights and points us toward Corby's mural. "I'll leave you alone with it," she says. "Take your time."

We stand before it, neither of us saying anything for a minute or more, our eyes moving up and down, back and forth. It's almost as if it's casting a spell.

Maisie's the first to speak. "Hey, are those pterodactyls?"

When I see what she's pointing to, I tell her, "No, I think those are blue herons. But I wouldn't be surprised if pterodactyls were their ancestors."

"Ancestors would be like their great-grandparents. Right?"

"Well, in this case more like their great-great-great-great-great-grandparents."

"Wow," she says. "Cool."

Mrs. Millman rejoins us, carrying a photo of the painting that was, she says, Corby's inspiration for the mural. "The artist was Pieter Bruegel the Elder, a Renaissance painter who lived during the sixteenth century. Most of his peers were painting commissioned portraits of courtiers and other prominent people, but Bruegel's subjects were commoners—peasants at work or play. This one's called *Landscape with the Fall of Icarus*, although the boy's death is curiously understated." When she points to it, I can see what she means.

Maisie butts in to ask her whether this library has any dinosaur books. "A couple at least," Mrs. Millman says. "Come with me and we'll have a look. Let's give your mom a little alone time with your father's painting." I don't know what Dr. Patel has told her, but I think Mrs. Millman gets the gist of why I'm here.

Thinking of Dr. Patel's advice, I speak softly, privately. "Corby, I'm here. I've come to see your mural." Saying it, rather than just thinking it, somehow seems necessary.

"I feel so moved by what you've created. I can almost see you working on it, bringing it to life day by day, section by section." I come closer, focusing on the brushstrokes, following them with the tips of my fingers. Doing this makes me feel closer to him than I did during those awkward hugs in the visiting room.

"I . . . I recognize that it's you in the foreground, looking down from some higher spot at those men floating down the river where we released your ashes this morning." I choke up, wait, and then go on. "One of those men in the inner tubes looks like it might be Manny. . . . I see Maisie and me on a path that runs alongside the river. . . . And Native women and men going about their lives like those peasants in the painting Mrs. Millman said inspired you.

"Oh, there's Mrs. Millman, wading into the water with Dr. Patel near those three boys who are skipping stones. When I met with Manny, he gave me a study you did of those boys. I had it framed and hung it in the hallway between Maisie's bedroom and mine. Ours until . . ." My voice cracks. I reach into my coat pocket and pull out a tissue. Wipe my eyes, my nose. "I could never bring myself to scatter your ashes until today, Corby, but this morning I was finally able to release you."

I dread saying the next thing, but why am I here if I don't? "Corby, I'm so sorry for your suffering, not only for the horrible way your life was taken from you by the virus, but also for all the ways you suffered having to bear the responsibility for Niko's death." I take another deep breath and will myself to continue. "The truth is, I bear some of the responsibility for our tragedy, too. I sometimes smelled alcohol on you when you slept next to me. And I knew you were taking more of those pills than you should have been. I wish I'd confronted you instead of telling myself that things would be okay again once you found another job. I wish I had been a better wife.

"In the time you were here, I regret that I only managed to visit you so rarely, and never with Maisie, even though I knew how badly you wanted to see her. During those times when I did come, I would sit across the table from you trying to cope with the confusion of emotions I was feeling: sorrow, anger, despair, love. Please know, Corby, that despite everything that went wrong between us, I never stopped loving you."

I'm struggling to continue, but I have to face the pain and keep going.

"I've thought many times about what I said to you in anger the last time we talked. When I found out why they weren't releasing you, I assumed the worst instead of listening to your explanation. I must have sounded as cold and unforgiving as my mother. But then last year I received an unexpected letter from Manny and we arranged to meet in person. He wanted me to know that you had been clean and sober in the almost three years you two had roomed together.

"I was in tears when he told me how horribly you suffered because of those guards and . . . and how they did something so ugly to you, I can't even say the word. Manny said you started taking that prescription to ease your suffering after that happened. When I learned what the circumstances were, I was finally able to get in touch with *your* pain instead of just focusing on my own. Corby, even though it's too late, I want you to know that I *have* forgiven you for what happened the day Niko died. I'm so sorry I withheld that forgiveness from you while you were alive."

I hear Maisie and Mrs. Millman somewhere else in the library. Maisie's enlisted her in the game she sometimes plays with Bryan.

"Triceratops?"

"Herbivore."

"Correct. Allosaurus?"

"Um, carnivore?"

"Correct."

"Corby, I need you to know that I'm going to remarry. Bryan is a carpenter and a kind, good man. We met at a grief group last year; his wife died from a cerebral hemorrhage, so he understands loss. They had always wanted a child but could never conceive. My child with him, a girl, will be born a month and a half from now."

"Here's a hard one. Oviraptor."

"Let's see. Carnivore?"

"Nope. Oviraptors were omnivores."

"Corby, Bryan and Maisie get along well. He's a good stepfather to her, but you will never be replaced. Sometimes she and I look at photos of you and I tell her about how much we loved each other.

"To this day, I can see you standing there at the door of that student apartment in your baggy yellow sweater, your hair rumpled and disheveled, those tired bags under your beautiful eyes. It makes me teary every single time. Maisie loves that story about your cross-country trip and wants me to tell it over and over. She and I filled a scrapbook with the drawings, notes, and cartoons you sent her and I'll sometimes see her take it off the shelf and look at it on her own. I will always help her to keep your memory alive. Rest in peace, Corby. I love you and I always will."

Looking closely at Corby's depiction of himself from the back, I spot a random bristle from his brush, lodged in his reddish hair where the paint was applied thickly. I pluck it out and hold it between my thumb and index finger. No bigger than an eyelash, it feels to me like a rare treasure.

I'm startled when Maisie, at my side, asks me whom I'm talking to. "Your father," I tell her.

"Oh. He was a good artist, wasn't he?"

"Yes, he was."

"Mom, can you pick me up? I want to see something up at the top."

I tell her no, sorry. She's too heavy for me to lift now because of the baby.

From behind us, Mrs. Millman says, "Hold on." She disappears, then comes back holding a step stool. "Just be careful," she says.

Maisie climbs the stool to the second-highest step and reaches toward something on the far-right side of the mural—a strange figure I hadn't noticed. Butterflies are flying free from what looks like a small, green chrysalis with a child inside. Oh, it's Niko! The baby moves inside of me as I watch Maisie reach up, high-fiving the image of her twin. "Hello, boy," she says.

ACKNOWLEDGMENTS

I can't believe my good fortune! That may be my name on the cover of this book, but I'll forever be grateful to the fellow writers, friends, and publishing professionals who supported my efforts, gave editorial feedback, and traveled alongside me during this six-year journey from the novel's first sentence to its last.

One of the most valuable things literary agents do is connect authors to those who might appreciate their work and make things happen. My longtime agent and friend, Kassie Evashevski, connected me to literary agent Bill Clegg, whose sharp insights, publishing expertise, and writerly instincts led me, in turn, to Marysue Rucci.

Marysue Rucci is editor/editor-in-chief of her eponymous imprint, Marysue Rucci Books, at Simon & Schuster. From start to finish, her editing of this novel has been insightful, thorough, thought-provoking, and collaborative. She challenged me in ways that helped me to strengthen and deepen my story. All that, plus she's one of the nicest people in the book business.

Marysue has gathered around her a crackerjack publishing team in the shepherding of this novel. They include editorial assistant/publishing associate Emma Taussig, copyeditor Jane Elias, senior production editor Sonja Singleton, art designer Michael Nagin, interior designer Hope Herr-Cardillo, marketing specialist Elizabeth Breedan, publicists Clare Maurer and Jessica Preeg, and managing editor Jessie McNeil. The book's publisher is Richard Rhorer. Thanks to them all!

Writing a novel is solitary work, but it's been my privilege for decades to work, converse, break bread, and laugh with a group of talented prose writers and poets who are some of my most treasured friends. We convene twice a month to offer feedback to one another on writing in progress: what's working and what might not be working yet. Group members include Denise Abercrombie, Jon Andersen, Bruce Cohen, Doug Hood, Leslie Johnson, Pam Lewis, and Sari Rosenblatt. Their responses to this novel have been invaluable.

Allyson Salazar deserves a special salute. I've known her since she was fifteen-year-old Allyson Cleveland, a high school student in my Honors English class. Since then, she has become a wife and mother, a teacher, a writer herself, and my office assistant. Allyson accommodates my foibles and eccentricities, compensates for my tech shortcomings, and responds to emails, requests, and a myriad of others tasks. She's also a great critic! Allyson is usually the first responder when I want to test-drive a new scene, a new chapter, a new idea. I take notes on what she says. And she's a hilarious storyteller! Thank you, Al.

My gratitude also extends to the following who have supported or enlightened me in a variety of ways: Ethel Mantzaris, Penny Balocki, Jamie Brickhouse, Jerry Spears, Toni Masciangioli, Chris Lamb, Justin and Jessica Lamb, Jared and Brenna Lamb, Teddy Lamb, Joe Darda, Joe Leonardi, Tom Hardecker, Michael Cox, Mark Croxford, Peter Kelly, Julie Anderson, Kevin Synnott, Ray Coggeshall, Simon Toop, Maria Garcia, my former students at York Correctional Institute, and Sadie the Dog.

ABOUT THE AUTHOR

WALLY LAMB is the author of six *New York Times* bestselling novels: *She's Come Undone, I Know This Much Is True, I'll Take You There, We Are Water, Wishin' and Hopin'* and *The Hour I First Believed.* Lamb also edited *Couldn't Keep It to Myself* and *I'll Fly Away,* two volumes of essays from students in his writing workshop at York Correctional Institution, a women's prison in Connecticut, where he served as a volunteer facilitator for twenty years. Lamb and his wife, Christine, live in Connecticut and New York.